NO QUARTER

NO QUARTER

a Matty Graves novel

Broos Campbell

McBooks Press, Inc.
Ithaca, New York

Published by McBooks Press 2006

Copyright © 2006 Broos Campbell

Cover painting by Dennis Lyall © 2006.

Dust jacket and book design by Panda Musgrove.

ISBN: 978-1-59013-103-9
      1-59013-103-7

                    Library of Congress Cataloging-in-Publication Data
Campbell, Broos, 1957-
  No quarter : a Matty Graves novel / by Broos Campbell.
    p. cm.
  ISBN-13: 978-1-59013-103-9 (alk. paper)
  ISBN-10: 1-59013-103-7 (alk. paper)
  1. Sea stories. 2. Historical fiction. I. Title.
  PS3603.A464N6 2006
  813'.6--dc22
                            2005029519

Distributed to the trade by National Book Network, Inc.
15200 NBN Way, Blue Ridge Summit, PA 17214
800-462-6420

Additional copies of this book may be ordered from any bookstore or directly from
McBooks Press, Inc., ID Booth Building, 520 North Meadow St., Ithaca, NY 14850.
Please include $5.00 postage and handling with mail orders. New York State residents
must add sales tax to total remittance (books & shipping). All McBooks Press publica-
tions can also be ordered by calling toll-free 1-888-BOOKS11 (1-888-266-5711).

Please call to request a free catalog.

Visit the McBooks Press website at www.mcbooks.com.

Printed in the United States of America

9 8 7 6 5 4 3 2 1

To the men and women of the Lady Washington.

Acknowledgments

It is customary on this page for the author to say that no book is ever written alone. It's a lie, mate.

Constructing a book that is at least readable, however, is very much a collaboration, one that calls for a power of patience, tact, and insight, with maybe a little eye-gouging thrown in for style—and that's just from the author. For their questions, encouragement and advice, I am particularly indebted to Patty Campbell, Bill and Judith Campbell, Frederick W. Campbell-Craven, Paul Mackinney, and Harry Shannon.

It is also customary at this point to complain that the golden age of editing—a perhaps apocryphal time when writers wrote and editors helped them do it—has passed. I have not found this to be the case. Throughout the editing of this book, Jackie Swift showed a diabolical ability to pounce on precisely those parts that I'd most hoped she wouldn't notice. For her enthusiasm, her skill, and, sweetest of all, her sense of humor, I am deeply grateful.

B.C.
Los Angeles, Calif.

POINT 1: First engagement with picaroons. POINT 2: Villon's camp. POINT 3: Matty rejoins the *Rattle-Snake*. POINT 4: Capture of *La Brise*. POINT 5: Encounter with *La Sécurité*. POINT 6: Second engagement with picaroons. POINT 7: Meeting with *Harold*. POINT 8: Encounter with Spanish frigate. POINT 9: Behind the mangroves.

NO QUARTER

One

The day after Christmas was a fine day for a funeral, I thought, as I sniffed the chill breeze blowing out of Baltimore-Town. Although the breeze stank of rotted manure and the bitter smoke of a thousand chimneys, I gloried in the day. Snowflakes glittered in the iron-gray sky, and fat cold tears dripped from icicles in the *Rattle-Snake*'s rigging. A fine day, a lovely day for a funeral, bleak and miserable for all but the most intimately concerned—and he was already bloating in his crypt in old Virginia.

Mr. Wickett dismissed the victualer's slaves at three bells in the forenoon watch. After that we cleared away the rubbish left from a week of stowing beef, biscuit and beans; powder and shot; canvas and cordage; water, whiskey and beer; pigs, goats, chickens and all the other needful things for a voyage of several months; and warped the schooner into the outer harbor. Now the Rattle-Snakes stood at divisions along the starboard side, toeing the deck seams and blowing on their hands as they waited for our captain, Lieutenant William Trimble—my cousin Billy—to appear.

I stood on the old-fashioned raised quarterdeck, gazing down at the men without actually seeing them. I'd learned few of their names yet. Most of them were so much furniture as far as I cared. What I cared about at that moment was the problem of hunching the collar of my greatcoat higher around my ears without attracting Wickett's notice. He'd rebuked me once already that morning for sneezing—said nothing, mind you, just stared, but our first lieutenant had a stare like a Gorgon. He towered beside me, all six-foot-something of him, aiming his pointed beak and gray eyes at this man and that, like an owl look-ing for rats. He missed nothing, did our Mr. Wickett.

He hauled out his watch and glanced at it. "My respects to the cap-tain, Mr. Graves," he said to me, tucking his watch back into his vest pocket. "Tell him it's time."

"I am aware of what o'clock it is," said Cousin Billy, poking his head through the after hatch. He was frowzy and ruddy, having spent the morning drinking his breakfast. Unsteady weren't in it—even his eyes jiggled, like a pair of coddled eggs on a wet plate. He belched softly into his fist before hauling himself up the last few steps of the ladder.

The hand-blowing stopped at once; but though the men were self-consciously glorious in their new pea jackets and pink-shaven faces, no foremast jack ever stands at attention. I found that Wickett and Sailing Master Rogers and I had arranged ourselves in a study of manly sorrow, as if maybe a portrait-painter lurked nearby. Corporal Haversham's Marines stood ramrod straight along the larboard rail, with their rifled muskets at the present, eyes front, with the flour turn-ing to dough in their hair.

"Do off hats," said Wickett in the formal way, and everyone save the Marines stood bareheaded in the damp.

Bracing his hams against the binnacle, Cousin Billy reverently ex-tracted a crisp document from his bosom and began to read. "December twenty-sixth, anno Domini seventeen hundred and ninety-nine," he said. "Long may this day be remembered." And there he had to stop to wipe his eye.

I looked the people over while we waited for him to collect himself. Sixty-two enlisted men, all of them clean and most of them sober—a good turnout, considering that nearly the entire lot had just come back from shore leave. The white hands had had a night and a day to at-tend church services, most of them opting for the Methodist meeting in Fell's Point, which was conveniently near any number of taverns and bawdy houses. Cousin Billy had even allowed the colored hands to go ashore, Baltimore being one of the few American ports where they could walk around unescorted.

I'd had a bit of a time myself, in celebration of my seventeenth birthday. It's awkward sharing a natal day with Jesus—the one tends to outglory the other—but as my mother and brother and sisters were dead, my father didn't like me, and my half-brother, Phillip, didn't believe in Christmas and other people's birthdays, I was long used to receiving presents only from myself. It suited me. I always knew what I was going to get, and it was always something I wanted. My gift that year had been a pleasant and charming redhead, about which I'll say no more, except that whoring ain't near as nasty as some people would have you suppose. I was content, anyway.

I became aware that I was smiling, and then I noticed that Wickett was staring at me as I smiled. And then I noticed that the port-wine stain in the middle of his forehead was contrasting in a strange way with the suddenly pale skin around it. He was all blotchy and mottled, like an angry octopus. Terrified that I might laugh, I hastily resumed my funeral face—the look of melancholic distraction that I had practiced in my bit of mirror below decks. The light northwesterly began to tickle my brows with snow, but with Wickett's eyes on me I dared not raise a hand to wipe it away. And my nose had begun to run. I sniffed furtively.

"The president," Cousin Billy was saying, "with deep affliction announces to the Navy and to the Marines the death of Our Beloved Fellow Citizen, commander of our armies and late President of the . . ." His voice fell away into a sigh. I caught "illustrious by his eminent virtues and important services" and "grateful country delighted to confer" something or other, but little else.

Not that I was listening much. I had no love for Our Beloved Fellow Citizen.

The snow gave way to drizzle, and still Cousin Billy maundered. A particularly large and icy drop from the mainsail boom hit me on the back of the neck and dribbled down beneath my collar. Caught by surprise, I sneezed.

Wickett reached out and caught me just above the elbow, and dug his fingers into the nerve on the inner side of the bone. You should try it sometime. It hurts like the devil, even through an overcoat.

"Desirous that the Navy and Marines should express," mumbled Cousin Billy, "in common with *something something* American citizens, the high sense which all feel of the loss our country has sustained in the death of this good and great man—"

Here he broke off to mop his eyes. Some of the older seamen did likewise, and I took advantage of it to get my arm away from Wickett and wipe my nose on my coat sleeve.

And at last came the end of it. "The President," Billy said, "directs that the vessels of the Navy be put in mourning for one week by wearing their colors half-mast high, and that the officers of the Navy and of Marines wear crepe on the left arm below the elbow for six months."

He refolded the sheet and tucked it next to his heart. "Carry on, if you please, Mr. Wickett."

"Do on hats," said Wickett. "Ready at the braces and slings." There was a rumble of feet on the deck as the men on watch ran to their stations. "Haul away!"

When the hands had finished scandalizing the yards—hauling them out of square as a sign of mourning—Wickett glanced at his watch and then shouted to the knurled, white-bearded man who waited on the fo'c's'le: "Master Gunner Schmidt, it is nearly noon. You may begin the salute when the fort does." In a fierce undertone he said to me, "Damn your eyes, Mr. Graves, stand by at the colors."

It was just as well that he did, because I'd entirely forgotten my duty and would have stood around watching Mr. Schmidt if I'd been left to my own desires. But no one likes to have his eyes damned, especially when he deserves it, and I tucked the little piece of resentment away to be savored at another time.

A few minutes later a puff of smoke appeared above the new brick ramparts of Fort McHenry. Before the sound reached us across the water, Schmidt shouted, "Fire one!" and the man at Number One gun, the farthest forward on the starboard side, pulled his lanyard.

The Stars and Stripes flying above the fort began the descent. At the taffrail, I solemnly lowered *Rattle-Snake*'s colors and raised them again halfway to the peak, savoring the smoke and thunder of the salute, and not least because Schmidt's German accent had caused his order to come out as "fire fun!"

I had seen salutes fired before, of course. We fired them every chance we got and demanded them in return, too, ever on the lookout for any impugnment of our honor. And our ships always required the utmost in ceremony from every port we entered, unless the captain had to pay for it himself. But the glorious waste of powder always thrilled me, and Washington's death rated a full twenty-one guns. Schmidt had to fire off all fourteen of our six-pounders and work halfway around again, until we were half-blinded and pretty near suffocated by the smoke. The *Rattle-Snake* and the tubby old *Aztec* were the only American men-of-war in port; but HM's thirty-two-gun frigate *Clytemnestra* lay near-to, and she and the more pretentious of the merchant ships joined in the din, rolling a continuous echo and re-echo of cannon fire around the harbor.

"Zalute gompleted, sir," called Schmidt when it was finished.

"Secure the guns." Wickett turned to Cousin Billy and raised his hat. "Salute completed, sir."

Cousin Billy lifted his hat in reply, his wisps of blond hair sticking to his shiny pink scalp. The hesitancy with which he returned the salute made him seem somehow pathetic, like a fat boy playing at soldiers.

"You may dismiss, Mr. Wickett," he said. "Then up spirits and give the hands their dinner, if you would be so kind. As for us, I've reserved a room at the Quid Nunc Club for after the procession." He looked sympathetically at his lieutenant, who was doing a fine job of containing his grief, it seemed to me, and said, "We will need a bracer by then, I'm sure.

"Cousin Matty—Mr. Graves," he said to me, "pass the word for my coxs'n, and see to it that my gig is hoisted out and all, there's a good fellow. And for heaven's sake, use your hankie; a very important personage is to meet us on the dock." He rubbed his hands together and smiled despite his recent tears. "He's our chance to be noticed, gentlemen. I think I need say no more than that."

A mean-mouthed man of maybe thirty, in square-rimmed gold spectacles and a fur-lined greatcoat, and with a hat that looked like a dead badger sitting on his head, stood waiting for us at the end of the Frederick Street wharf amid a pile of chests and valises and carryalls. Mr. P. Hoyden Blair, he yapped, was the assistant United States consul to San Domingo and not in the habit of waiting on anyone. "Not a one, neither kings nor dukes nor congressmen, and certainly not a pack of sailors. Port Republicain awaits. We sail at once."

A gun from the fort boomed in the gray distance, as it had done every fifteen minutes since the initial salute and would continue doing until midnight.

"Well, no. I am afraid we do not, sir," said Cousin Billy, looking embarrassed. "There's the procession, you know; mustn't miss it. And besides, we're still several officers short and not all the men are back yet, neither. I don't believe we can sail till morning."

"Morning! That ain't good enough, Mr. Trimble."

"Perhaps not even until tomorrow afternoon, sir," said Wickett. I could swear he hid a smile when he added, "And that is to assume the breeze stays in the north."

He didn't bother reminding Blair to say *Captain* Trimble, either. That, I thought, was interesting.

Blair peered at Wickett. "Mr. Trimble, who is this fellow?"

"His name is Wickett, sir, Lieutenant Peter Wickett. My first officer. He's been in the *Rattle-Snake* for longer than any of us. And this is John Rogers, our sailing master, and the short fellow is my cousin Matthew Graves, that I've rated master's mate."

I took off my hat to him, but he didn't spare me so much as a nod, which was just about exactly what I expected of him.

Rogers smiled as he held out a brawny hand and said, "The tide don't wait on us, Mr. Blair, but we must wait on it. Much as with yourself, sir."

"I know little enough of naval etiquette," said Blair, ignoring his hand, "but tell me this, Mr. Rogers: as a sailing master you are not on the ladder of promotion, ain't that so?"

"It is, sir, but I rank with a lieutenant all the same."

"Mr. Trimble," said Blair, "my impedimenta must be taken aboard at once."

"Yes, well, I suppose you can't just leave it sitting here on the dock," said Billy.

Rogers looked down at his hand as if surprised to see it still sticking out in front of him. He brushed back a long strand of dark hair that had come loose from his queue, as if that's what he'd meant to do all along, and said: "I'll see to the gent's baggage, Cap'n, and send the lads back again after."

The lads gave him dirty looks behind his back. No doubt they'd been looking forward to sneaking a few last hours of pinching wenches' bottoms and drinking flip beside a fire till Cousin Billy chose to go back aboard, and now they'd have to row around in the weather instead, slinging bags and boxes about and getting soaked through in the bargain.

But a sailor's life was full of hardship, and it was the sailing master's job to see to the stowing of cargo anyway. It was their bad luck and none of my own.

"There, you see, sir?" said Billy to Blair, when Rogers had gotten the boat's crew busy on the chests and valises and carryalls. "He'll have it all stowed away shipshape and Bristol fashion when we bring you aboard. And you will have my sleeping place in the great cabin. You will be my guest, sir. But we must away now to Baltimore Street for the procession, and after that we'll need something to take off the chill. I'm standing drinks at a little place I know."

"Indeed, indeed!" said Blair, brightening at last. "Was about to suggest it myself."

Baltimore-Town had been drearied up something awful, which was good of someone, I suppose. Black bunting festooned the three-story brick warehouses facing the waterfront, and more of it dangled from the lampposts and horse troughs along South Street. Church bells competed with the quarter-hour gun to see which could be the mournfulest. The shops were closed and the business district was near deserted, although light from a few imperfectly shuttered upper windows sparkled in the running gutters: commerce, like the tide and Mr. P. Hoyden Blair, waits for no man, especially not a dead one. The citizens we passed were wrapped in mourning weeds. We ourselves wore black breeches and stockings in honor of the day, with boat cloaks thrown over the blue and buff of our best uniform coats.

There was a great surge of people all bound for Baltimore Street, and in the press I contrived to get my heel stepped on. I stopped short, hopping on one foot and trying to keep from being pushed along by the crowd.

"Go on, gentlemen," I cried to Billy's back. "Go on without me, do!"

Wickett turned around to look at me. "What the devil are you on about?"

"I went and lost my shoe, sir."

"Well then, pick it up again. Don't you want to be in the parade? Look, the hawkers and pickpockets are already at work." And with that he disappeared into the crowd.

And a parade is what it was. Grief was on parade, and I resented it because I couldn't share in it. I kept thinking of the last time I'd seen my brother Geordie, and how Washington had let that bastard Hamilton bring down the weight of an army onto the heads of a few dozen men and boys. Washington should have prevented it. But an army was like a gun, I guessed: if you have one, sooner or later you just have to use it.

However, there was something of a holiday in the air, and as I considered the reason for the event, I couldn't be entirely uncheerful. The hawkers were shoving through the crowd with their barrels of beer mounted on barrows, and handcarts piled high with oysters; and a great many of the people were drunk. I spied a wall that was sheltered from the drizzle by an overhanging eave, and after shoving off a few smaller boys I sat me down. I bought a meat pie and a pot of beer, and after a while I could hear the parade shrieking and squawking down the street.

The mayor and his appendages were in the van, with an honor guard of local militia to push gawkers out of the way. Mr. Blair marched with the mayor, though it didn't look as though the mayor knew it. They were followed by a company of middle-aged veterans in their Continental uniforms, many with their handkerchiefs pressed to their faces—an affect sadly marred by the group of schoolboys who marched behind them, waving soggy paper flags and shrieking "Yankee Doodle." There was an Army band, of course, with sackbuts and serpents and cornets, doing their best to drum the poetry out of "Chester" and "The Old One-Hundredth." And then, while they were assaulting "Barbry Allen," the Presence hove into sight behind them.

The casket was set on a caisson drawn by a black-plumed horse draped in a black silk bard, with a pair of boots reversed in the stirrups, and was draped in more black silk with a crossed sword and scabbard on top, and yards and yards of black crepe drooping with damp all around—but I saw no Presence. What I saw was an Empty Box.

Not so the crowd. They moaned and wept over the unoccupied casket, and I hung my head in shame. It was like peering through a thrust-open door into a howling bedlam of madmen and idiots; but outside the fellowship, where I was, there was nothing but a cold grim emptiness. All I had to do was walk through the door and the inmates would welcome me in their fashion, but I could not. Though I did un-bend enough to wish that the West Indian bastard Hamilton had died instead. I had no doubt that in the three years since the election he had managed to hook his grapnels onto President Adams and had him firmly in tow.

"Here comes the Navy!" brayed one of the idiots. "Huzzah for jolly Jack Tar!"

I looked up to see Master Commandant Malloy leading my old ship-mates, the Aztecs, all bedizened in their shore-going finery, with shiny black tarpaulin hats on their heads and their long plaited pigtails hanging down behind. Staggering beside him was Cousin Billy, swabbing his face with his hanky, and behind him strode Wickett, now and then darting out a hand to save Billy from falling on his ear. I hopped down from the wall, following them from a safe distance until the parade broke up at the top of South Street and Malloy took his Aztecs away.

"Halloo!" cried Billy when he saw me. "There you are, Cuz! What became of you?"

"Lost my shoe in the crowd, sir."

"But you didn't miss the procession, pray!"

"No sir. I had an excellent vantage."

"Quite moving, hey?"

"I never seen anything like it, sir."

"And never will again!" said Blair.

"God, I hope not," said Wickett.

A few blocks south of Baltimore Street we swung to starboard into Lovely Lane, a narrow stinking misnamed alley, and entered a low doorway whose stones were black and greasy with age. Instead of the usual *memento mori* the question *quid nunc*—"what now?"—had been carved under the death's-head in the keystone to indicate that news and gossip could be gathered there.

Mr. Reynolds, the proprietor, bustled out of the murk as we entered, beaming and bowing as he worked his way through a party of *Clytemnestra*'s officers who had commandeered the common room. The British gentlemen all seemed to be singing, some of them even singing the same song. They ignored us, and we returned the compliment. Reynolds shooed us to a table in one of the back rooms, but it was the best back room, the one with windows in it, and snapped his fingers for the bar boy. The shutters had been closed against the weather. That and the candles and the great fire blazing on the hearth made the black-draped little cellar almost cheery.

Cousin Billy sank into the chair that Reynolds pulled out for him and said, "Whiskey all around, I think, gentlemen. Or would you prefer punch? No? Whiskey it is then, lad." He nodded to Fugwhit, Reynolds's mouth-breathing bar boy, and rubbed his palms together in anticipation. "Barley wine is fine, if it's been kept someplace cool, which it often hasn't. And claret's an obligatory yet unwelcome expense when it comes to commodores and patrons and such. Punch certainly would be welcome on a bleak postmeridian such as this one. Yet I think its warming qualities would lend an undue gaiety to such a solemn occasion as The General's being laid to rest." His voice made the initial capitals clear, and he lowered his eyes, bowing his head toward the black-draped engraving of Washington that had been set on the mantel and which blocked our view of Leda and the Swan that hung behind it.

"No," he continued, "I think that in such circumstances a dose of good old Monongahela rye is in order, or as close as these rooms will allow. Which is very close indeed, Cousin Matty," he said, laying a finger alongside his nose and winking at me, "being as I had one of our own barrels brought in this morning."

Some sort of answer was required, but I found it difficult to respond naturally. The Trimbles were important investors in Graves & Son, the family distillery outside of Pittsburgh. My half-brother, Phillip—the *Son* in the company name, and no plural about it—had hinted very heavily to me that it might be best not to tell Cousin Billy about "a temporary unease regarding our solvency." Phillip had built up a tidy little shipping business before the war with France—the undeclared war, the quasi-war, the war that wasn't a war yet killed men anyway—but privateers had since taken a heavy toll on his hulls in the Caribbean and the Bay of Biscay. Which meant little to me then, except that my allowance was threatened.

"Then that's very close indeed, *indeed*, sir," I joked.

"We're informal here, Matty! We're not on the quarterdeck, hey? Call me Cousin Billy, do!"

"Aye aye, sir, Cousin Billy, sir," says I, saluting him with both hands.

"That's the spirit, ha ha!"

Wickett had remained standing in the doorway, one hand on the lintel and the other on the ivory hilt of his sword, contemplating the Clytemnestras in the other room. He now came to the table, spread his coattails and lowered his long shanks into a chair, saying, "Yes, please do let's be informal," but his face held no clue as to whether he meant it. An uncomfortable silence passed, broken only by his breathing noisily through flared nostrils as we waited for the whiskey. He gazed at me without seeming to see me and pressed his bony hands together.

"Well," chirped Cousin Billy, "I have heard it said that entertainment is good for such occasions as this, to release the mind momentarily from its dungeon of grief. What do you think, Mr. Wickett?"

Wickett tilted his chair back, still staring at me. His eyes were as devoid of expression as any I'd ever seen.

"Oh, I don't know what would be appropriate, sir," he said. He shifted his glance to Billy. "Perhaps a draggle of street urchins to re-enact the conspiracy against Claudio?"

"Ah . . . no."

"What's this?" said Blair. "Conspiracy?"

Wickett looked at him. "Shakespeare, Mr. Blair."

"Mr. Wickett is having a little joke," said Billy. "And at a time like this, for shame. No, I . . . that is, I was speaking hypothetically. Off the cuff, as it were. To relieve the awkwardness of new companions thrown together at table. You see."

"*Much Ado about Nothing*, Mr. Blair," said Wickett.

"Oh, I dare say." Blair coughed into his fist, drummed his fingers on the table, and then opened his little eyes wide. "I've got it! Let's make the boy tell us a joke. That way he'll be of some use, at least."

I told him I'd rather not.

"Do not defy me, sir." He winked at the others. "And it better be a good 'un."

Cousin Billy frowned like a mule eating briars. "Another joke? Can't say as I much cared for the last 'un, Mr. Blair."

"Just to lighten our burden of sorrow a bit, Mr. Trimble."

Wickett regarded our captain.

Cousin Billy nodded, looking at the table. "Let us hear it: we need some relief on this terrible day—as you say, Mr. Blair. Tell us the joke then, if you must, Matty."

"Aye aye, sir," said I, trying not to glare at Blair. "I mean, Cousin Billy." Emboldened by the memory of my birthday present, I said, "Here's one I heard in the *Aztec:* What d'ye call a Tennessee gal who can run faster'n her brothers?"

Blair smirked around the table. "I've heard this one before. You'll never guess it, I bet."

Wickett steepled his fingertips and placed the tips of his index fingers against his bloodless lips. "A Tennessee gal," he said, "how droll and backwoodsian. Very American. Let us examine the clues provided: A young rustic female has the ability to best her male relatives in a sprint. Obviously, this being a jape, there is a point of humor that rests on information that is assumed, yet hidden to the recipient until the *pointe d'une plaisanterie* or 'zinger,' as I believe theater people call it, is delivered. I don't suppose the answer is 'a virgin,' is it?"

I had felt foolisher and foolisher as Wickett delivered his speech. Now I felt myself redden at the word *virgin*, and the rest of the company busted out laughing.

"Didn't I tell you!" Blair shouted. "A virgin, haw haw!"

Finally Fugwhit arrived with whiskey and water.

"Pour it, man, pour it," said Cousin Billy, and then he raised his glass. "Here's to General Washington: 'First in war, first in peace, first in the hearts of his countrymen,' as General Lee put it to Congress."

It was Light Horse Harry Lee who'd led the thirteen-thousand-man army across the mountains to put down what they in the East called the Whiskey Rebellion, as if a handful of farmers who tarred and feathered a few tax collectors constituted a threat to the republic. They constituted a threat to Colonel Hamilton's plans to establish an aristocracy, and to the value of some properties the president and his brother owned in the area, is the way I figured it. Hamilton and Washington had put on their old uniforms and ridden along as far as Bedford, where the Allegheny Mountains start getting rough. Washington turned back there, having made his point, and it was Harry Lee that the old soldiers had followed. But as a military man myself I couldn't fault an honest old warhorse for doing his duty. I had to drink up and like it.

Next came a toast to His Rotundancy, President Adams, he with his obnoxious Alien and Sedition Acts. That was followed by toasts to our squadron commander, Commodore Truxtun on the Leeward Islands station, and to Commodore Gaswell on the San Domingo station, who hated Truxtun and vice versa. Wickett offered the memory of John Paul Jones, hero of the Revolution and late admiral of the Russian navy. I drained my glass, Jones having been shorter than I.

Then it was my turn. I countered Adams with "good ol' Tom Jefferson," which got me a startled glance from Blair. Old Tom and his Democratic-Republicans were out of favor in those days, or so the Federalists claimed; and as Adams and his lady were rabid Federalists who believed the national government existed to reward their friends and punish their enemies, you didn't get to be the assistant U.S. consul to San Domingo without being one.

Finally Cousin Billy proclaimed a bumper: "*Cassandra*, may she be believed at last."

Blair, who apparently had no philosophy, gave him a blank look.

"Beg pardon, Mr. Blair," said Cousin Billy. "You don't know our history. It's simple enough, really: when the schooner was launched she was called *Cassandra*. Her name was changed when the Navy bought her."

"But why the doubt as to her veracity?"

"Cassandra was the daughter of the king of Troy," said Wickett.

"Met him once," said Blair.

"You fascinate me," said Wickett. "What I mean is, Apollo taught her prophecy. When she refused his advances, he condemned her never to be believed. She was taken by Agamemnon and murdered by Clytemnestra."

"Glad to hear it. A proper fate for a liar," said Blair. "But ain't it terrible bad luck to change the name of a ship?"

"Oh, lord no," said Billy. "It's done all the time, man. Why, there was—there was—what was there, Mr. Wickett?"

"Well, sir, perhaps you are reminded of the famous old *Alliance*, that took Lafayette back to France and was the last ship of the Continental Navy. She was the *Hancock* at one time, as I'm sure you meant to say."

"That's right," said Billy. "And there was—I'm sure there were more—"

"The *Ranger*, Paul Jones's sloop, that received our first salute—our first official one, I mean—was first called the *Hampshire*."

"Yes," I piped up. "And she was called *Halifax* after the British took her at Charleston."

"No doubt she was took for speaking without first being spoke to," said Wickett. "But the boy's right—and *Boston*, that was captured the next day—"

"I remember," said Billy. "She became the *Charleston*. And then there was the *Wild Duck*—"

"Sir, the whiskey stands by you," said Blair.

I was well on my way to getting knee-walking drunk when I became aware of a presence at my elbow: a tall, gaunt man with creases around his eyes and gray streaks in his beard. Under one arm he cradled a package wrapped in brown paper.

"Well I'll be a dog! Hello, Phillip," says I. "Was it something?"

He tugged at his chin whiskers and rubbed a finger across his shaven upper lip, as if he had expected a friendlier greeting but wasn't sure if he cared. "We departed on less than amicable terms yestereve, brother Matthew," he said. "I had not forgotten that it was thy natal day. Not that such things are important, truly, but I am sensible that they seem that way at times to the young."

"Oh, don't stand there, Cuz," said Billy, pulling out a chair. "Have a dram with us, that's a lad. Boy! Where is that fuckwit? Ha ha! I mean Fugwhit. Hey, Fugwhit! Another glass here, and another jug."

No, no, Phillip protested, pressing business awaited him; yes, yes,

Cousin Billy insisted, all business being suspended that day except tending bar, ha ha. Finally Phillip, to my surprise, relented "for familial duty," setting his black broadbrim on the table and his package on the floor by his feet.

After he had been presented to Wickett and Blair, and had returned Wickett's expressionless stare with an equal inscrutability, and had been induced to drink to "a prosperous voyage" but not "death to the French," Phillip turned to me and said, "A letter came from Father last week, along with certain items. I took it upon myself to bestow on thee other certain items already in my possession. If thou had not flown into a passion when I asked thee to accompany me to meeting, thou might have them in hand already."

"How is the old goat?" I said.

Phillip sniffed uneasily. "It is unseemly to call thy father a goat."

But he has horns, thinks I.

"Very well then, Phillip, how is dear old dad?" Father had donated a good deal of whiskey to the congressman who had gotten Billy his command and me my midshipman's warrant, and it wouldn't do if Phillip was to tell the old man I was ungrateful.

"He is well. As I was saying, Father wishes thee to have one thing and I wish thee to have another. As the Bible commands us to 'honor thy father,' I brought both." He indicated the package. "I will say once again, however, that I cannot fathom thy continued desire to sail under arms."

"Fathom! Hey, *fathom?*" Cousin Billy broke in, smiling around the table. "There's a nautical pun for you, hey?" Blair spewed out a mouthful of whiskey, and then snorted as Wickett stared at him.

Cousin Billy looked under the table at the package. "Open it, Cuz, do."

Phillip shook his head slightly.

"Well," I said, "I don't guess it'd be appropriate—"

"Nonsense," said Cousin Billy. "In fact, I order you to open it. There now, I've relieved you of your commendable modesty."

"He is my half-brother," said Phillip. "I think he will do as I say."

"And I'm his commanding officer," said Billy. "That's trumps, y'know. Military outranks family every time. Besides, I'm family, too— go on, Matty, open 'er up."

"Aye aye, sir." Pleased at the chance to annoy Phillip, I untied the string and pulled the paper aside, revealing two large leather-bound volumes and a polished triangular wooden case.

"Moreau's account of his stay in Hispaniola before the present unpleasantness," said Phillip, indicating the books. "He is frivolous at times, but he means well, and he is no shirker when it comes to detail. And it is in French, of course, which will enable thee to keep up with thy lessons, which I provided thee at some expense."

"Of which I am sensible and grateful, Phillip." I was vaguely aware that my French tutor, a refugee from the slave uprisings in San Domingo, which the Indians called Hayti, had been poorly paid when he had been paid at all. I examined the title page of Médéric-Louis-Elie Moreau de Saint-Méry's *Description topographique, physique, civile, politique, et historique de la Partie française de l'Îsle Saint-Domingue.* "A topographical, physical, civil, political, and historical description of the French part of the island of Santo Domingo," I translated out loud, "with general observations on its population, on the character and customs of its diverse inhabitants, on its climate, culture, production, administration, et cetera, published in Philadelphia by the author last year. Phillip, this must be worth a small fortune."

"A small one, yes. But it was acquired in lieu of a bad debt. I shan't ever see money for it, and besides, I read it before wrapping it up."

"Handsome of you, all the same."

I wasn't quite sure what to make of the literary windfall or what Phillip's reasons might be for bringing it—he who had given me nothing in my life but advice—and I felt like an ingrate for thinking such things in the first place.

"Now then, on to the case," he said, pursing his lips and nodding at the box, "and we can be done with this business. Father wished to see thee equipped with a set of pistols, but of course the Pacific Brotherhood does not countenance such requests."

He put his hand on the triangular wooden box before I could open it.

"This is a sextant case, I will have thee notice, and which thou will have deduced from its shape. I have no use for a sextant anymore. Most days, I can find my way betwixt office and home without recourse to azimuths and angles of declension."

Cousin Billy guffawed, pounding Phillip on the back. "Oh ho ho! Well said, sir, what a colossal pun—*declension!*"

Blair laughed too, though I doubted if he knew enough about navigation to get the joke.

"Please do thou not strike me, cousin," said Phillip, raising an arm to shield himself from the enthusiastic blows Cousin Billy was applying to his bony shoulders. "I fail to see—"

A malevolent triumph gleamed in Wickett's eyes. "The present mirth is rooted in a commingling of the words *declension* and *declination*," he said. "The former is a grammatical term, as you no doubt are aware. The latter is the angular distance of a heavenly body from the celestial equator, measured on the great circle passing through the celestial pole and that body, if I remember my *Practical Navigator* correctly—and I should be pretty far out of my reckoning if I did not. That is precisely what this grand instrument—" he indicated the still-unopened case "— is designed to measure. It tells us where we are at sea, so that—" he winked at me "—we will not be all at sea."

Taken aback by the joke coming from an unexpected quarter, Cousin Billy pounded the table till the glasses rattled. "Oh, capital, Mr. Wickett, capital! Fugwhit! Where is that lazy villain? Fugwhit, another round all around!" He fell silent, apparently struggling with a joke involving the juxtaposition of "round" and "all around," but soon gave it up.

"Curiously enough," Wickett went on, "declination also has to do with deviation and refusal, though such things are never countenanced at sea." He gazed with distaste at Phillip. "It is only on land that one must tolerate such stuff."

"Yes, I take thy meaning well to heart, brother," said Phillip, matching Wickett's gaze. "On land as in life, one must tolerate a great many indignities. Travail breedeth character, but thou will agree there are limits. I was ten years at sea." He rose. "And now, brothers, I have been too long away from business. Commerce waits for no man. Peace be with thee, brothers, and may thy contentions be resolved." With that he stood up, shook my hand, saying, "Remember how our brother George died," and left.

Blair was the first to speak. "My stars and body," he hiccupped, "what a bleak fellow. Must be pretty dismal having a brother for a sexton. I mean, a sexton for a brother."

"Half-brother," I said. "He's no sexton, he's—"

"Sexton! Sextant! Hey? Oh hoo ha," shouted Cousin Billy. "Another round before the meat comes, and let's have us a time! Fugwhit, where the hell's our dinner?"

Long after ten o'clock, as we were being rowed back to *Rattle-Snake*, and Cousin Billy had fallen asleep on Wickett's shoulder, and Wickett had shrugged him off and Cousin Billy had collapsed in a heap under his boat cloak, Blair whispered to me:

"Wha' th' sexton mean, 'Remember George'? Who George, hey? An' how'd he die?"

"Geordie, sir. My brother. My real brother, I mean." Liquor had taken the edge off the hurt. "He was killed in ninety-four."

"Nonny foe, nonny foe. Wha' happen in nonny foe?"

"The Reign of Terror ended, for one thing."

"Ha! An' that rascal Robespierre lost his head, snip snip!" He chopped his left palm with the heel of his right hand, to indicate the strike of a guillotine blade. "But say, was this Geordie a damn revolutionary, a what-d'ye-call-'em, them fellows without breeches: a sans-culotte?"

It would never do to pitch him into the water. "If you will, sir," I said, obscurely pleased that I could give him a mild answer. "But he never got farther away from home than Pittsburgh. That's where we're from. Or nearby, anyway—McKeesport, a few miles up the Monongahela."

I remembered smoke, and the fear on Geordie's face.

"No guillotine, then," said Blair. "No, was something closer to home." He sat, deep in thought, watching the oars biting the water. Then he snapped his fingers. "I got it! He was a Whiskey Boy! The Whiskey Rebellion. Some fellows wouldn't pay their taxes, and the president—God rest his dear soul—had to send out the militia to crack a few heads. Men from New Jersey and Maryland and Virginia, all marchin' on Pittsburgh. It was a triumph for Fed . . . Fed'ralism. Light Horse Harry in the van, and good ol' Alexander Hamilton there to see the rebels took their medicine an' liked it, ha ha!" He thought some more, and then shook his head. "Who remem'ers what *that* was about!"

"Aye," I said, "that's probably what he meant."

But I had no idea what Phillip meant, no idea what Phillip meant about anything. The Pacific Brotherhood were Quakerish in their contempt for violence, yet the "sextant," when I had snuck a peek at it while the others ate and drank themselves silly, had turned out to be a pair of dueling pistols.

Two

The rumble of the holystones and the slapping of the swabs drove me topside at first light. As I was weaving my way toward the seat of ease, I met a large man in the green coat and britches and red vest of a Navy surgeon. He greeted me in an expectant sort of way and then said, "Well, young sir, you don't look so good this morning."

He sported a wig and carried a cane, which gave him a genteel air, and he had a comforting smell of soap and tobacco. I liked him right off.

"Something I ate, sir. No, I tell a lie: Captain Trimble threw a dinner party yesterday, and I disremember if we actually ate anything at all. You must be Mr. Quilty."

"And you are Mr. Graves." Humbert Quilty put the back of one of his huge hands against my cheek, then used my chin as a handle to move my head this way and that while peering into my eyes. "You do not remember meeting me?"

"No sir. When did you come aboard?"

"Last night. You have forgotten it, then?"

"No, sir. I remember being in the boat, but after that it's a blur. No, I tell another lie: it is not a blur so much as a blank."

"Hmm. This is not a good sign, young man. I advise you to abstain from spirituous liquors, even though I realize you will ignore my advice for perhaps many years before seeing the wisdom in it." I might've taken insult at that, for a man's taking of liquor is no one's business but his own, but he said it in such a forthright way that I could not.

"However, to return to the subject at hand," he continued, "I remember you. You were singing. Or chanting, I should say: 'A-sailing down all on the coast of High Barbary' and 'Whiskey Johnny,' if I recollect aright."

"Oh no, sir, it comes back to me now. That was Mr. Blair. Mine was 'We're them derned ol' Whiskey Boys, hurrah hurrah hurrah.'"

"No wonder Mr. Wickett bundled you below directly. There was little he could do about Mr. Blair: he is aptly named, alas. Stick out your tongue. Say 'Ah.'"

He smelled my breath and then said, "You will live, though for a day or two you may wish you would not. Shall I give you physic? Castor oil or Chinese rhubarb would do the trick, or maybe some ipecac if you would rather void the poisons through the upper passage. No? Have some grog if you will, then, when the people have theirs. I find that works a treat."

I leaned over the rail.

"Recovery is at hand," said Quilty. "Come see me later, and I shall palpate your liver for you."

Wickett and Rogers were below, eating their dinner, when our last man came aboard. After Mr. Quilty's gaudy green and red, it was a relief to look upon the restful blue and buff of Dick Towson, my old friend from the *Aztec* and *Rattle-Snake*'s only other midshipman. Dick was as near enough my own age as made no nevermind, and that made us mates as much as anything. We were hardly peas in a pod, and that's a natural fact. He was better looking, for one thing—all rosy cheeks and classical nose and graceful limbs, with his long yellow hair clubbed in the back and held in place by a black velvet bow, and his crisp white neck-cloth rising to his perfect ears and contrasting exquisitely with the gorgeous blue stuff of his uniform, as if he'd been dreamed up by Rembrandt Peale, while I was banty and dark and grubby and tangle-headed—and for another he had a great deal of money, which he spent with an open hand, while I was forever on the lookout for an extra copper. I think I amused him. Behind him Jubal, his slave, a huge black man with a shaven head and arms as big as an ordinary man's thighs, stood easy with a pair of sea chests tucked under his arms and a great ham in a net bag dangling from one mighty fist. The sight of the greasy haunch set my stomach going again.

Dick whipped his handkerchief out of his sleeve and held it to his nose. "Downwind, sir, downwind!"

"*Europe,*" I groaned.

"A small continent, north of Africa," said Dick, patting my back. "There, there."

I wiped my lips with my sleeve and spat over the side. "How was your Christmas?"

"Prime! Turkey instead of goose, but I find I prefer it, and three kinds of pie, including sweet potato. Father says sweet potatoes are nigger food." Here he broke off to say, "You, Jubal! Don't just stand there. Get my things below. One of those fellows will tell you where. Strong as an ox," he said to me, "and as smart as one too. But anyway, our Bertha could make turnips taste like beefsteak. I *am* sorry," he said, as I paid another visit to Europe. "Forgot you don't like turnips. Oh, speaking of Father, he sends his regards and says you're an ingrate for not spending Christmas at White Oak." White Oak was the Towson plantation on Maryland's Eastern Shore. "But Mrs. Towson says she forgives you, as you are still a boy."

"I wish I *had* gone to White Oak," I said, though I was unhappy to think that Dick's young stepmother didn't think of me as a man—a notion I backed away from as soon as I thought it. "I calculated to spend Christmas with Phillip, but he kept dodging me. I saw him for a couple minutes yesterday. I was pickled, but he didn't look as sour about it as sometimes. He actually gave me a present."

"What, Bible verses stolen from the meeting house?"

"No, a box of pistols."

"Pistols! Won't the Brotherhood disown him?"

"He said the box was his old sextant and wouldn't let me open it where anyone else could see. He probably figures it this way: they're from the old man, so *he* ain't responsible. He's sly that way."

Dick grinned. "Yes, like the Quaker who says, 'Forsooth, brother, thou standest where I am about to shoot.'"

I grinned back, but said: "Him! He wouldn't bother. He knows there's always going to be someone else to do his fighting for him. But anyway, who's to tell on him?"

"Not I. Are they good 'uns?"

"They're handsome enough—walnut stocks, brass fittings, good steel barrels. But they're dueling pistols. Won't be worth a damn in a fight."

Dick's blue eyes glowed. "Dueling pistols! So you'll call Old Woman Malloy out at last?"

"You can't challenge a superior officer, Dick, you know that. The dog would just have me arrested, or ignore me."

"The man's a scrub. Why, if he'd struck me the way he did you, I'd have run him through right on the spot."

"I don't aim to get myself hanged. I'm delicate that way." When your captain's an idiot or a villain, all you can do is outlast him or leave him, I'd found. "Besides," I said, "you can't learn people manners by shooting 'em, any more'n shooting a dog learns him not to bite."

"Maybe not, but it keeps him from biting again."

"Captains have been beating midshipmen since forever."

"That was no simple caning. He—"

"Leave it lie, Dick, or I'll have to call you out in about a minute."

I said it sharper than I'd meant to, and Dick gave me a calculating look. It was some sharp calculating, too, for friends though we were, there was a feeling among the planting set that a man weren't a man till he toed his mark on the field of honor. We might have sailed into dangerous waters if he hadn't suddenly grinned and said, "I don't know what I would have done was I in your place. I meant no offense."

"None taken. Say, I bet you want to see my pistols. You won't be envious then, I bet. Not much!"

"But hold," he said. "Speaking of presents, look at what I have got!" He pulled a slim silver repeating watch from his vest pocket. He pressed a button and the lid sprang open. "It's a Graham Jackson, from

London. Just look at that engraving! Hold on." He frowned at the back of the watch, and then handed it to me. "I can't quite make out the inscription. What's that look like to you?"

I turned the watch around in my hand. It was heavier than it looked, all gleaming glass and solid silver, and crusted all around the rim with little dolphins and mermaids. Within a frame of laurel leaves on the front lid, a splayed eagle hovered over two frigates enwreathed in smoke: our *Constellation* capturing the French *L'Insurgente* last February, according to the inscription on the scroll in the eagle's beak.

But it was the back that Dick was pointing at. There, in a clearing between a sailor treading on a flattened crown and a bare-breasted Liberty brandishing the Stars and Stripes, a thicket of ornate letters had been engraved: R.T. TO M.G., XMAS MDCCXCIX.

"That's 'Richard Towson to Matthew Graves, Christmas seventeen-ninety-nine,'" Dick translated. "A happy Yuletide to you."

"You dog! I wish I had something—"

Dick waved his hand. "A trifle. It's from Father's lady, really, though she was vexed you didn't come. As was Arabella. She wanted me to hit it with a hammer." Arabella was Dick's younger sister, yellow-haired like her brother, pretty, just my size, and whose presence caused me to trip over my feet and forget what I was going to say.

"Oh, stuff," I said. "She only wanted me to come so she could torment me." I raised my eyebrows. "Not that I mind."

"That girl can outfight and outclimb any boy her size, all right, though I suppose she ain't so hard on the eye now that she has learnt to bat her lashes and cover her face with a fan." He glanced toward the blue coats on the quarterdeck and lowered his voice. "Speaking of matches made in heaven, how's Billy getting on with Wicked Pete?"

"Wicked Pete?"

"That's what they call Mr. Wickett below stairs. The wherry men told me while they were rowing me out here." He tapped his forehead. "They said he has the mark of Cain on him."

"It's just a birthmark. But I bet he'd be happy to lay the mark of *cane* on anyone who gets athwart his cable, ha ha."

"Yes, go ahead and joke about it," said Dick, and he said it in such a way that I stopped laughing and felt sick all over again. "And they said he's a hard driver, too. Think we should have stuck with Malloy?"

I glanced around before answering. Wickett was still below, and I hadn't seen Cousin Billy all morning.

"Oh, I don't know. He and Billy are getting on well enough. No sparks yet, not that Wickett ain't trying. He has a certain . . . I don't know, a certain manner, like he's mocking you. I suppose he resents it that he weren't given the schooner. Nothing out and out, I mean, nothing you can put a finger on, but it's there. Billy's ignoring it so far, if he's noticed it at all. He's a jolly soul, but I think even he will resent it in time."

"Him? Billy's not the sort to cross a man who shot his predecessor."

"Oh, that's only scuttlebutt. I don't believe it."

Dick smiled. "If Captain Tyrone had been born a gentleman instead of being made one, he'd have known how to deal with a rumor without getting himself killed in the process."

It was just like Dick to bring that up. Despite what the Navy might say about my being a gentleman, I didn't guess I was Dick's social equal by a long chalk.

"How you talk, Dick. My father's a merchant, hardly better than a mechanic. You know he runs his own distillery."

"Ah," said Dick, "but it's a very large distillery, and making whiskey is an art. My father says so. And they both farm, don't they?"

It'd be a waste of breath to point out that my father wasn't a *gentleman* farmer. He paid wages.

I said, "Wicked Pete or not, the people seem to like him well enough."

Dick made a face like he'd bitten into an unripe persimmon. "Sure they like him. They've sailed with him before. A sailor always trusts the devil he knows. But as long as they remember who the captain is, what do we care?"

"As long as *Wickett* remembers it. Listen, Billy told me something interesting: Their commissions are dated the same day!"

"Oh dear, and both of them lieutenants, ha ha!"

"Yes, I laughed too, till I thought about it."

"One thing I bet is true about Wickett," said Dick, "he ain't the sort who should take kindly to being made a dry nurse. No hand-holder, he."

"No, I'd resent it myself, but no fear about Billy: he's a fine seaman. He don't need his hand held. But sure there must've been a mistake—"

A voice rasped, "You don't mind if I shove in my oar, do you?" and we both jumped. With his hands clasped behind his back, Wickett glowered down at us and said, "Mr. Towson, I presume. Had a lovely holiday down on the old plantation, did we?"

"Indeed, sir, yes, thank you." Dick touched his hat and said, "You must be Mr. Wickett."

Ignoring the abbreviated salute, Wickett thrust out his pointed chin and said, "Crackers and colored paper, roast goose and creamed turnips, stewed cranberries and wassail, I bet."

Dick put his hands in his pockets and forced a smile. "Along with the ham and roast beef, yes sir, except we had turkey instead of goose. You ought to try it, it's quite as good—"

"And sixpences—I am no stranger to the glorious turkey, Mr. Towson, and you will kindly keep your hands out of your pockets while you are in my ship—and sixpences in the pudding, too? Or maybe Spanish pistareens is more your style."

"Not at all, sir. Father had some ten-cent pieces—"

"And perhaps an African wench afterwards, to warm y'self on a cold winter's night, hmm?"

Dick stiffened. "Really, sir! A gentleman resents being spoke to in such a way."

"I am sure he does. Now, sir, I met a man below, a very large and very black man, who said he belongs to you. He said his name is Jubal and that he's to be rated able."

"Oh, yes sir. We've been sailing on the Chesapeake since we could walk. Certainly he should be rated able."

Wickett pulled his thin lips down in such a deep snarl that the ends of his long, pointed nose and chin seemed to be trying to touch each other, like the tips of a new crescent moon, but his voice was soft. "If a man says he is an able seaman, then I believe him," he said. "His shipmates will soon set things right if he lies. There is no criminal so hated as a liar, at sea. No sir, that is not what I am about. You intend to pocket his wages, I assume?"

I could tell Dick was astonished, but he had the sense to hide it. "Of course, sir," he said. "You can't trust a nigger with money."

It wasn't unusual to ship slaves as seamen and keep their wages. It was frowned upon in some ships and accepted as a matter of course in others, and I'd never thought much of it until I saw the way Wickett took the news. He leaned over Dick, thrusting his face into his, and the farther Wickett leaned forward the farther Dick had to lean back, tucking his chin in till he looked like a turkey contemplating an approaching hatchet.

"When coming aboard," said Wickett, "it is customary for gentlemen to report themselves to the officer of the watch."

"That would be you, sir?"

"Of course that would not be me. We're at anchor watch, you pup—the gunner has the deck." In larger ships with larger crews, first lieutenants never stood watch. But Wickett was our only commissioned officer besides Billy, and the fact that he would have to take a watch once we got to sea must have stuck in his craw. As the color left his face the stain on his brow seemed to get ruddier, as if it was sucking up the blood. "Now, if it ain't too much trouble to you," he said, "we would like to get under way. Damned inconvenient for a fellow, I realize, but necessary if we are to get to San Domingo. Pray, would a gentleman object was he asked to lay aloft to superintend the setting of the main tops'l?"

"No, sir," said Dick. Then, as Wickett frowned even deeper, he touched his hat, said, "Aye aye, sir," and ran to the main shrouds.

"And do try not to issue too many orders, Mr. Towson," called
Wickett after him in a cheerful tone, as if they were the best of jolly
fellows. "I believe the topmen are acquainted with their business already." He watched Dick scamper up the ratlines. Then he leaned over
and said in my ear, "Won't he be annoyed when he discovers that
Mr. Blair has gone ashore after some misplaced letters, and we have
missed our tide. He'll have gotten tar all over his nice clean breeches
for nothing."

Rattle-Snake didn't weigh anchor till the beginning of the second dogwatch, as it turned out. There was considerable grumbling about bad
luck, and Wickett made mention on the crew's behalf (and in their
hearing) to Cousin Billy about tempting fate by sailing on a Friday.

"*Friday sail, ill luck and gale,* as the sailors' doggerel has it," said
Wickett. "I put no faith in it myself, sir. But because Jack believes it,
if anything untoward happens he will see it as having come from sailing on a Friday. And because he will expect bad luck, he will see it in
every sprung spar, in every blown-out sail, in every stubbed toe and
torn finger."

As it was the master's watch, Cousin Billy told Wickett to get on
about his business. Besides, he pointed out, a ship's day began at noon:
if Wickett had been ready to go when he had been asked to be ready to
go, it would still be Thursday, "a day that has no meaning whatsoever
to even the most superstitious foremast jack."

"One cannot command the tide, Captain," Wickett said, touching
his hat and walking away.

"Come back here, sir!"

Wickett turned and stared, and then strode back to the quarterdeck.
He touched his hat again and said, "Sir."

Said Cousin Billy, his jowls all a-quiver: "I won't stand for sloven-
liness, Mr. Wickett. You must salute me on my quarterdeck, and you
must do it proper. Let's get that clear from the beginning."

"Aye aye, sir."

Wickett doffed his hat, bent in a bow that was just this side of insolent, begged Billy's pardon in a flat ugly unreadable voice, set his hat exactly square on his head again, and stalked forward to his station down by the foremast.

The hands at the capstan had stopped what they were doing to watch. You couldn't blame them for it. It was shabby on Billy's part, ungenerous and ungentlemanly, however right he might be. And it was possible that Wickett had merely been making an observation, and that he'd meant no disrespect by the abbreviated salute, and that he'd never even contemplated the idea of lingering in harbor merely because it was Friday. But it looked bad.

And the men at the capstan were still staring. I recollected myself and shouted, "Here you, don't stand there gaping like ninnies!" They pantomimed shame. "Mr. Horne," I said to one of the bosun's mates, a broad-nosed, wide-shouldered, yellow-toothed Negro with a mass of long black wooly braids knotted at the nape of his neck, "mind what your people are about."

"Aye aye, sir." Horne shifted his wad of tobacco from one cheek to the other. "Hey, you," he said to the nearest man, "mind what you're about."

"It's just as easy to say a man's name as to say 'Hey, you,'" I said, even though I myself couldn't have placed a name to more than a couple of the faces around me. It was just the sort of thing an officer said.

Horne indicated how often he had heard it by grinning around his cud, but he answered mildly: "Aye aye, sir."

When the order came to commence heaving, a few of the men looked me in the eye when they spat into their hands before leaning into the capstan bars. Whether it was insolence or approval, only time would tell. They walked the schooner forward till the cable was nearly straight up and down, to the squeaking of the fife and to Horne's shouts of "heave cheer'ly! One more pawl! Get all ye can! Ready for the heavy heave—*heave!*"

"Mr. Rogers," said Cousin Billy, "I want to see how she handles. I have the conn, if you please."

"Very good, sir."

His hat in his hand for gesturing, Billy stepped forward to the break of the quarterdeck, where he could observe the ordered chaos aloft and alow, and shouted, "Make sail! Aloft sail loosers! Some of you men there, lead along your tops'l sheets and halyards. Tops'ls there, lay out and loose!"

Leaving Horne to finish seeing the cable rousted down, I ran aloft with the maintopmen. I had my usual secret moment of fear as I hung back-downward in the foothooks, the futtock shrouds, which are spread outboard as they pass around the cap, but there was no time to think about that. I threw myself across the topsail yard and felt with my feet for the footrope, and shuffled and squirmed out to the horse, which is an extra footrope at the end of the yard. The horse is necessarily hung close, making it an uncomfortable perch for a tall man but cozy for a half-pint like myself. It dipped and swung as the man next nearest inboard stepped on it, half on the horse and half on the main footrope. I clung to the yard with my elbows and began yanking gaskets loose with both hands.

"Anchor's a-trip, sir! Straight up and down!"

"Stand by," called Billy. "Let fall!"

"Main tops'l away!"

"Fore-tops'l away!"

"Lay in and down from aloft! Hop to it, lads. Man your tops'l sheets and halyards!"

Wickett caught me by the collar as I ran by. "How can you see what your men are about when you are out on the yardarm? An officer's job is not to do things, but to see they are done."

"Sorry, sir."

"I know you will do better another time." He slapped me on the back and said, "Look, the jib halyard is fouled. Get for'ard and see to it!"

The breeze pressing against her topsails gave *Rattle-Snake* sternway. Billy took a stance next to the tiller and said, "Put your helm alee." The steersman put the tiller over. "Helm's alee!"

Rattle-Snake's stern came around to larboard, eased along by the backed fore-topsail until the main topsail filled. The steersman put her helm over and she began to glide forward. "Hands to the braces!" The fore-topsail yard was swung around, the sail filled and we gathered speed. "That's *well* your braces! Hands to the mains'l!" With her square topsails braced around, the schooner glided out of the harbor, her great fore-and-aft mainsail rising as she went.

We turned south at two bells in the first watch—that is, 9 PM—with the light on Bodkin Point visible on the starboard beam and *Rattle-Snake* prancing to the white horses on Chesapeake Bay. The clouds had broken, swept away on the wind, and in the starlight the bay glittered like new-hammered steel.

Dick grinned at me, teeth chattering, and I grinned right back at him, thinking what a glory it was to be a sailor on such a night.

"There, that should do her," said Cousin Billy to Mr. Rogers. "Try not to run us onto anyone, and watch out for ice. Call me if in doubt or the wind gets up, will you?" He finished scribbling his night orders on the slate and said to me and Dick, "You may stand down now, gentlemen. Will you join me for a nightcap?"

"Thanks all the same, sir, if you'll excuse me," I said. "Mr. Wickett offered to let me stand the middle watch with him, so I guess I better turn in while I can."

"He'll *let* you stand the middle watch? Good lord. Will you join me, Mr. Towson, pray?"

"With pleasure, sir."

"Why dance with the mate when you can dance with the skipper," I muttered when Billy had gone.

"That's right, mate," said Dick. "No sense in polishing a rotten apple."

The schooner carried no guns on her lower deck, which was a blessing for it gave us some room to live in. But she had not been built as a warship, had not been designed to carry ninety-six men, boys, and officers with all their baggage and stores and livestock, and so even

I had to stoop under the deck beams. The air was already thick with the familiar fug of dried sweat, damp wool, and the manure sloshing around in the pigpen right forward, but it was warm. I made my way through the rows of men swaying and snoring in their hammocks till I came to the midshipmen's berth.

Our cabin was a canvas-screened cuddy on the starboard side, just forward of the mainmast. It was every bit as dark as the hole we'd lived in, in the *Aztec,* though smaller, but it was far less cramped with only me and Dick to share it. By slinging our hammocks diagonally we had near seven feet to stretch out in. It could have been worse—we could have had bunks, which we'd rattle around in the moment we fell in with any kind of a sea, and which would be forever damp from the working of the seams. However, some craftsman long ago had lined the timbers of our fourth wall with a convenient set of cabinets and drawers, with even a shelf with a hole sunk in it to hold a tin wash-basin. What deck space we had was mostly taken up by our chests, which we would use for chairs or tables as occasion demanded.

I stripped off my coat and boots and helped myself to a slab of Dick's ham, which Jubal had slung from a deck beam where it would be handy, and swung myself into the upper hammock. I had been asleep for what seemed only a few minutes when a shadowy figure staggered in and nearly knocked me out of bed.

"Rise and shine, starbowlines," came Dick's voice, whispering in the dark. "Here I come with a sharp knife and a clean conscience!"

"How many bells have gone?"

"The time is eleven and three quarters o'clock, or near enough as makes no difference. You know, that stout fellow Trimble broke out some damn fine whiskey. Father Graves is an artist, as I said once upon a when. Damn fine, laddy ol' mad, Matty ol' lad. He's a bit put out with you."

I peeped out from under my blankets. "Who, my father?"

"Mad Billy Trimble. You remember him."

"Sure, he's the captain."

"Say, you're right." He reached out a finger and poked me in the chest. "Surely you could find some other way to butter up the first luff than by spending a winter's night on deck with him and leaving your own cousin and best pal all alone."

"But that ain't—"

A third shadow joined us: Jubal, come to tuck Mars Dickie into bed. I pulled on my boots, grabbed my hat and greatcoat and went on deck.

The four chill black hours that followed were as miserable as I had expected, except for a curious thing. While Wickett was drilling me in taking lunar and star sightings, the sky having remained clear, he said, "You sir, you're a good Republican lad, ain't you?"

I said I guessed I was although I was too young to vote and didn't own the necessary property anyway, and to my surprise Wickett put his hand on my shoulder. I could not be sure in the dark, but he seemed to be grinning.

"Then you need never fear," said he. "I remarked your toast yesterday in honor of our good vice president. It is said Tom Jefferson is no friend of the Navy, but that is merely the Federalists' story, the concoction of royalty manqué, who fear democracy even more than they fear plays and poetry and love and everything else that makes life worth the trouble of living it."

He stared at me for a long moment in the darkness, and then continued, "However, we must recommence this interesting line of thought at a later date in more comfortable surroundings. In the meantime I should be much obliged was you to go forward and kick the lookout, if he has fallen asleep."

Three

We groped our way into Hampton Roads very early on Sunday morning under an icy fog and bucking a flowing tide. It was all hands but Billy on deck, with everyone straining eye and ear for any rumor of ships ahead. We had the lead going constantly, ready to throw all aback in an instant, with the cable roused out and the best-bower ready to let go. Unseen all around us, moored ships were tolling their bells or blowing on whistles or honking on conch shells. A man in the bows was shooting off a musket every minute.

"Ahoy the forward lookout," called Wickett. "What do you see?"

"No' a thing, sir." In an undertone that carried clearly through the fog, the lookout—one of four British deserters aboard that I knew of—added, "It's that gloamy a nicht, I could'na find mah mam's teats with twa guid hands."

Wickett turned to me and said, "Tell the captain we must come to an anchor."

I had no more business telling the captain what to do than Wickett had, but Billy's absence on deck was dangerous and unlawful. I rephrased Wickett's words in my head as I ducked below.

I could stand upright in the after-cabin, thanks to the raised quarterdeck above it, but a man of normal height would have to mind the deck beams. Underfoot was another matter. The cabin was crammed with desk and chart table, a sideboard filled with bottles and glasses and china, a locked chest for Billy's table silver, and another for cutlasses and pistols. Net bags of dried fruits, sausages, cheeses and other dainties swayed on the bulkheads. The scuttles and stern windows were shut against the fog, and whiskey fumes and the rat-stink of dead cigars pierced the aromas of the cheeses and sausages.

By the light of the taffrail lantern shining through the stern windows, I could see Billy in silhouette as he sat on the padded stern locker that served him as a sofa, transferring whiskey from a decanter to his glass. He was so intent on the task that he fell over.

He smiled beatifically up at me in the dappled lamplight when I helped him sit up.

"Ever notice how the glass is always empty?" he said. "You pour y'self a goodly dram, and then when you go to drink it, is empty. So you pour y'self another, an' 'en when you try and drink that, is gone too."

"Mr. Wickett's respects, sir, and he wishes to come to an anchor."

"Nanker?"

"An anchor, yes sir. Thick fog, baffling airs and a contrary tide. We're near south of Cape Charles, according to soundings. Let me get you a cloak, sir."

He started to fall forward and I propped him back up. My hand came away sticky.

"And Misser Wickett wansa drop anchor."

"Yes sir."

"Well, you can jus' go and tell Misser Wickett that I don't give a damn what he does, so long's he don't innerfere with my powwow with Misser John Barleycorn." He patted the decanter. "The Sec—Sec'tary may say Wickett's second in command, and Wickett may think he's *in* command, but we know who's really in command, don't we, Cap'n Barleycorn?" As he turned to regard the decanter, it slipped from his fingers onto the checkered strip of painted canvas that did duty as a carpet. "Uh-oh!" he said, throwing up his hands like a child playing a nursery game. "'Nother dead Marine."

"It ain't no matter," I said, setting it among its companions on the sideboard.

"Is of great matter! An empty bottle is an abomination! Is unnatural. Hey, Prichard," he called, trying to rise.

"Just sit tight, sir," I said, easing him back. I went to the door and told the Marine sentry to pass the word for Prichard, the captain's steward. When I came back Billy was lolling on the deck, giggling. Obviously he wouldn't be going topside, but I couldn't leave him lying there. I cajoled him to his feet and aimed him toward the jalousie door of his sleeping place before I remembered that he had given it to Blair. I turned him around and pointed him toward the corridor. "You're in Mr. Wickett's cabin now, sir."

"Unhand me! I can walk." He shrugged my hand away. "Been walkin' for years." But he stopped after a step or two, and with great care he bent over, one hand clutching the back of a gilt chair and the other covering his neck-cloth, and puked. It was an astonishing stream, prodigiously malodorous and prolonged, not to mention splashy, and it shot out of him with a straining, wailing, moaning sob that stood the hair of my neck on end.

"Ah. 'S better." He straightened up, took a step, whacked his head on a beam and fell with a wet smack onto the deck.

"Prichard!" I yelled.

"Well, hain't I coming just as fast?" Prichard opened the door and gave me a severe look, but his shoulders drooped when he saw Billy on the floor. He hooked him around the armpits and hoisted him more-or-less upright, his feet sliding in the goo. "Well, sir—get his feet up outa the muck and we'll have him in his cot in half a tick."

"Up-a-day," said Cousin Billy.

"That's right, sir," said Prichard. "Ups-a-daisy, here we go."

We swayed him down the corridor and into the wardroom to the aftermost cabin on the larboard side, which Billy had commandeered from Wickett. Billy's long-haired cat, Greybar, was asleep in the hanging cot when we came in. He stood up, stretching and purring.

Prichard stripped Billy to his shirt and upended him into the cot. He tucked the blanket around him and said, "There we go, sir, up tight and out of sight."

"Better leave his coat and boots handy."

Greybar stretched out on Billy's legs, Sphinx-like, and Billy murmured in his sleep.

"A bucket an' mop is more like it," said Prichard. "He hain't goin' nowhere."

"That ain't for you to decide, Prichard."

"And I haven't, neither. But he won't be going on deck, Mr. Graves, even if he could. And because why?" He lowered his voice. "Because he don't wish for to take a swim some dark night, that's because why."

Cousin Billy made his appearance toward the end of the forenoon watch. He was unshaven, his stockings didn't match, and he had a green and yellow goose-egg on his brow. "Where is Mr. Wickett?" he said. "Mr. Wickett, we seem to have come to an anchor."

"That we have, sir."

Billy glanced at the rough log for the night before and bit off what-ever he had a mind to say. It was all there—darkness and fog, falling wind, contrary tide. Wickett had done the only sensible thing under the circumstances.

"Ah. Hmm. Thank you, Mr. Wickett. I seem to have a bad head this morning."

The incident might have passed without further notice but for Blair, who had been in a snit ever since he discovered that Mr. Rogers and the boat's crew had managed to wet every piece of his clothing while hoisting his baggage aboard. The assistant consul was taking the air on the quarterdeck that morning, as was his right, and asked a question, which was not:

"Why was the captain not informed, Mr. Wickett?"

"He was informed, Mr. Blair."

"Yet it seems a surprise to him this morning."

"Thank you, Mr. Blair," said Cousin Billy. "I think all is well in hand here."

"Well in hand?" said Blair. "The man is practicing upon you, sir." He turned back to Wickett. "The captain was informed in what way?"

"I sent word down."

"By whom did you send it?"

"By Mr. Graves, here."

Blair looked expectantly at me, and I gazed politely back.

"Well?" said Blair.

"Yes, sir?" says I, determined not to be helpful.

"I was not aware that the day-to-day operation of the ship was of interest to you, Mr. Blair," said Wickett. What he meant was that how the ship was run was none of the consul's business.

"My interest is in arriving upon my station with as little delay as possible," said Blair. What he meant was that anything was his business if he wanted it to be. He had no official authority aboard, of course, but had pull that could make life miserable for an officer who crossed him.

Wickett looked to Cousin Billy, but he was bawling down the ladder for coffee to be sent up. "The captain was incapacitated," said Wickett.

"Oh? You are a physician?"

"I am not."

"Perhaps the physician was sent for?"

"We don't rate one. Mr. Quilty is merely a surgeon."

"Well, was he sent for?"

"Of course not, Mr. Blair. Why should he lose any sleep?"

"The captain's incapacity did not alarm you?"

"No."

"Please, Mr. Blair," said Cousin Billy, rejoining us. "Mr. Wickett believes I was the worse for drink last night, ha ha! He's trying to save me some embarrassment. In truth, I haven't been well, and of course Mr. Wickett can be trusted with as mundane a matter as bringing us to an anchor. We do things differently in these little vessels than they do in those big frigates. You'll find during our voyage that Mr. Wickett will take a great many duties upon himself. That is only right and natural when we have so few watch-keeping officers." Then a happy inspiration struck him, and he added, "Particularly at a time when my duties naturally must be focused on your comfort and convenience."

"And glad I am to hear you say it, too."

Cousin Billy looked around at the ships in the roadstead. "What of our convoy, Mr. Wickett? Are they here?"

Wickett indicated a nearby brig and schooner. "*Jane* and *Augustin von Steuben*. Their captains say they left *Anemone* and *Lighthorse* at New Castle, but expect them imminently. Oh, yes," he said as Cousin Billy raised his eyebrows, "the captains have been aboard and gone. I didn't presume to wake you."

Cousin Billy was caught by his speech about Wickett's freedom to take duties upon himself in his absence, but he puffed up a little anyway. "This will never do, Mr. Wickett. Not at all. Have you forgot the date? It's New Year's Eve, man! You must send a boat immediately and say I should be obliged of their company for dinner at three of the clock. I'd be glad if you'd join us, of course." He blinked companionably at Wickett.

Wickett bowed his head.

There were no white-gloved sideboys nor bosun's mates trilling on silver pipes, not for mere merchant captains. There was just me, in my second-best uniform with the standup collar, to greet Peavey and Spetters when they came aboard. Captain Peavey of the *Jane* was a sour-faced Eastern Shoreman of no more than my height but nearly twice my breadth, in a black frock coat that strained at the shoulders. Captain Spetters of the *Augustin von Steuben* was a robust Pennsylvania Dutchman in a bottle-green coat, flowered vest and pink britches. He clasped my hand in both of his and pumped it up and down, saying, "*Sie sind sehr junge*. You are seeming very young. Surely you ain't the captain?"

"No, sir. But if—"

"I am choking. I remember seeing you from when I before was aboard."

"Joking! Of course you are, sir." I led them down into the cabin and announced them.

The cabin had been made even smaller by a table the carpenter had banged together athwart the middle of it. There being little room left to stand in, Wickett and Blair had already sat down, Wickett at the foot of the table and Blair on Billy's right. They started to climb out from behind the table as we entered, but Cousin Billy was already waving Peavey and Spetters into seats. Then he remembered the need for introductions, and they all had to disentangle their feet, struggle half-upright and bow as best they could with their legs pinned between table and chair.

Cousin Billy waved at Wickett and said, "You've met my first lieutenant. And this gentleman is . . ." Blair's frown stopped him before he could commit the blunder of presenting the consul to his social inferiors, rather than the other way around. But the Marylander just stuck out his hand and said, "Esau Peavey. You must be that gummint cove I heard about. Say, anything to drink in this tub?" He looked the bottles over and helped himself to Madeira.

"This is Captain Spetters, sir," I said to Cousin Billy, who named him to Blair.

Spetters hadn't yet sat down. He clicked his heels and then laughed. "*Es tut mir leid,* fellows, but old habits die hard: I was a soldier once." He chuckled. "On the wrong side, it is true, but I soon realize the air off my face."

Cousin Billy waved him into a seat and gestured to Prichard to pour wine. "The error of your ways, sir?" he asked.

"Oh, *ja.*" Spetters tugged his vest down over his belly and reached for his glass. "I had the misfortune to be born a subject to the Prince of Hesse. I was a *Kaufmann,* a buyer and seller, in a small way. I imported some things, exported some others. I went me to Rotterdam and made several voyages, first as supercargo and later as captain. I have mine own ship. But soon came hard times and I am forced to return home and give up for taxes. I had not the funds yet to marry me, so refuge in the army I found."

"Here's to the army," said Peavey. "Poor sods."

Wickett noticed me. "Do not you have the deck?" he said.

"Not till the first dogwatch, sir. Mr. Rogers has the second, and then I'm on again till midnight. Cousin Billy—I mean, the captain invited me."

"Ah."

"But I do not answer your question, Captain Trimble," Spetters was saying. "Mine errors, *ja*. I had the pleasure of serving with England in your glorious rebellion. A pleasure because, because," he said, raising his voice as the others began to grumble, making a placatory motion with his hands, "it gave me the honor of seeing General Washington at close quarters at Trenton, Gott resting his soul."

All eyes turned to the engraved portrait of The General on the bulkhead. "Bless him," said Cousin Billy. "Aye" and "Hear him," muttered the others. I grunted.

"I had a mouseful of half-roasted goose at the time, as I recall. And I was wonderfully drunk—it being the *Weihnacht,* you know, the Christmastime, just as now."

"But hold," said Billy. "Not to contradict you, sir, but weren't the Battle of Trenton fought on December twenty-sixth?"

"Oh, *ja, ja,* and very early in the morning, too—but in Germany we celebrate from November until the *Heilige Drei Könige,* January the sixth, the day the three wise men in Bethlehem arrive. Any-how-some-ever, I remember General Washington quite well. He came in on his great white charger, waving his sword, and our men were running around in their underwear!"

"Oh, to have been a witness to that marvelous fight," said Blair. "We lost only four wounded that night, and captured over a thousand."

"*Ja,* but you lost several dead to the cold, poor fellows. I remember sitting in a snowbank chewing that mouseful of goose, thinking on the one hand that perhaps it was the last thing I would ever taste. I was *donkbawr*—that is, thankful—that my last sensation would be such a delightful one, though I wished for some wine to go with it rather than schnapps, of which plenty we had. And on the other hand, I remember suddenly realizing I was on the wrong side.

"You see, before, I hadn't realized there was such a thing as a right side and a wrong side in a war: there was only this side and that side. From where I have came, war was merely a disagreement among princes who had everything to lose. And by that I mean they had everything, and so what they lost from one hand they just up-grabbed again with the other. What did it matter to them that men might die to give them another few hamlets to tax, or to make these villagers call themselves Saxons or Prussians or Swedes or Poles? After the armies passed through, you just took up again your life and called yourself what you had before. And if you were in the army, you marched where you were told and shot at who you were told, and the fellows on the other side did the same. Principles were for princes, we thought."

"Here, sir, you're talking like a damn revolutionary," said Blair.

"Principles, princes—hey?" said Cousin Billy, hopefully.

"Hey, more wine here," said Peavey.

"But then," said Spetters, "as the fight swirled past me into the darkness, I had an *Epiphanias*—a change of outlook, a shaking up off my beliefs. How do you call that . . . ?"

"Epiphany," said Wickett. "Pray continue; you fascinate me."

"Epiphany," repeated Spetters with a sidelong look at Wickett. "Of course. And so I left my musket where it is and went off for the Continentals to join. They were annoyed with me for not bringing my musket, but other than that I was welcomed with friendship—" he glanced again at Wickett "—which of course is something to be cultivated in whatever soil it up-springs in, *ja?*"

"No sir, not entirely," said Blair. "We mustn't encourage friendship among the French, for instance. They are the enemy."

"How true that is, sir," said Cousin Billy. "How true that is. Come, come, Prichard, pour away."

"Well, hain't I doin' it just as fast, sir?"

A proper dinner in the captain's cabin called for a boy or a Marine behind each guest's chair, to pass the plates and keep the glasses filled, but there was no room for that. Prichard had only his mate to help him. They were having to shove their way behind the chairs or lean across the table to get to everybody, and little grimaces played across their faces as they snatched up the dirty plates and slapped the fresh ones down.

For all their carrying on, they served up an excellent dinner—

Chesapeake crabs and oysters for fish, followed by stewed mutton, roasted pork and a better-than-usual sea pie, with mashed turnips, baked onions and creamed potatoes for vegetables—but conversation lagged. Spetters had lapsed into a bashful silence, which left a hole in the conversation that was difficult to fill, and Wickett was engaged in an expressionless contemplation of the two merchant captains.

Peavey, who until then had parried all attempts to engage him in conversation by saying, "I'm just a simple sailor," wrinkled his nose when Cousin Billy tried to pass him the turnips. "Children's food," he shuddered.

Cousin Billy chuckled indulgently, winking at Wickett. "Ha ha! He'll think different once he's banged around in a bare-pole gale for a month straight, raw salt junk and ship's biscuit day in and day out, with cold boiled peas for pudding and rancid cheese for relish. He won't wish for a piping-hot dish of turnips then, eh, Mr. Wickett! —What?"

Wickett cleared his throat and was about to speak when Peavey sputtered, "By Jupiter, if that don't beat all! I been afloat most o' my life, sir! I been froze solid in Spitsbergen and sweltered down to a ghost o' myself in the Great South Sea! I boomed along in the Roaring Forties in a walleyed skiff with no more'n a toothpick for spars and a threadbare neckerchee for canvas! I drunk water that was more alive than wet and once et what I strongly suspect was my old mate Bill Higgins's right arm, on account of the mermaid tattooed on't, and said it was bully fare! No sir, I ain't a one to shy away from a plate o' grub, nor even when it's wigglin' around and lookin' back at me!" He calmed himself with a chug at his glass and then said: "Pardon me, gents, for speakin' sharp, but I tell you I don't cotton to turnips. They ain't no good in 'em, except for sloppin' hogs and midshipmen." He pointed his fork at me.

I guessed he was only fooling about Bill Higgins's arm—I weren't about to ask him, not the way he was waving that fork at me—but then Cousin Billy pounded on the table and roared, "Hogs and mid-shipmen, ha ha!" Even Wickett smiled.

"What's this?" Spetters said, peering around his belly at something under the table. "A cat! Good for hunting rats, *ja*, but ain't your people superstitious?" I mistrusted cats, myself, them with their fangs and claws and unpredictable tempers, but Spetters reached down a finger. The animal walked under his hand, letting the fingertip brush against the long hair of its back, and then went over and bumped his head against the leg of Billy's chair.

"Oh, no, my wee beastie don't eat rats, no," said Billy, patting his lap. "Up, Greybar. Come, sir." Greybar jumped up, blinked stupidly around the room, then sank down and closed his eyes. He kneaded Billy's thigh and began to purr. "The schooner does have a ratter, though," said Billy, shaking a thatch of loose fur from his hand. "Gypsy, the people call her. Horrible creature, as you'd expect from something that eats rats."

The others glanced with amusement at me, and I looked up at the deck beams. It was a commonplace slander that midshipmen supplemented their diets with rat.

"Bless me," said Wickett. "Rat toasted on a stick makes a welcome change from salt horse on a long passage, I dare say. How does that doggerel go? 'Old horse, old horse, what brought you here,' it begins."

"Anyone knows that," said Peavey:

From Whetstone Point to Bowley's Pier
I've carted stone for many a year,
Till killed by blows and sore abuse
They salted me down for sailors' use.

"That's one version of it, anyway."

"I like how you changed it from Britain to Baltimore," said Cousin Billy.

"It's more patriotic that way. Though I find Jack Tar to be pretty much alike wherever he's from. White, Dago, nigger, Chinaman or Mick—Svenskers, even—I don't give a hang so long as he can hand, reef and steer. The rest is:

The sailors they do me despise.
They turn me over and damn my eyes,
Cut off my meat and scrape my bones
And heave the rest to Davy Jones.

"Which is a timely reminder never to turn your back on a purser with a brine barrel to fill."

Wickett clenched his teeth, and the birthmark darkened on his forehead. "Well, one is what one eats, which makes our youngster here a turnip. Isn't that so, Mr. Turnip? Or perhaps I should say, Mr. Rat."

"Oh, I ain't never et a turnip, sir, if I could help it."

"Good on ye, boy," said Peavey. "Spoke like a man."

Wickett smiled patiently. "A rat, then."

I was saved from answering by a sudden yowl from Greybar. Gypsy, a lean calico whose ears had been chewed down to nubs in some long-ago battle, and whose nose and face had become deeply scarred in her ongoing war with the rats, had slipped in behind Prichard and was sharpening her claws on Wickett's chair. Little flakes of gold leaf sprinkled across the black and white squares of the deck canvas.

Cousin Billy clapped his hands. "Here, madam, stop that!"

She kept at it till Wickett reached down and scratched the back of her head. "Puss-puss," he said. "Mustn't mar the captain's furniture, there's a love." She stretched her neck toward the probing fingers and commenced a low, steady rumbling.

The bosun, Mr. Klemso, was calling the watch and the sun lay low in the west, piercingly bright off the flat water. Dick Towson paused in the companionway as if to get his bearings, clambered up to the quarterdeck and made his unsteady way to where I stood lounging at the taffrail. He saluted me with great care. "I relieve you," he said, taking my speaking trumpet and thrusting it under his arm. "Good ol' Cap'n Billy says if it ain't inconvenient, he'd be pleased was you to take a dram with him. Where're Rogers and Quilty and Schmidt? They're invited too."

"Taking a caulk below stairs. I told Mr. Rogers I'd stand his watch for him."

"Oh, don't be a toady. Let him stand his own watch. Go on along and hoist a few—I'll take the deck."

I shook my head. "I don't know that I'll ever drink again, Dick." I said it with great solemnity, for I meant it, but Dick just laughed.

"What, on New Year's Eve? Are you mad? Cap'n Billy wants *ev'*rybody to be happy." He flapped his arms at "*ev'*ry," and the speaking trumpet clattered to the deck. I snatched it up before it could fall down the rudder shaft.

"Thank you," Dick said, bowing.

"Not at all," I said, returning the bow but not the trumpet. "But maybe the gentleman can hold up my end of the party for me."

He bowed again. "A fellow as young and as inexperienced as myself shouldn't be entrusted with that kind of responsibility, but—" he paused to belch "—once more into the breach, my friend. Don't let the ship sink."

"I won't."

The gray clouds hung low, seeming barely to clear our maintop, but a streak of horizon was clear all around. A few stars glimmered out to sea. To the west the water gleamed and the lamps were beginning to shine in the town of Hampton at the mouth of the James. Beyond the point and up the river was Yorktown, where Rochambeau and Washington had turned Cornwallis's world upside down in 1781. French and Americans had been allies then. More than allies—we had been brothers. The French had been so impressed by the way we'd tweaked the British lion's tail that they'd gone ahead and had their own revolution a few years later. Of course, theirs hadn't turned out quite so well. And even brothers had to part sometime.

Unbidden, a vision of my brother's crooked smile came to me, the feel of his arm encircling my neck and gripping me close, the smell of homespun and sweat and dust. Geordie had approved of me. Geordie had always known when to help me, and when to stand aside. He would never have held my chin to keep me from drowning but not lifted my head out of the water, as Adams had said of the French while the Treaty of Paris was being ironed out. Geordie was the only person I ever trusted. He had snuck food to me, and taught me how to fight, and often slept beside me in the barn.

But Geordie was five years in the grave. There is no profit in thy tears, as Phillip liked to say, and the worms had eaten the dead of Yorktown before I was born. My father had been at Yorktown. If he'd been killed, I wondered, would I have had a different father or not been born at all?

All of its own accord, my hand rose up and struck me smartly across the cheek. Only a coward shrank from the gift of life.

I gazed around at the shipping to distract myself. Fat-bottomed Dutchmen and jack-ass brigs, snows with their trysail masts, pinks with the great doors in their pinched sterns thrown open for loading timber, and proper ships square-rigged on three masts rode to their moorings all about the great roadstead. And of course there was ketches and yawls and sloops from all up and down the coast, as well as your usual riffraff of Chesapeake bugeyes and log canoes.

Over behind one of the Dutchmen lay a sleek thirty-six-gun frigate, her yellow-painted hull glowing ruddy in the setting sun. She was the *Chesapeake,* launched last summer. It had been cheaper to maintain the frigates already in commission, and she had lain idle ever since. She was gaining a reputation as a hard-luck ship, yet I suddenly wished I was in her instead of Cousin Billy's leaky old schooner. All men drank, but Billy drank more than I remembered. If he meant to keep it up once we got to sea, I'd never distinguish myself under his trembling hand.

I wasn't supposed to be sitting or leaning, and I guiltily began pacing up and down the quarterdeck. *Cousin Billy.* That old soak shouldn't have taken me out of the *Aztec.* She was a converted merchantman, sure, but almost a frigate. Life hadn't been bad under Master Commandant Malloy—till last August, anyway, when he had cracked a seaman's skull for refusing to kiss the deck at his feet and then falsely accused the man of attacking him, and then knocked me down in public for daring to talk to him about it. I would have thought little of it if he'd confined himself to having me bent over a gun and beaten, because midshipmen have kissed the gunner's daughter since time began, I guess, but first Malloy had knocked me down with the back of his hand across my face. It was an unforgivable affront among gentlemen, but as I only held my rank by warrant, I didn't rate as a gentleman. Cousin Billy's promotion into *Rattle-Snake* and his offer to take me in had seemed a miracle of good luck at the time, and Dick had sweetened the deal by offering to come with me.

"Adventure's the thing," he'd said. "There's no excitement in a big ship. It's the little ones that go in harm's way."

His allusion to John Paul Jones had decided it for me—that and the chance to see the blank look on Malloy's face when I waved my orders under his nose and told him I was out from under his thumb forever.

I'd thought the joke was on *him:* a converted merchantman was not a frigate, no matter how many guns she carried, and the *Aztec* had only returned to Baltimore to be sold out of service. I'd been sure he'd quit in a pique and go back to his farm. But then had come word that Master Commandant Malloy was to be made post-captain and given a proper frigate. He was certain to be a commodore in time, the way he sucked up to Congress, and it would be my hard luck if I ever had to serve under him again.

My pacing took me back and forth past the companionway. I could hear them laughing down there, and I could smell the rye whiskey. *Cousin Billy is good and kindly,* thinks I, with sentimental tears coming to my eyes, *and I must take care of him. I owe him that.* Virtue swept over me like a warm blanket.

The next moment I cursed myself for a quiver-lipped child. Wickett was the man to watch. He was foxy, but the men obeyed him without question: they obeyed Billy's uniform, but they obeyed Wickett the *man*.

The blue devils dogged me through the rest of the evening. I couldn't shake 'em, even when I looked into the after-cabin for a moment at the end of the second dogwatch. Quilty and Rogers had come and gone. Peavey had curled up on the window ledge over the stern transom, muttering, "Jussa simple sailor" whenever someone poked him. Spetters was expounding at length on patriotism and potatoes, as far as I could tell. He had reverted to German and broad gestures, but Dick and the others seemed to follow him easily enough, being I suppose in the same state of mind, and Gunner Schmidt was drinking in the German so eagerly that his glass sat untouched before him. Cousin Billy was laughing. Wickett sat with his chair propped back against Billy's desk, an indulgent sneer on his lips and Gypsy on his lap, playing with his fingers.

"Hello, Mr. Turnip," Wickett said to me, waving at the various bottles and decanters. "Do have a glass of wine or whiskey or what-have-you. Many Marines have died for our pleasure." He peered around at the empty bottles and said, "Normally I might say 'beg pardon' at this point, but there are no Marine officers present." He raised his glass, shouting, "A toast! To the dead Marine: 'He has done his duty and is ready do it again,' bless him."

Though Wickett sat at the foot of the table he seemed to be at its head, as if Cousin Billy were a guest in his own cabin. Both wore a single epaulet: Wickett's on the left shoulder, to show that he was a lieutenant, and Billy's on the right, to show that he was a lieutenant who commanded a vessel. Billy had managed to unship his somehow. It dangled askew, and when I went down again four hours later, it had come off entirely.

"Gentlemen, it's nearly midnight."

I had to repeat it several times before they understood and began collecting themselves. Except for Peavey (who muttered, "Simp' sailor" after much prodding, but would not rise), and Blair (who said nothing at all, even when Cousin Billy wet his finger and poked it in his ear and Schmidt lifted his head by the hair and let it crash spectacles-first back onto the table), they all climbed slowly up the ladder and assembled on the quarterdeck to witness the ringing in of the new year.

At a nod from Wickett a gray-headed sailor with an enormous

beard, the oldest man aboard, struck four sharp double strokes on the bell. Immediately after, little Freddy Billings, the youngest of the ship's boys, struck eight bells again.

"Sixteen bells," Cousin Billy yelled to a chorus of cheers. "Let's splice the mainbrace, lads! Double tots for every man and beer for the boys! Happy New Year!"

All around the roadstead and on shore, people were shouting and bells were ringing. In the *Chesapeake*'s rigging a flurry of red, white and blue lights spluttered, and somewhere a cannon boomed. Under fife and drum, *Rattle-Snake*'s Marines marched up to the foot of the main-mast with a keg of whiskey and another of water and began doling out half-pint tots.

"Happy New Year, Matty," said Dick, smacking his monkey of grog against mine. "Or should I say, Happy New Century!"

"I don't think the new century begins till next year." There'd been a lot of debate lately on that very subject.

"Oh, stuff. It's 1800, and that's good enough for me. Cheers, ship-mate, and a happy voyage."

"A happy voyage," I replied, watching the Marines thumping and tootling up and down the deck, with Cousin Billy prancing at their head.

Four

Two days out from the Virginia Capes, at three bells in the forenoon watch, we spotted a pair of two-masters in the nor'-nor'west. Rogers, the officer on watch, was having difficulty keeping his glass on them as the *Rattle-Snake* rolled and plunged through the Atlantic rollers. He looked over to starboard at the roiling black mass of thunderheads building up in the east.

"What the hell are they doing standing toward us?" he wondered out loud. "And they're carrying too much sail, too."

The glass had been dropping steadily, and we were even then reaching north with *Augustin von Steuben* and *Jane* in an attempt to avoid the worst of the approaching storm. The men had been busy all morning lashing down everything in sight, except the guns. Those we'd save till last.

"Quartermaster," said Rogers, "bring us within hailing distance of the *von Steuben*." He sent a boy below to tell Cousin Billy about the strangers, and when we had closed the *von Steuben* he shouted across the water: "Cap'n Spetters! D'ye recognize them two sail?"

"*Ach, ja,*" said Spetters. "They are *Anemone* and *Lighthorse*, what were to meet us at the Capes but did not."

"Which is which?"

"*Anemone* is the brick, *Lighthorse* is the schnauer."

"Much obleeged, Cap'n Spetters." Rogers squinted at me. "What'd he say now?"

"I guess he means the *Anemone* is a brig and the *Lighthorse* is a snow, sir."

"Hell if *I* can tell a brig from a snow, bows-on at five miles," he snorted. "Here, take a glass aloft and tell me what you see."

The main t'gallant yard was slick with spray, even at that height, and the mast creaked and swooped in broad dizzy circles as we rolled along. I might've slipped if the lookout hadn't grabbed me by the collar. I took out my kerchief and lashed it around my thigh and the yard.

"Thank you—" I said, hoping the man would take the hint and tell me his name, but he was already scanning the horizon again. I didn't press it. I guessed I'd know everyone far too well by the time we got to San Domingo. I trained the glass on the approaching brig and snow, remembering to keep my unoccupied eye open but "lazy," the better to keep the object in view. I studied them for several minutes before I began to notice their differences. The one on the left had a large fore-and-aft mainsail footed to a boom. I shifted my glass to the vessel on the right. At that angle and distance I couldn't make out her "horse," a sort of half-mast stepped just abaft the main and which is a snow's distinguishing feature, but I could see that her fore-and-aft main sail was smaller and set loose at the foot.

"Deck there," I called. "The *Anemone* brig is to larboard, and the *Lighthorse* snow is to starboard."

"Very well. Let me know if—"

"Sir, the snow's heaving-to!"

"So we can see, Mr. Graves." That was Wickett, whose curiosity must have roused him when he'd heard Rogers shouting to Spetters. "Pray, *why* is she heaving-to?"

I'd forgotten they were catching glimpses of the sails down there, though the brig and the snow would still be hull-down from the quarterdeck.

"Something's wrong with her fore-t'gallantmast, sir." Her head shot up into the wind. "Looks like she's lost her forestay. I can't see what's—no, belay that. There's a man-of-war coming up on her, close-hauled on the starboard tack!" I handed the glass to the lookout. "Here, see what you make of her."

"Man-o'-war be a frigate, sah," he said after a quick squint. "French-built, look like. She heavin'-to. No, here she come again."

I relayed his observations and took the glass back. "The frigate's dropped a boat, sir. God, she's lost her fore-topmast!"

"What, the frigate?"

"Sorry, sir, I meant the snow. Her fore-topmast broke clean off above the cap. It's taken the main t'gallant with it." The frigate had braced 'round and gottten underway again almost before her boat hit the water. "The frigate's ignoring the brig and hauling toward us, sir."

Cousin Billy had appeared on deck, calling, "Where away the frigate?"

"Fine on the la'board bow, sir. She's sailing sou' by east, maybe a half east. We might weather her on this course, barely."

He shook his head and pointed at his ear. The rising wind was making conversation between deck and masthead impossible.

"Was she wearing her colors?" he asked when I had returned to the deck. His clothes and face were clean, and I could barely smell whiskey on him at all.

"Something red, sir. Couldn't tell more than that, but she looks French-built."

"Which might mean she's French, or might mean she's English," said Wickett.

He and Billy and Rogers put their heads together in a hasty council of war. I couldn't hear what they said, but I could follow their reasoning easily enough. The stranger's colors could be the red ensign of a British man-of-war, but the red I'd seen could just as easily be the red fly of the French Tricolor. That she'd sent a boat across to the snow without waiting to pick it up again made her more likely to be a Frenchman than a curious Englishman, however. An Englishman would merely have hailed her in this weather, and wouldn't have sent a boat unless something was seriously suspicious. That frigate hadn't waited to check the *Lighthorse*'s papers. She had captured her, and now she was ignoring the sure capture of the brig in hopes of a larger prize: us.

Cousin Billy peered up at his commission pendant. The wind was backing easterly. "Signal the convoy to scatter," he said. A trick of the light made his face seem pale. "Point us as close to the wind as may be on the starboard tack. Get the tops'ls in but shake the reefs out of the course and fores'l, please, Mr. Wickett."

"Aye aye, sir. If I may, we will make less leeway if we keep the reefs in."

"This is true, Mr. Wickett, and if I want your opinion I will surely ask for it." When Wickett still hesitated, Billy said soothingly, "We'll see how she handles, first, if you please. But be ready to take the reefs back in again like lightning, should I give the word." He looked over at the thunderheads. "In any case we'll need the upper yards sent down and the topmasts struck too, I think."

"Very well, sir." Wickett cupped his hands and bellowed, "Topmen, lay aloft to take in tops'ls! Sail loosers, stand by to shake the reefs out of the course and forecourse!"

The wind continued to back easterly, until the quartermaster said, "Please, sir, I can't steer this heading no more."

"Steer as small as you can, then," said Cousin Billy.

The strange frigate, hull-up now from the deck, was having even more difficulty making her easting than we were. The more the wind backed, the more northerly she had to sail, and *Rattle-Snake*'s fore-and-aft rig allowed us to lie a full two points closer to the wind.

It was an odd way to be chased. With the wind now north of east and both of us close-hauled on the starboard tack, the strange frigate was actually leading us at times and pointing slightly away. But if we were to come about on the port tack we'd be sailing right into the heart of the storm, and the frigate would cut us off if we tried running to the west. Her best point of sailing would be with the wind on her quarter, and ours was with the wind before us. But the way the wind was shifting, sooner or later we'd have to run before it or sail right up to her. Either way, she'd eventually catch us—I spat into my palm and touched wood—she *might* catch us unless she carried something away. And once we were within range of her guns, we'd be forced to surrender: in that sea, one well-aimed broadside could deal the *Rattle-Snake* a fatal hurt.

It soon became obvious that the wind was pushing us crabwise down toward the frigate faster than we could headreach on her. Cousin Billy, who could do spherical trigonometry in his head, drunk or sober, faced the same set of facts and came to the same conclusion.

"Bugger," he said. "Shorten sail, Mr. Wickett."

If Wickett was pleased at having been proved right, he hid it, but the crew did not. They nudged each other, grinning as they took their stations. One topman said, "Billy Shakes has met his match," and laughed out loud.

"Silence, there!" rasped Wickett. He pointed at the man who'd laughed. "Stotes, I know you. I shall have your spine out for that!"

Cousin Billy turned away, his face white. I didn't know what he was upset about. He was a fine sailor, and if the sea had been a little less lively, if the wind hadn't increased when it might've steadied, his plan would've been the correct one.

With his shoulders sagging, he said, "Be sure to strike the topmasts too, if you please, Mr. Wickett. I am going below to . . . to see about Mr Blair."

"Aye aye, sir," said Wickett, as if he were accustomed to captains who left the deck with a possible enemy in sight and the bottom dropping out of the barometer. "We'll be wanting the jeer capstan, Mr. Graves."

I snuck a look aloft as I worked. Dick and the foretopmen were tucking the clews well into the furled fore-topsail to keep the wind from snatching it apart on its way down to the deck. He grinned down at me and waved. His crew rigged the yard rope and tripping line, and then with the jeer capstan taking the strain we eased the topsail yard down the topmast backstay to the waisters waiting to strike it below. Then we did it all over again with the main topsail yard, with Wickett roaring, "Handsomely! Handsomely, lads, or we will tear the bottom out of her!" If the yard got loose it'd plunge like a lance through the deck and possibly right on through the hull. "Belay!" said Wickett at last, and the waisters hustled the yard below.

A dark line of wind on the water raced toward us, the sea choppy and broken before it and flat with rain beyond. It would be on us before we could get the topmasts in. Wickett called for two more men to help the pair already at the tiller. They braced themselves as the squall struck us on the starboard bow.

One instant I was dry as toast in my pea jacket, and the next I was as wet as if I'd taken a header over a waterfall. The *Rattle-Snake* shuddered as green water swept over the bow and rushed aft. The weight of it forced her to stand up even as the wind tried to set her on her beam-ends.

The rigging shrieked as the first awful gust passed through, and then the noise of the wind lessened, and there came a different shriek. I looked up to see two figures against the sky. The stockier one was kicking and waving as he tumbled toward the sea. The thinner one seemed unconscious, his limbs fluttering loosely, but trailing a line from one ankle. The wind whipped away the splashes they made as they hit the sea.

I grabbed the loose line as it whipped toward me, threw a bight around a belaying pin and braced my feet on the deck. I was congratulating myself on my quick thinking when the moving deadweight on the other end of the line yanked me off my feet and then pinned my hands between line and rail. At the other end of the line bobbed a body in buff breeches and a plain blue jersey. Its face broke the surface and then sank again.

"Oh Lordy," I cried. "Dick!"

Men grabbed the line and began hauling it in. Someone snatched me out of the way—Horne, the big bosun's mate—and looked at my hands before chafing them between his rough palms. "Ain't no bones broke," he said. "Gonna smart like Billy-o, later, though. A handful o' turpentine rubbed in well should fix it." He gave me a friendly swat on the shoulder. "Another time, white boy, tail on *behind* your bight, hey?"

"Lemme through! Oh law', lemme through!" called an urgent voice: the monster Jubal, scattering men as he ran to the main shrouds and swung himself over the side. I ran to the rail to look. As Dick's body surged alongside, Jubal leaned out from his perch down in the main-chains and snagged his jersey. He heaved the body out of the water with one hand, draped it tenderly across his shoulder and climbed back over the rail, knocking the helping hands away.

"Y'all stan' aside," he said, easing the body onto the deck. He rolled it face downward and began pushing down on the rib cage. A stream of seawater gushed out of the open mouth.

Coughing and sputtering, Dick said, "Get off of me, you great lump!" and sat up. "Jubal, whatever were you doing?"

"I thought you's drownded sure, Mars Dickie!"

"Well, I *ain't*," said Dick. He looked around at the staring faces. Some of the black ones didn't look as happy as they had a moment before. "Glory, did I fall?"

"Not half you didn't," I said, kneeling beside him. "Will you live?"

He felt his head. "I don't see why not." Then he laughed in delight and said, "When we shipped that sea, the mast whipped over and suddenly it wasn't there anymore. Nothing but *air*." He rubbed the side of his head and said, "Something fetched me a blow—I'll say it did!"

"Get on about your business, you mollygawkers! You, Jubal," said Wickett, "get him below and make sure he shifts his clothes. Move, lads! Those topmasts will not get themselves down."

No one said anything about the other fallen man, drowning at that very moment in our wake. In a rough sea with an unidentified man-of-war giving chase, there was no stopping for a man foolish enough to fall overboard.

I watched the men running aloft in the pouring rain and saw what I was afraid to see. The lost man was the lookout who'd kept me from falling not two hours before.

Everything about the frigate said she was a Frenchman, from the sharpness of her bows to the elegant rake of her masts. She *could* have been British, as Wickett had said—the Royal Navy's superior seaman-ship had captured many a Frenchman in nine years of war—but there was something about her that was too jaunty and sleek for her to belong to King George.

Cousin Billy had returned to the deck. His eyes were too bright, but he was calm. "Here, Mr. Graves, she signals. What does she say?"

I ran to get the signal book from the flag locker and took a telescope from the beckets.

"Can't read it, sir, but it ain't the recognition signal. And she's fired a gun. And that's definitely a Tricolor she's flying."

"I suppose he wants us to heave-to. I shan't, I guess, but what can we do?"

Wickett and Rogers glanced at each other. Wickett cleared his throat.

"We could clear for action, captain."

"That's not what I meant," snapped Cousin Billy, coloring. "Well, don't just stand there. Clear for action and beat to quarters, if you please, Mr. Wickett. I'll have the guns loaded and run out too, I think."

There was no question of engaging the frigate. She was half again as long and twice as wide as *Rattle-Snake* (and deeper, too: her hull reached past the uncertain surface into the calmer water below, giving her less leeway and making her a steadier gun platform), and she could be counted on to carry at least twice as many guns as well. Plus they would be much larger guns, giving her perhaps ten times our firepower. Even John Paul Jones might have refused such odds, but beating to quarters would please the men now and look good in the papers later. If we lived to read about it, I thought with a gulp.

The gawky Marine drummer boy brought his sticks to the present and began his tattoo. Men poured out onto the deck and splashed through the rain to their action stations. There was a shower of sparks to leeward as the peg-legged cook and his mate heaved the galley fire over the side. Gunner Schmidt fetched the key to the magazine from Wickett and then sent a quarter gunner back up with the flintlocks for the great guns. The gun captains snapped the cocks of the locks to make sure the flints sparked before screwing the locks into the breeches of the guns, and then covered the locks with the little canvas hoods to keep out the rain. Tin match tubs were brought up in which coils of slow match were set to smoldering, in case the flintlocks failed in the wet.

Bosun Klemso and his mates started to get the boats into the water, where they wouldn't be shot to pieces, but Wickett stopped them. "Belay! Towing them will only slow us down, and I have no intention of abandoning them. Fill them with water in case of fire." He started to go down into the waist to his fighting station at the guns.

"A moment, please, Mr. Wickett," said Cousin Billy. "It occurs to me that some words might be in order. Have the people assemble aft.

"Lads," said Cousin Billy when the people had gathered at the break of the quarterdeck, "over there is a French frigate." He pointed and they all looked, although everyone aboard had had plenty of time to examine her already. "She expects us to give up." He smiled expectantly, as if he'd made a little joke. When they looked at each other and then back at him, he shuffled his feet and looked over at me. I smiled and nodded encouragement, rainwater dribbling from the brim of my hat, but it didn't occur to me to say anything. That was his department.

He faced the men again.

"Well." His voice sounded far away in the wind and the rain. "Let's *don't*. Give up, I mean. The ship." When the men still didn't respond, he looked pathetically at me.

I waved my hat over my head. "Give us a cheer, men!" I felt foolish.

But just then Dick bounded up to the quarterdeck, buttoning his coat with one hand and holding his hat on with the other. He snatched off his hat and waved it, yelling:

"Hip, hip—"

"Hurrah!" shouted the men, as if they meant it.

With an embarrassed little smile, Billy shooed them away. "To your stations, lads. You'll, erm, do your duty, I expect. Now then, gentlemen," he said to the rest of us, "gather 'round me, please. Here's my plan. I want it to appear as if I mean to come about on the port tack. He'll expect us to do that anyway." He checked the frigate's position.

"Yes. We're headreaching on her now, but it ain't enough. She'll yaw as soon as she sees us start to go about, to fire into us. I'm betting that she'll continue to come around. She'll figure we're trying to get away—" he pointed southeast "—that way. But as soon as we are sure he's going to follow us around, we'll change our minds. We'll fall back on the starboard tack instead and head that way." He pointed northwest.

What Cousin Billy said made sense, even if he wasn't speaking sensibly. He was as soaked as the rest of us and his knees were shaking. "The instant you see she has committed to her turn, Mr. Wickett, you signal from the fo'c's'le, like so." He demonstrated. "We'll slip under her stern and catch her flat aback. Give her a good what-for with the starboard guns, hey?"

"It might work, at that," mused Wickett, stroking his long chin. "But 'twill be a disaster if it's timed badly."

"Then, sir, I trust you shan't time it so," snapped Cousin Billy. "Mr. Rogers, I shall take the conn myself. Should—should I fall, know that I mean to come about and let her go by to windward. You understand? Good. Oh, and Matty," he said, laying a shivering hand on my shoulder, "hoist our colors, there's a lad."

I ran the Stars and Stripes up to the peak. The crimson and ultramarine and pure white silk were lovely against the dull sea and sky. I shifted my gaze with morbid fascination to the frigate, so close now that I could count her gunports as they opened and the snouts of the guns appeared. A thirty-eight, she was, with what looked like eighteen-pounders on her gun deck and short nines on her quarterdeck and fo'c's'le. I did a quick unhappy calculation in my head. She could throw three hundred and twenty-four pounds of iron per side, not counting the nine-pounders. Certainly more, if the French bothered to double-shot their first salvo. It didn't compare favorably to the *Rattle-Snake*'s puny forty-two pounds per side.

Forty-nine and a half, I corrected myself, if you counted my murdering pieces, the five one-and-a-half-pounder swivel guns mounted on the rails on each side of the quarterdeck. More oversized shotguns than cannon, they would be useless against the frigate's oaken sides, but supervising their loading gave me something to do. And if we got close enough I might even have the chance to give a couple of Johnny Crappos a face full of something they wouldn't like.

Already I could make out the officers on the frigate's quarterdeck as we began our turn. The French tried a ranging shot, but I didn't see where it went. My teeth were chattering. The wind had begun to blow up awful chill. I felt as if the world and my place in it had become entirely too temporary.

The leading edges of the frigate's sails came a-shiver. She began to turn toward us.

"Watch your luff! Watch your luff," called Cousin Billy. "Make it look good." Then, "Ready about!" He let her drop off a bit, as if he meant to gather way for going into stays. "Now bring her a point into the wind. Steady. Keep her at that." He peered forward at Wickett. As the *Rattle-Snake*'s bow came into the wind, she began to lose the momentum she had gained by turning away. On the fo'c's'le, Wickett dropped his arm.

Billy raised his speaking trumpet. "Brace in the mainyard—up helm! Shift over the headsheets!" The wind came around on the starboard quarter. "Haul aboard! Haul out!" Deft hands flew the jib sheets. "Brace up!" The jib sheets were hauled aft and the *Rattle-Snake* came smartly to her new course, running free with the wind on her starboard quarter.

I glanced back at the frigate. "She's missed stays! She's in irons! She's all aback!"

"Quit that chattering, Mr. Graves." Rogers studied her. "No, by thunder, she's boxhauling."

It was a rare maneuver, endangering masts and sails in any kind of a rough sea, and called for an exquisite sense of timing and balance. I had never heard of anyone doing it except in the direst of need.

Rogers shook his fist. "Go ahead and show away, ye frog-eatin' fuck! And may ye carry away all!"

I stared as the frigate braced her head yards right around on the other tack and hauled up her mainsail and spanker. Squaring her afteryards, she hauled her jib sheet flat aft and began a circular stern board toward us. I glared at the gilded letters glinting on her stern in the dull light: *Fraternité*, a stupid name. If she was going to pound us, I wanted her to have a cruel name—*L'Invincible*, or *Férocité*, maybe, not *Brotherhood*. Her bow swung around to larboard and then her lethal side began to present itself. I watched, entranced, as the guns foreshortened and started to bear. They belched flame and smoke, one after the other all along her larboard side, and my awe changed to indignation. No warning shot, but her whole damn broadside! The sea in our path turned suddenly white. An instant later the thunder of the cannon rolled across the water.

Cousin Billy jumped up and down in glee. "She's fired too soon! She's fired too soon! Oh, gracious, I think—"

Whatever he thought was lost as our guns began to bark—like a terrier teasing a bear, I thought. It was fine sport, as long as the bear didn't get his licks in.

Wickett strolled aft, loosing our broadside gun by gun, calling, "Wait for it. Take your time. Make each shot count. Fire as they bear and no sooner."

The Rattle-Snakes gave a great yell as the *Fraternité*'s fore-topmast leaned forward, slowly at first, and then pitched over the bows like a drunkard tripping over a paving-stone. Then, with her foresails no longer checking her stern board, her backed main and mizzen topsails pushed her farther to leeward and turned her battery away from us.

The men waved their hats and shouted themselves hoarse while Cousin Billy smiled shyly by the weather rail and we sped away downwind.

"Silence!" Wickett had been shouting for some time. "Silence fore and aft!" With the mark on his forehead bright against his brow, he clasped his hands behind his back and stuck his chin out. "You did not shoot that spar away—it was the wind. She will be on us soon enough, my buckos, and our convoy scattered who knows where. It will be a long stern chase right back to Hampton Roads, and pray we keep out of reach till nightfall."

He turned to look at the captured snow, and so did we all. Someone in her was even then raising a jury topmast, and a Tricolor streamed above her Stars and Stripes. When he turned to look back at the frigate diminishing in our wake, all eyes turned with his. Her mizzen topsail had burst and was flapping like Mother O'Brian's laundry, and her main-topmast had followed her fore-topmast by the board, but her crew was dealing with the inconvenient wreckage by simply hacking it away.

Cousin Billy had stopped smiling. "I'm—I'm not quite sure that's entirely true, Mr. Wickett," he faltered, but when the first lieutenant rounded on him he fell into a confused silence.

If Wickett wanted to continue his tirade, he thought better of it. "Shall I secure the guns, Captain? A late dinner and up spirits, hey?"

The rest of the afternoon was anticlimactic and unreal, even when we recaptured the *Lighthorse*. The French prize crew hadn't finished securing the jury topmast and took to their boat as we approached. Despite Wickett's threats, the Rattle-Snakes lined the side and took to the rigging to jeer the French sailors, who hooted right back at them, their boat nearly swamping as they dropped their oars to make rude gestures at us. I didn't translate what they said, for fear someone might shoot into the boat. Which didn't matter in the end—the last we saw of *Fraternité* before the storm fell upon us in earnest, she was throwing out lines to her boat's crew, who'd managed to stove themselves in against her side.

Five

Oilskins make about as graceful a garment as a Franklin stove, but they keep a man dry so long as he don't move around too much. Since coming on watch at 4 AM I had mostly hung onto the lee lifeline, trying not to think about the weather while waiting for the sun to rise if not shine. Experiment had shown me that if I faced just so and kept my shoulders straight, most of the rain and spray running off my sou'wester did not go down my collar.

The main force of the storm had passed us by to the south, and we were hove-to on the starboard tack, flying just enough canvas to keep us bows-on to the seas. The wind had blown lustily but unvaryingly through the morning watch, and though it had veered steadily, we'd barely touched a rope. The men at the tiller had a time of it, though, and had to be relieved every half-glass. Dick and I had taken our turns, and while it was strenuous work to keep her balanced in the choppy sea, I for one thought it was great fun.

My father had made me memorize "The Maid of Norway" when I was a boy, and bits of the ancient ballad had been running through my head. I couldn't get rid of them nor quite put them in proper order. I'd gotten stuck at the part where the storm catches Sir Patrick Spence on his way home from fetching back the king's daughter:

Loath, o loath were our guid Scotch lairds
To wet their cork-heel'd shoon,
But lang or a' the play was play'd
They wet their hats aboon.

I'd asked my father what "aboon" meant. He'd clopped me on the ear and made me start over—by which I gathered he didn't know, either.

Off the starboard quarter the sky began to lighten. It wouldn't properly be morning until we could "see a grey goose at one mile," but I doubted if we could have seen a pink elephant at a hundred yards. But I could make out Wickett, standing motionless by the weather rail. Cousin Billy had sequestered himself with Blair shortly after supper last night, and all I'd seen of him since had been his nose when he stuck it out from time to time to see if we had sank.

I went back to the beginning of the poem and chanted it to myself. It came more easily now, with the rising of the sun. There was a line about a "gurly sea," whatever that was—stormy, I supposed. The wind had bated enough that I could hear my own voice again, and at blessed last I came to the final verse, where everyone dies:

Half o'er, half o'er to Aberdee'
In waters fifty fathom deep,
There lies guid Sir Patrick Spence
Wi' the Scotch lairds at his feet.

That was a sailor's life for you: Sir Patrick had been ordered to sea against his own good judgment and got drowned for his trouble.

I shook myself alert and got a bucket of water down my back. A pale blur began to take shape across the roiling water abaft the larboard beam: the *Lighthorse,* hove-to in our lee. Her captain had worked his crew through the night, repairing the rigging torn away when she lost her topmast. They had replaced the spar with a spare topsail yard: odd-looking, but serviceable.

The wind continued to slacken, but the rain kept a-falling. I could hear Wickett issuing orders, though he stood ten feet away and was hardly shouting. Lookouts ran up the rigging in response to his gestures as much as to his voice, and a messenger-boy scampered below. Another bravely followed the lookouts aloft. He came down again almost immediately and reported to Wickett.

"You are certain?" I heard Wickett say.

"Aye, sir," said the boy, all big-eyed at being addressed by the first lieutenant. "'Twas the cap'n of the foretop hisself what tole me, and he wouldn't lie."

"Of course he would not. My compliments to him, then, and I trust he will keep me apprised."

"Yes sir! I mean aye aye, sir!" said the boy, and scampered aloft again.

Wickett beckoned me to his side. "Run below and tell the captain there is a man-of-war on our weather bow, scudding toward us under double-reefed fores'l and main tops'l, but shaking out canvas as she comes. I'm going to make sail and come about." He was calling for all hands as I slipped under the canvas fearnought screen stretched over the after hatchway.

As I felt my way through the darkened wardroom, I could hear an odd, high-pitched giggling coming from Wickett's cabin, where Billy was berthing while Blair was aboard. Along with the giggling came Prichard's voice, hissing, "Catch him! Damn your hide, boy, there he go again!"

When I poked my head around the door, I saw Prichard holding Cousin Billy in a bear hug from behind while the boy tried to guide Billy's feet into a pair of trousers. He got them halfway up, but Billy kicked them off again.

"Don't want trousers!" cried Billy. "Where the hell are my breeches? There they are, hanging from that deck beam, ha ha!" He looked at me and crowed, "H'lo, Cuz! Hell of a morning, hey? Ha ha!"

"Give us a hand, sir, please!" said Prichard.

It'd be a while yet before the strange frigate was anywhere near us. I leaned in the doorway and grinned at Prichard.

"You're unusual polite this morning," I said. "Something wrong?"

"First he wants trousers, Mr. Graves, then he wants britches, an' then he wants trousers an' now it's britches again. P'raps can we get both his feet in the air at once we'll stand a chance. But please, sir, I'll need your help, sir."

Holding Cousin Billy's thrashing ankles and ignoring his giggles, I grunted, "Mr. Wickett's respects, sir, and there's a man-o'-war a-coming down on us from windward. (Haul up them britches, boy. That's *well* your britches. 'Vast heaving.) He's called all hands and is getting us before the wind."

"Oh, he is, is he?"

While Billy was distracted, the boy guided his feet into long wool stockings and buttoned the knees of his britches over them. Billy grabbed Prichard's shoulder to haul himself upright, and then leaned against the bulkhead while Prichard got him to step into his sea boots.

"Hand me my coat," said Billy. "No, leave the oilskins. Look ridiculous." He shoved past us and tottered through the wardroom.

The deck tilted as the *Rattle-Snake* came about, fetching him up against the ladder, but he didn't seem to notice, and he gained the deck with the help of a mighty shove I gave him from below. He reeled over to the binnacle, shouting for Wickett as he went.

The wind had dropped to a moderate gale, but the rain had increased and the sea showed no sign of calming.

Wickett swung down from the main shrouds and said, "Strange frigate off the sta'board quarter, sir. I've taken the liberty of getting us under way."

"You do take liberties, sir, and I mislike it. I mislike it very much, d'ye hear me there?" He scanned the horizon, such as there was of it in the rain, but missed the gray sails of the frigate not two miles away. "Well, Mr. Wickett, is it that Frenchy again or ain't it? We'll look awfully silly, running away if it ain't."

"We should look even sillier with our legs shot off."

"Say *sir*, if you please. We'll keep civil tongues in our heads in my ship." He stuck his head down the hatchway and shouted, "Damn your mangy hide, Prichard, bring me a great pot of coffee, piping hot!"

"An the galley fire was lit, sir, I could get it!" retorted Prichard below, but he was already making his way forward and was gone before Billy could reply.

"Deck there," hailed the mainmast lookout, "it's that British frigate what was in Baltimore for the funeral. *Clytem*-what's-it."

His Britannic Majesty's frigate *Clytemnestra*, thirty-two, had her lower ports closed against the heaving sea, but she ran out her quarterdeck and fo'c's'le guns as she loomed up alongside. Cousin Billy had nearly sobered by then, and meekly hove the *Rattle-Snake* to in her lee while the *Lighthorse* cracked on sail and slipped away in the rain. King's officers had a nasty habit of finding British deserters among the crews of American merchantmen, which was doubly irksome in that sometimes they really were British deserters. At least four of the Rattle-Snakes, who in theory were untouchable because we were a national ship, had already found excuses to go below while their mates covered for their absence.

A bored voice with a fashionable simper hailed us: "What ship is that?"

Cousin Billy nodded at Rogers, who cupped his hands and replied, "United States armed schooner *Rattle-Snake*, Lieutenant William Trimble commanding, as ye know goddamn well."

Cousin Billy frowned. "Really, Mr. Rogers, there's no call for bad language."

"His Majesty's frigate *Clytemnestra*, Captain Sir Horace Tinsdale," said the bored voice, finishing the routine exchange before adding, "From your reply I have no doubt you are indeed an American, but do you send a boat with your papers anyway."

"The hell he says," muttered Rogers. "Impudent whelp of a one-eyed bitch."

"Better we send a boat to him than he send one to us," said Wickett. He called for the bosun: "Mr. Klemso! Hoist out the captain's gig."

"Good thinking, Mr. Wickett," said Cousin Billy. "That way I shan't be at his mercy but may come and go as I please." He raised a hand as Rogers's grumbling grew louder. "Tut-tut, sir, let's not provoke him."

"But Cap'n, he has no right—"

"Tut-tut."

"Sir—"

"*Tut*, Mr. Rogers. There is nothing amiss with our papers. Once we've satisfied him, we'll be on our way again and no harm done. Come along, Mr. Graves. The rain's letting up: let's get into our number-ones and go a-visiting, hey?" He seemed pleased at the prospect. "Prichard! Prichard there!"

Prichard popped his head out of the fore hatch. "Hain't I just got the galley fire lit, sir? Your coffee hain't ready yet, nor it won't be—"

"The joke's on you, you lazy rascal, ha ha! Lay out my best uniform coat and my sword." Cousin Billy rubbed his chin sadly. "No time for a shave, I guess. Ah, well. They'll understand, of course. Ah, Mr. Blair, you're on deck. Will you pay a call with us?"

Blair looked across at the frigate. Great Britain: neutral in theory, often hostile in fact, yet engaged with us in an informal alliance with the black general Toussaint L'Ouverture to wrest San Domingo from French control.

"The social call is meat for a man in my profession, sir," he said, "but I am to avoid unnecessary contact until I have taken up my station, and you know how these navy types are with their oceans of paperwork. My name will be mentioned, be it even in the dim recesses of Whitehall, and I cannot have it."

The captain himself met us at the frigate's entry port. He was shaved, powdered and bewigged, and no doubt full of breakfast, and resplendent in a superbly tailored undress uniform that was beaded with the drizzle. He made his leg pleasantly enough, but the smoke rising from the slow match in the tubs on the quarterdeck and fo'c's'le put the lie to his graciousness. He waited until Cousin Billy had put his hat back on and the wailing of the bosun's pipe had died away before he spoke:

"Welcome aboard, sir. You are?"

"Lieutenant William Trimble, sir, captain of the schooner. I take it you are Sir Horace? Allow me to present Mr. Graves, the most promising of my young gentlemen."

"The captain himself, by Jove! I expected a junior lieutenant." Which was an obvious lie, I thought—Sir Horace wouldn't have bothered attending the side otherwise. "Pleased to make your acquaintance, Captain Trimble. Allow me to name my first officer: Lieutenant Stone."

Stone, who drew himself up to his full height the better to stare down his nose at us, was the owner of the bored voice that had hailed us earlier. He put one hand on his hip while languidly holding out the other.

"I b'lieve you Brother Jonathans clasp hands in greetin'." After clasping Cousin Billy's hand—or allowing him to hold it a moment, rather—he drew a lace handkerchief from his sleeve and wiped his fingers. Me he ignored. "You've brought your papers, sah? No, don't hand them to *me*, Lieutenant. Excuse me—*Captain*. Give them to that young gentleman." He waggled his fingers at a pimply blond midshipman, who thanked Billy for the papers before handing them over to Stone, who handed them to Sir Horace, who tucked them under his arm.

Sir Horace said, "Glass of something whilst I look these over? This way then, if you please, sir." He turned to the pimply blond midshipman. "Look after Mr. Graves, will you now?" He took Cousin Billy by the arm and turned him toward the quarterdeck, saying, "Now, Captain Trimble, we're looking for deserters. Need every man we can get, with the French poised to strike across the Channel. Don't mind if we have a look? Good, excellent, capital!" He nodded to Stone, and then disappeared aft with Cousin Billy on his arm.

It had been done so deft that I was struck stupid for a moment. Cousin Billy had been making an ass of himself with his drinking, but had done no lasting mischief yet. Allowing British marines to search the *Rattle-Snake*, however . . . not only was it against orders, but he might as well save everyone the trouble and just send our best topmen over. Despite my worry, I almost smiled as a dozen redcoated British Marines preceded the smirky Lieutenant Stone over the side into their longboat. Wouldn't Wickett be mad!

The pimply blond midshipman held out his hand, fingers straight and thumb up like an American, and said, "Paul Gordon."

"Matty Graves." I shook his hand. It was long and boney but had a strong grip and was rough with honest calluses. "Gordon, hey? You don't sound like a Scotchman."

"No. Had it beaten out of me at school."

Gordon, six inches taller than me and a few years older, looked like he was made out of sticks and twigs. The cloth of his coat was every bit as gorgeous as Sir Horace's, though its sole decoration was a pair of white cloth patches on the collar: the British equivalent of the gold-embroidered lozenges I wore on mine. A good two inches of knobby wrist showed below his cuffs, and instead of britches he wore loose slop trousers. I had to look at his silver-buckled shoes twice before I realized what had struck me as wrong about them, besides their great size. They had been made so that one was shaped for the left foot and the other for the right.

Gordon smiled faintly, holding out his wrists to exaggerate the shortness of his sleeves. "Father had his tailor make me three of every-thin', in three different sizes. I've already grown out of the third set. Thank heavens my feet haven't grown as well."

You got that right, mate, I thought. If he ever fell overboard, he could use one of his shoes to paddle around in, just about.

I smiled in spite of my worry. "Me, I don't think I'll ever get my growth."

We clasped our hands behind our backs and drifted toward the fo'c's'le. When we were out of earshot of the officers on deck, Gordon said:

"What's the date of your warrant?"

"September ninety-eight. I'm rated master's mate."

"You figure on bein' a sailin' master, then?"

"Not I, mate. I'm going to be a captain someday."

"You don't say? I think I shall be an admiral."

"Captain suits me—we don't have admirals. How long you been a midshipman?"

"*Passed* midshipman."

"Passed? What's that?"

"July ninety-five—*passed* means I've passed the lieutenancy exam but haven't been promoted yet. Frightful exam, with five captains shootin' questions at you before you've finished answerin' the previous one. Are your lieutenancy exams hard?"

"We don't have 'em. If you've got good stuff, you get promoted pretty quick. That's the beauty of a new service. Most of our captains and lieutenants were masters and mates in merchantmen, and privateers before that. Some of 'em go right back again because it pays so much better and the discipline's easier, but there's still lots of competition. Competition's the thing: makes it easier to get rid of the bad 'uns."

"Assumin' they're willin' to go."

"Why should they stick around where they ain't wanted?"

"Don't know. But if they have interest, they'll get promoted whether they deserve it or not. And if they haven't any interest, there's always their half-pay to squeak by on. Frightful embarrassment to join the merchant service after bein' a King's officer, you know." He shot his cuffs again, which apparently was a nervous habit with him.

"Why wouldn't they be interested?"

"Interested in what?"

"Interested in being promoted."

"Oh! Ha ha, no. *Interest* means pull, influence. Someone higher up with an *interest* in seein' 'em get ahead, y'see. But with a democracy, you needn't worry about that. All men created equal, what?"

"You'd be surprised, mate."

"Oh! I do beg your pardon." He was a polite cuss, even if he was British. He glanced aft to where Billy and Sir Horace had disappeared. "Mr. Stone says I talk too much. Will I show you around, then?"

It'd been a while since I'd been in an honest-to-God frigate—the *Aztec* didn't count—and I gaped around like a booby. The *Clytemnestra* was enormous compared to the *Rattle-Snake,* of course, more than twice as broad and a good sixty feet longer. Her backed main topsail was nearly as large as *Rattle-Snake*'s fore-and-aft mainsail.

Despite the shaking she must have gotten during the storm, the frigate was spotless. What brass hadn't been smeared with blacking gleamed in the morning light that had begun breaking through the clouds; the rope ends were carefully faked down in French coils; and the deck, steaming in the sun, was as smooth and white as a tablecloth when the parson's expected for dinner. Wickett kept the *Rattle-Snake* clean in a utilitarian sort of way, but the *Clytemnestra* was flawless. It was intimidating as hell. I was pleased to find, as I followed Gordon down the main ladder, that her lower decks stank as much as any other ship's of stale farts, sour beer and ancient bilge water.

The gun deck, painted red to hide blood spilled in action, glowed in the eerie light of the battle lanterns. The twelve-pounders on either side were bowsed up hawser fashion, with a messenger cable passing through the eye, then hauled taut and secured to the cascabel of each gun. Obviously Sir Horace hadn't considered the *Rattle-Snake* worth the effort of getting his main battery even ready to be run out.

Gordon followed my look and said, "Sir Horace says the guns can be cleared for action faster this way, and Mr. Stone thinks it's prettier than just housin' the guns. Look here," he said, stepping over the messenger cable and motioning me alongside. Squatting down behind one of the guns, he pointed forward along the line of barrels. "Each one is elevated at precisely forty degrees, no more and no less. Took us all mornin' to get them exactly so. Mr. Stone would be very unhappy indeed, was we to undo that work for nothing. Dear me—awfully sorry."

For nothing, I grumbled to myself as I followed him up the after ladder, which wasn't a ladder so much as a broad wooden staircase. I felt puny and shabby. Professional interest dispelled my sulk, however, and I eyed the quarterdeck guns with excitement. In addition to a pair of elegant long brass nines were six squat iron monsters, short-barreled, wide, and mounted on slides rather than trucks. I ran my hands over one of the brutes.

"Carronades, by gad!"

"Have you never seen 'em?" said Gordon. "They're all the go with us. Had 'em at the end of the American war, but it was over before we had a chance to try 'em out." He blushed. "But haven't you fellows any?"

"Sure we do. The *Constellation*'s got some twenty-fours. She's our flagship, but I ain't been in her since she got 'em."

"We call 'em *smashers*, because that's what they do when you get close in. Pack a real wallop." He shot his cuffs again. "Or at least they do against empty beef-barrels. Confess I've not seen action yet."

"Your tough luck, mate," I said, offhanded-like.

"Have you, then?"

"Sure I have. We wrassled catch-as-catch-can with a French forty-four just yesterday. *Fraternité*, a razee frigate with long twenty-fours on her maindeck. Oh, yes we did so!"

Gordon had raised an eyebrow but said nothing.

"Very well," I grinned. "I 'low I tell a lie. She was an eighteen-pounder thirty-eight. But they were long eighteens, and we exchanged broadsides all the same. She lost her main-topmast and her fore-topmast, and her mizzen tops'l split like a fat man's britches."

He still said nothing, still looking at me from under that raised eyebrow.

I crossed my heart and laughed. "God's truth! Only it was the storm that took her topmasts, and he was shooting where we weren't, and all we wanted to do was cut on out of there. But admit it, that's like you taking on a seventy-four!"

Gordon held up a hand and quoted an old gunroom couplet: "*He who once a good name gets, may piss the bed and say he sweats.* Rather than continue the action, sir, I strike my colors."

"Speak of the devil," I said, staring over at the *Rattle-Snake*.

Someone was hauling down the Stars and Stripes.

The redcoats had drawn up around Stone and Wickett, while our blue-coated Marines were trying to push them aside. Wickett and Stone stood glaring with their heads thrust forward, like fighting cocks

waiting to be loosed at each other. From my vantage high on the frigate's quarterdeck, I could see Stone had the tip of his sword pressed
against Wickett's breast. Apparently the sailors had been mustered by
divisions, but now they were breaking up into furious groups. Some
were reaching for handspikes or rammers, while the ones nearest the
mainmast were snatching up the boarding pikes kept in racks there.

"I think maybe we'd better warn the captains," I said.

"Here they come now, looking as angry as Raw Head and
Bloody Bones."

"No time to hoist out my barge," Sir Horace was saying as he and
Cousin Billy puffed by. "Let us take yours, shall we, sir?"

Etiquette demanded that a ship's commander be the last in and the
first out of his boat, and the captains were already approaching the
entry port. I slipped over the side onto the main channel, the platform that spreads the base of the shrouds, and used a deadeye strap
as a handhold to drop myself into our gig. Gordon tumbled in right
behind me.

He whispered with a grin behind his hand, "I'll wager ol' Stony is
stampin' his goatskin boots on the deck right now."

I didn't see what was so damn funny about it. A year back, three
British sail of the line had detained the USS *Baltimore* off the Havana.
Officers from HMS *Carnatic* had paraded the American crew and pressed
fifty-five men. The British commodore, Loring, eventually returned all
but five whom he claimed as deserters from the Royal Navy (which
they probably were), but the incident had caused an uproar. The American captain, Phillips, had been dismissed from the Navy for "passive
submission," despite having obeyed Commodore Truxtun's written orders not to fire on British ships. The Secretary of the Navy had since
decreed that "on no pretense whatever" should a Navy captain allow
his men to be taken, so long as he was able to fight his ship.

I gloomily wondered how long the Secretary expected us to fight if
the *Clytemnestra* pressed the issue. I glanced at the two captains in the
stern sheets. Cousin Billy looked worried and a bit woozy: no doubt
he'd been guzzling sherry wine while Sir Horace pawed through the

Rattle-Snake's papers. Sir Horace seemed quite certain of himself, as well he might with his vastly superior force—though surely he was intelligent enough to back down should Billy find his backbone. England didn't want to force the United States to patch things up with France.

As Sir Horace and Cousin Billy made their way to the *Rattle-Snake*'s quarterdeck, with Sir Horace somehow contriving to lead the way, everyone fell silent. The lobsters and Corporal Haversham's Marines formed into separate companies. Stone and Wickett stepped apart, Stone's sword making a small *snick-click* as he returned it to its scabbard. Surgeon Quilty and Mr. Blair stood unobtrusively against the rail in the background.

Cousin Billy snorted. "What have you done now, Mr. Wickett?"

"We have struck our colors, sir. We demand these gentlemen accept our surrender at once."

"We do?"

Rogers stepped up. "Hell yes. It's the only way to get 'em to leave us be, Cap'n."

Sir Horace smiled quizzically. "Surrender? 'Fraid I don't understand."

Wickett glared at him. "On the contrary, I think you understand very well, sir."

"Well, *I* don't," said Cousin Billy. "What's happened here?"

Rogers jerked a thumb at Stone. "This puke comes aboard and orders the men—*orders* 'em, mind you, with naked steel in his hand—to line up by divisions. As he's got a thirty-two-gun frigate right next door we do like he says. He demands all the people prove they're citizens. And you know how many of 'em have papers: damn near none, that's how many. 'And why the hell should they need 'em in a man-o'-war?' says I. But he starts counting 'em off anyway, saying this man's an Englishman, and so's this one, and so's this one. Fifteen hands he wants to take, sir, a quarter of our foremast jacks, and not a landsman among 'em."

"They all have British names, Sir Horace," lisped Stone, unperturbed. He waved his handkerchief under his nose. "Mostly Scotch and Irish trash, but they are *our* trash, don't yew know. Don't see what all the fuss is about, really. Didn't touch their—what do they call 'em? Ah, yas: darkies." He sniggered. "Didn't touch their darkies, Sir Horace. Mustn't touch private property, what?"

The Rattle-Snakes weren't saying anything, but they hadn't dropped their weapons, neither. Both sets of marines stood waiting for orders, the whites showing in the corners of their eyes as they tried to watch everyone at once. Cousin Billy and Sir Horace raised their hands in soothing gestures.

"Tut, tut," said Cousin Billy.

"Now, now," said Sir Horace, "Jay Treaty, what?"

Cousin Billy looked to the assistant consul. "Well, Mr. Blair, it is legal under the Jay Treaty, ain't it?"

Blair folded his arms at the mention of his name. The sunlight reflecting on his glasses masked his eyes, but he was frowning, you could tell. "Among other things, the treaty gives Britain the right to examine vessels for contraband and to take off deserters," he said carefully, looking like he regretted having come up on deck to see what the commotion was. "But exactly what constitutes contraband, and whether an American citizen can be said to have deserted from foreign military service—and involuntary service at that—are questions for lawyers and diplomats to argue. Regardless, it applies only to private ships. Perhaps the lieutenant was overzealous in his duty."

"Overzealous?" snarled Wickett. "He committed acts of extreme provocation. This is an armed vessel of the United States *Navy,* not some New England rum tub. If these gentlemen wish to start a war with the United States, then by God I am for it!"

Stone sniggered, but Sir Horace cut him off with a gesture.

Cousin Billy blinked at Sir Horace. "We've got you there, haven't we?" He took a deep breath. "Well, Sir Horace, if you intend to, erm, offer battle, I must give you leave to quit this ship so you may prepare to defend yourself."

Sir Horace bowed, his front leg angled out just so, like a gallant saying good night to a lady who'd unexpectedly shut the door in his face.

"You have got the weather gage on me, sir, and I find I must decline your offer of combat. A shame to—"

Whatever else he was going to say was cut short by a lookout hailing from the *Clytemnestra*'s masthead. A nearer cry came an instant later from our crosstrees:

"Sail ho! Deck there, a sail fine on the starboard bow!"

Cousin Billy looked up, shading his eyes. "What is she?"

"It's that Johnny Crappo we shot at yesterday, sir. She ain't seen us yet—whoop, she's hauled her wind. Don't think she likes the look of us, ha ha!"

"Damme, my man saw her first," said Sir Horace, rubbing his hands together, "and I claim the honor of single combat. You shot at her, eh? Good on you, sir! What is she?"

"Shan't tell you, Sir Horace," said Cousin Billy.

"Oh, dear fellow, that's no way to do," said Sir Horace.

"*Fraternité,* sir, thirty-eight, with eighteen-pounders on her gun deck." Gordon threw me an apologetic look as he spoke. "She lost her fore- and main-topmasts as well, though one expects she's rigged something up by now."

Sir Horace beamed. "Excellent, Mr. Gordon, you've been listening instead of talking." He turned eagerly to Cousin Billy. "A frigate duel, eh? I beg you don't interfere, sir, whatever the outcome. Shot away some spars, did you? Good on you, sir, good on you!"

The *Rattle-Snake* and the *Clytemnestra* together could easily take the Frenchman, which no doubt was why she was clawing her way upwind. It'd make an interesting problem for a prize court: the Rattle-Snakes and the Clytemnestras would be entitled to equal shares, but national pride would preclude admitting the other's claim. The money could be tied up for years.

Gordon held out his hand and was obviously relieved when I took it. He glanced at Lieutenant Stone shooing the British Marines into *Clytemnestra*'s longboat, then pulled out his handkerchief and fluttered it under his nose. Affecting a bored simper, he drawled, "Duty calls, don't yew know. Well, sah, 'fraid I *must* dash."

The British pulled so lustily for their ship that the shafts of their oars bowed with the strain.

In answer to Wickett's look I said: "I told Mr. Gordon about the frigate, sir. I didn't realize it was important."

"Oh, let's leave them to it and hope they shoot each other's legs off," said Cousin Billy, rubbing his hands together. "All's well that ends well, I say. Get us underway, if you please, Mr. Wickett. Mr. Rogers, lay us a course as easterly as may be till we've cleared the Gulf Stream, please, and let's see if we can't find our convoy. Smooth sailing from here on out, hey?"

"Aye aye, sir," said Wickett. "All sail in conformance to the weather— immediately we have dealt with Stotes, I take it."

"Oh," said Billy in a small voice. "I had forgot about him."

"Thank God I cannot mete out more than a dozen without the say-so of a court-martial," said Cousin Billy. "Are you sure you won't have a dram, Cuz?"

"No thank'ee, sir."

In the dimness of the after-cabin, Billy's face looked lined and gray. Regulations set the limit at a dozen lashes, but it was a limit that was widely ignored. Malloy in the *Aztec* had routinely ordered up three or four dozen for drunkenness, theft, swearing, dirtiness, lagging behind, and anything else that provoked him, and he wasn't alone in that. I didn't see what Billy was so all-fired uneasy about.

"The old salts calculate it takes at least a dozen to make an impression," I said.

Billy looked at me like I'd cut him across the face. "Whether it makes an impression on *Stotes* is beside the point," he said. "The purpose is not to cure him of a loud mouth but for me to show confidence in my first lieutenant. He said he would have Stotes flogged, and I must go through with it."

I'd meant that it would take at least a dozen strokes of the cat to make an impression on the ship's company, who'd grown up watching men's backs laid bare at the red-painted public whipping-post that stood in every public square from Boston to Savannah. They were hardened against such things.

"Billy," I said, "Stotes has it coming. What was Wickett supposed to do, just knock him down and forget about it?"

"That's what a good petty officer would've done."

"He ain't a petty officer. And anyway, surely he ain't just trying to put you on the spot."

"Oh, you think not?"

"For chrissake, Billy, it's only a dozen licks."

It weren't as if Billy hadn't never flogged a man before. Surely that couldn't be.

I was wondering how to ask him that when little Freddy Billings poked his head in the door and piped:

"Mr. Wickett's respects, sir, and the people are mustered to witness punishment."

"Seize him up," said Wickett.

Horne removed Stotes's shirt and hung it across the condemned man's shoulders. Then Horne and Elwiss lashed his wrists and ankles to the hatch grating leaning against the mainmast and removed their cats-o'-nine-tails from their red baize bags. The cats had wooden handles about a foot long, covered with red cloth, and nine white cords of eighteen or twenty inches whose ends were whipped rather than knotted. Some bosun's mates knotted their cords, but that was just pure cussedness. After half a dozen lusty strokes, the knots would start ripping little gobs of flesh out of a man's back.

"Mr. Quilty," said Cousin Billy, "is this man fit for punishment?"

"I have examined him, sir," said the surgeon, "and found him physically fit." Quilty's post was next to the condemned man, so as he could see the punishment wasn't "excessive," which meant as many things as there were surgeons.

"Men," said Billy, gripping the quarterdeck rail, "what the law says you shall have, you shall have. Carry on then, Mr. Wickett."

"Show me your hands," said Wickett.

Soft-hearted bosun's mates had been known to conceal red ochre in the fists, through which they ran the tails of the cat after each stroke to untangle them. The ochre of course would leave a red mark upon the man's back that looked like blood, letting the bosun's mate go easy on him. Horne and Elwiss held out their hands to show they were empty.

"Do off hats," said Wickett, and the entire ship's company but the Marines uncovered themselves. "Do your duty, bosun's mates, and do not favor him or you shall take his place."

Stotes rolled his eyes in terror as Elwiss removed the shirt from his shoulders. "Oh God, I'm a-gonna be whupped by a nigger," he said, staring over his shoulder at Horne, and then hung his head.

As it happened, Elwiss was left-handed. Some captains kept both a left-handed and a right-handed bosun's mate so their alternating strokes would leave what they considered an aesthetically pleasing cross of blood across the condemned man's back, but Elwiss and Horne had both been rated bosun's mate before Billy came aboard, and he couldn't be faulted for that.

At a word from Corporal Haversham, the Marine drummer boy commenced an ominous shuffling beat.

Horne reared back his right arm and swung his cat whistling through the air. The ends struck Stotes's naked back with a smart crack. Stotes started, but he didn't cry out.

"One," said Bosun Klemso, who served as our master-at-arms.

Elwiss was skinny for a bosun's mate, but he was tall and had a long reach. He laid down a crossways stripe from the opposite side, making Stotes jump. A line of blood dribbled down Stotes's back, but still he kept his mouth shut, and the men looked on with something like approval.

"Two," said Klemso.

The third stroke produced a moan. A man or two shook his head.

Stotes cried out as Elwiss laid on the fourth stroke, and some of the men looked at each other.

"Eyes front," said Wickett.

By the tenth stroke Stotes was weeping and screaming, and the men looked disgusted.

"Mr. Quilty," said Billy, "is he fit to continue punishment?"

Quilty felt his pulse and examined his back. "He is physically capable of withstanding the two remaining strokes," he said, "but I cannot speak for his mind."

"Then pray do not, sir," said Wickett. "Carry on, bosun's mates."

Stotes collapsed, sobbing, when he was at last cut down.

"Do on hats," said Wickett. "Punishment completed, sir."

"Ship's company dismiss," said Billy, and ducked below.

Stotes's messmates carried him down to the sick berth, and none too gently, neither. He had shamed them by his capers.

I heard Billy vomiting below decks—sick with whiskey, I guessed. I felt a little queasy myself. A couple of men sloshed buckets of seawater across the spattered blood and squilgeed it into the scuppers.

Six

The Caicos Bank stretched away to starboard in a wide, milky, sub-aqueous band dotted with coral heads and clumps of weed. Below us on the sandy white slope our shadows rose out of the blue depths of the Turks Passage as if we were a squadron of Montgolfier's balloons drifting over a snowy mountain range. Five large shadows: *Rattle-Snake, Jane, Augustin von Steuben, Anemone* and *Lighthorse.*

A larger shadow swept across ours like a cloud gone mad, disappearing, reappearing, shifting shape and direction, until with ten thousand bright flashes of silver fins a shoal of baitfish broke the surface. Barracudas and wahoos tore through them, leaving winking scales and puffs of blood in their wake. Overhead, hundreds of screaming birds circled and dived.

"It's a wonder we've maintained station," Dick was saying as Jubal reloaded one of my pistols for him.

I glanced at the merchantmen. The wind had turned fluky, and they hadn't been able to wander far. "If you can call it that." I followed a gull with my pistol.

"If they've maintained station, it ain't due to superior seamanship," said Rogers, who had stepped over to watch our shooting. "Nor to close attention to the common good." No merchant captain gave a hang for that. "It's due merely to the lack of a breeze."

"I'm surprised to have 'em within hailing distance," said Dick. "Come on, Matty, will you shoot or not?"

"It's early yet," said Rogers. The creases around his eyes deepened as he squinted against the glare. A lifetime at sea had aged his face beyond his forty-some years, and black and silver whiskers stood out on his broad upper lip and square chin. "Subtle differences in the current will have us all over the passage by the first dogwatch, you mark me," he said. "Won't surprise me if we have to haul someone off the bank afore dinner."

The hell with Rogers, I thought. It was his duty to worry about such things, not mine.

Dick punched my arm. "Shoot."

"They're on to us, Dick. They won't alight."

"If the enemy refuse battle, you must go to him," said Wickett, raising his hat to the quarterdeck as he stepped up from the waist. "May I try?" He examined the pistol that I uncocked and handed him, hefted it in his hand, sighted along its barrel. "Will it shoot straight?"

"Never saw a dueling pistol that did, sir," said Dick.

"You are familiar with the Code Duello, Mr. Towson?"

"All Southern gentlemen are, sir," said Dick, standing tall. "And if I may say it, sir, I hear you've killed your man, as well."

"I'm sure I have, Mr. Towson. I sail to places and shoot at people: it has been my occupation this past year and more. But you ask if I have killed my man 'as well.' Are you a killer?"

"No, sir. I mean to say—"

"You mean to include me in the honorable fraternity of duelists, and to utter earnest hopes that you, too, will one day be enrolled in that select company. Is not that so?"

"Indeed it is, sir."

"There is no glory in dueling, Mr. Towson." Wickett cocked the pistol. "You merely sneak out to some lonely place where you try to kill someone before he kills you. Afterwards, one of you has breakfast."

"At least the more skilled marksman wins, sir."

"The only meritocracy to be found among the ruling class," said Wickett. "I really ought to favor it." With his left hand on his hip and his right leg extended, he raised the pistol and stalked a gull with it.

"Surely you do not suggest, Mr. Wickett," said Rogers, pretending to be haughty, "that our government is not composed of the finest of men."

Wickett grinned. "I do not suggest it, John: I say it."

"Tut-tut. You court sedition, sir." Rogers took the other pistol from Jubal. "Blast away and—say, that was a sweet shot!"

"I did not aim at that one."

Attracted by the noise, Cousin Billy and Mr. Blair quit their breakfast bottle long enough to have a go. I made a quick two guineas off Blair before he tumbled to it that Billy was a crack shot, pie-eyed or not.

"I'll pay you later," sniffed Blair. "I'm good for it."

"Ha ha, don't you believe it, Cuz!" said Billy. "He told me himself he's a great welcher—it's cash on the barrelhead with him, or you'll have nothing at all."

"Fah! Boulders!" cried Blair, but with everyone watching he had no choice but to fork over. He rooted around in his pockets until he'd found his purse, and then he rooted around in that until he'd found a pair of sovereigns. But gold being too good for a midshipman, he thrust and poked around in his purse some more till he'd given me nine dollars in greasy state currency. That was still twelve dollars short in my reckoning, and after eyeing my outstretched hand for a while he gave me half a crown and a few Spanish dollars, heavily shaved, with the air of a man trading a child a shiny new penny for a nasty old sixpence. But even after cheating me he still looked so put out that I asked if he would tell that joke he'd told me the night before.

He cheered right up. "Listen, gentlemen, this one's a corker. A fat man and a thin man are to fight a duel. Fatty's all in a lather because the fellow he's up against has such a bigger target. So his second draws two lines up and down his waistcoat and says, 'Anything outside them lines don't count.' *Don't count*—ha ha!"

Then he was madder than before, because no one laughed.

Two days later we lay becalmed in the Bight of Léogane, with Guanabo Island bearing three leagues south, and the rugged mountains of

Hispaniola rising up all around us to the north and east and marching off into the far southwest. With the famously reliable trade winds making not so much as a ripple on the glassy sea, and the sun beating down like a hammer, the watch below had curled up in what shade there was and gone to sleep.

I lowered my quadrant, wishing that Phillip's package really *had* contained a sextant—an infinitely more elegant instrument than the quadrant—and waited for Wickett and Rogers to finish quarreling over their calculations. Their noon numbers were always within a few seconds in latitude of each other's, and the presence of prominent landmarks all around us that morning made our exact position inarguable in any practical sense, but it was a routine they had fallen into. It was one area in which Rogers had the final say, he being the officer charged with the navigation of the schooner, and overruling Wickett gave him great pleasure. I didn't think Wickett minded. It was a way each had of reminding the other that his presence was merely tolerated, and first lieutenants as a rule are loath to upset tradition even when it goes against them.

Rogers glanced at my figures for form's sake and then patted me fondly.

"The boy agrees with me, Mr. Wickett."

"Then he is a greater booby than I took him for, Mr. Rogers."

"Yet I concur with him." Rogers took two steps to his right and wrote our position on the slate hanging from the binnacle. Then he shot the sun once more and said, "I make it noon, Mr. Wickett."

Wickett clasped his hands behind his back and said, "There you are sank, Mr. Rogers: it is not noon until Captain Trimble declares it so. As he is our lord and master, so too he is lord and master of the very sun itself."

Rogers reached for the half-hour glass, but stayed his hand.

"Mr. Graves," he said, "why don't you hop along below and make the suggestion to him?"

The sun king was helping himself to whiskey when I knocked and entered. He was dressed in nothing but his shirt, with Greybar drowsing stupidly in his lap. The whitewashed bulkheads gleamed in the sunlight streaming in through the open stern windows.

"Oh, 'tis you, cousin," said he, not at all chipper.

"Mr. Wickett's respects, sir, and it's coming on noon if you please."

"Respect! Thirteen days at sea with the man, and his sense of humor yet amazes me." He rubbed his head. "What is it you came down here for again?"

"To tell you it's noon, sir," I said before I thought.

He waggled a finger at me. "You mean, to tell me Mr. Wickett *believes* it to be noon. Well then, make it so, make it so, otherwise I shall have to come up on deck and fiddle around with a sextant myself. What a bore." He grabbed the hem of my monkey jacket as I turned to leave. "No, don't leave us yet, Mr. Midshipman Graves; I haven't said 'dismiss.' He must have a toast with us, first. Mustn't he, yes, puss-puss-puss." Stuffing the cat under his arm, he fetched another glass from the sideboard. "Water in yours? Nay, nay—fish fuck in it." He hoisted his glass. "Here's to . . . what shall we drink to?"

"Confusion to the French?"

"But the French are *always* confused. Oh, very well: Confusion to the French."

We drained our glasses. I was finding I enjoyed whiskey less the more I craved it.

"Whuffah!" He slammed his glass onto the table and made Greybar stare. "Now then." He waggled his finger at me again. "Special orders of the day; see that you inform Mr. Wickett. I have much to do. I am to be disturbed under no circumstance whatsoever. *No circumstance whatsoever.* Tell *that* to the 'respectful' Mr. Wickett, and see how he likes it."

He looked so sad sitting there with Greybar still hanging from his arm that I couldn't bring myself to leave.

"Billy," I said, "can I ask you something?"

He looked up from under his eyebrows. "What?"

"Well, we're family and all."

He brightened. "Yes, yes, of course we are." He pointed at a chair.

"Sit, Cuz. I've always been fond of you, you know that. So tell your ol' Cousin Billy what's on your mind. Are the duties too onerous? I can fix it, you know. I'm pretty important around here."

"Well—"

"Come, come, out with it! You can tell me anything. That's what family is for."

"Well then, Billy . . . why do you get drunk?"

He threw back his head like I'd swung at him. Then his eyes narrowed.

"Why do I get drunk, say you? Why oh why do I get drunk." He put his chin in his fist and pretended to ponder. "I have spent a great deal of thought on this, and I do not answer lightly. The answer has cost me many a night of long, lonely, intense scientific investigation. However, I shall tell you, dear Cuz, because we are family, and I know what great store you put in *that,* you who get on so well with your brother and father both. I get drunk," he said, looking right through me like I was miles away, "because I put whiskey in my mouth and swallow it. Now get out of my sight, God damn your eyes."

I could hear him weeping as I closed the door.

"Cap'n says make it noon, sir, and he ain't to be bothered on any account."

"Very good, Mr. Graves," said Wickett. "Quartermaster, strike eight bells." He faced forward and bellowed, "Call the starboard watch!"

"About time, mate," muttered the helmsman to the man who had been waiting to relieve him, though not so loud that Wickett would have to notice. As he relinquished the tiller he announced the course, the purely hypothetical and optimistic course, to his relief, who repeated it. Rogers, whose watch it now was, decided after a moment's hesitation and a glance at Wickett that the starboard was the weather side, and took his station there, saying, "I relieve you, Mr. Wickett."

Dick ran up the companionway, still tucking in his shirttails. "And I relieve you, Matty."

"Get off my quarterdeck!" roared Wickett. "What do you mean, sir, stepping up here half naked? And why were you not here when we took the noon sight?"

Dick tucked in his chin and raised his eyebrows, as if he were astonished at Wickett's interest in his dress. "I beg pardon most humbly, sir," he said. He returned to the quarterdeck a short time later in coat and hat, saying, "I relieve you, Mr. Graves."

"Watch yourself, Dick." I kept my voice low. "Billy's already drunk, and their lordships are at it again."

"Storm clouds brewing?"

"I'll say so, and in shoal water, too. First they can't agree on our position, then they keep changing the figure on the slate, and I ain't entirely certain they're joking anymore. I'm afraid Billy—"

"Hist, Matty! Clap a stopper on your tongue."

Wickett glanced at us as he strolled by, his hands clasped behind his back and his fingers working against each other. "Is it duty that makes you linger on the quarterdeck, Mr. Graves?"

"No, sir."

"A word with you, then. You will forgive us, I am sure, Mr. Towson." He took me by the arm. A casual observer might have assumed the gesture to be a friendly one. "Come stroll with me, Mr. Graves. Let us take the air and indulge in idle chit-chat. Now, sir," he said, after he had steered us clear of the quarterdeck, "kindly tell me what that was about." His fingers rested over the nerve in the inner side of my arm.

Wickett was capable of applying an agonizing pressure to the nerve, but I'd be damned before I let him know it hurt. I kept my face expressionless and my voice steady as I said, "Merely advising Mr. Towson as to the weather, sir."

"Very kind of you, to a certainty. One can examine the sky and the slate, but a word from the officer coming off watch is always welcome, eh?"

"Yes, sir."

"You mentioned shoal water, I believe, Mr. Graves. Whatever can that mean?"

I pointed a thumb toward Guanabo. "The current seems to be taking us toward l'Île de la Gonâve, sir."

He cocked his head, as if I had said something clever. "Say that again."

"We seem to be drifting."

"No, no, the part about the island."

"You mean Île de la Gonâve? It's the French name for Guanabo, sir."

"*Mais oui,*" he said, and continued in Canadian-accented French: "Your pronunciation is very good, very high-tone."

I slipped into French without effort. "Thank you, sir. My father insisted I learn in honor of my mother, who was from Saint-Louis in Louisiana."

"And mine was Canadienne." He removed his fingers from above the nerve and merely held my elbow, as if we were friends. "But unlike your English, your French does not sound as if it had just blundered out of the back woods."

"Very many thanks, sir. I learned from a man who once owned a plantation in the Artibonite, the great river valley of Saint-Domingue. He had been educated in Paris."

"No doubt he was compelled to leave his holdings in a hurry and had need for employment," said Wickett. A wave of bloody uprisings had swept the colony after the French revolution, and civil war raged there yet.

"I suppose so, sir. It never occurred to me to ask."

"Oh, careless youth," he said in English, shaking his head. "Your conversation just now had no other signification?"

"I don't know what you mean, sir," I said, also in English.

"Stand easy, Mr. Graves, stand easy. Sometimes an officer's duty takes him into uncharted waters, if I may belabor your metaphor." He released my arm and clasped his fingers behind his back. "We are—" He switched back to French as a seaman sat down nearby with a full mess kid. "We are in shoal waters, indeed. I have had my eye on you, Mr. Graves, and I have decided that the time has come for you and me to speak frankly. Will you take an early dinner with me at one o'clock?"

"*Quelle bonté,* how kind," I said with truth. I usually ate at noon with the men, ship's fare being ducks to me, having been raised on salt pork and cornmeal mush; but I had been anticipating with distaste the Wednesday dinner of rice, cheese and molasses.

"Until two bells, then, Mr. Graves."

He strode forward, his fingers twitching behind his back and his long nose and chin preceding him.

I was surprised to find that the wardroom dined on ship's rations too. But the wardroom steward had made a glutinous pudding of the officers' rice, biscuit and molasses, plus a handful of nuts and currants, and accompanied it with chopped boiled eggs and a chicken.

The wardroom wasn't accustomed to having its dinner until two o'clock, and none of the officers who shared the mess was present. Surgeon Quilty stuck his head in, but Wickett assured him that a brace of birds lay in reserve and he needn't fear going without.

"Then I shall let my pudding cool," said Quilty. "It's too hot to eat anything without it has sat awhile." Wickett shut the door after him.

"Speaking of cooling, sir," I said, reaching for the clay jug that sat on the table, "how did you get cold cider?"

"The steward wraps the pot in a jute sack, which he then soaks with seawater. As the water evaporates, it takes heat away from the liquid inside. *Et voilà.* And it is my cider, too, so do not worry about saving any for the others."

He had insisted that I loosen my stock and remove my coat. He had not even considered putting his own on, after all, not in such dreadful heat, and except for being in his presence I wasn't entirely uncomfortable. A little air came in through the scuttles in the cabins on either side, and the room could've been pleasant if the door and the skylight had been open.

We had been discussing politics in French, Wickett having tried my

Latin and Greek and found them wanting. As a rule it weren't genteel to discuss politics at table, but there was only the two of us, and it'd become clear to us both that we shared a profound contempt for the Federalists. As the bulk of the officer corps was Federalist, it seemed only natural that two Republicans who found themselves alone together would wish to express sympathies ordinarily kept under wraps. Wickett was expounding on what he called the myth of Mr. Jefferson's enmity toward the Navy.

"Which," he said, "is a base subterfuge concocted by Adams and his Anglophiliac brethren. I hope I was not so rude as to mention it at your cousin's vigil for the late president."

"Not that I recall, monsieur."

"Yes. Good. But anyway, what they mean is that Jefferson is no friend of the Federalists, which is hardly the same thing. They will have us bowing and scraping to England again if they have their way, and then we shall have to settle the question of our independence all over again."

It was my duty as his guest to argue if he wished it. "But isn't it a legitimate fear," I said, "that a strong navy could be an instrument of oppression in the hands of a tyrant?"

He nodded. "So the Antifederalists say. The Republicans, I mean. But even the Royal Navy was unable to stop our smuggling before the Revolution. Neither can we, for that matter. Our little fir-built navy poses no threat to our own commerce. And as for the West, should we sail across the Appalachians, guns blazing?" We both laughed. "We could sail to Pittsburgh, I suppose," he continued, "assuming the Spanish let us use the Mississippi, and we could get anything larger than a gun galley past the Falls of the Ohio, and buckskin-shirted riflemen did not pick us all off from ambush along the way. An army would be much more useful for the purpose. No doubt that is why Hamilton insists upon having one."

I remembered standing in the doorway watching Geordie marching backwards up the lane in his deerskin jacket, waving his hat all the way and with a big grin on his face. He had Father's old infantry musket across his shoulder. My father was caressing my hair, and I wondered if he was aware of it. When at last Geordie had reached the brow of the hill and strode off down the other side, still waving his hat, my father smacked the back of my head and said: "Grain don't get itself in, boy. You have got a man's work to do now, if you're up to it."

Wickett was looking at me and I realized I had stopped laughing. "An army's been used for that purpose already, monsieur, with Washington at its head and Hamilton prodding him along like a milk-cow."

"Well, metaphorically speaking, I suppose." He hesitated, then: "Monsieur Graves, forgive me if I speak out of turn, but I recall now that you had some family tragedy during the, er . . ." In English he asked, "What's the French for 'Whiskey Rebellion'?"

I shrugged. French is a great language for shrugging. *"Je crois, Rébellion Whisky."*

"Oui. Rébellion Whisky."

I ran a finger through one of the wet rings my glass had left on the table. "My brother was killed."

"I am sorry. Pardon me." He said it so softly that I looked up at him. He resumed in French: "And yet I cannot help but remark that you have volunteered for the country's service."

"And why not?" I wiped my hand on my loose cotton trousers. Billy had let us switch to lighter clothing when we crossed the tropic of Cancer. "America is my country."

"But you do not love Washington and you do not hate the French."

"No," I said. "What should either matter?"

"Your pardon again. I do not mean to make the interrogation. It is merely an eccentricity of mine to learn why other men have joined the Navy. May I help you to another slice of pudding?"

"Thank you, monsieur." I held out my plate. "Well then, I shall indulge you. I thought we were going to fight the Barbary pirates, which you will recall is why Congress reinstated the Navy in the first place. Or better yet, to fight the English."

He smiled his weird death's-head smile. "You dislike the English, then?"

"I dislike King George."

"Because he is mad?"

"Because he is king."

"I despise kings, churches and aristocrats," he said. "They combine great power with gross stupidity. I thought the French had the right idea when they invented the guillotine. At first, anyway."

That was my thought exactly, though I thought perhaps it had one last use. "They should chop off Talleyrand's head," I said. "He's not much of a foreign minister. They could have avoided this whole mess if he had talked to our emissaries without demanding a bribe first."

"Or least not such a large one. A quarter of a million dollars! Can you imagine such a sum?"

"For a certainty." Among my tutor's little hoard of books had been Galland's translation from the Arabic of *Les Milles et une nuits.* "I have often pictured myself holding up a lamp in Ali-Baba's cave and seeing the glint of gold as far as the eye could reach." I drank some more cider while I wondered what Wickett was up to.

"But as for all that," I said after a time, "it is true I serve at the president's pleasure, monsieur, but it's my country I serve, not him or his Federalists."

"And she is my country too, bless her. Yet sometimes I wonder about this noble experiment of ours. Well, perhaps *noble* is an unfortunate word, but it occurs to me that Washington and Hamilton came out of the, shall we say, Monongahela misfortune admirably situated to gain what they most desired: a strong central government to control the states and a standing army to control the people."

"Monsieur forgets we have no standing army."

"Ah. But what would you call the thirteen thousand men who marched on western Pennsylvania five years ago last fall?"

"Militia."

"Yes . . . but they were not all Pennsylvania militia. And it was a larger army than Washington ever commanded during the Revolution, was it not?"

"It was." I clutched my cup. "They came from Virginia, Maryland, even New Jersey."

"Very clever, that. The federal government has a ready army, yet the states pay for it."

I concentrated on eating boiled eggs. The wardroom steward had cut them up with onions and tossed them in some fluffy sort of white sauce that tasted of olive oil and egg yolk. It was pretty good spread on ship's biscuit.

"The militias belong to the states," I said at last.

Geordie had sent word that he was sick, and my father had let me go look for him. As I came into the village where he was laid up, I saw Virginia dragoons kicking in doors, dragging women and children into the street, and a house burning across the common where the liberty tree had stood for nearly twenty years.

"Exactly," said Wickett. "So how was Hamilton able to . . ." He switched to English again. "What's French for 'call them up'?"

I took another swig of cider before answering, also in English: "The Militia Act made it all perfectly legal, as I calculate you know, sir, and the president got a certificate from a pet justice on the Supreme Court saying so. You make your point, Mr. Wickett."

"The Whiskey Rebellion was all but over before the army even marched, was it not?"

I remembered Rogers's remark the other day about sedition. I'd thought he was joking, but Wickett's utterances were indeed dangerously close to criminal. The Bill of Rights notwithstanding, men had already been locked up under the Sedition Act for making unflattering comments about the federal government. Legally you couldn't even suggest that John Adams was fat, when you came right down to it. That man's skin was thinner than a drunkard's alibi.

"It was pretty much over but the shouting when the army marched, Mr. Wickett, as you say. The Whiskey Boys were already going home. Or trying to." With a shaking hand, I pushed my knife away out of reach. "Please, you made your point."

"Have some cider."

"Thank'ee."

But Wickett had not given up: he was merely coming about on a new tack. In French he said, "In this war with France, Hamilton has got an army, a national one I mean, albeit a small one, and he will not relinquish it when this war is over, you mark my words. It is extermination of the Indians next, and then war with Spain. She is rotten as an old whore. Perhaps he means to seize the Floridas and New Orleans, and perhaps even all of Louisiana—which we could not do without British help, in exchange for which we must necessarily return to the arms of the empire."

Those were wild ideas I'd never even thought of. The Mississippi was our natural boundary. We could never hold onto an empire that reached beyond it, even if the people would abide such an evil thing. I shook my head.

"If he tried to make an empire," I said, "he would be hoist on his own petard."

"His own farts would lift him in the air? You fascinate me."

I snorted cider through my nose. "*Pétard*, not *péter*," I said, laughing and choking at the same time. "A sort of bomb for blowing open gates and such."

"The French, it is a funny language. But seriously, how do you arrive at this conclusion?"

"It is simplicity itself. Resistance to the excise tax wasn't confined to western Pennsylvania, you know. Were the West to get strong enough it'd break away. Kentucky, Tennessee—everyone west of the mountains would ally themselves with Spain to send their goods through New Orleans. And the British have yet to vacate their forts in the Northwest Territory. I doubt Adams could raise an army big enough, even with Hamilton's help. Or especially with Hamilton's help."

"And the reason being?" said Wickett like a teacher prompting a pupil.

"Because the Virginia militia would never march behind a Boston prig and a New York lawyer. Washington was the crucial element, of course. If Tennessee and Kentucky got mad enough, if they saw a chance for true independence, it'd be Concord Bridge all over again, with the United States on the wrong side. I speak *impromptu,* you understand. But anyway, I thought you said Hamilton wanted the army for stamping out democracy."

"Exactly! What is more undemocratic than an empire, and what is an empire but a group of dissimilar states controlled by a strong central government?" He drummed his fingers on the tabletop. "However, we have taken a very roundabout road to reach our objective."

"And the objective being—?"

"The objective—well, perhaps I should say the *point.* The point, my young friend, is that the primary purpose of any organism, be it the smallest of worms or the most beneficent of governments, is to ensure its own survival. Any other purpose is secondary."

The steward came in to remove the dishes, and Wickett said in English, "Will you take some cheese, Mr. Graves?"

"Yes thank'ee."

When the cheese had come and the steward had gone, Wickett continued in French: "Any purpose is secondary to survival: what do you make of that?"

"I think it is true enough as far as it goes, monsieur, but it sets us on a dangerous road from which there is no turning back."

"Any action is dangerous when one is under attack, monsieur. But inaction is fatal."

"Oh, foo. We're not under attack, *monsieur le lieutenant.* We're not even officially at war."

"This vessel is not under attack at the moment, no. But it rots from within."

"From within? Is there mutiny afoot?"

"Never smile at that," snapped Wickett. "There have been grumblings."

"All sailors grumble, as monsieur knows. It's their right, as they have no others."

"Ah. But they're American sailors, and so they *believe* they have rights. They do not realize that their rights have been taken from them. There is more to fear from a man who has lost his rights than from a man who has never had them. There is only one thing they lack."

My heart was thudding so hard I was having trouble thinking. Except for Stotes, I couldn't think of any man who'd shown open contempt. And Wickett had fixed that—Stotes was even then malingering in the sickbay, but his only complaint now was that his mates were shunning him. And Prichard had said Billy was afraid to go topside at night, but I'd just guessed he meant he didn't want to risk staggering over the rail when he was in his cups.

So I had to ask. "And what is it the men lack?"

"A strong leader to bind them together."

I looked at him jerking his long fingers and twining them around each other, like a hoodoo priest muttering over his mojo bag.

"And that leader would be you, Mr. Wickett?"

"What?" His forehead paled around the birthmark.

I threw down my napkin, despising myself for having stayed so long.

"I am no toady, sir, and you are a dangerous man. I had wondered why you kept the door and skylight closed." I went up on deck without looking back.

Seven

Muffled shouting woke me. I was in my hammock, shirtless and bare-foot, staring up at the deck beams. I had had a snootful of Mr. Wickett's cider and then I had fallen asleep, I remembered, but beyond that my recollection was fuzzy. I wondered drowsily what time it was, and thought maybe I would go back to sleep. But there was that shouting again, and the rumble of feet overhead, and a clatter that I couldn't place. I ran up on deck.

Under Bosun Klemso's supervision men on either side were slip-ping the sweeps—a very long sort of oar—into the rowing ports, which accounted for the clatter. Another gang was striking the awnings. In the larboard main shrouds with a glass to his eye, Wickett was staring toward the island of La Gonâve, while Dick was doing the same on the quarterdeck rail. Rogers was facing forward with an unnaturally uninterested expression on his face, clearly wanting a look but know-ing that Wickett would tell him all he needed to know. Surgeon Quilty stood next to him, looking grim.

I went over to Dick and said, "What in tarnation is everybody so puckered up about?"

He handed me his glass and pointed south toward La Gonâve. "Picaroon longboats. About ten of them, maybe a dozen. Here, you'll want to stand on something if you want to see. They're barely on the horizon."

Still stupid with sleep, I balanced on the rail with my arm around a backstay, focused the glass, looked, wiped sleep out of my eye and looked again. They were difficult to see at first through the heat waves, but once I knew what to look for, the boats crammed full of men were quite clear. Sunlight winked on cutlasses and muskets. Red no-quarter flags drooped from lateen yards. A curious shimmer alongside the boats confused me at first, until I realized I was looking at their oars flicking back and forth. Refusing to let my voice quaver, I handed the glass back and asked, "Rigaud?"

"That's what Mr. Wickett thinks."

Benoit Joseph André Rigaud, one-time goldsmith and a veteran of the Continental Army, commanded the mulatto forces in the nominally French colony of San Domingo. He had quit his alliance with his former friend Toussaint L'Ouverture, commander of the black armies, and the two were now engaged in a savage civil war. Neither had broken openly with Paris, but that was prudence, not loyalty. Rigaud controlled San Domingo's southern peninsula and La Gonâve, and he maintained a large force of what he pretended were privateers here in the Bight of Léogane. So far they had attacked only unescorted merchant ships.

"How many men do you think they have?"

"Three, four hundred easy."

I feigned nonchalance, but my heart had begun to pound. "Sounds about right." I hopped down.

Just then Freddy Billings scrambled up from below, squeaking to Wickett, "Please, sir, cap'n's coming on deck." He hid himself behind me.

Bleary-eyed and furious, Cousin Billy squinted up at Wickett in the rigging. "Come down, sir! Come down at once and explain yourself. I left explicit instructions that I was not to be disturbed under any circumstances. Any circumstances, sir! Was there some unclarity in my wording that left you in doubt?"

Blair had followed Cousin Billy on deck. He squinted up at Wickett with disapproval, the sunlight flashing on the lenses of his specs.

Wickett swarmed down the shrouds and dropped lightly to the deck. "Your words were as clear as the purest crystal, Captain. But I thought you might be interested—"

Cousin Billy stamped his foot. "Mr. Wickett, how many times must I tell you that I am indifferent to what you think? I want officers who obey me, not think for me." He glanced up at the limp sails and looked around the horizon without seeing anything, and then took in the commotion on deck and got mad all over again. "And what are you about, striking the awnings and putting the people to work in this heat? I'll not have half the people laid low with sunstroke."

"If you please, Cap'n," said the sailing master, "I really think you ought to hear him."

"I do *not* please, Mr. Rogers. Oh, *God.*" He rubbed the back of his neck as if it pained him. "Very well, don't *sulk,* for all love. I suppose I must indulge you two, or I'll never get my rest. What is it you think will interest me?"

Wickett pointed. The boats were just visible to the unaided eye now, though still miles off on the horizon, seeming in the shimmering heat to hover between sky and sea. "Picaroons, sir. A dozen barges. I make it three hundred sixty men, say thirty in each. They usually mount a gun in the bows, just swivels or three-pounders mostly, but the larger ones often have something heavier."

Cousin Billy opened his mouth and closed it. He looked at Wickett, looked at the approaching boats, looked around at the scattered convoy wallowing on the long, low swell coming down through the Windward Passage. The *Rattle-Snake* carried not quite a hundred men, boys, officers and Marines; the four merchantmen carried fifteen or sixteen men each—a force of a hundred and sixty or so, all told. To the *Rattle-Snake's* fourteen 6-pounders the merchantmen could add three or four smaller guns each, assuming their crews knew how to operate them, which it was a good bet they did not.

Cousin Billy let his breath out slowly. Taking Wickett's glass, he clambered a few feet up the shrouds, set his hanky on a ratline, settled his plump backside on the hanky and peered at the approaching boats.

A faint pounding of drums, keeping the rhythm for the picaroons at their oars, came to us across the water. Down in the waist, Horne, his wild braids tucked into a stocking cap and the sweat rolling down his broad chest, answered it with a sweet husky chant for the Rattle-Snakes at the sweeps:

"*Saro Brown be a bright mullata—*" he sang.

"*Way, hey, roll an' go!*" responded the rowers, putting their backs into the stroke.

"*She drink rum an' chew terbacca—*"

"*Ah spends my money on Saro Brown!*"

The Navy did not approve of chanteys much beyond "one-two-three-*heave*," but Wickett ignored the singing in the same way he ignored my bare feet and chest.

They'd thrown Saro over and were courting her daughter instead by the time Billy came down again, breathing heavily from his climb. He looked around without seeming to see anything. He smoothed his shirtfront, drew himself erect, and announced:

"I am afraid—that is to say, I'm afraid we should never prevail against such odds. I shall surrender the *Rattle-Snake*."

I disrecall what the others were doing, but I was looking at Wickett. He rubbed his forehead before replying, his fingers leaving white streaks around his birthmark.

"I beg pardon, Captain Trimble," he said, putting ever so slight a sneer into the word *captain*. "Surely you did not say what I think you said."

"Now, see here, Mr. Wickett," said Cousin Billy. He looked around for agreement, but found none except perhaps in Blair. "See here. These pirates have us outnumbered and outgunned. Unless a breeze comes up soon, they will be on us in an hour or so. Perhaps less. The point is, we cannot escape, and we cannot fight. We *cannot* fight," he repeated, as Wickett started to break in. "If we do, they will kill us all. Pirates only kill when they are resisted, Mr. Wickett, everyone knows that. I'm thinking of the men's lives, of course. We can't resist. It'd be worse than impossible—suicidal. We must bow to the inevitable, I'm afraid."

It was the third time he'd said *afraid*. It was a bad word in a captain's mouth.

Wickett cleared his throat. "It is not just our right to defend ourselves, *sir*, it is our obligation. Is not that so, gentlemen?" he said, turning to the rest of us.

"Yes!"

"Hear him!"

"Sir, you must listen!"

Cousin Billy shook his head. His jowls quivered. "No, Mr. Wickett, we must not resist. Once they have had their way, they will carry off what they can and leave us. There will be ample time later to deal with them. I am not thinking of myself, Mr. Wickett, but of the people, as I said."

"Eight long years I rolled with Saro—"

"Ah spends my money on Saro Brown!"

The sweeps came around through another long stroke, hauling us forward another fathom or so.

"These are not ordinary Caribee pirates, Captain Trimble," said Wickett. He turned away and then faced Billy again. His hands clenched behind his back. "They are Rigaud's butchers. They have executed whole regiments of their own men. They have slaughtered entire towns. They have massacred Frenchmen and Englishmen and women and children, and you believe they would hesitate to do the same to us? They are man-killers, not sneak thieves!"

He had been whispering in his fury, but the last words broke out of him in a shout, and the men at the sweeps stared up at him.

"C'mon me boys an' keep your stroke there—" sang Horne.

"Ah spends my money on Saro Brown!"

A couple of curious heads poked up from the fore hatch.

Wickett gazed at his own raised fists, and then put his hands behind his back. He took a slow breath and said: "We are a national ship, sir. It is not our right to submit to dishonor."

The off-duty men had been sent below to keep out of the way of the men at the sweeps, but they began drifting up in ones and twos and gathering on the fo'c's'le.

"Dishonor?" said Cousin Billy. His eyes widened at the word. "Do you accuse me of dishonor, sir? Did I not see us safely through the encounter with that French frigate?"

"Yes, and you let the British come aboard us without a thought."

"Say *sir*, you insolent dog!"

"Please, sir," said Rogers, "before you surrender for the people's sake, you got to at least ask 'em what they would do."

"Lord," I whispered to Dick, "if Billy puts it to a vote we're sank."

He jerked his head in a nod, red-faced with anger.

In the Continental Navy, it hadn't been uncommon for captains to ask the crew's opinion about whether to give battle. And oftentimes they'd voted with their backs whether they were asked or not.

Cousin Billy straightened his coat. "Will you stand by their decision?"

"That's how we did it in the last war, sir," said Rogers. He looked at the whispering knot of men on the fo'c's'le, at the quartermaster standing beside him pretending not to hear.

"And you, Mr. Towson?"

"The Revolution is over, sir," said Dick, low and scornful.

"Mr. Graves?"

"A man-o'-war ain't a democracy, sir." I hung my head, unable to look at him.

"Of course, sir, we will *not*," said Wickett quietly, but with such intensity that we all stopped and looked at him. "The decision and the responsibility are ours, not theirs."

"The decision and responsibility are *mine*, sir. I take it you will consider it an advisory vote only, then. And what about you, sir?"

Quilty had been gazing calmly at the ever-closer picaroons. "I abhor fighting," said the surgeon. "It gives me too much work all at once. But I think I will have much less to do in the long run if we fight than if we submit."

Gunner Schmidt and Bosun Klemso and the other warrant officers had gathered on the quarterdeck at the first sign of trouble, and
Corporal Haversham had assembled his Marines.

"Vot by t'under is goink on?" said Schmidt.

"Democracy in action," said Wickett. The men looked up anxiously
from their sweeps as he stepped forward and rasped, "Carry on sweep-
ing, you men. The rest of you gather 'round. Your captain would have
a word with you." He stepped back again.

Cousin Billy showed them his kindly face. "Lads," he began, "I'm
afraid we are faced with a difficult situation." They listened carefully
as he outlined the prospects for them, explained their options. There
was a low muttering as they talked it over. Finally Horne pulled off
his hat and said:

"Sir, if it's all the same to you, I think the lads'd rather fight. I
would, anyway. I don't aim to stand around while some frog-eatin'
Johnny Crappo slits my throat and paws through my duds."

The hands liked that. "Amen, brother," they said, and "Go it,
big man!"

"I don't reckon—" began Stotes, standing in the back of the crowd,
but one of his mates quickly knelt behind him and another toppled
him over with a shove, accidental like.

"There you have it, Captain Trimble," said Wickett. "The people
have spoke. Now, sir, my plan is—"

"Your plan is to get us *all* killed," said Billy. "How democratic. I
will have none of it," he said, his voice rising. "If you men want to
have your throats cut by pirates, then I wash my hands of you! But
Mr. Wickett," he said, shaking a finger under his first officer's nose,
"I do not countenance it. We are meddlers here, dilettantes and in-
terlopers. It ain't our fight. I shall be in my cabin, and when we are
boarded by pirates with blood in their eyes, just you remember that
I counseled against it. Don't gape at me, sir—tend to your guns and
cutlasses, and when you are tossed in pieces to the sharks, you just
remember I could have saved you! All these good men will have died
for nothing."

All the good men who weren't laughing at his bizarre speech gave him a chorus of boos.

"Silence!" roared Wickett. "Silence, fore and aft!"

"Well," Billy said in the sudden quiet, "I'll be in my cabin. Come, Cuz . . . there's no reason why you should throw in with this idiocy."

I swallowed. My mouth was producing so much saliva that I thought I might choke on it.

"I can't, sir," I said. "I'd prefer to die fighting than die without a fight. Billy, I . . ." What I'd have preferred was not to die at all, but I was too frightened by what Dick and Wickett might think to join him.

He went below. Blair scurried after him, muttering something about getting his papers in order.

"Mr. Rogers," said Wickett, wiping his face and hair with his kerchief, "for as long as possible, I want the picaroons to think we are a big, fat, blubbering ninny of a merchantman, trying to hide while others do our fighting for us. We'll keep our ports shut until they are alongside, with the Marines and most of the people hidden behind the bulwarks." He swabbed out the inside of his hat and placed it back on his head, adjusting it just so. "Then we'll open up all at once and give them a great surprise. Perhaps that will convince them to withdraw."

"By gom, dot'll show 'em," said Schmidt, smacking his fist into his palm. "Mr. Vickett, I shall require the use off the magazine key, if you please." He went off with his mates, jiggling the key in his hand and waggling his gray beard as he chuckled to himself.

"An excellent disguise, Mr. Graves," said Wickett, condescending to notice my naked chest and bare feet at last. "But an officer must be conspicuous in battle. The men will be more confident if they think he will be shot first."

I jumped down the ladder, ran to the midshipmen's berth, yanked on some socks, stuffed my feet into shoes, slipped into a shirt and vest, pulled on my coat—there was a note pinned to it, which I stuffed in my pocket—belted on my midshipman's dirk, grabbed my hat and ran up on deck again.

"Terrible news, lads," Wickett was saying. "The heat has spoilt the beer, and we must make do with whiskey from now on." He put his fists on his hips and grinned as they laughed. "Oh, and one other thing: some sea robbers have come to annoy us. We are worth five times what they are. They don't know it yet, so it is up to us to teach them. They will give no quarter. Neither will we."

"Well that's only fair, ain't it mate?" said a man in the front.

"That's the spirit, man!" Wickett raised his hand over the grinning faces like a preacher blessing his flock. "And when we open fire, let us give a great shout: *No quarter!* Are you with me?"

"Aye!" They were eager but sober, looking expectantly to him for orders.

"Then go to your stations in good order, quietly, and when the word comes to fire, do so cheer'ly. I expect every man and officer knows his duty. And remember, mute as mumchance until you hear otherwise." He turned to Corporal Haversham: "You, sir, get half your Marines ready to go into the tops and put your others on the fo'c's'le. Have them load their muskets with buckshot. And keep them out of sight until the last moment. And you, Mr. Graves, remove the murdering pieces from the rail: I don't want 'em seen yet. Wait until I give the order for the guns to be run out. Mr. Rogers," he said after a moment's hesitation, "you'll have to take my place at the great guns. Mr. Towson is your second; I have found him to be useful in that capacity. Be ready to take command should I fall. Above all, gentlemen, keep hidden until I commence the action. Surprise is essential."

If any man or officer was distressed by the change of command, none showed it. Each went quietly to his station, crouching low so as not to reveal himself to the approaching enemy, some of them even chortling behind their hands about what a joke we were going to play on the picaroons. Gunner Schmidt sent up the flintlocks for the six-pounders and slow match for the swivel guns. The boys hustled up from below with cartridges in their wooden boxes while the men picked out the roundest shot from the shot garlands.

I felt an odd sensation as the boarding nets rose, as if a dreadful weight sat on my shoulders that only mayhem could lift, and I seemed to see myself from a great distance.

"You'll be fine once the first gun is fired," I whispered to myself. The words kept repeating in my head.

The pair of Navy pistols I hooked onto my belt felt ridiculously large. My fine dueling pistols were stowed in Billy's cabin for safekeeping, but they weren't suited to the present purpose anyway. A service pistol comes with a spike along the left side for hooking it in your belt, which prevents your losing it at some inconvenient moment, and it is a sturdy thing, with an iron butt-cap that makes it an admirable skull-cracker.

Someone handed me a monkey of grog. I forced myself to sip it, not down it. My legs were jigging. The need to find a new rammer for one of my gun captains gave me a distraction from the growing noise of the approaching drums. I could hear the rhythmic splashing of the picaroons' oars. I could hear mulatto voices counting cadence in island French, and I found the Creole inflections comforting in their familiarity. My mind raced from thought to thought. I wondered what horror had caused my French tutor, a mulatto as imperious as he was poor, to exchange his much-lamented villa for two dirty rooms in Fell's Point. And I wondered if Geordie had ever gotten a chance to fire that old musket.

My men and I squatted on the quarterdeck beneath the hammock nettings as the *Rattle-Snake* crept into the middle of the becalmed convoy. I could see the masts of two of the merchant ships to starboard across the far rail from me, and a third about fifty yards off the larboard bow. I couldn't see *Augustin von Steuben* from where I crouched, but I knew she had drifted some way off in the current and had gotten a boat out. I hoped cheerful old Spetters could tow within range of our guns before the picaroons reached him.

Wickett, in shirtsleeves and a wide straw hat, stood at the break of the quarterdeck with one hand raised. In the other he held his uniform coat.

"In sweeps!" he called. "No time to stow them—pile them fore and aft between the masts, there. Mr. Graves, hoist our colors! Mr. Rogers, I'll have the guns run out, if you please!" He threw the straw hat away and thrust his arms into the sleeves of his coat. "Wait for it . . . Mr. Graves, get those swivels into action! Wait for it . . . *fire!*"

I didn't bother trying to answer over the roar of the six-pounders. As soon as I had run up the colors, I had grabbed the nearest murdering-piece and dropped its pivot into the receiving hole drilled in the gun-wale, squawking at my crews to follow my example. They knew what they were about and set to, loading the swivel guns with langridge— old bent nails and bits of scrap metal—and joining in the general shout of *No quarter! No quarter!* I looked over the side.

A longboat crowded with men was surging toward *Rattle-Snake*— toward *me*. An intent group was bent over the gun in its bows, while behind them the rest of the crew boated their oars and snatched up cutlasses and grapnels. A picaroon with a smoking linstock in his hand waved his loaders aside and looked up. Our eyes locked.

"Fire!" I yelled. "Oh, boys, if you love me—" just as all five starboard swivels blasted into the boat. The iron whirlwind ripped the mulatto gunner to rags and splattered his friends with blood. Men were falling around him. Momentum crashed the boat's bows into *Rattle-Snake*'s side.

From the other side of the quarterdeck a load of chain shrieked overhead through the boarding nets. Bits of cut cordage snaked down onto the deck. Out of the corner of my eye I saw Horne racing aloft with marline spike and stoppers to repair the damage. I could hear the Marines' muskets snapping in the tops. Behind me Wickett rasped, "Boarders! 'Hawks and cutlasses. Lively now!"

"Stop your vents," I called. Only a few seconds had passed since we'd fired, but I should have been working faster. The gun captains jammed their leather thumb-guards down over the smoking touch-holes. "Sponge! You there, number-two gun on the larboard side—I said sponge your piece! D'ye want to blow your mate's hands off?" Iron-shod wooden grapnels were clattering onto the deck. "Load!" The grapnels skittered across the deck and caught on the bulwarks.

"Prime!" A man came up the starboard side on a grapnel line, thrusting himself between the netting and the rail. I hauled out one of my pistols and shot him in the face. "Fire as you will!"

Another man followed the first, and I smashed him across the ear with my empty pistol. In my hurry I got the pistol wrong side up. The cock lodged in his skull and he took the gun with him when he fell back into the boat, knocking down the men behind him as he went.

I had a brief impression of waving arms and legs before we fired into the boat again. Momentum broken and in confusion, the mulattos sheered off and tried to escape. Their flight took them under our main battery, and boat and crew disintegrated in a gust of shattered timber and pink spray.

Inertia buoyed the boat's bow for a moment. A man hauled himself from the water onto the bow gun, clinging absurdly to its barrel as the bow slapped forward and dumped them both. A trail of bubbles followed them to the bottom.

The water was as clear as gin under the surface froth. I could see the man lying on the bottom, struggling to get out from under the gun as gaily colored fish eyed him curiously.

"Cease fire," Rogers was shouting in the waist. "Cease fire, dammit!"

A final gun discharged into the sea. Wreckage and dead men bobbed alongside. The rest of the picaroons hastily pulled their boats out of range while the Rattle-Snakes hollered and stamped.

Wickett had found his proper hat and had been waving it on the end of his sword. He settled it back on his head and said, "Let's not start kissing each other yet. They'll be back, my lads. Ship the sweeps again, we're falling off our station—bless me," he broke off, glancing toward *Augustin von Steuben*. "It seems Captain Spetters is about to have his painter cut. You there," he said to the nearest boy, "run down to Master Gunner Schmidt with my compliments and ask him to meet me on the fo'c's'le."

Mr. Schmidt arrived in his list slippers, which he wore in the magazine to prevent sparks, and muttered into his beard as he eyed the pair of picaroon longboats converging on the far side of *Augustin von Steuben*. Spetters was popping away with his four-pounders but having no luck. Schmidt ran his hands over the shot in the garlands, setting aside three of the truest balls, and loaded the brass bow-chaser himself. No one but he was allowed to touch it, not even to polish it.

"No time for but more than three shots," he said to himself. He patted the long brass gun. *"Gott im Himmel,"* he said, "now the time it is for to do your shtuff." He allowed four quarter-gunners to run *Gott im Himmel*'s snout out through the forward port on the larboard side, and then bent down to squint along its length. He cranked the elevating screw around and then had his gunners traverse the gun with hand-spikes. *"Ja, so,* dot'll do her," he said at last.

His first shot flew straight as a rifle bullet between the *Augustin*'s masts, but it sailed right over the picaroons' heads as well.

"Ach, so," he said. "It is der hide unt der seek mit uns they play, eh? Vell, ve show them somethink, by gom by gombo." He swabbed out the piece, gave the elevating screw half a crank, and reloaded with a reduced charge.

His second shot took off a picaroon's head, but on the way it also clipped off a chunk of the *Augustin*'s far rail.

"Es tut mir leid, Kapitan Spetters!" he called across the water.

"Es macht nichts, mein Herr!" cried Spetters in return. He gave a jaunty wave, and then the picaroons were swarming aboard like ants on a beetle.

"Ach, mein Gott," said Schmidt. He hefted the six-pound shot in his hand, and then lobbed it in disgust toward the *Augustin von Steuben*.

There was nothing to do but watch. The Augustins held up their hands, but the picaroons cut them down where they stood, and jostled for room at the rails to take pot shots at the ones who jumped overboard. The devils took great sport in it, laughing and pointing. No swimmer completed the gantlet.

"Oh, der hell mit it," said Schmidt. He loaded canister on top of ball and fired into the mulattos milling around in the *Augustin*'s waist.

Splinters and body parts splattered the limp sails. The picaroons ducked out of sight.

There was a lull punctuated by some shouting, and then a line of dark figures trotted in tandem toward the fo'c's'le. Behind them, a fat man in a bottle-green coat and pink britches kicked and jerked as he rose to the yardarm.

Toussaint had a good deal of sympathy in America, but then so did Rigaud. I even once heard an otherwise sweet old lady liken Rigaud to "a levee holding back a wicked tide of blood-maddened nigras," the fear being that once Toussaint's army of ex-slaves had plundered the entire island of Hispaniola they'd turn their attention to our Southern plantations. As I held up my hand to block the sight of Spetters's body I glanced around *Rattle-Snake*'s deck, and it struck me how many of our men were black or mulatto.

I was roused from my daze by Wickett calling, "Here they come again! Give us a cheer, lads!" And the Rattle-Snakes—whites, Dagos, niggers, Chinamen and Micks, even Svenskers—roared back, "No quarter! No quarter! No quarter!"

I went back to work, sick with fear and hatred.

This time the picaroons gained a foothold on the fo'c's'le. I saw Dick crying, "Boarders away!" with Jubal and a party of seamen at his back, his dirk in one hand and a pistol in the other, but he went down, and I lost sight of him. Wickett pointed his sword that way, and Horne and his mates dashed into the smoke. Rogers arrived with a group of sailors armed with tomahawks and boarding pikes, and the mulattos scampered back into their boats. The forward guns gave them a load of grape as they went, and the picaroons once more hauled out of range.

I sprinted forward to where Jubal was bent over Dick.

"Bung-up and bilge free, sah," a sailor told me. "Jus' a tap on him coconut, is all."

Dick stood up, grinning, wiping a stream of blood away from his face. He held still while Jubal knotted his kerchief picturesquely over the gash on his brow. Then he said to me:

"Hello, shipmate—hot today, ain't it!"

"Oh, Dick, can you stand it?"

"Bully! Ain't it grand!"

"Permission to check on the captain, sir."

Wickett was standing at the quarterdeck rail, gazing toward La Gonâve. He turned to look at me. His left eye was red and watering, and that side of his face was black with spent powder. His cheek was torn open, and blood had run down his jaw and soaked his white neck-cloth and shirtfront. Blood dripped from the handkerchief in his hand.

"Permission denied." He held out his glass. "Run aloft and see what you can see."

I settled myself in the crosstrees and opened the telescope. "Deck there," I called down, "the boats are pulling for Guanabo. They've got *Augustin von Steuben* under tow. No sign of prisoners."

"Anything to seaward?"

Nary a cat's-paw marred the surface of the water. "No, sir."

"Very well. Stay there until I call you."

I had little to do while I waited. The picaroons were occupied by their long haul back to La Gonâve and the sun was making me sleepy, so after a time I began looking through my pockets for something to amuse myself. In the pocket where I had jammed it, I found the note that had been pinned to my lapel.

SIR [*it read*],

In your haste to depart you left this your coat apon the back of your chair. It ocurr^d to me after a moments Reflection that perhaps I express^d myself badly, leading to a Misapprehension of my thrust, which was that there can be no Fire without it has a spark. Experience has eyes that Innocence does not. Be assured I remain

your humb^l ob^t s^vt &c,

P: Wickett

The "your humble obedient servant, et cetera" was pure pro forma, of course. I had been indignant when I left the wardroom, but I already viewed the early afternoon as a time apart and long ago. The way I remembered it—the passing of time fogging our memories as it does—I had kept my voice level and remembered to speak in French, saying, "I had wondered why the skylight remained closed, Mr. Wickett. I hope I shall never be asked to resume this conversation."

He had looked stricken. "Alas, what have I done!"

I had coldly thanked him for dinner—I was pretty sure I'd thanked him—bowed, and gone on deck.

He had followed me up a few minutes later, humming the opening bars of a newly popular ditty as he fell in step with me:

Hail Columbia, happy land!
Firm, united let us be . . .
As a band of brothers join'd . . .

I had gone below in a huff, thinking that the only malcontent in the *Rattle-Snake* was her first lieutenant, and that he meant to involve me in some sort of intrigue. I glanced down at him now as he walked back and forth on the quarterdeck talking with Rogers, at his bloody shirt and ruined cheek. And I thought maybe he was, and maybe he did, and maybe he had his reasons. *The proof is in the pudding,* I thought with a snort, as I remembered the way Billy's buttocks had jounced as he scuttled below before the shooting could start.

"Well, Mr. Wickett," thinks I, "if it was mutiny on your mind, you've pulled it off sweet as pie." We were all in it with him, now.

I raised my glass and looked again toward the island.

"Deck there!" I called down. "They're throwing out their dead and wounded. The shallows are full of 'em. But they got a passel more men on the beach. They're taking on shot and powder." I counted them as best I could, masses of men hauling wounded or dead men out of the boats and piling aboard in their place. "They have at least as many replacements as men already in the boats. Hunnerds of 'em. Here they come again, sir."

"A word with you, Mr. Graves."

Wickett was daubing at his face with a handkerchief when I returned to the deck. The flesh around the rip in his cheek was puffed and purple, and mottled with black gobs of dried blood.

"Another time," he said in a low voice, "I'd wish you to deliver such information to me quietly rather than risk alarming the entire crew." He leaned over the side and spat out a bright stream of bloody spittle. Then he reached into his mouth and pulled out a molar and contemplated it sourly. "There's some time yet," he said. He put the tooth in his pocket. "You may go see how your illustrious kinsman does."

The door to the after-cabin clinked against a spilled chamber pot when I opened it. Apparently Billy had been reluctant to use his private head in the quarter-galley, though it would have given him a slap-bang view of the fight. The wooden deadlights had been shipped over the stern windows to help prevent shattered glass from flying about, but the skylight and a pair of shot holes in the side let in enough light to see by. Cousin Billy was crouched with one knee on the padded locker at the transom, head bowed over a glass. A muffled keening came from beyond the closed door to the sleeping place.

To make my report in the proper way I would have had to mention Wickett's name, which seemed very much the wrong thing just then. "Bad news, I'm afraid, sir," I said instead. "We've lost Captain Spetters and the *Augustin*." He took a drink, but said nothing. I repeated myself, and again he said nothing. I said, "Are you well, Billy?"

He looked through me. "Is horrid. Hell down here. Such a thundering. Not knowing what's going on makes it worse. You can't imagine what is like. Not even whiskey help." He poured himself another. Liquor splattered on the deck. "Well, don't gape at me like ninny. I'll be on deck to offer surrenner momentarily. You'll just have to tell those ruffians they must wait till I'm damn good an' ready. No sense caving in to their every whim or they'll be making most outrageous demands." He patted my arm. "You had your doubts about good ol' Cousin Billy, but I'm glad you're still alive to see was right. The very fact that you're here to ask my sur—surren . . . for my sword proves that they're more gennelmen than even I gave 'em credit for. I admit it fully and most graciously. You must tell 'em so." He bowed, spilling the rest of his drink. He poured and swallowed another. "Well, what must be done must be done. Sword's around here somewhere. Strap 'er on and let's get over with.

"Oh, Cuz," he said in sudden boozy remorse, "so sorry. So sorry so sorry so sorry. Never thought end this way. Must forgive. So sorry." Forgetting what he was intending, he reached again for the decanter. "Empty again, dammit. Where Prichard? Hey, sentry! Pass a word for steward!"

"That's all right, Billy." I eased him sprawling onto the locker. "Prichard's needed at number-four gun. He'd much rather be down here with you, I'm sure, but there you have it." I plumped a cushion and he dropped his head onto it.

He waved an arm in the air. "Oh, that Peter Wicked behind this, I know. Have him up on charges. Won't he look funny *then*. He had it in for me. And the people, too. The people. Allus gotta call 'em *people*, not *men* . . . Had it in for me from first, and Peter Wicked is their leader. Goddamn mutineer. Well, misser, I'll have you dancing on air, I will, and the whole country laughin' at you then, you sonabitch. Hey, you, Prichard," he said to me, "fill up 'at fucking decanter and get out my sight, there's good fellow, you thieving li'l prick ah ha ha."

He closed his eyes and folded his hands across his paunch. A stain spread across his crotch and dribbled down one britches leg. Prodding him produced only a snore.

I couldn't leave him to be found like that, but he was too heavy for me to shift his clothes myself. I rapped on the door to the sleeping place.

The keening stopped with a hiss.

"Mr. Blair? Sir, I—"

There was a bang and a crack, and chunk of the door splintered out right above my head. I hit the deck in a splatter of piss and whiskey.

"Stay back!" called Blair. "I have another pistol!"

"Don't shoot, Mr. Blair," I called. "It's just me—Matty Graves."

"Get back!" Another bang and another chunk out of the door, lower this time, followed by a shriek as he realized he'd emptied the second pistol. "I have . . . I have a *third* pistol!" I heard the sound of a wooden case being dropped—the one my dueling pistols came in, I had no doubt—and a rattle as of lead shot pouring out onto the deck. "Goddammit goddammit goddammit to hell," said Blair under his breath.

I saw no reason to wait around while he reloaded. Damning Billy for a drunk and Blair for a lunatic, I took Billy's key from his desk, closed the door behind me, locked it, dropped the key into my vest pocket, told the sentry to let no one in without the captain's say-so and ran back on deck.

Wickett was talking with Dick and Rogers. "Mr. Graves," he said, "what was that noise?"

"An accident with a pistol, sir."

"A brace of pistols, I believe." An empty smile bloomed on his face.

"But no one was hurt, sir."

The smile faded. "Ah. Our brave captain yet lives, then?"

"He sends you good cheer, sir," I lied, "and admits that it is only pride that prevents him from returning to the quarterdeck. He leaves it in your hands to fight the ship, sir, and trusts that victory is ours."

Wickett exchanged looks with Rogers before looking back at me. "Truly?"

"Well, sir, it's true he ain't able to take the deck at the moment."

He smiled again, and again the smile faded.

"It's a damned shame about Spetters," he said. "I'd have thought he would give a better account of himself." He glanced toward the *Augustin von Steuben* in the distance, still under tow and forever beyond our reach. "The picaroons are laying off for the moment, but they're just watching the current. Now *Jane* is getting away from us, I believe."

Lighthorse and *Anemone* still lay a short way to starboard. *Anemone*'s main shrouds had come afoul of *Lighthorse*'s bowsprit, but a fluke of the current to larboard was pulling *Jane* away from us. Recognizable even half a mile away in the same dreary black coat he had worn when I first met him, Peavey was helping to sway *Jane*'s single boat over the side.

"At least they are going to run for it," said Rogers.

"Perhaps," said Wickett. "But I do believe they mean to take her under tow, brave fellows."

"Brave fellows mine arse, Mr. Wickett. That's probably the only undamaged boat they got left, and they won't all fit in."

"Wasted effort, anyway, Mr. Rogers. They'll never get way enough on her with just the one boat."

It had been awful to lose jolly Spetters. I couldn't bear to lose Peavey, too, and I thought somebody should do something about it. Dick might like the job—then I recoiled from the thought like a man who suddenly finds himself on the edge of a cliff. Shame, not courage, had kept me on deck instead of following Billy. A black pit of self-hatred awaited me if I kept on that road. I stepped to Wickett's side and touched my hat.

"Beg pardon, sir," I said. "Was I to take a boat I might be able to help tow the *Jane* back in time, or at least get the rest of her crew off. If they won't come, maybe I could help fight her."

Wickett gripped my shoulder and said, "Steady fellow!" For an odious moment I hoped he'd said "Steady, fellow"—that he was saying it was a daft idea—but no, he was looking at me with something like approval. "I'll ask the people myself," he said. "A few might harbor some unfair resentment against you. Lads," he called out, "Mr. Graves has handsomely volunteered to go to the assistance of *Jane*, over there. Who is not afraid to follow him?"

Eight

I felt pretty confident as we set out for the *Jane*. My blood was up, damn me if it weren't. I wanted to fight some more. I knew things would go well. Horne had picked out eleven volunteers, mostly from among the swivel-gun crews but also including a few of his particular mates, the biggest and blackest men in the schooner. He had also chosen our cook, who was called Doc, as man-of-war cooks always are. I wouldn't have chosen him myself. He was missing an eye and a leg, and because he was a warrant officer and an absolute monarch in the galley, he had gotten the idea that he could decide whose orders he would obey. But if I had any worry at all, it was that among those big black men I felt pale and childish, a moo-calf among bulls.

But they couldn't have been kinder. Horne, pulling stroke oar with long, smooth draws, suddenly chuckled.

"Ain't nothing more pleasant than a little boat ride in the sunshine, Mr. Graves," he said.

"An' a nice supper waitin' at da end ob it," said Doc. He grinned. "Some dancin' too, I 'spec."

"How can you dance wif a ol' peg-leg?" asked Wilcox, one of my swivel-gun men.

"Shoo, dat don't slow a man down if he a *man*, any more'n havin' only one eye make him blind to da ladies. Hey, Mr. Graves, you think we'll get liberty in San Domingo?"

"Aw, stow your gob," said Horne.

"Shush yo' mouf. You don't outrank me."

"No, but I'm bigger'n you."

"I'll bust yo' head," said Doc, but everybody laughed and so did he.

"Boat your oars," I said. "Get that boat hook ready."

I was not expecting gratitude from an Eastern Shoreman and was not disappointed. Peavey leaned over the rail with a blunderbuss in his hands and shouted, "Yer a bit premature to be claiming salvage, young man! Stand off and mind yer own business!"

"Back water. Way enough." I shaded my eyes against the bright sky as I looked up at him. "We only get salvage for *recaptures,* Captain Peavey." Although I couldn't see the picaroons from down in the boat, I knew he could from where he was. "But suit yourself. We'd just as soon come back later anyway."

"Hell he says," muttered Wilcox. "We just got here."

"Watch an' learn, boy," said Horne.

Peavey looked toward La Gonâve and the faraway *Augustin von Steuben.* "I'll heave you a line," says he.

The Janes in the boat seemed glad to see us, anyway. Their faces were red and the sweat was streaming down their bare backs. Peavey's mate waved his hat from the stern sheets and cried, "Huzzay for the *Rattle-Snake!*"

By themselves they were barely managing to tug the *Jane* through the water, but when we took up the slack on our line she crept along willingly enough. I ought to have put us in tandem, with the smaller boat in the lead, but we weren't rigged with a towing post, and there was no time, and I didn't want to give up any momentum. And it wasn't my aim to outrun the picaroon longboats, anyway. I just wanted to get within pistol-shot of the *Rattle-Snake.* Even getting within a few hundred yards of her would do the trick: Gunner Schmidt and *Gott im Himmel* could play ninepins with the picaroons at that distance.

I didn't care for the work, such of it as I did. My contribution was limited to making encouraging noises. Horne wouldn't let me touch an oar—because I was a quarterdeck officer, he said, but more likely because he didn't trust me to keep the stroke. The sweat ran down the Rattle-Snakes' bodies and dripped from their arms and hands, and in the soupy, overheated air they were soon gasping for breath. I had nothing to do but sit in the stern sheets and pretend I'd meant to remain in the boat instead of going aboard the *Jane,* as a more experienced officer would have done. The men began to cuss, too, between breaths. I should have told them to stow it, but I was too hot in my coat to play the tyrant.

"Hey . . . Mr. Graves," said Doc, pulling at his oar, "whyn't you . . . whyn't you pour some . . . some water on our heads."

"Good lord, no. Fever's endemic in these islands."

The men grinned. Wilcox actually laughed: "No disrespect, sir . . . don't know diddly . . . about no endemic. Dat's to worry about . . . *later.* A bit of a chill . . . feel powerful good . . . about now."

"Dat's right," said Doc. "You just pour dat water, boy. We'll worry . . . 'bout catching our deaf . . . some *uvver* time. G'wan now."

"Very well, then. Don't blame me if you get pneumonia." I scooped up a bailer full and raised it over Horne's head.

"I don't need no water poured on me, white boy," said he. "Sir."

Before I could dump the dipper over the man behind him, a shower of spray did the cooling-off for me. There was a blur and a buzz as a cannonball skipped over our heads.

"Pick up them oars!" Horne yelled. Men guiltily snatched them up again and looked to him for orders.

"Don't look at *me*," he said. "This ain't my boat."

I cast the towing line loose. "La'board side, back water! Sta'board side, give way!"

I swung the tiller over and glanced first to starboard and then astern as the boat came about on the opposite course. The horizon seemed filled with picaroon longboats, all crowded with men. Three were headed our way, one of them with smoke rising over its bow.

A second longboat fired its gun. The ball touched sea with a little splash, skipped once, twice, and then plowed into the *Jane*'s boat. Pieces of planking and oars and men traced the ball's path as it passed through the boat and into the sea.

I steered toward the half-dozen survivors. Horne glanced around forward to see where we were going, and gave me a look, but he didn't say anything.

I soon discovered the reason for the look. It's impossible to reason with a man in the water if he can't swim, and the Janes nearly swamped the boat with their grabbing. And when one white-faced man began screaming about sharks, the Janes threw themselves into the boat any which way they could. We nearly turned turtle—I'd have gone overboard if Horne hadn't grabbed my coat—and we shipped a great deal of water, but soon enough all were aboard and I pointed us once again toward the *Jane*. The Janes collapsed around our feet and didn't so much as offer to bail out the boat.

"Here, you," I said, hauling on the mate's jacket. "Take the tiller." I bailed her out myself.

They didn't stand on ceremony when I brought them alongside the brig, either. Despite my shouts and the Rattle-Snakes' offended protests, they scrambled over the low railing and under the raised boarding nets. When the last of them except the mate was aboard, I followed with the Rattle-Snakes behind me. The mate came last, looking sheepish.

"I see we've doubled your force, Captain Peavey," I said.

"That's what you think," said the mate. "Come back here, ye goddamn swabs!" As soon as we'd turned our backs, five or six Janes had jumped down into our boat and were now pulling for the *Rattle-Snake*. A picaroon longboat put its tiller over to cut them off.

With a strangled growl, Peavey snatched up his blunderbuss and blasted at the runaways. A couple of them squawked as if they'd been stung, but the range was too great for whatever bits and pieces he'd loaded it with to do them much harm.

"Ah, well," said Peavey. He handed the blunderbuss to his mate and looked at me. "But don't go getting ideas, now, Mr. Midshipman Whoosis. I'm just a simple sailor, but I know my rights. This here brig is still *my* brig, see?"

"Yes, sir, but I guess we'd better handle the guns."

The *Jane* carried a pair of long three-pounders on either side. They were tiny guns by Navy standards, the least of the so-called great guns, about four and a half feet long and weighing seven and a quarter hundredweight apiece; but when a long three is hot and loaded with good powder, it can throw a three-inch ball of solid iron well over a mile.

"Horne," I said, "you'll command the sta'board battery and I'll take the la'board. Captain Peavey, where's your powder?"

He indicated a small keg by the mainmast. "That there."

"You, Samuels," I said to a tall, shaven-headed man, the best of my swivel-men. "You're our gunner. Take that keg into the cockpit, if there's no magazine, and make sure no candles are burning. You four Janes, you're our powder monkeys. You'll answer to Samuels, and yes you'll take orders from a Negro if you love life." All the Janes were white. "Do you have any cartridges made up, Mr. Peavey? Very well then, fetch us up some sturdy paper and we'll make 'em out of that."

I checked on the picaroons—still a quarter of a mile off, coming at the bow to avoid our guns for as long as possible. I guessed we had about fifteen minutes to get squared away. Then one shot apiece, maybe two, and they'd be on us.

"You have more muskets, captain? Then I suggest you lay them out. You'll have use for 'em soon enough."

I wasn't happy with the guns. They were too old to have flintlocks, but that wasn't it—slow match would do very well—and the shot in the garlands was rough with rust, but that shouldn't matter at close quarters. I ran my hand along one of the barrels. Bits of black paint flaked away from the pitted surface, as if each of numerous coats had been laid down over years of corrosion. I hated to think what they looked like inside.

"Captain Peavey, d'ye have any musket balls?"

"A few, aye."

"No, I mean in the cargo. Lots of 'em, that we can use for grapeshot."

"No, I just have the muskets. All the ammunition's in the *Augustin*."

I had no idea what he meant by that, but I didn't have time to ask. Instead I asked if he had any scrap we could use.

He scratched his chin. "Well, I allow as how I might have a barrel of nails somewhere. But nails ain't cheap, y'know. It'd be a shame to waste 'em."

"You disappoint me, Mr. Peavey. Ain't you the fellow that boomed along in the Roaring Forties with a toothpick for a mainmast and a threadbare handkerchee for a mains'l?"

He looked at me sideways. "Well, what of it?"

"I'd a thought you'd take more interest in your own defense. Ain't you never had to fight afore?"

He scowled. "Now—now see here!"

"Your guns're a disgrace. You ain't never fired 'em, have you?"

He grinned like a dog shitting peach pits. "Wull, I always been able to show my heels to just about anything afloat. Besides," he said, drawing himself up, "I was kinder countin' on the Navy's protection, see?"

"That's what we're here for. Now how about fetching up them nails."

"I already told ye, nails ain't cheap!"

"I'll use the silver in your pockets if I have to, Mr. Peavey."

He fetched the nails.

Then here was Samuels, reporting that the powder was of the poorest kind and much of it ruined by damp. I took off my hat and rubbed my forehead. "Find an empty keg to dump the most suspect powder in, then. Send us up a cartridge each of the best-looking stuff, and have another couple of cartridges each standing by."

The fifteen minutes burned away, but the Rattle-Snakes worked quickly with little need for orders. A pair of them grabbed *Jane*'s old-fashioned galley, a deck-mounted wooden box filled with sand, and dumped the fire overboard. Others cleared the decks by tossing the crates stacked on *Jane*'s deck after the coals.

"Avast!" roared Peavey. "Do you know what them crates is worth?"

"What's in 'em?" I said.

"Muskets! D'ye have any idea what a musket's worth in San Domingo these days?"

All the more reason to toss them, I thought. With a sudden dread, I realized I expected the *Jane* to be captured.

"Tommy," Peavey said to the mate, "keep a list of everything that's lost. I'll have every last penny accounted for, by gad."

I hoped the picaroons would bugger the old miser. But we were out of time, and I sent the men to the guns.

"Out your tampions! Check your guns!" I called. With Samuels down in the cockpit and Horne commanding the guns on the other side, I had to be my own gun captain. Straddling the nearest gun, I felt down its barrel with the worm. There was no charge down at the bottom, but the inside of the barrel was caked with rust. I figured the first shot would blow it clear.

"Sponge your guns!" That might get rid of some of the inner filth, anyway.

"Load your guns!" I grabbed the pound of powder in its paper cylinder that a worried-looking *Jane* handed me and stuffed it into the muzzle. It fit well. Samuels had found a bottle or a drinking glass to use as a template. I put a wad of old cloth on top of the charge and tamped it home with the three-foot bit of dowel that served as a rammer.

"Shot your guns! Nails on top of round shot!" The load called for a smaller charge, I remember thinking, but the guns obviously weren't hot yet and I didn't think it would matter. I rolled the truest-looking ball in on top and shoved it down. Now to add pepper to the pot.

"Get me some o' them nails here," I called. "Come on, shake a leg!"

They were six-inch nails, twice the width of the bore, which wasn't good, but they were all we had. I put another wad of cloth on top of them and pounded all home.

"Run out your guns!" Wilcox and his mate and I heaved on the tackles and ran the gun out.

"Prime your guns!" I shoved the pricker down the touchhole to pierce the cartridge.

The *Jane*'s mate brought us gun-flour in a pewter flask. I sprinkled the fine silvery stuff into the touchhole until it formed a little heap, and passed the flask along.

We used handspikes to traverse the guns as far forward as they would point. There was a flashing and popping as Peavey and his mate opened up with muskets on the fo'c's'le.

A picaroon longboat whipped into sight from beyond the bow. It mounted a twelve-pounder carronade, a short fat ugly gun with no accuracy to speak of, but crushing power close in. The gunner was twirling a piece of slow match around his head to keep it lit, and waving with his other hand at the tillerman. *"Le barre dessous! Babord!"* he shouted, and the tillerman put down his helm and brought her around to larboard.

I too had a length of smoldering match in my hand, and my gun crew was watching eagerly, but the boat was too far forward to reach. I watched the maw of the carronade as it swung around, widening into a perfect circle, and for a dizzy moment I thought I could see right down the barrel. Then the opening narrowed again as the boat finished its turn. There was a burst of smoke and sparks around the gunner's hand as he thrust the end of his match into the touchhole of the carronade.

A twelve-pounder, even a short gun like a carronade, is too loud to hear when it's fired at you at close range. The noise is a physical sensation, very much like being slapped across the ears. It rattles your ribcage and you forget to breathe.

A canister of musket balls whined through the open rail, knocking the men at the forward gun into bloody lumps.

The boom of another twelve-pounder answered Horne's two guns popping off behind me. The shot came across the deck and shattered the rail beside me. Wilcox's mate fell screaming with the jagged ends of a splinter protruding from either side of his thigh.

The boat on our side was momentarily dead in the water. But no! The recoil had given her some sternway, enough to bring her into my sights.

"Wilcox, stand clear!" I glanced along the pitted iron barrel of my gun, stepped to the side and jammed my slow match into the priming. Red sparks and a fountain of smoke shot up out of the touchhole, and then . . . nothing.

The picaroons bent to their oars with a yell. A grapnel landed in the netting. Picaroons were coming up the side.

I drew my dirk and bleated something about repelling boarders. Then the boarding nets were full of struggling determined picaroons, and we were busy swinging and slashing and smashing.

I had a pistol in my hand. I stuck it in a man's belly and pulled the trigger. I dropped the pistol and jabbed the next man with my dirk. The point bit bone and I couldn't pull it out again. I braced my foot against his chest and heaved. I lost my grip on the bloody hilt and fell backwards to the deck. A mulatto in a blue coat tried to stick me with his sword. Something blew his face open from behind and he fell on top of me.

I'd clonked my head on the gun carriage. As I lay dazed on my back beside the three-pounder, Wilcox reached across it and grabbed my hand.

Then a long red crack shot down the side of the gun and all the shadows disappeared. The sky rocked and dimmed, and the world went away.

Nine

"You return to us," a voice remarked in beautiful French. "You had the nasty shock when the gun exploded, *hein?* Ah, you speak French, *mon cher petit ami—c'est bon!* Can you see my hand? How many fingers? Excellent! You may dispose of that disagreeable souvenir now."

Somebody was holding me upright. My head lolled and most of me lay sprawled on the deck, and the rails and rigging rode past my vision as if I was drunk and a storm was blowing. I was clutching something: a black man's lower arm, ripped off near the elbow, its hand clasped in mine. Splintered white bone protruded obscenely from its end. I tried to heave the thing overboard, but it flopped against the smoking shards of the three-pounder and fell wetly to the deck. A picaroon kicked the thing into the sea.

"*À bonne chance,*" said the same voice, "my men are able to recognize a military uniform, though it be soaked in blood. You are an American officer, yes? On the strength of this, I have prevented the hanging of yourself and your sailors for the time being. The civilian officers of this ship, however . . . Disgusting, is it not?"

Here I was aware of a delicate honey-brown hand whose manicured fingers and pink palm compelled my eyes to follow its gesture and look up at Peavey and his mate, Tommy, dangling by their necks from either end of the mainyard. Filth dripped down Tommy's legs.

"Perhaps you would be so kind," continued the voice, and I bobbled my head around, looking for its source, "as to help me sort out your sailors from the men who belong to this ship. The first are to be interned at the jail in Guadeloupe. The others are smugglers who must be disposed of as justice dictates."

I shook my head, and the world spun nauseatingly. *"Tous le miens,"* I managed.

"They cannot *all* be yours," said the voice. "You must be confused. Understandably so, *hein?* No matter. There will be time enough to hang everyone once we have returned to our base and a citizens court can be convened. Ah, but as you can see, we are arrived."

The picaroons were towing the *Jane* into a natural harbor through a break in the reef. It was a long and narrow anchorage, not easily visible from the sea, but it was deep enough for the *Augustin von Steuben* to ride there at anchor and for the *Jane* to slip in beside her. Field guns peered from thickets on the headlands at either side.

I twisted around to look to seaward as we passed through the reef. Away off to the north through the open railing I caught a glimpse of the sails of the still-becalmed squadron, tiny with distance, a smoky mist hanging over them. They looked terribly far away on the broad bright sea.

Astern, half a dozen picaroons rowed our gig into the cove, with no sign of the runaway Janes but the blood on their hands.

From General Villon's left temple to the point of his swarthy chin ran a crooked purple scar. He needed a shave, but his black hair had been carefully dressed in shiny ringlets. His dark blue *uniforme national* had been brushed recently, but the gold lace was cracked and blood had dried black on the scarlet cuffs. His pantaloons, white under gory splatters, were tucked into a pair of Hessian boots, one of which still boasted a gilt tassel. The red tip of the Tricolor plume on his round hat had broken off or had been shot away.

We were seated on crates beside a smoky fire, near an orderly hamlet of weather-beaten tents. My uniform was singed and ripped, but, except for a queasy stomach, some blistered skin and an aching head, the explosion that had torn Wilcox apart had left me unharmed.

Villon was examining my watch, his fingers dark against the silver, turning it this way and that and holding it up to his ear. He sucked at the clay pipe between his teeth, but it had gone out.

"It is a disagreeable subject," he said politely in French, reaching an ember out of the fire with a bent twig and applying it to his pipe, "but there is still the difficulty of sorting out your men from the merchant sailors. Except for that large *nègre* with the profusion of braids, they wear no uniform, nothing to mark them as being in the military. As a naval officer you've noticed this before, of course, but as I am of the artillery it has only recently come to my attention." He made a face. "This tobacco is worse than horseshit. I hope there is something better in the ships we took. What were their names?"

Despite the violence and murder I'd seen that afternoon, or perhaps because of it, I wasn't afraid of Villon. I was wary and anxious, yes, but in spite of that I liked him.

"I don't know all their names," I said. "I'm not sure I could remember now, anyway." I felt sick with shame and grief.

"All their names? There were only two."

"Oh, you mean . . ." What were the words for brig and schooner? "You mean the vessels you took."

"The ships, yes. There were two of them." He held up one finger and then another: "One, two."

"*Augustin von Steuben* and *Jane*," I said, my finger trembling as I pointed out which was which. "Fifteen days out of Norfolk, captains Spetters and Peavey. I don't know what their . . ." I groped for the word for "cargo" while trying to fight back the memory of Peavey's feet swaying as he hung by his neck. "I don't know what they carry."

"*Augustin von Steuben*, he carries ammunition," Villon said. "Everything from round shot to musket balls. Not much powder, unfortunately." The unscarred side of his black-freckled face broke into a grin. "According to the manifest, *Jane* carries nearly a thousand stand of muskets. French 1763s, mostly, that we sold you for your own war of independence. Very amusing, no?"

"Amusing? What is?"

"Why, that we sell you arms that you might gain your freedom, and twenty years later you sell them to our enemies to keep us from gaining ours. Does the irony not amuse?"

He seemed to want an argument. So I said the first thing that came to mind: "But monsieur, I thought all Frenchmen were already free."

He smiled—a faint smile, a mocking smile, but a smile all the same.

"Bien entendu!" he said. "Of course! All Frenchmen are free. Not a slave in the bunch. Yet some are freer than others. That is, some will more readily be able to prove their loyalty when the Republic finally sees fit to reoccupy Saint-Domingue and put an end to this nonsense."

"But is not Toussaint L'Ouverture the legal commander-in-chief of all French forces in the island?"

Villon pursed his lips. "His appointment was mere expediency, Paris being so far away. When a proper field marshal arrives, this bloody imbecility will stop."

I licked my lips. "Do you plan to kill me?"

He drew back in surprise. "This is a terribly blunt question."

"I have, monsieur, a pressing interest in the matter."

He waggled a finger at me, and chuckled. *"Là,* my friend, you are jumping from the rooster to the donkey. We will discuss all things in their proper time."

I felt like a four year old in wet pants. I said, "A 'proper field marshal,' monsieur? Did not the Directory appoint Toussaint?"

He tipped his hat back on his head. "Toussaint merely happens to command the larger force in the island *at the moment.* Saint-Domingue is the richest colony in the world! Its product alone is twice that of all of Great Britain's possessions. Do you think for one moment that the First Consul intends to let a bunch of *nègres* take it away from him? Your own economy might outpace it, you know, if you would stop this nonsense of cooperating with the English. Go back to fighting

them instead of us, *hein?* What are you, a gang of ungrateful rustics?"
His pipe had gone out again, and he spat into the fire.

"As it happens, monsieur," I said, "I am entirely of your mind about
the English."

He nodded, as if it was a matter of course that I'd agree with him.

"But . . . I beg your pardon, monsieur," I said, "but who is this First
Consul you mention?"

"Who . . . ? Who is the First Consul? Where have you been?"

"At sea, monsieur."

He slapped himself on the forehead. "But of course, and we just
heard it ourselves last week. There has been a coup d'état, my friend,
on the eighteenth of Brumaire—that would be your ninth of November.
When Général Buonoparte finished setting things right in Egypt, he returned to Paris, abolished the corrupt Directory and created a new gov-
erning body. Naturally he has put himself at its head."

Last I'd heard, Buonoparte's army had been stranded in Egypt after Nelson destroyed the French fleet at Aboukir Bay. But I dared not
mention that. Instead I said, "Abolishing the Directory, monsieur, is
not necessarily a bad thing. But is it not compounding an error to take
power from a very few men and invest it in one?"

"No one ever acts alone," said Villon. "Buonoparte is merely the
voice of the people. He is the chief of three consuls. He is the most
powerful of them, of course, but is not as if he has brought back the
tyranny of the monarchy. He has not crowned himself king, after all."

"One needn't be a king to be a tyrant, monsieur." I had admired the
little general's courage and audacity, and was shocked to think of what
he might now become.

"The mob is the greatest of tyrants and the most dangerous," said
Villon. "But you! You unshod ingrates, you Americans. You owe us
money, but do you pay? You do not. You owe us loyalty, but do you
help us? You do not! You owe us friendship, and what do you do? You
build a navy and attack our ships!"

"There I have you, monsieur. We wouldn't have built a navy if
French pirates would leave our merchantmen alone."

"*Corsairs,* not pirates!" he snapped, and the smile left my face. "There are rules, you know, legalities to be observed. Except for the occasional show of temper, there is no wantonness." He patted my knee. "But what else can poor France do when her ships are fired upon without provocation? Why, the jail in Guadeloupe is filled with American seamen, who of course cannot be exchanged because no state of war exists between our two nations. We want nothing but the peace. Why must you cause trouble?"

"You will forgive me, monsieur, if I point out that the trouble is precisely that France has attacked us."

"Attacked you?" He spread his hands and looked sad. "Where? When?"

"The French navy steals our ships and jails our men."

"For trading in contraband items with the enemy."

"Free ships make free goods, monsieur. Our position on this is quite clear."

He knocked his pipe against his boot. "I think this tobacco really *is* horseshit. Hey, Citizen Prêteur!" he called out to a grizzled white man in the remnants of a French sailing master's uniform. "Wasn't there any tobacco in the what-do-you-call-them, the ship's stores?"

"Perhaps, Citizen Villon," said Prêteur. "It happens I got a full pouch at the moment. Want a pipeful?"

"I take that as a great kindness," said Villon, snapping his fingers for Prêteur's pouch. "And I should take it as a greater kindness were you to deliver at least a kilogram to my tent before morning."

"I'll see what I can do, Citizen Villon. I already arranged for the booze to be placed under your protection, along with a few other dainties that would only encourage unrevolutionary decadence among the men. There were several chickens and pigs and a goat, as well. Maybe I should go supervise their slaughter to make sure that nothing loses its way between the chopping block and the carving board."

"But no!" said Villon. "Save the goat for the milk!"

Prêteur grinned. "Save it for the flies, you mean. It was killed in the attack."

"Ah well," said Villon, packing his pipe contentedly. "And when the goat has been coaxed into digestibility, perhaps you will be so good as to join me for supper."

"*Mais oui, Citoyen Villon!*" Prêteur hustled off, probably to make sure that the best cuts were reserved for Villon and himself.

"Now there's a rover," said Villon. He lit the fresh tobacco in his pipe, drew in a lungful and exhaled with his head back and his eyes closed. "I make no doubt that he had stolen all the tobacco for himself. However, he has impeccable revolutionary credentials; could take the next ship home to Toulon and retire on the earnings from his captures—" he coughed decorously "—not all of them American, I assure you—and could probably buy the estate he was whelped on, yet he insists on staying here. I don't know, perhaps he thinks chatteldom under one system is no different than villainy under another. Sometimes I think he merely likes fighting, or he has an inconvenient number of wives." He sighed. "Speaking of inconvenient numbers, we really must settle this question of which men are yours and which must be otherwise disposed of. We've only so much food, you know."

"But I told you, monsieur, they are all of them my men."

He pretended to be surprised. "And I have told you, I can scarcely believe this."

I shrugged. "If it's a question of provisions, perhaps you should just let us go."

"Perhaps. Perhaps, but I could do with some decent seamen instead of these jackals I have." He shrugged, his eyes unreadable. "Maybe I'll keep them instead of hanging them, though that could be difficult when my men have recovered from their day's work and the women have counted the dead. I tell you what we do, *mon cher petit ami*. I keep your men and this fine watch, and you keep your life. Not a bad bargain, *hein?*"

"But—this is the Devil's bargain, monsieur!"

"*Nous avons discuté tout ce temps en pure perte,*" he said, meaning, "We have argued all this time to no purpose." But it was just an old saying, and he uttered it absently, like he was already thinking of something else. He smiled fondly at my watch before tucking it into his vest pocket. "Until my supper is ready I will take a much-needed rest. Will you promise not to run away?"

"I will, monsieur," I said—thinking, *I will promise if it occurs to you to actually ask.* Anyway, I wasn't a commissioned officer and he had no right to ask my parole.

"*C'est bon,*" said he, yawning. He put his hands in the small of his back and arched his spine till the bones cracked. "*Merde,* such a life. Well, see you later." He waved absently and shuffled over to a tent that was larger and cleaner than the others. He went in past a pair of sentries, but in a moment he came out again with my dirk in his hand and bent himself in an ironic bow. "For his gallantry, I return the gentleman's sword."

"*Merci, monsieur.*" I slipped it back into my scabbard. The ivory grips had been stripped from the tang, but the foot-long blade was a good one and I was glad to have it back.

"Please promise not to kill anyone with it." He yawned again.

"I'd prefer not to."

My head hurt and I was having trouble thinking. But—as far as I was concerned, anyway—I'd stated a clear preference for not wanting to promise anything. If all my life was worth to him was a silver watch and some seamen, I aimed to up the exchange rate a bit.

All the picaroons that I could see were on the other side of the tents. Several boats were drawn up on the beach a few hundred yards away, including *Rattle-Snake's* gig. There were very few of the picaroon longboats about. I guessed they used a base that was more convenient for launching attacks. I could handle the gig myself. It'd be clumsy and slow, but I could do it. All I had to do was stroll down to the beach . . . and be shot for my pains. *Non merci, Général Villon,* thinks I.

One thing was certain: I was under no obligation to continue roasting by the fire. With mosquitoes swarming my face and ears as soon as I left the smoke, and flies buzzing over the gore that crusted my coat, I began poking around the camp. Nothing in the gentlemanly code said I couldn't take note of whatever my captors allowed me to see.

Most of the picaroons simply ignored me. Quite a few were still busy off-loading *Jane* and *Augustin von Steuben*. And my Janes and Rattle-Snakes were being made to help them.

"*Attendez! Ne bouguez pas!*" I said to Prêteur, the gray-haired sailing master. "Hold it! They're to be detained, yes, but not as prisoners of war."

"*Détenu? Prisonnier?* What the fuck's the difference?"

"It means you're supposed to lock them up, not use them as slaves."

"Lock 'em up where?" He looked around, as if searching for a jail. "And anyway, 'slaves' is a bit harsh."

"Well, you're still not supposed to use them this way. Hear how that one groans—poor fellow!"

"Go on! He's one of ours, and he knows if he wants his dinner, he's got to work for it. Same as your chaps."

"I still say you can't work my men."

"And I say I can. If they want to eat, they got to work—that's only fair. So far as I know, the only thing I can't do is kill 'em till I get the say-so. 'Less they try to escape, of course. Which I wish they would," he muttered.

"This is too much," I said. "Just because Général Villon is sleeping is no reason for you to take liberties with my men. If I have to bring this to his attention, I'm sure it will not go well for you."

The old man snorted with laughter. "Go on then, gossiper! Here he is now!"

"Citizen Prêteur," said Villon, his eyes puffy and his ringlets crumpled, "I had hoped to wake to a peaceful supper for once, but instead I have been roused by the familiar sounds of squabbling. Pray, what is the matter this time? *Mon dieu*—" He broke off as he recognized me. "How I wish we hadn't abolished the saints, so I could beseech them. Why are you still here?"

"Monsieur," I said, prim as a parson, "my men are being misused."

"He thinks 'prisoners of war' can't be made to work, Citizen Villon."

Villon massaged his temples. "They cannot be prisoners of war, because we are not *at* war. I have explained this, *hein?*"

Prêteur rolled his eyes and grimaced. "You don't know the first *thing* about being a pirate! Let me clear it up for you. Again: we take the ones who want to join us and send the others away. Otherwise it's bad business."

Villon clenched his teeth. "We are not pirates! We receive our authority from Rigaud himself!" He sighed. "Citizen Prêteur, are you almost finished here?"

"Damn near. Last tier of crates. Nothing after that but the turds in the ballast."

Villon turned to me with a graceful little flourish. "Only a few more crates, monsieur, and then the men will eat. Why quibble now, when it is almost done?"

I bowed to the inevitable. *"C'est bon, monsieur,"* I said, then raised my voice and called:

"Mr. Horne!"

"Sir!"

"The French have no legal authority to make you work," I said, which wasn't true, by the way—not because we were prisoners of war but because we weren't, if you follow me, but Villon was as sketchy on that point as I was. "But the sooner the work is done, the sooner you'll be fed. Carry on for now."

"Aye aye, sir."

"You heard the man," said Doc. "I ain't workin' no mo'!"

"You ain't been working at all, fool," said Horne. "Now get out the way so we can finish up."

"They discuss the fastest and most efficient way to finish the unloading," I told Villon in French. "Although they realize they are under no obligation to work. It is the natural *bonhomie* of the American sailor."

Villon waved a hand toward the cooking fires and I fell in step beside him. "Naturally, the *nègre* has a proclivity to labor that we *gens de couleurs* do not share, we being mostly white. However, between the *nègres* picking things up and the *petits blancs* telling them where to put them down again, the business shall soon be done."

"Moreau goes on in great detail about the fine racial distinctions made in Saint-Domingue," I said. "'Negroes,' 'people of color,' 'little whites'—and 'great whites,' too, before the present unpleasantness—dozens of classes and subclasses. It's fascinating, monsieur, do you not agree?"

"Ah, you have read the *Description topographique!* These distinctions are a matter of great importance here. How else does one know where to sit in church, or even if one may enter? It is refreshing, is it not," he continued as he, Prêteur and I sat down at a table covered with a much-stained cloth, "to watch three inherently unequal races working together toward a common goal. This is something one becomes accustomed to in Saint-Domingue. Yet I find that, each time I observe it, it merely stokes my revolutionary fire. Do you not agree, Citizen Prêteur?"

"Makes me hungry," said Prêteur.

"Everything makes you hungry." Villon lifted the cover of a dented silver dish and examined its contents. "Toad of the sea," I thought he said. "A local delicacy. Some say it is not worth the fishing, but when the bones are removed it is palatable."

"I'm not sure I agree," I said, "if monsieur will pardon my saying it, that the three races are unequal—or rather that they are *naturally* unequal."

"You have seen evidence to the contrary?" He poured me a glass of pale yellow wine. "We must speak in the terms scientific, *non?* To do otherwise would obviate the argument, *n'est-ce pas?*"

"*Au certainement.*" I sipped the wine. It tasted thin and sour, but wine to me meant claret or Madeira. "Take Horne, for instance, that big petty officer with the profusion of braids, as you put it. Black as Adam, but as intelligent and quick as any white man."

"There are exceptions, yes. This of course assumes that intelligent white men are not exceptions themselves."

Prêteur was making good time with his fish, and we had to hurry to catch up. When the fish things had been taken away and chipped soup plates were being set in front of us, I said, "When I said that Horne is as quick as a white man, what I meant was that he is quicker than most *men.*"

"Ah, yes?" said Villon, as his servant began dumping stew onto our plates. "So your *nègre* is of superior intelligence. Does it do him any good?" He loaded a mound of well-done goat and stewed vegetables onto the back of his fork and lifted it toward his mouth. "Niggers occur in the highest strata here in Saint-Domingue. Toussaint is an example." He chewed and swallowed. "But I submit that he is the exception rather than the rule—an unfortunate accident, a freak of nature. To offset his example I offer his lieutenant, Général Jean-Jacques Dessalines. Now there's a nigger who likes his work, his work being to kill people. Especially white ones. I think he'd exterminate them even were it not necessary. Fortunately for you, my friend, I have much more enlightened views."

I sipped from a glass of red wine that was remarkably good at keeping the goat-meat down. "There was some talk in the papers of excesses. On both sides, as I recall."

"*Excesses?*" Villon set down his fork. "Toussaint ordered the murder of five hundred persons of color when he retook Mole Saint-Nicolas. Picked them arbitrarily: 'You-you-you, bang-bang-bang.' This is mere excess?"

"I apologize if I have touched upon a sore spot, monsieur. But Rigaud slaughtered unarmed whites when he attacked Petit Goâve, merely to slow Toussaint down, did he not?"

Prêteur looked up briefly from his plate. "Sure he did. And when you gents have solved our differences, maybe one of you could pass the salt."

"Apparently there was a gap in the government," said Villon

sometime later, when the conversation had worked around again to Buonoparte's coup, "like a hole in a rotten tooth. Everyone knows how ineffectual the Directory turned out to be. So Buonoparte abolishes it, and establishes the Consulate with himself as its head. You know what this means, of course?"

"No, monsieur. Will you not tell me?"

"But it is obvious! A strongman as head of the government means an end to a France muscle-bound by bureaucracy. And when Buonoparte decides to devote his attention to this fever-ridden gold mine of ours, which no doubt he will as soon as he can, it will mean not only an end to American influence—and profits—but an end to Toussaint's de facto rebellion as well. The niggers will go back to work, and we men of color will have our rights at last."

"How true that is, monsieur."

I nodded and smiled, hoping the tangle of fear and pity that rose in my breast didn't show on my face. French regulars would reoccupy Saint-Domingue, the black rebellion would be crushed, and the particularly cruel brand of slavery practiced in the Caribbean would again extend its bloody hand across the colony. And Toussaint—he had to choose between horrors that I couldn't even imagine. He would not survive to see the hope he had planted bear fruit, I was sure of it—and yet he carried on. I felt a sudden admiration and even love for him that I hadn't expected in myself. But I nodded, and smiled, and said "hmm!" and "you don't say!" at the proper places.

I felt as logy as one of Dr. Mesmer's automatons. It seemed suddenly possible that the Federalists had been right to treat the French revolution with cynicism and contempt. It was nauseating to think that Hamilton could be right about something so important, and worse to think of Buonoparte as a traitor to liberty. I wanted to crawl away somewhere.

I smiled, I nodded. Hard cheese and rancid nuts came and went.

The mosquitoes got worse at sunset. Villon and Prêteur puffed happily on their pipes, and I sniffed the fumes and wished I had one, while the camp settled down for the night. A few men shouldered muskets and trudged toward the batteries. Others spread tarpaulins over every piece of equipment in sight.

"Against the evening rain," said Villon, following my glance. "Rains nearly every night this time of year. I'll be going to my tent soon, to avoid a soaking. Everyone else who isn't an idiot will seek shelter, too. Hard to keep a good lookout that way." His voice had fallen to a murmur. "It would not surprise me were someone to take a boat and leave this place."

"It'd be uncomfortable, maybe even dangerous, in a little boat all alone on the sea," said Prêteur. "But a damn sight better than sticking around to be hanged in the morning, *hein?*"

We crouched in a sandy depression at the edge of the woods, peering out at a man on the beach. Campfires flickered down at the south end of the cove, off to the right where the tents were, but the man on the beach was the only picaroon who might see us. I counted the dim forms around me.

"Horne," I whispered, "where are Doc and Samuels?"

The big bosun's mate scratched his head. "Right at this very moment, sir?"

"No, next week. Where are they?"

"Well, gone to scrounge tobacco, sir. You were asleep, and—"

"Me? Asleep?"

"Yes, sir. Do you want to wait for 'em?"

"You shouldn't have . . ." But it was my fault. Everything was my fault. I had to fix it if I could. "No. Keep everybody else here until I signal."

"What're you going to do, sir?"

I peered out from under the trees again. The man on the beach wasn't carrying a musket, but he had something in his hand that I couldn't make out. Moonlight glinted on it. I eased my dirk out of its sheath.

"No, Mr. Graves. You can't." Horne gripped my shoulder.

"Get your hand off me, damn your eyes!"

One of the men snorted in the darkness, and I suppose it did sound funny, an undersized boy scolding a grown man in the middle of an enemy camp.

"I just meant I'd do it, Mr. Graves."

Don't think I wasn't tempted. But I guessed if I let him take my place I'd never get my authority back.

The sand dragged at my shoes as I worked my way down toward the water, studying the man's back as I approached. Should I stick him in the kidneys? Disembowel him? He was too tall for me to count on reaching his throat from behind.

I wondered if he had a wife. Maybe he had children. He had a mother, certainly.

I froze as the man turned. He was Villon.

I was keenly aware of every sensation—the roughness of the coral sand underfoot, the touch of damp air on my sweaty skin, the iron stench of dried blood on my clothes and the salty stink of sea wrack rotting along the shore. Insects throbbed in the forest, the wind sighed in the trees, the blood drummed in my ears. The stars and moon shone as if it were any other evening, as if nothing of importance were about to happen. For a dizzy moment I imagined myself walking high up among the silver walls and black canyons of the clouds. I thought very carefully about the chance Villon had given me and the quibbles and half-promises and twisted words I had given him in return.

The clouds parted for a moment, and in the moonlight I could see his ringlets and Hessian boots, and that the glinting thing in his hand was merely a bottle. As he saw me he raised it toward me.

Past his shoulder, white flashes of surf showed the reef and the way through it, and then the clouds closed over the moon again. My only obstacle was the life of one man.

I sheathed my dirk and went down to where he stood.

It was good French brandy in the bottle. I took a fiery swig and handed it back to him. He patted my shoulder and said, *"Bonne chance, mon cher petit ami."* Then he strode down the beach toward the battery on the northern headland.

I scampered down to the nearest longboat and waved at the trees. No one appeared. I waved again. I made a hissing noise with my teeth. Then I stood up and waved. "Hisst! Ssst!"

No answer but the rustling of the wind and the chiming of insects in the trees.

Fearing that the men had decided to take a last-minute vote on it, I selected a conch shell from the beach and flung it toward the trees. I was rewarded with a *clonk* and a muted, "Ow."

The noise of the insects stopped dead, as if a door had been closed. I held my breath, not daring to move. Then one started up, and then another, and then the night lifted again with noise.

A moment later a shadowy Jane flitted from beneath the trees and crunched across the sand toward me.

"The big buck says he gon' send ever'body 'long one by one."

"Move along down to the stern, but stay in the shadows," I said, pleased that Horne was using his head. The Janes and Rattle-Snakes came along one by one, as the sailor had said, and I lined them up in the shadow of the boat as they came.

When Horne arrived he said, "That's all of 'em except Doc and Samuels, sir. They never showed."

We eased the longboat into the water, slipped the oars into the locks and pulled as quietly as we could across the lagoon, towing Cousin Billy's gig behind us. In the stern sheets with the tiller tucked under my arm, I eyed the headlands. If Villon knew his business, the trajectories of the guns there would cross at midchannel. That would take care of most large intruders. A slight traverse would take care of smaller intruders—or escapees, if I had read him wrong. Unless . . .

The tide was nearly at slack water, even beginning to rise, but there was a strong breeze out of the west and the two captured merchantmen strained at their moorings. I whispered to Horne and swung the tiller over, making for the *Jane,* praying Villon had not thought to leave a guard in her. We couldn't hope to escape in her—we'd never get her under way before the picaroons discovered us—but she had another use.

No one challenged us as we crept under her bow and Horne used my dirk to saw through the cable. Using the oars just enough to keep us under way, we ghosted toward the channel beyond the headlands. Pushed by the wind, the *Jane* slowly followed.

I thought again of the batteries protecting the cove. If we passed close enough to the guns, they couldn't be depressed enough to hit us, and if we hugged the gap between the reef and the shoreline until we were out of range, they couldn't traverse enough to hit us, either. Or so I hoped.

I nudged Horne. "Get for'ard," I whispered. "Watch for coral heads. I'm going to shave that point inside the reef."

We edged toward the point in the increasing offshore breeze, touched bottom once—twice—then emerged from the shadow of the headland into comparative brightness. If the sentry was awake up on the point and happened to glance down, we'd find out soon enough if the guns could reach us.

As I craned my head around to watch the battery, a fat raindrop hit me in the eye. Others plopped into the water around us, and the trilling of the insects died away. I wiped my face with my sleeve and looked up again. I thought I'd seen movement.

Then a voice asked, quite distinctly in the sudden silence, *"Qui va là?"*

I held my breath—absurdly, as the Rattle-Snakes continued to row, gently but steadily. Some of them glanced toward the voice, but they didn't miss a stroke. A raindrop hit my hat with a loud *plock*. Trees waved beyond the headland, clouds scudded across the moon behind them, and somewhere up on the point a man with a musket wanted to know: *Who goes there?*

"Qui va là?" he called again.

I debated whether to say *"c'est moi"* and let him figure it out, or to tell the men to row for their lives. Whatever I did, I would have to do it before he challenged us again. The next query might be delivered by a musket ball.

But then Villon's voice said, *"C'est moi,* René—don't be jumpy like a flea! Here, I've brought a jug."

"Ah, Citizen Villon, you're a saint among men. I mean, a hero of the people. You're a—"

There was a flash-boom behind us. I turned around and saw the dark blur of the *Jane* swinging around broadside to the reef. There was another flash-boom as a second cannon on the far point fired.

Then rain was falling straight down in a blinding, choking torrent. Far away against the roar of the rain I heard Prêteur shout, *"Don't shoot, don't shoot, God damn your balls,"* but his words were cut short by a scream.

It took us two days and nights to cover the eighty-some miles down to Port Républicain at the bottom of the Bight of Léogane. We spent the first night negotiating La Gonâve's northern tip. I stood farther out to sea than I might have, but better safe than sorry, I thought. I could hear the surf roaring on the reef even through the rain. And at least we managed to get some rainwater into the breakers that were kept stowed in the bow cuddy. The downpour vanished with the dawn, and a good stiff breeze rose with the sun, whisking away its heat. The Janes' natural patina of grime would protect their skins from burning, I thought as I looked them over, and I guessed the Rattle-Snakes' black skins wouldn't burn at all, but I would have to make do with the shade of my hat.

The Janes took their ease while we raised the longboat's mast and hoisted her sail. You would have thought we were out for a pleasure jaunt, the way they jeered and jabbered about this and that and complained at the lack of food and the miserly way I doled out the water as we whisked them along. But it was just as well—it kept them out of the way, and kept the Rattle-Snakes from squabbling, being dead set against lubbers and ingrates, and determined to show themselves to be man-o'-war's men. I was tempted to put the Janes in the gig, but I guessed they'd get tired of rowing pretty quick and would get them-selves lost.

I offered once to put in to see could we steal some eggs from the birds that crowded along the creeks, but the Janes and Rattle-Snakes alike indignantly reminded me that the streams in those parts were full of caimans.

"Some of 'em's seventy foot long an' twelve foot wide," said a Jane.

"It's a lie, mate," said a Rattle-Snake. "Who ever heard of a river seventy foot long and twelve foot wide?"

"Nay, mate," retorted the Jane. "The *caimans* is seventy foot long and twelve foot wide."

"Oh, how you talk. They don't come bigger'n forty foot, tops."

I scanned the shore for fruit trees as we coasted along, but all I could see was the poisonous Caribbean dwarf apple, which the Spanish call *mançanilla*. Lieutenant Bligh's account of his adventures after the *Bounty* mutiny was much in my mind, their weeks without food and then their shellfish soups once they reached the Great Barrier Reef of New Holland, but only as a way to keep up my spirits. We were in no danger, not of starving, anyway, but I was a failure. I hadn't saved the *Jane*, and I'd gotten men killed and lost. I dreaded going back to face the wrath of Wickett, but I didn't know what else to do.

Ten

We raised The Princes—the islets that had given Port Républicain its pre-revolutionary name of Port-au-Prince—on the evening of the second day and passed into the harbor, where we spotted the *Rattle-Snake*'s familiar silhouette against the moonlit sky. The harbor stank of sewage and dead animals. When I closed my eyes it was very much as if we were crossing Baltimore's inner harbor, except the bloated carcasses were human, and faintly on the offshore breeze I could hear the weird throbbing of voudou drums. There were no French warships in the harbor, of course. Fear of invasion had compelled Toussaint to close his ports to them, except those carrying emissaries from Paris. Us and the British he allowed to trade at Port Républicain and Le Cap François, the colony's principal city in the north. It was guns and ammunition he wanted, and Paris would only deliver those in the hands of French soldiers.

Dick's voice hailed us as we approached the *Rattle-Snake*. Horne shouted back, "No, no," meaning we were a Navy boat but he had no commissioned officer aboard and expected no ceremony.

I was filthy and weary and felt like my stomach had been tied around my spine, and my backside was too well acquainted with every grain and splinter of the thwart, but beyond that I felt well enough as we hooked onto *Rattle-Snake*'s side. She was battered from the fight with the picaroons, but I didn't care. Despite my apprehension at the dressing-down I was sure to get, I found myself nearly in tears to get aboard her again, for she might have sailed as soon as she had delivered the merchantmen. I didn't doubt we'd been given up for dead.

"Well, I swan," said Dick, looking over the rail. "Now I can tear up that letter I was writing to Arabella." He was the only officer on deck, and he had a strained look as we shook hands. I had rehearsed my homecoming in my mind, and this weren't at all the reception I'd expected from him.

"Sweet jumpin' juniper berries, Dick, ain't you glad to see me?"

He put a finger to his lips and tipped his head significantly toward the Marine sentry nearby.

"Of course I am, mate," he whispered. "But look around you."

The sentry stared with distrust at the sailors pouring aboard. Lanterns burned at the taffrail and in the rigging, and little sparks of light twinkled across the water from the town. At the forward hatch loomed another Marine. Like the first, he was in full kit, with coat buttoned and bayonet fixed. At the after hatch stood another Marine, likewise turned out. Corporal Haversham surveyed Rattle-Snake's waist from the quarterdeck rail, his feet exactly shoulder-width apart, one hand clasping his cartridge belt behind his back and the other gripping his spontoon, which is a sort of spear that sergeants and corporals carry.

"How come the sojers are turned out?" said I. "And why ain't anybody on deck?" Then I stopped short and stared. "Glory! What a mess."

The rigging was all ahoo and draggled, and cut up some bad in places, and grape and chain had gouged up the masts and bulwarks pretty considerable. I was shocked to see it—not that I didn't expect a mess after a fight but because Mr. Wickett should have had the carpenter's and bosun's crews working round the clock to set things to rights. At the least, someone should have swilled the blood off the deck.

"What happened, Dick? Last I seen, Elwiss and Mr. Klemso was splicing everything shipshape again."

"They hit us twice more after you . . . after you left. It was touch and go for a while."

"But that don't—"

Again with the finger to the lips. "The captain's cat is missing," said

Dick, as if that explained all. "I dasn't say more right now." In a louder voice he said, "When did you eat last?"

"Dunno." I guiltily recollected my duty. "Me, I'm more thirsty than hungry right now. Horne, see if you can't find the men some cut-and-come-again. Beans, hardtack, anything'll do, and all the water they want."

"I expect the lads want grog more'n anything, sir," said Horne.

"No spirits. Food and water only, Mr. Horne," said Dick. "Take one man to help you, no more. The rest of you men wait on the fo'c's'le. And as for you, chum," he said to me, "you'd best get shipshape before making your report to the captain."

"Where is he, anyhow? If he's going to call out the sojers, you'd think he'd be on deck."

Dick motioned me closer. "Listen, there's a, um, a dispute about the action," he murmured. "Your cousin's claiming credit for running off the picaroons. He's also saying Mr. Wickett locked him in his cabin a-purpose, so he'd get the glory. Don't know how he figures to reconcile the two stories, but the upshot is that Mr. Wickett's under arrest and the people don't like it, so everybody's been sent below."

"Under arrest! For what?"

"Defiance, I suppose. But really I think it's for killing that cat."

"Why the hell would he kill Greybar?"

"I doubt anyone did. He's been missing since that scrap with the picaroons. So's Gypsy. They're just hiding in the hold, I expect. You know how cats are. But listen," he said, "I'd sluice my face and shift my clothes, was I you."

I didn't want a wash and a change. I wanted everyone to see the powder-stains and splattered gore, as if I were the only one who'd had a rough few days. Besides, it was my duty to report immediately.

The sentry outside the cabin looked doubtful, but he didn't stop me from knocking. Billy opened the door himself. There was a murmur of conversation behind him.

"Bet you never thought you'd see me again, Billy," I grinned, holding out my hand.

For a moment his eyes registered relief—or perhaps mere recognition.

"Well, if it ain't Wickett's fart-catcher," he slurred, and then held up a hand in sudden horror. "But look at you! That's no way to report for duty. Don't come back here till you're fitted out proper. And clean!" He slammed the door, muttering something about unwashed brats.

I made my way forward in a snit, just looking for a man who would dare stand in my way, but no one did and by the time I reached the midshipmen's berth I was nearly in tears. As I tore off my vest and flung it against the cabinetry, an unfamiliar key fell out of the pocket. I can still remember the clink it made when I tossed it into the little pewter cup I used to keep my toothbrush in, though I thought little of it at the time. I splashed myself with seawater—it should have been fresh, in port—yanked a comb through my curls and ran my fingertips across my chin and cheeks. My whiskers were not as prolific as I had hoped when I first glanced into the bit of mirror. Most of the foliage turned out to be grease and gunpowder, which vicious rubbing with a corner of my shirttail soon removed. But I scraped my face with Dick's razor anyway: raw cheeks and chin would proclaim a painstaking toilette. More-or-less fresh linen, dry socks, dark blue pantaloons, and my second-best monkey jacket pulled on over all, and I was ready to face Cousin Billy and his drunken whims. Something to eat or a cup of hot coffee would have been grateful, but there was no hope of that.

As if in answer to a prayer, Jubal kicked at the door. The tray in his hands bore a steaming mug of coffee and a thick smear of deviled liver between two pieces of biscuit.

"You have a soul to be saved," I said.

"I dint have nuffin to do wid it, suh."

"Then thank Mr. Towson for me," I said through my mouthful. "This is excellent biscuit."

He smirked. "Weren't Mars Dickie, neither, suh."

"Well, who was it, then?"

"Oh, I gots my ways, suh. I gots my ways."

The bread and potted meat were manna, the coffee ambrosia—steaming hot, thick from long simmering, heavily sweetened, and fortified with some sort of spirits. I inhaled its fumes and took another molten gulp. "Ooh-yah! What's in this?"

His face betrayed nothing. "Just coffee an' 'lasses, suh, so far's *I* know."

I took another gulp. Rum, probably. Rum was considered low where I grew up, not so much because it was a by-product of slavery as because it competed with the local whiskey, and I'd never tasted it outside the Caribbean. No doubt the lower deck was awash in it already. It would be a poor sailorman who couldn't find liquor within a few hours in port, even without going ashore, and it would be a poor 'tween-decks leader—and Horne was a natural leader—who couldn't commandeer a portion for his mates. The thought was as warming as the rum.

"Tell Horne I'm refreshed and obliged," I said, handing the empty mug back to Jubal and brushing crumbs from my coat.

"Hmmph," he muttered as he left. "Where ol' Horne s'posed to get potted meat an' biscuit dat fine? Dat's what *I* wants to know. White boys think dey knows everthang."

The people were all in their hammocks, with lights out except for the night-lantern at the mainmast. The usual little group of smokers up forward around the galley was missing, and the silence in the rest of the 'tween-decks was entirely too complete to be natural. Three more Marines were posted abaft the mainmast, kneeling in the low space with their muskets at the ready.

I made my way aft past the other warrant officers' sleeping places and the diminutive wardroom with the senior officers' cabins on either side. A light shone through the jalousies of the aftermost door on the larboard side—Wickett's cabin, which presumably he was occupying again now that we had delivered Blair to his destination.

I shrugged my jacket straighter on my shoulders, the sentry knocked, Billy roared, "Come in!" and I stepped into an odd little scene.

The table had been put back in and Billy lolled like a lord behind it—as of course he might, being the captain—but he had an uneasy look in his eye as he reached across the bottles and glasses and grabbed me by both hands. "About time you came back to us, Cuz!" he shouted, as if he hadn't cut me to the quick just a few minutes before. "Can't tell you what a relief it is to see you! Have a drop." The old soak handed me a tumbler of whiskey and, his hostly duties done, fell back again on his cushions behind the table.

Rogers sat to his left, with an untouched glass in front of him and sweat shining on his face. He shook my hand and then went back to staring into his glass.

Blair was there, too, sitting across the long way from Rogers. Ignoring me, he reached out his hand, set it down, reached out again, set it down again, and finally pointed at the whiskey decanter. "The wine sits by you, sir," he said. Rogers shoved the "wine" down the table to him.

"Hello, Mr. Blair," I said. "Ain't you gone ashore yet?"

He shot me a quick nasty glance. "And who are you to question my whereabouts?"

"No one a-tall, sir. I just thought you was in a hurry to take up your position."

"Well, it's the middle of the night. The government offices are closed, ain't they?"

Rogers looked up. "Leave the boy alone, Mr. Blair."

"Well who does he think he is, bursting in here amongst his betters and questioning their whereabouts? Seems to me, young sir, as you should be accounting for *your* whereabouts." He gave me that nasty look again.

"I'll be glad to give my report to the captain as soon as he wants, Mr. Blair."

"Yes, Cuz," said Billy, rousing himself as if from a dream. "What the devil have you been up to, hey? Quite a tale to tell, I reckon, ha ha! Sit sit sit, and tell us all about it."

Sitting with glass in hand, I wondered at the wisdom of pouring more liquor into myself until I'd had a proper meal and some sleep. I pretended to sip, just wetting my lips, but even so it had some effect. The cabin gently rose and fell. A breeze was drifting through the open stern lights, carrying with it the stench of the harbor and the sound of the drums.

Billy blinked and nodded as I recounted the hanging of Peavey and his mate, the men who'd been killed in action, our capture by the picaroons, Villon's kind treatment (except for stealing my watch, of course) and our subsequent escape.

"I also lost the cook and seaman Samuels, sir, one of my gunners," I finished.

"That's quite a butcher's bill," said Billy. "Doc's been killed, hey?"

"No sir. I mean I left him and Samuels behind."

"You abandoned the ship's cook?"

"*And* this Samuels fellow," said Blair. "Abandoned two good seamen, the blackguard."

I looked at the smug bastard, swilling Billy's whiskey and poking his nose into places it didn't belong. But whether it was his business or not, I had to answer him while Rogers at least was there to bear witness.

"No I didn't, Mr. Blair. Doc and Samuels weren't there when it was time to leave. In my judgment it would've jeopardized the whole party was I to go back and look for them."

"In your judgment? And who were you to take that kind of responsibility on yourself?"

"The officer in charge, is who he was," said Rogers. "He had a hard choice to make, and he made it. Would you have done any different?"

"Damn right I would," said Blair. "I'd have shot 'em on the spot. Taught 'em a lesson."

"What, and wake up the whole camp?" said Billy. He squeezed one eye shut, concentrating. "But anyway, that ain't the point. What was the point again? Oh yes—I remember. You've got to keep an eye on your people, Mr. Graves. Can't have 'em jumping ship right and left. It won't do. No sir, no sir, won't do at all."

"Aye aye, sir."

"Well, anyhow, it couldn't have been too bad," he said, eyeing my pink cheeks and fresh clothes. "You're hardly even smudged. You must learn to fight hard if you're going to be any kind of asset, Mr. Graves. Have you anything useful to tell us?"

"No sir," I said, wondering if his brain had gone completely soft. "Oh, wait, I do: General Buonoparte's abolished the Directory and declared himself First Consul. Apparently the revolution's over."

"So we already heard, Mr. Johnny-Come-Lately," said Blair. "And just the fellow for it, too. Knocked the rabble tits over teakettle with grapeshot, right on the streets of Paris. Served 'em right, too. We could do with that sort of man ourselves."

"Have you no scruples, sir?" muttered Rogers into his glass.

Blair looked at him. "Can't keep a republic together if you let people take to the streets anytime you do something they don't like, Mr. Rogers. Stands to reason. And I'd watch my words, if I was you."

"Yes, yes, I'm sure," said Billy. "But listen, Cuz. Hearken well to what I'm about to say, because it's important."

"Yes sir?"

"Yes. Well. No doubt you've heard rumors already of our present situation." He mopped his face with his hanky. "There's always rumors aboard ship, and they're almost always wrong. Let me clarify 'em for you. You will not credit it, but Mr. Wickett claims our recent victory, the dog. I came down to my cabin to secure certain documents when the picaroons attacked, and when I went to go on deck again, I found myself locked in!" He drained off his glass.

"I'm surprised to hear you say that, sir," I said.

Rogers looked embarrassed. Blair just looked shifty. With creeping alarm I realized whose key it was that I had found in my pocket.

I ventured, "Perhaps some good Samaritan was concerned for your safety, Billy."

"You mean Wickett?" He sniffed. "To measure his concern for me would require an apothecary's scale, it is so minute. The man has no concern for anything but his own career. He would sacrifice me to Congress and pirates *both* to get a command of his own. *This* command. He pretends to be a slave to duty, but it is ambition that drives him. He would sacrifice you and you," he said, pointing at Blair and Rogers in turn, "if it served his end. He's already turned the people against us. They were sullen and disobedient from the start, but now they flirt with mutiny. There was round shot rolling on the deck at night as we made our way down here, and if that ain't a sign of mutiny, what is? And to compound his infamy, the coward murdered poor Greybar!"

Rogers had lifted his head at the word *mutiny*, and Blair squawked like an indignant hen. But when Billy mentioned the cat Rogers looked more worried than angry.

"I do not admire Mr. Wickett, sir," he murmured, with his head back down, "but I do not think he would stoop so low as to kill a dumb beast."

"He as much as admitted it, Mr. Rogers! He said, 'Who gives a fig about your cat'! And he didn't say 'fig,' neither."

"He was agitated, sir. I'm sure he didn't mean it."

"What could agitate him to the point that would excuse such talk to his captain?"

"Well, sir, he's touchy about getting his due, as any officer would be, and he did hold us together in the fighting off Guanabo—"

"Watch yourself," said Blair.

Lips trembling, Billy held up his hand. "I had intended to bury poor Greybar at sea with full honors when his time came. Now I'm denied even that comfort. The man's a menace. Do you know, gentlemen, that he came into this cabin during the battle to taunt me?"

"Indeed!" said Blair. "I took a shot at the snake. Two shots. I only regret that I missed."

Rogers frowned. "Did Mr. Wickett ever leave the deck during the fight?" he said.

"Well, who's to say otherwise?" said Blair. "Mr. Graves here missed half the battle. He can't say what happened after he left, now can he?"

No one answered.

I could hear screams mixed in with the drumming, faint and far away.

A fly had gotten into my drink. I fished it out with my finger.

After a long lull, I said, "May I talk to you alone, Cousin Billy? A family matter."

"Yes, yes, dear Matty. You're the only subordinate left I can trust."

Rogers left with his head hanging and wouldn't look at me.

Blair stopped to survey us from the doorway. "My work here is done, Captain Trimble," he said. It was the first time I'd heard him address Billy properly. "But you know where to find me should you need me." He tipped Billy the nod and left, shouting as he climbed the ladder, "Mr. Bosun, fetch me a boat at once! Port Republicain awaits me, and neither kings nor dukes nor congressmen shall stand in my way."

As I came hoarse and trembling out of Billy's cabin a quarter of an hour later, the sentry tapped on Wickett's door. Wickett stuck his head out and said, "Mr. Graves, a word with you," in a low voice. As he stood aside to allow me to squeeze into his cabin, his shoulder brushed against the lantern in its gimbals, throwing crazy shadows around the room. He put something into the Marine's hand and shut the door. "Take a seat, I pray," he said.

There was no place to sit but on his hanging cot, and so I sat there. At the foot of the cot was a basket with an old towel in it, and on the deck in the corner was a chipped china dish containing some scraps of fish. Next to the dish lay a knitted mouse with leather ears and a spun-yarn tail—the work of some kindly seaman, I supposed. A little bad-smelling air came in through the open scuttle, and in acknowledgment of the heat Wickett had taken off his coat and neck-cloth and rolled up his sleeves.

He leaned against the door. "Did you note that sentry's face?" His voice was so low I could barely hear him.

"No sir," I said, keeping my voice equally low. "All the sojers look alike to me."

"Pay more attention another time. The man can be bribed, and is not to be trusted. But anyway, I wished to congratulate you on your escape. I was afraid they had hanged you."

"Oh, it was nothing, sir."

"You are too modest. You must overcome that if you are to get ahead."

"Aye aye, sir, but I mean it really *weren't* nothing. They killed Peavey and the others in a passion, but after they cooled off they just wanted to be rid of us—of me, anyway. It was pretty humiliating, I can tell you, being brushed aside like that. He aimed to press the men. Rigaud ain't got too many sailors, apparently."

"Yes, we have a way of relieving him of what few ships he has and detaining their crews. Did you learn anything useful about the pica-roons? What their plans are? Who leads them?"

"They didn't say anything about plans, but they're led by a general who calls himself Villon, like the poet."

"A *nom de guerre,* no doubt. And no doubt your cousin was relieved and gratified to see you safe after such travails?"

"So he said. Villon's an interesting fellow, sir. I liked him, except he stole my watch. Borrowed it, maybe. Only I didn't think it'd be smart to ask him to give it back afore I left, in case I'd mistook him."

He turned his hands out, palms up. "Exactly so. Motives are easily misconstrued. Should you like some dainties?" He lifted the napkin from the single place laid at his desk. "From out of my private stores, but I find this oppressive heat has taken my appetite away."

On a plate lay some more of the biscuit and deviled liver that Jubal had brought me, but the jam was even better and I spooned it up in mouthfuls. There was the earthenware jug of cider, too, sweating through the sides in the tropic heat. He reached and poured even as I looked.

"And sometimes the foulest of deeds can be recast," he said, setting the jug down again. "What does he say about me?"

"That you absquatulated with his cat, and maybe squiffed it."

"Watch your tone, sir. I do not care for flippancy." He reached out and grasped my arm, his fingers resting over the inner nerve above the elbow. He smelled of old sweat and rotted teeth. "You must decide where your interests lie, Mr. Graves. The Rattle-Snakes are very unhappy with things as they stand."

I took his hand off my arm and looked him in the eye. "That's not needful, sir. I was on my way to see you anyway."

"Truly?" He dropped his arm to his side and sighed. "The situation is ridiculous, or too perilous, I should say, for us to be worrying about a goddamned *cat*. I did not kill the animal, by the way. It must have disappeared during the fighting. Cats are easily offended, you know. Gypsy only reemerged this evening. She is under the bed."

I looked under the cot and saw a pair of green eyes reflecting the candlelight.

"I have been unable to coax her out. I expect she will come out again once she has forgotten what frightened her. Truly, I did not kill Greybar."

"I believe you, sir. About everything." I spread some potted meat on a biscuit and held it out to the cat. "It was me that locked him in his cabin, you know. I put the key in my vest pocket, which I forgot about until just a little while ago. It's in the midshipmen's berth if you want it."

There was already a piece of biscuit with meat smeared on it under there. I put mine in my mouth and stood up.

"How droll," said Wickett, not smiling. My hand was on the knob, but I didn't turn it. He moved past me and sat on the cot. "No, I think the captain's key belongs to the captain, don't you?" He swung his feet up and put his hands behind his head. "You may go now."

"I told him all about it, sir, which is what I was coming to see you about. He'll be calling for you in about a minute."

He sat up. "Then pray take your hand off that door knob and tell me what's on your mind."

"I spoke with him in private. I am his cousin, you know."

"I am aware of this."

"Yes, sir. I told him I would refute his statements if it came to a court-martial. His own cousin, refusing to stand by him—I guess it'd look pretty bad."

"It bodes ill for both of us."

"As the commanding officer of record, he takes credit for the victory. That's understood."

"One should not expect otherwise."

"And you're released from close arrest."

"Naturally." He reached for his neck-cloth and wrapped it around his throat. "There yet remains a great deal of work to be done. Until the decks and rigging are set to rights, our shame is on view for all the world to see."

"And you're to stand watch and watch until further notice, and not go ashore without permission."

He threw up his hands. "Phaw, four hours on and four hours off, day and night!" he said. "It's nothing. Duty has kept me on watch and watch since he came aboard, and I dare not go ashore anyway, for fear he will surrender the schooner to a bumboat while I am gone. But, pray tell me, how long am I to be under this shadow, this implied rebuke?"

"Until he can discuss the matter with the commodore, he said. Also, I'm to stand watch and watch with you."

"The better to keep an eye on me?"

"The better to learn my duty, sir."

"Oh, I think you know where your duty lies," he said, rolling down his sleeves and reaching for his coat. "But then so do I." He grinned like we were a couple of schoolboys plotting mischief. "It would seem we are in the same boat, you and I."

Billy held a dinner in honor of my return, talking little and drinking heavily, and it broke up as soon as the toasts were drunk and we could decently turn away from each other again. For days he came on deck only rarely, lurching along the weather side of the quarterdeck as we beat to windward along the northern coast of San Domingo, supporting himself with one hand on the hammock nettings, taking little notice of anything around him except to peer aloft or glance at the compass now and again. Mostly he kept to his cabin and drank, and never set foot on deck after dark.

We found the *Constellation* off Le Cap François, she being newly arrived from the States. Billy took me over to the frigate for his confab with Commodore Truxtun, but he said nothing in the boat except to mutter, "We'll soon see who's in the right of it." He left me in the care of Lieutenant Sterrett, who had made a name for himself in the fight with the *L'Insurgente* a year ago come February.

I lifted my hat and said, "Mr. Sterrett, it's an honor to meet you, sir," but Sterrett merely looked down his long nose at me, tucked in his already weak chin, and turned me over to the midshipman of the watch.

"Why if it ain't Jemmy Jarvis," I said, shaking his hand. "I know you from when you and a bunch of your mates come a-visiting in the *Aztec* with a case of Porto wine."

"Which we had stole from the captain," he said with a grin. We'd had to drink it all, of course, thinking to dispose of the evidence that way, but even though there was a dozen of us to do it, we were all three sheets to the wind by midnight and had to kiss the gunner's daughter in the morning. The beatings were well deserved, we'd all agreed—and well worth it, too.

Jemmy put a finger alongside his nose and motioned me over to the skylight on the quarterdeck. After making sure Sterrett weren't watching, Jemmy put a finger to his lips in warning, and we cocked our ears.

"If you can't handle your officers," Truxtun was shouting, "by Jasper I'll get someone who can, sir! And mark what I said—you get me a mess of them Johnny Crappo pirates. I aim to show Gaswell how 'tis done!"

Jemmy gave me a wink and a friendly poke with his elbow, but I was too dispirited to sock his eye for him.

And so it was that we prowled the Bight of Léogane instead of rejoining our squadron on the Leeward Islands station. One bright exhilarating morning two days later off the tip of San Domingo's northern arm, with columns of spray rising against Môle Saint-Nicolas in the distance, we came upon a trim little sloop under French colors having her way with a merchant brig flying the Stars and Stripes.

"Sir," said Wickett, lifting his hat, "pray, may I make a suggestion?"

He did it so humble and proper and it was such a gorgeous morning that Billy had to say yes.

"May I suggest, sir, that as she does not seem to have noticed us and we have her under our lee, that we take her by boarding rather than fire into her? She will be much more valuable if we can take her whole."

It was an agreeable suggestion, and Billy nodded, smiling in the beautiful sunshine. "Of course, of course, Mr. Wickett, and of course again! Detail a party of boarders to your liking—except Mr. Graves, here, whom I need at the swivel guns."

"But sir!"

"Tut-tut, Mr. Graves, Mr. Quilty has excused you from duty for several more days yet."

"But I'm fit, sir!"

"*Tut*, Mr. Graves."

I knew he was getting back at me, but there was only one thing left to say: "Aye aye, sir."

I watched jealously as Gunner Schmidt and Bosun Klemso, and Horne and Elwiss, and Dick and Jubal and just about everybody but me and Billy armed themselves with pistols and cutlasses and tomahawks and boarding pikes and got ready to go. Even Surgeon Quilty came on deck to take the tiller, and the ship's boys manned the braces.

So intent were the French upon their mischief that they absolutely failed to notice *Rattle-Snake* until Quilty thumped us alongside them and we threw our grapnels across.

"Never mind, Mr. Quilty," called Wickett, as the grapnel men lashed us firmly in place. "It is only paint. Boarders away!"

With horrible shrieks and maniacal laughter, the Rattle-Snakes flung themselves across and waded into the pirates. I saw Jubal with a belaying pin in each of his mighty fists clearing a path for Dick, and Schmidt's silver hair flying as he ran straight across the sloop's deck and on up the merchantman's side. The Marines and a bunch of foremast jacks followed him, while others darted below on the heels of the fleeing Johnny Crappos.

I heard shrieks and the clanking of metal on metal, and the swooshing and snapping of blades cutting through flesh and bone, and then for several awful minutes there was no sound at all.

Then Wickett appeared on the deck of the French ship, which was a sweet little four-pounder sloop of eight guns, and said, "We've lost not a man, sir, and everything seems in good order."

"Thank you, Mr. Wickett. Come make your report when you are ready." Billy saw me standing by at the swivel guns and said, "You may ease yourself now, Cuz. The danger is past."

I was stung. "You ordered me to stay here at Mr. Quilty's suggestion, sir." I had been plagued by nauseous headaches since the explosion in the *Jane*.

"Yes, and probably no one will think the worse of you for it. One must always remember that a good commander does not *do* things, but causes them to be *done*. Forget that at your peril." But high spirits—or perhaps relief that regulations forbad a captain to accompany a boarding party—overcame his urge to lecture and he smiled. "Come have a glass with me while we wait on the good lieutenant's pleasure."

"Congratulations on your *victory*, Cousin Billy," I said when we had seated ourselves and Prichard had brought whiskey and a jug of water. "My *admiration*, if I may." I gave him a mock salute with my glass. It was a shabby attempt to wound him, but he took me at my word and my shot went wide.

He beamed. He continued to beam when Wickett knocked and

entered, bearing the captured sloop's books and with the soaking wet merchant captain lurking behind him, carrying his own books. The value of the merchantman's hull and cargo were argued over and agreed upon, a percentage of which was due us as salvage. After Cowan, the merchant captain, had signed the necessary documents and offered taciturn thanks for his rescue, he drank a glass but was not encouraged to stay.

Cowan seemed to have taken the excitement of the action with him once he'd squelched away, and Billy and Wickett lapsed into an embarrassed silence. They looked at each other almost bashfully.

"Well sir, we lost not a man, I am pleased to say," Wickett finally offered. "Not even a scratch, though Jubal flung Mr. Cowan overboard by mistake and we had to fish him out of the drink."

"Ha ha!" said Billy. "No wonder he was gruff!"

Even Wickett laughed. "Yes sir. Fortunately he apparently fired off his entire arsenal of oaths at the time, or we should have had an earful in here, ha ha! Ah me. At any rate, our momentum carried us across to the merchantman, where we chased the French below decks and killed them all. Likewise in the sloop. It was just as well, as it turns out. The Frenchmen had no letter of marque and reprisal, no official permission to commit what amounts to theft and murder on the high seas, which is piracy, and we would have had to hang them all anyway."

"Glad we were spared that unpleasantness," said Billy.

Wickett had been glancing through the sloop's books. "She is *La Brise,* out of Cayenne," he said. "And a pack of villains they were, too. Took three Americans, it says here: *Charlotte and Katie* out of Savannah, bound for the Havana—"

"Ha ha! Savannah—La Havana, hey?"

"Yes sir, ha ha, as you say. —*Candice,* off Saint John, Porto Rico, no homeport given; and *Molly Best* out of Baltimore. *Molly Best . . .*" He ran his finger along a line, peering at the handwritten French. "She was just in from the Guinea coast, no cargo listed. Slaves, no doubt, but it omits to say what they did with them. Nor does it say what they did with the crews, though they would have landed them at Guadeloupe or one of the other French islands, had they owned a letter of marque and reprisal. Pirating is quite the profitable business, apparently."

"Privateering, I think you mean, sir!" laughed Billy.

"Hmm? Oh indeed, sir. I must have misspoke."

Billy picked up a pencil and made a few calculations, and chuckled at the result.

Wickett turned the pages consideringly before saying, "And a good thing for us she had so many men away in prizes, sir. She carried four score or more when she set out, and might've put up a fight." Privateers were notoriously overcrowded, to allow for prize crews.

"Don't be modest in triumph," said Cousin Billy, raising his glass in a toast, "lest people think your triumphs are modest."

Wickett sipped his whiskey, gazing into the past. "I remember *Molly Best*," he said. "A sharp-built schooner with a fine turn of speed—the fastest slaver on the Bight of Benin, as I recall. Her master was an unkempt man with a nasty habit of spitting. I meant to shoot him one day in Whydah, but I had forgotten to take a pistol with me that morning, more's the pity."

Now *that* was a piece of his past I hadn't heard before, but he turned another page and the moment was gone. "Also a British whaler bound for the Great South Sea—they'd have done better to wait till she got back, I'd say—and several Dutchmen not worth mentioning."

Cousin Billy reached for the decanter. "Is France at war with Holland again? I can never keep track."

Wickett hesitated before replying. "Well, sir, France has absorbed the Austrian Netherlands. Maybe you mean the so-called Batavian Republic."

Cousin Billy looked up from his glass. "Hmm? Oh, yes, yes, I'm sure. But I was thinking . . . A trim little island sloop and a sweet sailer, from the look of her. Could catch anything smaller and evade anything larger. In harm's way one moment and haring off in front of the pack the next, hey?"

"*La Brise?* I suppose so, sir, yes."

A silence followed, with Trimble and Wickett both fidgeting. I had opened my mouth to excuse myself when Trimble busted out:

"Well, dammit, that was a handsome action, sir." He flushed.

Wickett almost smiled. "The gun and head bounty will be welcome, I'm sure, sir. The Navy Board is bound to condemn her, especially as no one is left to say otherwise. But anything that can float and can carry a gun will be a help to us."

"Yes. Yes, my point exactly. 'Anything that can float and carry a gun,' just as you say. I, erm . . . ahem—" As if he had just recalled my presence, he broke off and frowned at me.

I had been contemplating the logistics of what I guessed Cousin Billy was about to offer Wickett. *La Brise* was too small to be a lieutenant's command, really, but she was awfully sweet and looked like she would be nimble and swift in the right man's hands—*in the right man's hands* being the important point. And although each foremast jack could claim an equal share of the crew's portion of the prize, he couldn't claim it until she had been condemned by a prize court back in the States. Even then he wouldn't get his money until the end of the cruise, and perhaps not until his one-year enlistment was over. In the meanwhile, it wouldn't be unheard of was Billy to use her as a tender while we were on detached duty, hunting down Rigaud's picaroons in the bight. And having two ships increased our chances of taking more prizes. I didn't guess the crew would object to that . . . It took me a moment to realize that Billy and Wickett were waiting for me to go away.

"Oh! It's nearly eight bells," I said, "and Mr. Rogers will expect me, I bet. Will you excuse me, gentlemen?"

A great deal of work needed doing in *La Brise* to clear away the mess from the short but vicious battle. I was unpleasantly reminded of how much blood the corporeal envelope contains and how it seems to go everywhere once it is released, as I directed a party of waisters dragging the bodies (and parts thereof) out from below decks and throwing them overboard. I wondered who the man had been whose grimacing head I held by the hair, and what he must have thought seeing his body across the cabin without him. But thinking like that would never answer, and I tossed the thing to the sharks and went to make sure the waisters were rigging the pump properly.

The lubbers had gotten the hose shipped despite themselves and were rinsing the blood into the well. Topside, the rest of my party tailed into the washdeck pump and squilgeed the streams of pink water out through the scuppers.

The warrant officers had descended on *La Brise* like locusts. Klemso and his mate Elwiss, a scrawny, talkative waterman from the Eastern Shore, were going through the vessel's bosun's stores, examining the rigging, counting the paint pots, going over the spare anchors. It was illegal to loot a prize that way, but it was often done. Hess's Adam's apple bobbed as he scribbled in the bosun's log, and Klemso was uncharacteristically cheerful as he contemplated his newfound bounty. Down in the locker, the sailmaker was rubbing his hands over *La Brise*'s canvas, while Gunner Schmidt and his mate had disappeared into the little magazine. *La Brise*'s four-pound shot was useless for *Rattle-Snake*'s six-pounders, but her store of grape would serve us nicely, and her powder was money in our pockets.

Then Wickett dropped into *La Brise*'s waist with a thump. Gypsy jumped down beside him, squinting in the sunlight as she twined herself around his legs.

"Hold, gentlemen," said Wickett. "Put everything back where you found it. She's mine, now."

As he stalked about his new command with his fingers twitching behind his back and Gypsy following him, I remembered what he'd said about the Marine he had bribed. Yet I didn't hold his words against him. I envied him.

Eleven

"A regular *flag* officer, is our Admiral Trimble," said Wickett, snapping his telescope shut as yet another group of flags rose in *Rattle-Snake's* rigging. "Can you read what that says exactly, Mr. Graves?"

"Well, sir, I think he means—"

"I asked what it says *exactly*, Mr. Graves."

"It says *Form line of bottle*, sir."

If sending lots of signals was the main duty of a squadron commander, Billy had the job squared away. He hadn't dared to affect a commodore's broad pendant, but he had seized the opportunity to practice "fleet maneuvers" with *Breeze*, as he had renamed the sloop, and that meant innumerable messages and replies. Worse, Dick didn't know the signal book as well as he might, and often spelled out words rather than use the three-flag codes that we had adopted from the Royal Navy.

"Hoist *Signal not understood*, Mr. Graves," said Wickett. He grinned. "And ready the acknowledgement."

"Aye aye, sir." The hoist lay ready at hand, as we'd been having plenty of occasion to use it, but all the same I kept my eye on the signal rating while he bent it on.

Flying *Form line of battle* at last and firing a gun to emphasize the order, *Rattle-Snake* wore around and came charging up to us.

"Hoist *Acknowledged*, Mr. Graves. Ready about! Ease down your helm!"

"Ease down the helm, aye aye, sir."

"Ease off the jib sheets, there. Haul in the mains'l boom, handsomely. Helm's alee! Let fly your jib sheets!" The bow swung across the wind's eye. "Let go and haul!"

We circled around behind *Rattle-Snake* and into her wake. She tacked, determined to catch us up; we wore, determined to get on station astern of her. We both had completed a circuit and were halfway through a second, with *Breeze* gaining due to her superior speed in stays, before *Rattle-Snake* gave it up and straightened her course. With his jaw set but his eyes sparkling, Wickett promptly reduced sail to keep station astern.

"Flag's hailing, sir," said a grinning seaman.

"So she is, Atkins," said Wickett, taking his speaking trumpet from its beckets and heading forward. "Wipe that smile off your face or I'll stop your burgoo."

"Aye aye, sir," said Atkins, still grinning. Burgoo was the boiled oatmeal, sometimes a gruel, sometimes a gluey mass, that sailors to a man hated despite eating it nearly every morning of their lives at sea.

Billy was not pleased. Every ear on *Breeze* could hear him roaring down the wind: "What are you at, Mr. Wickett? Didn't you see my signal?"

"I did, sir, and a strange one it was, too."

"I mean the second one, God damn your eyes!"

"Plain as day, sir: *Form line of battle,* unless I miss my mark. But the way you were twisting around—"

"I'll talk to you later about twisting things around, Mr. Wickett. In the meantime, put yourself twelve miles to windward on the sta'board tack. Is *that* plain as day, or would you like it in writing?"

"Twelve miles to windward it is, sir."

"See that it is, Mr. Wickett. And stay within sight of my signals or you'll answer for it!"

Wickett's "aye aye, sir" was mild enough, but he was tight-lipped and the skin around his birthmark was pale as he called out his orders for the course change. When we had come about he said, "You have the conn, Mr. Graves. Steer nor' by west until you judge we have reached our station, then call me." Rubbing his forehead, he went below.

The headaches that had plagued me since the action aboard the *Jane* had gotten worse, and as I admired the play of light along the water and the dazzle of the spray as we swooped and thumped our way to windward, the first probing fingers of pain wrapped themselves around the backs of my eyeballs. "A quiet dim room and a vegetable diet," Quilty had said, both impossible in a vessel of war. He had given me a supply of willow bark to chew when the "migrams" became unbearable, though I thought clutching my head and screaming would have been just as helpful.

I imagined it was my conscience at work, toiling away without consulting me, as if I could have persuaded Billy to resign the service if I could just have found the words. But I would have had to speak out of love and compassion, and I was having to grope deeper and deeper for that.

I pulled my hat low on my forehead and went to stand in the shade of the mainsail. That helped a little. I was able to see normally again, anyway, except for the little flashes of light dancing around the edges of objects. Thinking of the pain as some sort of punishment made it bearable, as did a shadow passing over the sun: raggedy black clouds scudding before the northeast trades. The wind grew gusty and rain began to fall in scattered bursts.

I felt as dark and sullen as the clouds. *Breeze* didn't need two officers, and I couldn't figure out why Wickett had asked for me. He could have taken Dick as second in command, or either of the bosun's mates, Horne or Elwiss. Dick was the obvious choice, having excellent political pull in the form of his father, but there was something about him that got Wickett's back up.

I would've taken Horne. He'd grown up in the merchant service and would hold his master mariner's warrant before he was twenty-five, you could bet on it. But he'd had precious little education beyond his letters and figures.

Me, I'd had two years at Judge Brackenridge's academy in Pittsburgh, where I'd learned my classics along with the gentlemanly arts of ear-twisting and eye-gouging. I read Greek and Latin easily, which it isn't bragging to say because I spoke them badly, and I could argue that Hector or Odysseus was the true hero of the Trojan Wars, whichever you wished. And Wickett did wish it, taking us on long voyages over Homer's wine-dark sea most afternoons while our meat sat untouched. Anyway, everything was gravy to me as long as I was out from under Billy's bloodshot eye.

While I'd been ninnying about, I'd completely lost track of where we were or where we were going. *Rattle-Snake*'s sails were just visible on the horizon, when it occurred to me to look. Or perhaps that white patch was nothing but an odd cloud formation.

"Masthead," I called. "How is *Rattle-Snake* heading?"

"West by south, suh. She hull-down from here, suh. And now she signalin'."

Sweet mother of pearl, I thought—if I got out of sight of *Rattle-Snake,* Billy would rebuke Wickett and Wickett would savage me. "Boy," I said to Freddy Billings, snapping my fingers, "my respects to the captain. We're on our station and I'd like to come about. Also tell him it's blowing up squally." Then I took a glass and scrambled aloft.

The bunting in *Rattle-Snake*'s rigging was just readable at that distance, despite the increasing chop that sent *Breeze*'s mast around in erratic circles. I knew the signal book and my cousin well enough to know already what he had to say. I managed not to jump when Wickett called from the deck, "Mr. Graves, what are you doing up there?"

"*Rattle-Snake*'s signaling, sir."

"And what does he say?"

"Well, it's difficult to read, sir. He's nearly dead to loo'ard, and the flags are blowing—"

"Pray do not toy with us, Mr. Graves. Can you read it or not?"

"Yes, sir. He says, *Why are you not on station?*"

He clasped his hands behind his back and said, "Indeed, indeed. And how should I answer him, Mr. Graves?"

"I don't know, sir."

"That answer would be entirely too honest, I think. Where's my signal rating? Hoist *Acknowledged*. Helmsman, come la'board two points."

I put my glass to my eye. "Deck there: new signal." I called down the familiar numbers to the signal rating, who translated: *Why have you not answered my signal?*

"Tell me now, Mr. Graves, what shall I reply to that?"

I was sunk. *"Inattention to duty*, if you please, sir."

"Oh, no, that would not please me at all. Observe and learn, Mr. Graves." To the signal rating he said, "Hoist *Signal not understood*, and let it become jammed in the blocks for a time."

I was glad to have avoided a chewing-out, and even gladder when I happened to glance toward the rugged gray line of the Cuban shore.

Two bright shapes against the gray: two pale quadrilaterals that narrowed and elongated again even as I raised my glass.

"On deck! Sir! There's a brig that's just hauled up, making east-sou'east or maybe sou'east by east."

"Where away?"

"A point abaft the sta'board beam, sir."

"Ready about! Clear that mess away and signal *Strange sail in sight*. Mr. Graves, let me know what *Rattle-Snake* says."

We continued on our course for several anxious minutes as we waited for *Rattle-Snake*'s reply. Flags broke out on her hoist.

"Deck there! *Rattle-Snake* says—can't quite make it out, sir. It looks like—no, a squall has hidden her."

"Very well. Lay alow from aloft, Mr. Graves, I need you."

By the time I had shot down the backstay to the quarterdeck, the signal rating was already running up the chase's bearing and we were coming about to intercept her. The lookout called down that *Rattle-Snake* had hauled her wind and was heading easterly.

"Load all but the foremost guns with chain, Mr. Graves, and run them out on the larboard side."

Squalls forced us to reduce sail, but the chase had to shorten down as well. Our fore-and-aft rig let us sail closer to the wind than she could, and the weight of the guns run out to windward helped to steady *Breeze*'s keel and stiffen her.

"Larboard battery ready, sir!"

"Thank you, Mr. Graves. Now, d'ye see what I have done here? We close steadily on the chase, walking up to windward to meet him—on a bowline I can sail three miles to his two. He cannot keep his present course without coming under range of our guns, and if he tries to run down to leeward he will fetch up on the Cuban shore."

"Is she French, sir?"

"Who's to say? All I know is that he is trying to run away, and naturally I want to ask him why."

She was hull up from the deck now, thrashing into the wind. We were having a rocking time of it ourselves, as we slapped our way through the swell. Wickett was grinning, one arm hooked around a shroud and his glass in his hand, his hair streaming in the wet wind and his hat lost someplace in our wake.

"We should see her teeth soon, if she has any," he said. "Hoist our colors, Mr. Graves."

I sent our ensign with its fifteen stars and stripes up to the peak. Perhaps it was the fresh air, perhaps it was excitement, perhaps it was the sight of the crimson and cobalt crackling and snapping against the gray sky, but my headache lifted suddenly, as if a window had opened in a stuffy room, and in joy of it I snatched off my hat and cried, "Hurrah, boys! hurrah!" and the men hurrah'd me back with an enthusiasm that made the hair on my arms stand up.

The brig also hoisted an American flag as we edged up toward her, an old one with red, white and blue stripes and the stars in a circle. It was nonsense, of course—her name was picked out in gold on her transom: *La Sécurité*, which she must know we could see by now, and if she was a prize she'd show it by wearing American or British colors over French. She even seemed to have women aboard. That was an old pirate trick, dressing as women to lure other ships within striking range. It was also entirely unnecessary, as we were determined to catch her.

"Hoist the challenge of the day," said Wickett.

"No response, sir."

"Lay a shot across her bows."

The sea was too rough to show the fall of the shot, and I judged its effect by watching the brig. She yawed away from us.

"Run in the larboard guns," said Wickett.

The brig came into the wind, almost missing stays but settling down again on the starboard tack. Wickett anticipated her, and we were on her new course before she was. It was glorious weather for a chase, too—whitecaps slashing the gray sea, the wind singing in the rigging and the salt spray whipping along the deck till we were soaked to the bone—with the sky all bleak and gloomy and the splendid reek of gun smoke mixed throughout. Three more times we fired, but the brig never hove-to.

As we hauled within long pistol shot, the "ladies" all went below.

"Run out the guns on both sides, Mr. Graves," said Wickett. He raised his speaking trumpet.

"Ahoy the brig! Heave-to or I shall fire into you!" He repeated the order in French. The wind blew his words away, but his meaning must have been clear.

There seemed to be a scuffle in the brig, and then Old Glory came down and the Tricolor went up.

"She shows her true colors," said Wickett. "See if you can't shoot away a spar or two, Mr. Graves."

"Aye aye, sir—look there! Someone's waving a handkerchief on the fo'c's'le. I believe they want us to hold our fire, sir."

"I'm sure they do," said Wickett, "and yet someone else is running out her guns. Put us across her stern," he said to the quartermaster, and then: "Mr. Graves, fire as they bear."

I gave her a rolling broadside from the larboard battery—*pok! pok! pok! pok!*—aiming high as we crested a roller. *Breeze* gave a little twist as the roller passed under her, and the shots walked right up the brig's mainmast. It was infernal luck, and I don't say so out of modesty.

La Sécurité's main-topmast took the fore-topmast with it when it tottered. Lines and shrouds snapped as the intricate balance of stays and backstays went all to hell.

"Stop your vents!" said I.

"She hesitates!" said the captain of Number Two gun. "Look at her fly ahoo!"

"Sponge!"

"Naw, mate, she's got a good hand at the wheel," said his sponger, looking up from his work. "See her recover!"

"Stop that chattering!" said I. "Load!"

But then her mainmast went by the boards with a mighty crash. The wind kicked her nose to leeward, a roller picked up her stern and she drove herself under the sea.

By the time we got a boat in the water, there wasn't much more to see of the brig than her forecourse, floating in the waves like a drowned island. Not a man was left alive—nor woman nor child, though there had been plenty of both on board, judging from the bodies that churned about us.

We could see it all, now that it was too late. She had been carrying a shipload of refugees, perhaps diehard holdouts from Le Cap bound for the French-speaking communities in Spanish Louisiana. She'd mistaken us for a privateer, as skeptical of our colors as we had been of hers. Someone had tried to surrender while someone else had tried to fight, and this was the result.

The bowman hauled another small body alongside and held it up on his boat hook. "Dead 'un," said Stotes, and the bowman let the child drift away again.

La Sécurité's forecourse gave up its burden of air with a sigh and fluttered away like a great ghost beneath the waves. I watched it go. Then I put the tiller over and returned to the *Breeze*, my eyes stinging and vomit rising in my gorge, but my hands steady and my manner perfectly composed.

Twelve

Peter Wickett sat in *Breeze*'s cuddy with Gypsy draped across his knees. An untouched glass of brandy stood on the desk beside him. The bulkheads glistened with damp and the purser's dip had flavored the air with smoke, but he didn't seem to notice. He sat with his chin resting on his steepled fingers, staring at—but apparently not seeing—the local pilot, who sat across the desk from him, blinking solemnly, with his eyes gleaming in his black face.

"It's near six bells, sir," I said.

Wickett stirred himself. *"Excusez-moi, monsieur,"* he murmured to the pilot. Then he glanced at me and said, "Precision is not your strong suit. How near?"

I pulled out my watch and looked at it. "Four minutes, sir." Just shy of three o'clock on a January morning, and the mercury in the thermometer above Wickett's head stood at seventy-nine degrees.

"We have a little time, then," he said, holding out his hand for my watch. "What happened to that dainty Graham Jackson that Mr. Towson presented you?"

"Villon stole it, sir."

"Yes, I recall it now. And where did you get this iron turnip?"

"Off a bumboat in Port Républicain, sir."

He jiggled the monster in his hand. "We could use it for shot, I suppose, should we shoot all ours away tonight. I hope you didn't pay more than a few shillings for it."

"Three dollars in silver, sir. And lucky to get it at the price, too."

He handed it back. "You were twice robbed, my pigeon: valuables removed from fleeing planters fill Port Républicain, and can be had for cheap." Gypsy squeaked as he unhooked her claws from his nankeen trousers and settled her in his chair. "When we have returned from cleaning out this pirate's nest tonight," he said, as the pilot and I followed him up the ladder, "mayhap we will go clean out another, you and I."

The breeze backed to the west as we rounded Cap Dame-Marie and headed south along the tip of San Domingo's long lower finger. In our wake came the *Walnut* cutter and the *Choptank* frigate from Commodore Gaswell's Santo Domingo squadron, with *Rattle-Snake* bringing up the rear.

Captain Oxford of the *Choptank* had been godlike in his wrath when he'd discovered *Rattle-Snake* and *Breeze* loitering off Jérémie—units of a rival squadron poaching on his territory, as he saw it, until it had occurred to him that, as senior commander in the area and the only post-captain, he could double his force by temporarily attaching us. It was his job to root out privateers in the southern bight and the Jamaica Channel, particularly Rigaud's picaroons. They had vanished from Guanabo Island, as he called La Gonâve, but a clutch of them had hatched among the creeks and coves of a shallow bay south of Cap Dame-Marie. *Choptank* drew too much water and *Walnut* was too lightly gunned for Oxford to have accomplished much before, but with us as ferrets, so to speak, he was now ready to drive the rats from their hole.

Wickett had taken me along to see Oxford present his plan aboard the *Choptank*. A few other midshipmen were there, but not Dick, and we hunched together in the shadows, keeping out of the way and our mouths shut while the lieutenants drank sherry wine and talked among themselves. Billy had been cleaned and shaved, but his face was blotchy and his belly made noises and he exuded a faint but pervasive stink. He didn't give me so much as a nod.

He and Wickett were senior to all of Oxford's lieutenants, including Lewis, who commanded *Walnut*, but Oxford soon had that straightened out. Wickett, in the *Breeze,* was to have the honor of leading *Walnut* and a squadron of boats into the bay, there either to take the three vessels lying at anchor—the *Augustin von Steuben,* the *Jane* and a snow—or chase them into the waiting arms of *Rattle-Snake* and *Choptank.* Billy was to take command of the squadron should Oxford fall, which flattered Billy and strengthened our resolve.

"You have—" Oxford had consulted one of the sheets of paper in front of him "—good lord, Wickett, do you mean to tell me you have only fifteen men and officers, including yourself?"

"Sixteen, counting the crumb-bosun, sir," Wickett said, with no discernable expression.

Oxford had tugged on his side-whiskers, but said only, "We'll leave the ship's boys out of this, I guess. Never mind, I can loan you some people." He looked around the cabin. "Has anybody else anything to add? No? How about you young fellows in the back, there. Mr. Smiley," he said, looking at the lanky redheaded midshipman next to me, "you've usually got an opinion on everything."

Smiley shuffled his feet. "No, I reckon not, sir," he mumbled.

The lieutenants chuckled to see a snotty put in his place. All was right with the world.

"And you, the little curly-headed fellow in the back," said Oxford, fixing me with his eye. The midshipmen drew away from me. "Have you any useful advice for us, or are you just here to take up space?"

"Well, sir," I said, because he had told me to speak, and I had to say something or I'd be shuffling my feet, too. Billy frowned and Wickett looked amused. "Just that the brig, *Jane,* is pretty old-fashioned in her rig. She's got no footropes in her, and furls her sails under the yards. And she carries four three-pounders, but the after gun on the la'board side is out of action, sir. Least it was when I was in her last. I dunno if they replaced it."

"Ha ha!" said Oxford. "That's the ticket. Now why couldn't one of you other young gentlemen have spoke up bold like that? Very well, then: Mr. Smiley, you'll take a party up into the *Jane*'s maintop and drop the main tops'l. And you, Mister—"

"Graves, sir," said Wickett. "A fire-eater."

"Is he? Good, good and good. Mr. Graves, you'll see to the fore-tops'l and the heads'ls. Is that well with you, Mr. Wickett?"

"It is well, sir, but I shall need those extra men you mentioned."

"And you'll get 'em. Now, Jack," said Oxford to Mr. Oakham, his tough little captain of Marines, "you'll attack the main body here at the far end of the bay, and Trimble, we'll land a party of Rattle-Snakes at the battery here on the north headland . . ."

"You were with Malloy in the *Aztec,* I believe?"

I jumped. A man was heaving the lead in the bow, softly singsonging, "No bottom, no bottom with this line" as *Breeze* whispered along under a mass of stars. Someone stifled a cough on the crowded deck. Wickett's face was a pale blur in the hooded light in the binnacle, and he had spoken so quietly that it was possible no one had heard him but me.

"Yes, sir," I said, also speaking low. "From ninety-eight till I joined *Rattle-Snake.*"

"So," Wickett continued, "you were there when Bainbridge lost the *Retaliation* to *L'Insurgente* and *La Volontaire.*"

"A year ago last November, yes sir. Off Guadeloupe. But I only saw it from a distance."

"Bainbridge gave up his ship without a shot, and yet no stigma attached itself to him. And why should that be, I wonder."

"Well, sir," said I, "*L'Insurgente* was a thirty-six and *La Volontaire* was a forty-four, while the *Retaliation* was only a fourteen-gun schooner no bigger'n the *Rattle-Snake.* He was hopelessly outgunned. And he kept his head, too."

"Did he so?"

"Yes sir. After he was took, he exaggerated our strength to the French and they called off the chase."

"You witnessed this yourself?"

"Oh, no sir. We never got within gunshot. I read it in his report, later."

"Ah. The *Aztec*—by which I mean Malloy—was running away at the time, was he not?"

"No sir," I said, stung. Then: "Not at first, I mean. We'd been chasing two other sail to the west, and we thought the frigates astern of us were English—"

"Yes. Tell me, Mr. Graves, is there any substance to the rumor that you called him out?"

"No, sir. I was strongly cautioned against it."

"Is he that good of a shot?"

"I doubt it, sir. He disapproves of dueling."

I didn't know if we were joking or not. The sky was brilliant with stars, but there was no moon, and although that kind of light is sufficient for seeing large things—ships and whales and islands, for instance—it ain't so good for faces.

"The other story," said Wickett, "is that he threatened to arrest you if you tried to challenge him."

"That's no story, sir. That's the truth of it."

"I am not surprised. One refuses a challenge from an inferior: think of the opportunities for advancement, else."

The pilot muttered a course correction in French. Wickett passed it along to the quartermaster, who passed it along to the steersman at his elbow.

"Still," said Wickett, "all he had to do was say no."

He took a turn or two along the landward side, peering out into the darkness. He had us cast the log—three knots and a fathom, sir, if you please—and when all was quiet again he said:

"Forgive my harping on the subject, but Malloy is a mystery to me. It is said that he shows, shall we say, a certain reluctance to come to grips with the enemy, and yet he has been promoted to post-captain and will be given a frigate, now that the *Aztec* is to be sold. Would you say he is shy, at all?"

"Oh no, sir, he's as willing to risk his men's lives as any captain."

"And yet his men like him?"

"No, sir. They call him the Old Woman behind his back."

"Yes, well. I read one of his reports once. He was anxious to point out to the Secretary that he saved the Republic a great deal of money by never firing his—"

We had been listening to the leadsman with the backs of our ears, so to speak, and Wickett immediately shut his mouth when the whispered chant of "by the deep" changed to "by the mark." The water was shoaling. Saturn was setting in the west, and Mars was rising between a pair of steep peaks on the larboard beam. I took a bearing on the northern peak—east-southeast a half east—and then the other.

"*Le point de repère,*" said the pilot, pointing at the peaks. He knew his directions and his fathoms, but he didn't speak much more English than that.

"There is our landmark," Wickett translated for the quartermaster. "There, do you see those two peaks?" He snapped his fingers. "Mr. Graves, the time."

"Three fifty-seven, sir," I said, glancing at my watch in the binnacle light. When I looked up I found I had lost my night vision.

"Very good. Signal *Walnut* that I am coming about."

I found the dark lantern at my feet by its heat and smell, and felt my way past the man at the tiller to the taffrail. I lifted the shutter three times, waited three seconds and flashed the light twice more. After thirty seconds I repeated the signal to be sure it'd been seen.

By the time I returned to Wickett's side I could see again. We had opened up a bay at the foot of the twin peaks. Campfires dotted the shore at the far end of the bay, with a white cliff behind them gleaming in the starlight. You could hear laughter and snatches of song drifting across the water.

The boats from the *Choptank* and the *Rattle-Snake* shaved our stern, swift as ghosts, with a drawled "Ahoy the *Breeze*—yoicks and away" from Jack Oakham, Oxford's captain of Marines.

"*La barre dessous,*" said our pilot.

"Down helm," said Wickett.

"Down helm it is, sir," said the quartermaster.

The admirable and steady wind came across our stern and then forsook us as we entered the bay, leaving us wallowing in baffled airs for agonizing minutes before we picked up the offshore breeze.

"Keep her as near as she will lie," said Wickett, translating the pilot's instructions. "Thus. Very well thus. Now bring her to." And in the same calm tone, as if he was drinking a dish of tea in some biddy's front parlor, he said: "Boarders away."

Breeze was towing her jolly boat and a pinnace borrowed from the *Choptank*. The boat-tenders pulled them alongside and the boarders snatched up their pistols and tomahawks and cutlasses and poured in. Oxford's sailing master, whom we'd picked up earlier, had the pinnace and its twenty-five Choptanks. I had the jolly boat with seven men.

"Good luck, Mr. Graves." Wickett shook my hand and I dropped into the boat, awkward with the cutlass I'd remembered this time. *Handsomely, handsomely,* I said to myself. I was as giddy as a girl in a store-bought frock. Sweat trickled down my chest and arms, but I guessed maybe it was just from the heat.

"I've checked that their pistols are at half cock, sir, so some fool don't blow his balls off by accident," muttered Horne, on loan from *Rattle-Snake*. I was unhappy to see Stotes, the grumbler, sitting behind him.

"Thank you, Mr. Horne." I felt the locks of my pistols, grateful to the big bosun's mate for the tactful reminder. I managed to ship the tiller in a seamanlike fashion and remembered to put a gruff in my voice when I ordered, "Give way."

Three bright flashes off on the left, three echoing booms and three sudden spouts of water alongside nearly made me squeak.

"Christ!" cried Stotes. "They seen us! The fuckin' shore batteries is a-gonna git us!"

"Clap a stopper on it," said Horne.

"Say, nigger," said Stotes, "who died and made you cap'n, that's what I'd like to know!"

"Shut your goddamn mouth." I suppressed the urge to take the flat of my blade to him. But we could do all the shouting we wanted, now. The attack had started too early.

I thought Wickett might recall us—but no, the *Breeze* was filling, working her way close-hauled up the bay. With a weird groaning, another salvo from the northern point straddled her without hitting her. Of course they weren't shooting at us, I realized, and the self-contempt drove my fear away. Then I could hear shouting and the crackle of small-arms fire around the shore battery to our left. The muzzle flashes looked like a crazy swarm of fireflies. As we pulled across the bay I could hear the ringing of steel as the sailors spiked the guns.

Breeze was making for the snow, the largest of the three vessels in the little bay. *Walnut* hauled alongside *Augustin von Steuben* and let loose with her larboard guns, lighting her up with an eerie red glow.

I followed the boats closing on the *Jane* brig, steering us around to the larboard fore-chains as the longboats hauled alongside to starboard. There was a thundering and a flurry of wild yells from her far side, and then I was leaping from the jolly boat up into the fore shrouds with Horne right behind me. I was too excited to be frightened even while hanging backside downward in the futtocks as I scrambled into the top.

The topsail yard was sitting on the cap, of course, several feet over my head. I swung around the topmast shrouds and squirmed up onto the yard. Shouting in exhilaration (or terror, which is much the same thing), I ran out to the end of the yard, wildly waving my arms for balance until I found the topping lift and snatched hold of it.

Someone behind me had forgotten his coaching about the lack of footropes. He slipped off the yard with a screech and thumped onto the deck below. But another man had followed me out, two men were straddling the other end of the yard, and Horne and two others had stayed in the top to cast off the buntline. I might've stayed there in safety, but I guessed this was a time for leading, not pointing.

"Loose and let fall!" I unknotted gaskets, and the sail tumbled open, pale in the starlight.

I glanced down. A mass of men struggled around the base of the mainmast, but the fo'c's'le was clear. I shouted and pointed, sprang over the man inboard of me, leaped for the forestay and by the grace of God remembered to let myself down hand over hand instead of sliding. I landed on canvas, pleased to still have the skin on my palms.

"Horne," I called, examining the canvas with my hands, "her fore stays'l's already bent on."

"Fore stays'l aye!" he said, following me to the deck by the same route I'd come. The others were slipping down the braces, landing softly barefoot on the deck.

I couldn't see a thing in the shadows underfoot, but I could smell the rotten bottom-ooze on the anchor cable. I groped around till I found the slimy thing—one cable only. She was riding to a single bower.

"Here," I said.

Horne unshipped his broadax and swung it in a smooth arc, sinking its bit into the cable, hefting the ax again.

The fighting had concentrated aft. I prodded my men toward the pinrails, saying, "Cast off your tops'l gear. Man the tops'l halyard."

As the fore-topsail yard swayed up, I stepped on something soft and warm and wet at the foot of the foremast: Stotes, broken and bloody on the deck. His head was turned at a ghastly angle.

"You and you," I said, grabbing two men. "He's a dead 'un. Get him out of the way."

They tossed him over the side.

With her cable cut and her fore-topsail backed, *Jane* began to turn her bow away from the breeze.

"Sheet home! That's *well* your sheet!" I called. "Clear away the fore-topmast stays'l!"

I cast off the staysail downhaul and ran to give a tail to the men at the halyard. They hauled away as one—*heave! heave! heave!*—bringing in the line as fast as I could haul it through the block.

Then a pistol ball thumped into the block, sending a numbing shock up my arms, and the picaroons were on us. I threw a couple of hasty bights of the halyard over its belaying pin, hauled all a-taunto, yanked my cutlass out—and promptly got knocked down. I lost my cutlass. People kept stepping on my hands while I groped around for it. Blades clashed overhead. Men grunted and swore and shrieked, and the air stank of sweat and blood—and piss and shit, too, to tell the truth of it.

And there I was right spang in the middle of it, scrabbling among the milling feet, looking for my blasted cutlass. Someone kicked me. Then someone else kicked me, and I grabbed his bare foot and bit it. I was rewarded with a jerk and a howl. I think it was a French howl, but I was so mad I didn't give a damn whose foot it was. Then Horne arrived and cleared a space with his ax, raining blood in a broad arc. A seaman hauled me to my feet.

"Thank you," I said, indistinctly. The toes had left a nasty taste in my mouth. "Look, there they go!"

The picaroons were leaping into the water or running below. An American quartermaster was steering for the open sea, the sails were drawing, and a lieutenant and the sailing master from the *Choptank* were strutting around the quarterdeck as if they owned the place—which in fact they did.

"Give us a cheer, boys," said the lieutenant, and how we roared!

A glow in the east lighted our way. *Walnut* led with *Augustin von Steuben* meekly following her across the creamy green water of the bay. The *Choptank* and the *Rattle-Snake* lay hove-to on the imperial blue ocean beyond. *Breeze* escorted the snow astern of us, with Venus glowing like a lantern in her rigging. Along the shores of the bay, fires broke out, pale in the sudden dawn, as the Marines put the picaroons' boats and huts to the torch. Dead men lay sprawled among the toppled guns on the northern headland, their blood bright against the dazzling white sand. As for the rest of the picaroons, the Marines and sailors in the shore party would handle them. A pretty good night's work, I thought, and I hadn't done so bad myself.

Then I remembered that I had lost Stotes. And I had lost our jolly boat, too, which I had forgotten to secure before boarding the brig. I felt small and cold in the morning light, and infinitely disgusted as I contemplated the dressing down that Wickett would give me.

➤ ➤ ➤

But we were all too busy next morning to worry about dead men and jolly boats. Nine prisoners had been taken during the night action, and Oxford had summoned all the sea lieutenants to decide what should be done with them. I was ordered to appear as translator.

Choptank was only a twenty-eight, tiny compared to, say, a forty-four-gun bruiser like the *Constitution,* but she boasted a wide after-cabin, beautifully lit by a great, curving, many-paned stern window. A long table had been placed parallel to the window, backlighting the officers who sat there and making their faces difficult to read. Oxford sat in the middle, with Brownstone and Halliwell, his first and second lieutenants, on his left; Wickett sat on his right; Lewis of the *Walnut* and Cowper, third of the *Choptank,* sat on the ends; and I sat at a table off to the side with the clerk. In the middle of the deck, six of the defendants huddled in manacles with a pair of stout Marines lurking over them. The arrangement had the appearance of a military court, although strictly speaking it wasn't. The prisoners were accused of piracy, they'd been caught with the goods (the vessels we'd taken from them), and by custom immemorial Oxford could hang them out of hand if he chose.

"Many of the picaroons went over the side during the action," Billy was saying. Oxford had appointed him as the "friend" of the accused, although Wickett was the abler man. "But these men stayed. Surely it says something in their favor that they elected to put themselves in our hands rather than swim for it."

"That's no argument, sir," said Lewis, a New Hampshireman who at first glance seemed to be all flowing side-whiskers and nose hair. "Most sailors can't swim! It's one of Jack Tar's defining characteristics. He don't wish to tempt fate with such Hebrews."

"Hebrews?" said Wickett.

"Aye, sir, *Hebrews,*" said Lewis. "A learned word, Mr. Wickett, taken from the Greek. It means putting on airs."

"You are very kind, sir." Wickett had allowed himself just a touch of raised eyebrow, but then he caught me looking at him and had to mask his smile with a cough.

I expected Billy to shout, "Hebrews—hubris, hey? Ha ha!" But he didn't, being uncommonly sober.

"Such Hebrews," Lewis continued, unnoticing, "such overbearing pride as to take his fate into his own hands should he fall in the drink is anathema to Jack. Why, the very Furies would be upon him. The gods'd strike him down."

"Surely there's but one God," murmured Cowper.

"He means it in the Greek sense," said Wickett.

"Just so," said Lewis.

"Jack is a superstitious chap," said Oxford, leaning back in his chair and casting a contemptuous look at the prisoners. "Everybody knows it. No need to flog a horse that's already dead. But the obvious explanation here is that these sons of bitches were more afeared of a certain drowning than they were of a possible hanging. What d'ye say to that, sir?"

Billy wrung his hands like a parson at a kissing-bee. "Consider the possibility, gentlemen," he said, "that these men were pressed into service, that they joined not out of greed or depravity but because they were afraid for their lives."

The picaroons nodded hopefully as I translated.

Oxford frowned. "And yet they undeniably went a-pirating."

Downcast looks from the picaroons.

"I feel compelled to point out, sir," said Brownstone, "that we have a delicate situation here. There are our men in Guadeloupe to be considered. What happens to them if we hang this lot?"

"Don't translate that," said Oxford. "Let 'em sweat for a bit. You've got your finger on it, though. It chaps my hide to say it, but if they believe they were acting under lawful authority then they must be given more consideration than they deserve, the dogs. Treated as prisoners of war, begad. What a damnable fiction that is."

"We could carry them to the commodore ourselves, sir," said Brownstone. "If we put in our own two cents' worth, we might hang 'em yet."

Oxford and the lieutenants put their heads together and murmured awhile. At last they sat back and Oxford said:

"We've reached a decision, and it's this: We find the defendants guilty of piracy, for which the punishment is death."

I know my face went white, for when I turned to the prisoners to translate the verdict, they were already looking at me with horror. *"Coupable,"* I said. Guilty.

"However," said Oxford, and I could swear he and Brownstone were looking very pleased with themselves, as if they had just pulled off a colossal joke, *"however,* despite their obvious guilt they are to be detained until such time as amicable relations are restored between our two nations or France agrees to a proper exchange of prisoners."

The picaroons brightened with relief when I translated, and some of them wept.

"There goes a case or two of shitten-arse, ha ha!" said Oxford as they were led away. "Next!"

The sergeant-at-arms brought in Doc and Samuels, the *Rattle-Snake*'s cook and my best gunner, that I had left behind in La Gonâve. Their weeks with the picaroons had left them nearly unrecognizably filthy and ragged, but they protested their innocence with a vehement and thoroughly American expectation that right would prevail. Life among Rigaud's rebels hadn't taken that away, but sharpened it.

"We was on dat brig to take her," Doc insisted. "We'd never ob been on dat island, else. Mr. Graves, here, he knows we's loyal an' true. Dint we volunteer to help him take back dat merchantman? What was her name—*Jane.* And dint we fight till we was struck down and couldn't fight no mo'?"

"Yes sir, that's exactly what happened," Samuels chimed in. He was blinking rapidly, and both men shone with sweat.

"Jane? Ain't that the brig we cut out last night?" said Oxford. "Mr. Graves, how did these men come to be ashore if they were with you in the *Jane?* And what makes 'em say *you* retook her, and not Tommy here?"—giving a nudge to Brownstone, who was the lieutenant I'd

seen on the *Jane*'s quarterdeck when we cut her out.

"They were captured with me off Guanabo a couple weeks ago, sir, in that first fight we had with Rigaud's men—"

He held up a hand. "We haven't established whose authority they were acting under, if any. Continue."

"Yes sir. *Jane* had drifted out of range of our guns, but Captain Peavey wouldn't give her up. The picaroons had murdered several men in *Augustin von Steuben* when they tried to escape, and they'd hanged her captain. He was a jolly fat fellow, sir, no harm to anybody. And I thought the same would happen in *Jane*. I asked Mr. Wickett if someone shouldn't go over to see if he could help, and Mr. Wickett said I was welcome to try. All the men who went with me volunteered, sir. And Doc and Samuels both acquitted themselves well."

"We'll decide who is acquitted here. Now then, Mr. Graves, when you escaped, as I assume you did seeing as you're here—" he looked around for a laugh and got it "—where were these two?"

"I can't say, sir."

"Don't play the sea lawyer with me, young man. Why was it that these men weren't with you?"

"I was told they went looking for tobacco, sir."

"Hearsay," said Billy. "Gentlemen—"

Oxford cut him off with a gesture. His hand was as blunt as his manner, the nails cut square and the palms as callused as a foremast jack's. "You mean they ran."

"Oh, no sir, they wouldn't neither one of 'em desert. I'm sure they meant to come back."

Billy cleared his throat. "Shouldn't Mr. Graves be sworn in, sir?"

"No need, Trimble, a gentleman is always truthful," said Oxford. "Sergeant-at-Arms, take those fellows outside a minute." After they'd been taken away, clanking, he said, "Damme if I remember any of this in your report, Trimble."

"My report, sir?" said Billy, licking his lips.

"Certainly, your report. There was an assistant consul or some politico—" He snapped his fingers. "What was his name?"

"Blair, sir," said Brownstone.

"That's right: Mr. Blair. He gave an account of the action to a correspondent to the *Aurora*, I believe—one of those democratic, freedom-hating Philadelphia papers, anyway. Your report appeared alongside it."

"You doubt my veracity, sir?" Billy glanced at Wickett, who shook his head slightly.

"Of course not," said Oxford, surprised. "Didn't I just say it was a *Philadelphia* paper? It's just that, except for his giving himself the starring role, with a cutlass and pistol in every hand and a couple more in his teeth, just about, his account bears a remarkable resemblance to your own."

"Well, we exchanged observations, of course," said Billy.

"And notes, too, no doubt," sniffed Lewis. "Fellow must have cribbed like a common schoolboy."

"If I may make a suggestion, gentlemen?" said Wickett. "Doc and Samuels are Rattle-Snakes—"

"Yes, that's right!" said Billy. "I can vouch for them. And if they're to be tried for their lives, I must insist we bring the matter before the commodore."

"And he won't like it anymore than we do," said Cowper. "Probably have to send it back to the States, where some civil court will claim jurisdiction—"

"And some ninny of a Republican," said Lewis, "will stand up in Congress and say the Navy's a tyrant's bludgeon—"

"Not to mention every man jack in the squadron bleating about sailors' rights and demanding it be put to a vote every time we so much as want to change course or shake out a reef," said Brownstone.

"And yet sailors *do* have rights, gentlemen," said Wickett. "That is our reason for fighting France in the first place, let us not forget. And besides, have you ever known a sailor worth his salt who did not submit cheerfully to punishment if it was just? He could not look his messmates in the eye ever again, otherwise. And yet men who are punished unjustly will eventually declare themselves to have had enough."

"True, true," said Cowper, looking depressed. "Muttering, shirking—and worse. It ain't safe on deck, alone on a dark night." He shut his mouth suddenly, as if he had said more than he meant to.

"Aye," said Lewis. "And if a man be punished wrongly, as Mr. Wickett says, especially as severe a punishment as abandoning his post in the face of the enemy deserves—a hundred lashes, death, even . . ." He let the sentence trail off.

"This, I believe, is an internal matter, gentlemen," said Wickett. "I never put *R* next to their names in the muster book. And why not? Because I never thought they *had* run."

"Yes, yes, you make your point," said Oxford. "You agree, Trimble? Very well, I think we've heard enough."

When Samuels and Doc had been brought back in, the lieutenants said, "Not guilty," from juniormost to seniormost, in the formal way, and Oxford added, "Not guilty of piracy for these two, and Captain Trimble may take what action he sees fit at another time. A couple dozen at the grating to remind them of their duty, *I'd* say—" (Billy went white at the suggestion, and I knew it would never happen) "—and maybe now, gentlemen, you understand better the Secretary's wisdom in proscribing the enlistment of niggers." Oxford raised his voice. "Sergeant-at-Arms, bring in the next prisoner. He's the last one, I hope," he muttered. "It's nearly time for dinner."

I had an unpleasant feeling that I knew who the sergeant-at-arms had gone to fetch. When Oxford had mentioned dinner, he had looked to see what o'clock it was on a fancy silver watch that he had taken out from under his papers.

Villon in handcuffs and leg-irons was not the man I remembered from La Gonâve. All insouciance had left him. In its place were bags under his eyes; dirty, unshaven cheeks; slumped shoulders and a stink of despair. When he saw me, however, he squared his shoulders and looked Captain Oxford in the eye.

Oxford said, "D'ye speak English, sir?"

"*Non, m'sieur le capitaine.*"

"Ask him why he's wearing a French uniform, Mr. Graves."

"He says because he's a French officer, sir, and as such he'd like his chains removed, please."

"I think not—General Villon, as you call yourself. That ain't a general's uniform. Ask him his true name and rank."

"I am François Villon Deloges," I interpreted, "after the famous rogue-poet. The captain has heard of him, yes?"

"Sure, sure," said Oxford, though I doubted it. "And his rank?"

Villon puffed out his lips and glanced at me before replying. "I am a major on the staff of General Rigaud, temporarily commanding the division of boats in the Bight of Léogane and the Jamaica Channel. I am sorry for the untruth I spoke before to Mr. Graves. It was a harmless exaggeration that I hope the gentleman will pardon."

Here Billy interrupted. "I think perhaps, sir, the prisoner should be sworn in if he is to be made to testify. Even though he obviously is a gentleman—"

Oxford frowned. "Very obviously he is *not,* sir. He's a goddamn nigger—a quadroon at best. And pirates don't need to be tried anyway, not when they're caught red-handed. Those weren't their ships we recovered, and I'm sure any amount of stolen stuff will be found in them. Now, then—where was I? Oh, yes. If he's on Rigaud's staff, what was he doing with the pirates? Ask him that, Mr. Graves."

"He denies that they're pirates, sir. He says he was under orders to harry our shipping in the bight and its approaches."

"Then where are his orders? Where is his letter of marque and reprisal?"

Villon unhappily indicated the torn breast of his filthy uniform. "Lost in the fighting, perhaps? Burned up in my tent along with my commission? I cannot say. But I am a soldier: I hear and obey. All that I did was pursuant to the rules of war."

Oxford rubbed his hands together. "Ah, but as General Desfourneaux in Guadeloupe is so fond of pointing out when we ask for the return of our sailors, the United States and France are not *at* war. You took ships that did not belong to you, you plundered them, and you murdered their crews. Ergo: you, sir, are a pirate."

"Non, non! C'est faux! Je ne suis pas un pirate!" Villon actually fell to his knees and clasped his hands. "I swear to heaven it is not so!"

"Get up, you damn fool," I hissed at him. "He's toying with you."

"Just translate what's said," said Oxford. He held up the watch. "This was found on his person. Mr. Graves, is it yours?"

"It . . . it looks similar to one I used to own, sir, yes."

"Come, sir! Mr. Wickett recognized it without difficulty. It's a Graham Jackson, I believe."

"I suppose it could be the same one, yes, sir."

He turned the watch over and read the inscription: "'R.T. to M.G., Christmas seventeen-ninety-nine.' That's—" he consulted another note "—that's 'Richard Towson to Matthew Graves,' ain't it?"

"Yes, sir. I guess it's mine."

"I don't understand your reluctance to claim it, Mr. Graves: it's a fine piece. You may have it again when these proceedings are closed, which will be quite soon unless I miss my guess. Now then, Captain Trimble's report was sparse as to details regarding your adventures as a captive. Pray tell us what transpired when you were in this man's infamous hands." Oxford really did talk like that, as many men do when they think they'll be in the papers and quoted in Congress. The clerk at my elbow redipped his pen and scribbled away, spattering himself and me with ink.

Villon's hands didn't look so infamous clasped in a pair of iron darbies, and the fine fingers were torn and bloody. But pity was a luxury that wasn't mine to give. In a few words I told of my capture, of Villon's kind treatment despite his threats, of our midnight escape.

"Do you mean to tell us you just took a boat and left?"

"Yes, sir."

"And with his full knowledge, gentlemen," said Billy. "I must stress that."

Oxford didn't bother to look at Billy. "And why, Mr. Graves, should he want you to leave?"

Villon shrugged when asked. "Because it is not my business to fight public ships."

"But you attacked the *Rattle-Snake,* sir," said Oxford, "an armed vessel of the United States Navy."

"I did not realize her status until the attack had already commenced, monsieurs, and for this I have received the reprimand. I am engaged as a raider of commerce, not a navy captain. Besides, I wished not to kill the boy, and I could hardly recruit any of the private seamen were he still around. So I let him go. He fooled me, this one: I did not know he would take the sailors with him."

Oxford turned to Billy. "As I recall, you indicated in your report that you saw the picaroons murder the crews of the ships they captured. Ain't that right, sir."

Billy glanced at Wickett, who locked eyes with him but said nothing. "The picaroons were observed murdering the merchant crews, yes sir," said Billy. "That is essentially correct."

"Don't quibble. Did you see 'em or not?"

"I was otherwise engaged at the time, sir."

Oxford blew air through his nose, annoyed. "But Mr. Wickett, you saw them?"

"Yes, sir."

"And you, Mr. Graves, you saw it too?"

"Yes, sir. But I don't guess it was Villon's idea, sir. He saved as many of us as he could."

"We are not interested in guesses, Mr. Graves. What about the *Jane*'s officers?"

"I didn't see them hanged, sir. They were already—they were already so when I came to."

"Came to?"

"Yes, sir. A gun had exploded and knocked me witless for a time. That was how I knew the *Jane* was missing one of her guns, y'see."

"Extraordinary. You will have to tell the whole story one of these days, Mr. Graves. *Someone* ought tell it, anyway," he muttered, and Billy and Wickett exchanged looks again. "But dammit, I'm ready to splice the mainbrace—I'm dry as a desert, begad. Now then, to business. Tell him what we've just said. You may shorten it to make it all a-taunto and watertight, if you wish. Oh, and tell him that we are sensible of his kind treatment of you and our sailors, and so on."

Villon bowed in his chains, obviously relieved.

"Which," Oxford continued, "in no wise mitigates his crimes: murdering captains Peavey and Spetters, stealing a valuable watch, et cetera, et cetera, et cetera. Sir, by ancient law it is my right and duty to find you guilty of murder and robbery on the high seas, which is piracy, and to hang you by the neck until you are dead. Gentlemen, we're adjourned."

Thirteen

A table had been set under an awning on *Choptank*'s ample quarter-deck. I had hoped Wickett or Billy would find an excuse to send me back to the *Breeze,* but Captain Oxford had invited me himself, with a pat on the shoulder and a whiff of the tobacco rotting between his teeth, and I had to stay whether anybody else liked it or not.

In my pocket was a letter that Villon had written to his wife, and it hung on me like a weight. He had asked me to come to him in the lieutenant's cabin that had been set aside for him, and such pallor and trembling you never saw. It annoyed me that he would fall so easily for Oxford's prank.

"Haut les coeurs! Cesse de faire l'enfant!" I said to him. "Raise the heart! Stop playing the child! Captain Oxford has condemned the others, too, but they are all to be held until this quasi-war is over. Oxford dare not hang you—think what an evil inspiration it would be to Desfourneaux in Guadeloupe, where our own captured officers are held."

"Mais oui, mon cher petit ami," he said. "But tell me, what is that noise the sailors are making upstairs?"

"They joke about the noose they have run up to the yardarm. Seamen have a crude sense of humor. Pay it no mind."

He went ashy, and grasped my arm with amazing strength. "Quick! The door stands open behind you! The sentry has absented himself from the passage!"

"Calm yourself, sir," I said, pulling his hand off me a finger at a time. "It amuses the captain to frighten you with a macabre joke. You did the same to me, if you'll recall."

"*Pour rire?* But yes, a joke!" he gasped. "See how I enjoy it, ha ha! But listen . . ." He clutched at me again, getting my number-one uniform coat all grubby. "If you would be so good as perhaps to close the eyes, I could swim for it."

"Here—let me go." It irritated me when he said "close the eyes." *Connive* sounds downright elegant in French, but was I to help him abscond it'd get me dismissed the service, if not disrated and flogged round the squadron and round the squadron again, till five hundred lashes had removed the flesh from my back entirely. It was Oxford's purpose to terrify Villon—I was pretty near sure of it—and he'd succeeded far more than even he might've expected. Poor Villon had fallen apart.

I removed his hands from my coat, resisting the impulse to knock him down and run away.

"I couldn't just close my eyes," I said, making a pretense of surprise. "I'd have to go with you, and then where would I be?"

"But I helped *you* escape," he said.

"Yes, at no cost to yourself. And my life was in danger whereas yours is not, I tell you. Oxford is playing a cruel jest. How many times must I tell you? Besides, we're miles from shore. With those handcuffs on, you'd sink like a stone."

"But a boat, even perhaps just a little skiff—"

"Speaking of boats," I snapped, "I went to plenty of trouble to bring the captain's gig back when you stole it, sir, and it was aswim with innocent blood. Has the gentleman forgotten that?"

He fell into a chair and put his chained hands to his face. "No, I do not forget."

His little gesture struck me in the guts like a cold blade. He was sinking in a sea of despair, and I had to do something to pull him out before he dragged me in.

"Tell me something, monsieur," I said, chiding him. "What did that old rover Prêteur say when he found I had made off with all the men, *hein?* Some pretty choice words, I expect, ha ha!"

He dropped his hands to his lap. "That was a cruel ruse you yourself played, monsieur, at l'Île de la Gonâve. When you set the *Jane* adrift, the gunners on shore thought someone was stealing her. They fired several rounds before they could be stopped. Poor Prêteur!"

Villon had cut deep into the emptiness inside me, and now he was turning the blade. All I could do was stand there and let it hurt. I owed him that.

Not wanting to know, I asked: "But what happened?"

"Did you not hear his screams? His legs were shot off." He shrugged, making his chains clank. "*Lá,* these things happen in war." He laughed bitterly. "But I forget, we are not at war."

"But monsieur . . ." I could have touched him, made some comforting gesture. But I didn't. "I am sorry about Prêteur. I liked him."

He shrugged again. "He still breathes, last I see him. Maybe now he will finally return to France. With his money he will live like a lord. Or the way they used to, before this . . . this stupid war with England. And you, you *lourdauds,* you clodhoppers, how could you do this to *la belle France?*"

Gently, I quoted him: "*Nous avons discuté tout ce temps en pure perte, hein?*"

"Yes, we have argued all this time to no purpose." He looked up then, managing a smile. "Ah, you remember our amusing conversation, *mon cher petit ami.* I am glad."

I assumed a bantering tone: "Now, as for you, monsieur, you'll be staying at some rich man's town house in Philadelphia until Talleyrand agrees to see our ministers, which will happen soon enough at the rate we're taking your frigates." I forced a smile. "If you wish to blame someone for our being in this war, blame Talleyrand, him with his demands for huge bribes. I had no idea there was so much money in the world, outside of Ali-Baba's cave."

"Open sesame!" he said, holding up his hands and jingling his manacles. His smile viciously twisted the scarred side of his face. "But alas, they hold fast. Perhaps the magic words do not work on iron chains, *hein?* And you tell *me* not to play the child."

Desperate to distract him, I pointed to the desk where he'd been working with pen and paper. "Maybe you could dash Talleyrand off a line or two while you wait."

He shrugged. "Yes, Monsieur Graves, no doubt he will heed the words of a man of my importance. Certainly, I shall get on it immediately."

"And while you await the favor of his reply, you will take your ease in the capital. Philadelphia is often compared to Paris, you know. It is the finest city in all of North America. No harm will come to you. The hand on the conscience," I said, which is French for *cross my heart and hope to die.*

He gripped my hand in both of his and then let it go. "I am greatly comforted by our little talk, monsieur," he said, standing up to see me out. "How kind it was of you to call! All the same . . ." Turning to the desk, he folded the piece of paper he'd been working on, dribbled candlewax on it and pressed his ring into the wax. "If ever you have occasion to be in Jacmel on the southern coast of Saint-Domingue, perhaps you would be so kind as to deliver this note. A lady lives there who would know of my fate."

Now every time I closed my eyes, I saw his feet dancing in the empty air.

It helped to think of Spetters and Peavey, as I lifted my fork and opened my mouth and chewed and swallowed, and as I was always hungry I did myself credit. Certainly Oxford and Brownstone showed no loss of appetite: "'You're going to take a stroll up Ladder Lane and down Hawser Street,' I told him, by gad!" said Oxford; "Ha ha, sir," said Brownstone around his pudding. For his part, Wickett emptied his plate through the various removes with his usual efficient indifference, while Billy merely mangled his food and concentrated instead on drinking.

With a bellyful of food, a noseful of wine, and a job well done behind him, Oxford grew expansive. "Hughes," he said, referring to the earlier governor of Guadeloupe. "When I said General Desfourneaux,

I almost said Governor Hughes. Brownstone here tipped me the high sign. I was on top of it, of course, but I admit I almost blundered. Hughes . . . that's a hell of a name for a Johnny Crappo, eh? I wonder where he got it. I say, where do you suppose he got it, Mr. Wickett?"

"I suppose he got it from his father, sir."

"Eh? Ha ha, yes—from his father! But, say . . . I've only been on station a month and haven't had a chance to take in the local color." Forgetting the fork in his hand, he reached over and thumped Lieutenant Cowper on the chest. "Local color, ha ha!"

"Yes, sir: ha ha," agreed Cowper, dabbing at the gravy spatters on his vest.

"Ha ha!" said Billy.

Oxford gazed at me with an unwholesome leer. "And how are they, young fellow?"

"How are what, sir?"

He laughed again, and Brownstone grinned. "Why, the wenches, man! How are the ladies of a certain reputation?"

"Oh! Quite nice, I've heard, sir."

"Look at the fellow blush! 'Quite nice,' he says, and 'so he's heard.' Ah, beardless youth. Well, any port in a storm, I always say, and twice in fair weather. Course, it don't do in the light of day—the enthusiasm of the she-nigger is matched only by the ardor of the buck, I'm told, but it don't do to look at her face. Which reminds me, Brownstone tells an interesting story about how niggers got to be so damn ugly. Eh, Tommy?"

"Yes," said Brownstone, swirling the wine around in his glass and allowing a mischievous sneer to curl his handsome lips. "Seems that when Satan saw God had made Adam, he decided to do him one better and make himself a man, too. But God discovered what he was about and turned the man black, so no one would confuse the devil's work with His own. Well sir, Satan got so vexed that he knocked his brute down. Hit him so hard that it spread his nose and lips all over his face. That's what the niggers say, anyway. God's truth."

I'd read that story in Moreau's *Description topographique*. I'd also read there that some blacks believed God had made them first and that whites were imperfect creatures whose color had faded.

Lieutenant Halliwell, second of the *Choptank,* glanced uncomfortably at the Negro stewards as they took away the pudding and set out nuts and cheese and Madeira. Although the Secretary of the Navy had directed his officers not to enlist black sailors, high wages in the merchant service meant that the directive was commonly ignored. Even *Choptank* had some black foremast hands, though they were all slaves whose wages went straight into the officers' pockets.

"Captain Trimble," said Halliwell, "you haven't described your battle for us."

Billy rolled his eyes toward Wickett, who smiled politely back at him. "Yes, do edify us with your valuable insights, sir," said Wickett. To the table at large he said, "Captain Trimble tells the battle astonishingly well, gentlemen. Each time he tells it, the story is as fresh as if newly made—I could scarce believe it, had I not seen it with mine own eyes."

"Hear, hear!"

"Tough luck, losing half the convoy."

"For shame, Cowper—he *saved* half the convoy."

"Let him tell it, let him tell it," said Oxford, raising his voice to be heard. He whittled himself a chaw of tobacco and stuffed it into his cheek. "You may fire when ready, sir: we are all ears."

Billy had been glaring at Wickett, but he could hardly refuse a chance to toot his own horn without arousing astonishment and suspicion. "Well," he began. He took a pull at his wine, which went down the wrong way. After Brownstone had pounded him on the back and another cautious gulp had soothed his throat, he regrouped and sallied forth. "Well, as you know, gentlemen, we were becalmed not too far from here—about three leagues sou'-sou'west, I'd say. Ain't that so, Mr. Wickett?"

"Near enough as makes no difference, sir. Pray continue."

"Yes. Well. Knowing what a difference surprise can make, I . . . er, we kept our gunports sealed, so the pirates would think we were just another merchantman. Erm . . ."

Here Wickett made like he was pulling an oar.

"Yes, that's right," said Billy. "Under sweeps, we took station in the middle of the convoy, so." Warming to his task, he placed the wine in the center of a squadron of loose nuts and scattered a dozen bits of cheese to one side to represent the French. "Twelve longboats, filled with desperate characters—fifty or sixty to a boat, we guessed. Ain't that so, Mr. Wickett?"

"Not above seventy, sure."

It was twenty-five or thirty to a boat, as I recalled, but no sense in ruining a good story with the facts.

"Say, five or six hundred bloodthirsty mulattos, all told, with red flags at the peak." Billy moved the nuts and cheese and wine around. "When the people saw the red flags, did they blanch? They did not! Said turn-and-turn-about was fair play, and they'd allow no quarter, either. Shouted it out, so they did. You could hear 'em from . . . well, from every part of the *Rattle-Snake*, I imagine. The pirates rushed us from all sides, but we gave 'em a taste of grape and they hauled out of gunshot to think about it a while. *Augustin von Steuben* had drifted out of our range . . ."

At length he got through a creditable telling of that bloody afternoon, helped along by hints from Wickett, hesitant at first to claim credit but warmly embracing it by the time the *Jane* and I were disappearing beyond the distant tip of La Gonâve. "Twice more they set upon us that afternoon, gentlemen, even gaining a foothold upon our very decks. But as my presence here today bears witness—" and here he shot Wickett a triumphant look "—I prevailed."

Oxford and the others applauded when he had finished. "But why," asked Oxford, "did you put so little of this in your report?"

"Eh . . . my report?"

"Captain Trimble is so very modest at times, gentlemen," said Wickett, "that one might think him shy."

"What?" cried Oxford. "Surely not shy!"

"Perhaps *shy* is not the word I mean, sir," said Wickett. "I cannot abide a shy man." He gave Billy a sideways glance. "But *retiring* seems not quite the right word either."

Oxford had mentioned "rumors" earlier. He was like to bust his belly with questions, and although he couldn't very well ask a direct one at his own table without being unpardonably rude, post-captain or no, he did need to be assuaged. Here's a nice problem for Billy and Wickett, thinks I: for Billy because he could be charged with coward-ice, and for Wickett because he could be charged with mutiny. And so could I, I remembered with sudden dread.

Billy muttered, "An internal matter, sir."

"Captain Trimble is the soul of tact," said Wickett, when the others had all turned their eyes to him. "In point of fact, one of our officers did not perform as expected." He cracked a nut and ate it.

"A shirker! That would explain it," said Brownstone. "Not to pry into the sordid details, of course, but how d'ye deal with someone like that?"

"Andy Sterrett in the *Constellation* ran a fellow through with his sword during the fight with the *L'Insurgent*," offered Cowper.

"Don't be an ass," said Brownstone in horror. "One can't very well go around running officers through with a sword, you know—it was a common jack that Andy stuck. The coward tried to leave his post," he said, picking up the thread of Cowper's thought. "The commodore omitted it from his report, naturally." Mutters of "certainly," "indeed" and "aye" coursed around the table. "But Andy bruited it about back home, and now they'll never get it back in the bag."

"Sterrett will never make captain if he does not learn discretion," said Wickett.

Oxford shot tobacco juice toward the spitkid. "You talk like a po-litico, Mr. Wickett."

"Nay, sir, say not so. I merely wished to observe that a good officer knows when to keep his mouth shut, not for his own good but for the good of the service—and knows when to open it again, as well."

"Oh, nicely turned," snickered Brownstone, but he professed

only earnest admiration for a *bon mot* when Wickett turned his gaze upon him.

Oxford and the lieutenants had forgotten me entirely. I and Smiley, the only other midshipman at the table, were eating as much as we could and saying as little as possible, which was everything that duty and custom demanded of us.

Oxford had steered the conversation back to safer waters, pontificating on which was a better antiscorbutic, sauerkraut or lemon juice, and supposing it was the former, how best to get the people to eat it. "First of all," he was saying, "open 'er as far to loo'ard as ye can and give 'er plenty of air, so the reek don't put the people off their feed," but everyone knew that. Billy said he'd heard Surgeon Quilty say that citrus fruits were the recommended treatment now for scurvy: the Royal Navy had been putting lemon juice in the men's grog for years now. Brownstone pointed out that while lemon juice certainly was a valuable remedy, limes and oranges seemed wanting in that regard.

"Yes, in the amounts the juice is given," Wickett said. "Perhaps if the people were given more than a spoonful. An ounce or two, say."

"Oh, come, sir," said Cowper. "Where are we to get it in such quantities?"

"Where indeed," said Wickett. "The Caribbean, perhaps? But according to Captain Cook's journals, any fresh food will do, even seal meat, so long as it is not cooked overmuch. And fruits are particularly advised."

"What, raw fruits? That's begging for cholera. No, the people would never submit to it."

"Boil 'em, then," said Brownstone.

"What, the men? Ha ha!"

"*The men?* Ha ha, Cowper," said Brownstone, "you are a rare one."

But the conversation broke off there, which I thought was just as well for Cowper and Brownstone: a dangerous gleam was building in Wickett's eye. A hail had come from the masthead and all eyes except Oxford's flicked aloft, as if they could see through the sailcloth awning, and immediately back to Oxford, who had unexpectedly switched over to steam engines and why they would never provide a practical means of propulsion. The officer of the watch came over and muttered in his ear, quite as if we hadn't already heard the lookout shouting out that a cutter was bearing down on us from the northeast.

"*Hermes,* no doubt. Our mail cutter," said Oxford. He frowned down at us at the far end of the table and said, "Mr. Smiley, why don't you take Mr. Graves, there, and show him around the ship?"

"Is she really called *Hermes?*" I asked when we had settled ourselves in the mizzentop, out of sight of the officers beneath the awning and with a fine view of the approaching cutter. Her starboard side was a startling yellow in the lowering sun, and her shadowed larboard side so nearly matched the silver-blue sea behind her as to make that side of her nearly invisible. "*Hermes* is coming it pretty high for a cutter, ain't it?"

"She's *Harold,* actually, H-A-R-O-L-D, but we call her *Hermes* on account of she's a *herald* of the gods—"

"Oof!"

"—God being Commodore Gaswell, in our case."

Scratching and farting in contented sloth, we watched a midshipman with a dispatch bag under his arm judge his moment, leap from the cutter's rail to the frigate's side, lift his hat to the quarterdeck and disappear under the awning. Other men were busying themselves with fend-offs or hoisting up net bags of mail and groceries.

Smiley entertained me by pointing out peculiarities in the frigate's spars and rigging, none of them inordinately peculiar that I could see except that in light airs *Choptank* wore a ringtail sail on her taffrail flagpole "just like the *Constitution,* and her a big ol' forty-four!" He opened his green eyes wide when he said it, to show that I should be impressed, and I yawned, to show that I wasn't.

Scarcely five minutes had passed after the midshipman disappeared under the awning before Billy and Wickett stepped out from under it. Wickett had his hands clasped behind his back and carried himself with a grimly satisfied air. Billy was red-faced and tottering, and clutched a letter to his breast.

The scuttlebutt in the *Breeze* was that Commodore Truxtun had summoned us to join the Leeward Island squadron at last, where we might expect some easy prizes of two or three guns and half a dozen men instead of barges full of raggedy-arsed picaroons armed to the teeth and with nary a sou in their pockets. A competing faction claimed that Commodore Gaswell desired us to visit him at his base in Le Cap François so he could buy the *Breeze* into the service and fill their hats with gold and silver. I told the jacks who asked that they'd find out when we got there, by which they reckoned I didn't know, either. The gold-and-silver men lorded it over the others when we set a northward course with the *Rattle-Snake* toward the Windward Passage, but the others took the ribbing with good grace. Either outcome was pleasant to think about.

We slogged eastward past the southern coast of Tortuga all one night, following the same route that Columbus had sailed some three centuries ago, a few days before his sailing master had fallen asleep on a pleasant evening just like this one and torn the bottom out of the *Santa Maria*. The stars and planets drifted westward, fireflies winked in the trees on shore, and a late light in Port-de-Paix to starboard marked our progress. The angle of the wind was such that we made good our course without touching a rope, but the contrary current took some of the benefit out of it. By dawn the promontory that marked Port-de-Paix was still in view astern.

After we had stood down from quarters and Wickett in his nightshirt had gone back below, I stood at the rail in the golden morning, slurping a mug of heavily sweetened black coffee and gazing at the hills of Tortuga rising from the waves to larboard. I was as fascinated by pirates as anyone who's ever read Defoe—and by "pirates" I mean buccaneers and filibusters, not your low picaroons—and I eagerly took in the stone tower and the road leading across the ridge to the old governor's mansion beyond, and here, closer in but not uncomfortably so, the long line on the water that warned of the reef that guarded Cayone Roadstead, the island's single harbor. It wasn't a good harbor and honest seamen had abandoned it long ago, but shady rovers had found it convenient for many years, and no doubt used it yet.

After a while I moved over to the starboard rail, out of the way of the men scrubbing the deck with sand and holystones. There was little enough to see on that side—nothing but a desolate waste of pesty mangroves and a pink monotony of flamingos, and dense dark pine forests climbing the jagged peaks on and on into the clouds—so, after a glance aloft to make sure the lookout was attending to his duty, I set my empty mug on the binnacle and took the spyglass out of its beckets.

Half a mile ahead, *Rattle-Snake* braced her topsails around as she passed out of the island's lee and caught the northeast trade wind. A mile beyond her, *Harold,* not obliged to stay with us because she carried dispatches, had already cleared Point Mason and was scooting toward the horizon.

The mandarin-orange disk of the rising sun colored the water like burnished copper, and I had to wipe my eye before raising the telescope again. I heard the sounds of Wickett dressing below as a man stepped to the belfry and struck three double strokes. Fifteen minutes later little Freddy Billings, the crumb-bosun, with his blond curls all smushed down on one side of his head, popped out of the forward hatch, wandered sleepily across the deck carrying a tray on which stood a coffee pot, a mug and a covered dish, and disappeared down the after hatch. After Wickett had breakfasted, I knew by now, he would step on deck precisely at eight bells.

The men hosed the sand into the scuppers with jets from the pump, squilgeed the puddles of water into the scuppers, and began beating the deck dry with swabs. How Wickett could maintain his good humor each morning despite the din it must have caused in his cuddy, with the deck timbers only inches above his head, I couldn't fathom, though I guessed if I had my own command I could tolerate a great many nuisances.

Wickett had confided that, according to the letter he'd received in the *Choptank,* Truxtun had fobbed the *Rattle-Snake* off on his enemy

Gaswell, who was summoning Billy merely to send him home. And, one man's bad luck being another man's fortune, Wickett obviously expected that the schooner would soon be his own. I was of mixed emotions about it. Wickett deserved the command, I thought—he had the necessary seniority, experience, and willingness to fight—and sending Billy quietly home would be doing him a kindness, but as his cousin I expected I'd be encouraged to leave the service as well.

I guessed I mightn't come out of the scandal too badly, all in all. Phillip would probably take me into Graves & Son in some capacity— but he would never add that *s* to *Son,* and by Jasper it would be dull. If I knew my half-brother at all, he would expect me to work for little more than room and board as a way of helping out the family, but it wouldn't occur to him that family obligation might work both ways. My head began to throb. I chewed some willow bark and climbed to the crosstrees in search of cool air.

The lookout made room for me, and I sat watching *Rattle-Snake* and *Harold.* The cutter's breeze held strong and steady, and she was increasing the distance between them.

"*Rattle-Snake*'s signaling, sir."

"Yes." Even before I looked I knew what Billy had to say, and a glance confirmed it: our number followed by *Keep closer station.* We already carried all the sail the angle of the wind and our present course would allow. I looked at the hoist again and noticed that one of the flags had gotten entangled with itself. "Deck there," I called, "any one of you, hoist *Signal not understood.* Do you know the number?"

The seaman who had been nearest or fastest was bending the familiar response onto the signal halyard. "Oh, aye, sir." In an undertone to his mates he added, "Who don't by now?" and someone stifled a laugh.

"*Harold*'s coming about, sir," said the lookout.

Her main course disappeared and reappeared as her boom swung over and she ran for *Rattle-Snake,* signaling as she came, but I couldn't make out the flags against the sun. New bunting under our number rose to *Rattle-Snake*'s peak.

"Deck there," I called. "My respects to the captain, and *Rattle-Snake* reports that *Harold* is signaling *Warship in sight.*"

Harold continued on her new course, signaling again, and again the sun obscured the signal. I looked at *Rattle-Snake,* but she was asking *Harold* for a bearing.

"If you please, sir," piped Freddy from the deck, "Cap'n says his compliments and call him should you do see anything yourself, on account of he ain't et his breakfast yet."

"Very well."

I thought I could see a white speck on the horizon beyond *Harold.* It might be a sail, or a cloud; there would be plenty of time to tell which. I guessed Wickett must think I was pretty foolish to bleat at the first rumor of an enemy, and only possibly an enemy at that. He knew better and I resolved to follow his lead: *Harold* and *Rattle-Snake* would tell us the news as soon as they knew it. Seven bells came and went, and all that I had gotten from my time aloft was a sore arse.

Rather than shorten sail, Cousin Billy spilled his wind from time to time, allowing us to close up the gap. *Breeze* rocked in the rollers as the wind faded and our way left us, then the first few puffs of the trade wind whispered against my cheek. "Hands to the braces," I called down. "Lively now!" Soon we were swooping along on a bowline in a manner that pleased me like thunder, because of the way the people had jumped to their stations, trimming the sails with a minimum of fuss and no further orders from me.

The speck on the horizon had become two white specks close together, with possibly a smaller one behind them. *Rattle-Snake* had sent up *Keep closer station* again, which I acknowledged but otherwise ignored—what did Billy expect us to do, fly?

Definitely there were several white specks now: two stacks of rectangles, a suggestion of triangles afore, and a trapezoid abaft: the sails of a square-rigged ship. She was under all plain sail and royals, which almost certainly meant a man-of-war, but there was something odd about her rig.

"She ain't French," I said to the lookout.

"No, sir, that she ain't. She's got no rake on her a-tall, just about."

"She could be Spanish."

"Well," he began in that deferential tone that seamen use with idiots and midshipmen. "Sure and it's possible, sir."

I had no idea how many men-of-war Spain had that far north of the Main. The Havana in Cuba and Saint John's in Porto Rico were too well fortified to need much naval presence. Spain still occupied the eastern two-thirds of Hispaniola, but it was only a matter of time before Toussaint invaded. He needed to seize every port in the island, was he to keep the French from landing an army.

I shifted my glass. Still no new signal from Billy. I resumed my examination of the distant ship. She was hull up now, and I could see a single row of gunports, and perhaps a raised quarterdeck. Yes, definitely a raised quarterdeck, giving her an elegant but archaic look. She even had a poopdeck, all ablaze with gold leaf.

"She's a frigate, sir," said the lookout.

"So I see."

I cogitated. It was months too early for the treasure *flota* from Vera Cruz and the Havana, so there was no reason for any Spanish vessel larger than a *guarda costa* lugger to be lurking about this section of the coast. And even then she'd be off station—by Spanish law, the *flota* always entered the Atlantic via the Gulf of Florida. Yet there she was, and not trim enough to be French, not flash enough to be British, not sturdy enough to be American, too graceful to be Danish or Dutch or Swedish. Besides, even from seven miles away and despite her golden poop, she looked shabby.

I was half-conscious of eight bells being struck and of the hands jabbering as they went to their breakfast.

"Was it something, Mr. Graves?"

On the quarterdeck, with a cup of coffee in one hand and a piece of hardtack with jam on it in the other, and Gypsy the cat twining about his feet, Wickett stood looking up at me. When I told him (with a surprised glance from the lookout) that a Spanish frigate was bearing down from the northeast, he asked at what distance she lay. "Very good," he said then, and leaned against the rail, munching his biscuit and sipping his coffee. Then he licked the crumbs and stickiness from his fingers, set his mug on the binnacle next to mine and told the boy to "clear that junk away" before commencing a leisurely ascent of the rigging.

I didn't know if his composure was assumed, but I found it as soothing as the seamen obviously did. In the crosstrees, the lookout and I having removed ourselves to the topsail yard, Wickett studied *Rattle-Snake* and *Harold,* and then turned his glass to the horizon beyond the cutter.

"You have better eyes than I, Mr. Graves," he said with faint sarcasm, "to be able to tell her nationality at such a range."

"I believe she's carrying a crucifix in her maintop, sir."

"By jingo, so she is. She certainly looks like a Don, too, with that gaudy poop, and *Harold* does not seem too worried about her. Probably bound for Port-de-Paix. Hello—she's bending on some bunting there. Not much activity on deck . . . gunports still closed . . . but let's beat to quarters anyway, shall we?"

Harold had come about again, and we three were sailing in a miniature line of battle toward the approaching frigate by the time she finally hoisted her colors. The red and yellow of Spain broke out at her peak and then from every mast, including the archaic spritsail topmast on her bowsprit, with Jesus staring sadly down at his flock from his perch in the maintop. She was unlikely to have any active hostility in mind: despite their uneasy alliance with France, the Dons had no overt quarrel with us and preferred to pretend we didn't exist.

"I shouldn't cross his hawse if I were you, Mr. What's-Your-Name," said Wickett, staring at *Harold* through his glass. "I'd ruin your paintwork with an iron ball, so I would. Ah, he goes about."

Harold came smoothly around on the starboard tack, angling to pass the frigate astern so as not to provoke her, but Billy stayed his course— from obstinacy, maybe, or perhaps to prove his nerve—but at any rate it was a close thing whether the frigate would cross *Rattle-Snake*'s bows or the other way around. Of course the Spanish captain had no intention of yielding to a little thing like the *Rattle-Snake*—and indeed he was showing great restraint by not sending a ball into her—but Billy was gaining, and for a few minutes it seemed he would just shave the frigate's bows.

And then it was obvious he could not. With the frigate's sails momentarily masking the wind it would have been easy enough for Billy to come about on the starboard tack, with no chance of missing stays and just avoiding a collision. But he wore instead of tacking, and his momentum as he came about fetched him up broadside against the frigate. There was a great screeching and scraping as the frigate shouldered *Rattle-Snake* aside; and then, instead of veering to get clear of the frigate and gain time to recover, Billy compounded his error by continuing to wear.

"Fuck!" cried a hand, "he's coming right at us!"

"Ready about!" shouted Wickett, and I was already bawling, "Ease your jib sheet! You men, to the braces there!"

"Put down your helm," said Wickett. Then, "Helm's alee!"

Breeze was coming up into the wind—so neatly, so nearly so. "Tops'l haul!" I said as the square topsail came aback, pushing our head over, and we almost made it.

But then the *Rattle-Snake*'s bowsprit hooked our starboard shrouds and dragged us to a halt. The mainsail boom swung across the deck, we ducked, and the sail pierced itself on the schooner's bowsprit, while the frigate continued on her stately way, her officers shaking their fists and shouting—about ruined paint, probably—and her sailors all hooting like baboons and pointing at their arses. And as we bobbed in her wake and while the shouting faded into the distance, there was among us a long, shocked silence.

"Mr. Wickett," came Billy's voice at last, "I trust you have a good explanation for this."

Fourteen

We didn't rig for church on Sunday morning. Instead, Wickett read aloud from "An Act for the Better Government of the Navy of the United States," a supplement to the *Marine Rules and Regulations* of 1798. We'd received a copy of the new pamphlet from Captain Oxford, all commanders being duty-bound to read it aloud at least once a month so no man could claim ignorance of what it said.

After reading through the several articles dealing with desertion, mutiny, murder, sleeping on watch, theft, quarreling, sodomy and other mischiefs that men are prone to get into when packed together for months at a time, he came to a trio of passages that caused the Breezes to pass meaningful looks among themselves:

> *Every commander* [he read] *or other officer who, upon signal for battle or on the probability of an engagement, shall not use his utmost exertions to bring his ship to battle or shall fail to encourage, in his own person, his inferior officers and men to fight courageously, such offender shall suffer death . . .*
>
> *If any person in the navy shall treacherously yield or pusillanimously cry for quarters, he shall suffer death . . .*
>
> *Every officer who shall, through cowardice, negligence, or disaffection, in time of action withdraw from or keep out of battle, or shall not do his utmost to take or destroy every vessel which it is his duty to encounter, or shall not do his utmost endeavor to afford relief to ships belonging to the United States, every such offender shall, on conviction thereof by a general court martial, suffer death . . .*

Each of the three articles ended with "or such other punishment as the court shall adjudge," but the implication was clear. Billy might be lucky to sneak away in disgrace.

The Breezes passed the afternoon glaring at the *Rattle-Snake* and muttering about "that bunch o' lubbers"—most of them quite forgetting that, to the Navy Board at least, they were as much Rattle-Snakes as those presumably equally unhappy men in the schooner. I was too ashamed to discourage them, and calculated they'd defy me if I tried, anyway, which would end unhappily for everyone. Wickett sent the main course aloft again as soon as we could stitch it shut, its raw, cross-shaped patch standing out like an accusatory scar on the weather-stained canvas.

Feelings ran high in the *Rattle-Snake* as well. Her people's shame found expression in the shoddy way they repaired the damage to her bowsprit and in the way they handled her, letting the sails flap like Mother Hubbard's laundry and leaving a wake that would break a snake's back.

There was no chance of presenting a united front to Gaswell's squadron, even if anyone had wanted to. After we had refused her offers of assistance, the *Harold* cutter had raced ahead to Le Cap François. Word of the bungled and unnecessary encounter with the Spanish frigate would soon be common knowledge there.

It was an angry lot that entered the harbor at Le Cap on Monday morning.

Commodore Gaswell's *Columbia* frigate was already flying our numbers and *Captains repair aboard flag* by the time the local pilots had guided the *Breeze* and the *Rattle-Snake* through the harbor's northern entrance. Once we'd picked up our moorings, Wickett left me in charge of the deck and had himself rowed over to the flagship. There, a curious pantomime occurred.

Billy arrived at the *Columbia* just after Wickett did. Wickett had his boat's crew back water so Billy might go aboard first, but Billy took his sweet time about it. Apparently somebody said something, for Billy suddenly shouted at Wickett and threw his hat at him. Wickett stood up and drew his sword, Billy recoiled—and Wickett calmly plucked Billy's hat out of the water with the tip of his sword and held it out to him with a bow.

Pausing in his stroll along the deck, Elwiss, our acting bosun, laughed: "Old Shaky's on a pisser this morning—not half he ain't!"

I clasped my hands behind my back and regarded him loftily—which wasn't easy, as he was several years older and a head taller than I—and said, "Trimble, tremble . . . 'Old Shaky.' That's wit, Mr. Elwiss! Did it come to you sudden, or did you lie awake all night thinking it out?"

His Adam's apple bobbed gratifyingly. "Beg pardon, Mr. Graves," he said, ducking his head. "I forgot you're kin to him."

And well he might forget it. I wished I could.

Wickett returned at half a glass after two bells in the forenoon watch and invited me to take a late breakfast with him. "Well, Mr. Graves," he said, rubbing his bony hands together over his lobscouse, which is salt junk hashed with potatoes, onions and pounded biscuit, "it's all set. Your cousin will leave for Philadelphia as a passenger in the *Harold* in a few days. I'm to have the *Rattle-Snake*—pending confirmation from the Secretary, but I'll be her custodian in the meantime. I asked Commodore Gaswell if we could keep the *Breeze* as our tender. He said no, as you might expect—she has to be condemned in an American port first, and of course the men expect their share of the prize money, cash on the barrelhead. But he said he would consider buying her into the service. I managed to insinuate the idea into his head that he could do worse than to have you for her skipper, young and foolish though you are, and instead of getting his back up he said he would think on it. He said he 'wouldn't hold it against that fine young fellow,' 'it' being your cousin's remarkable behavior during the fight with the picaroons.

"Oh, yes," he said as I gaped at him, "scuttlebutt is a remarkable means of communication. The truth of the matter, with a few personal aggrandizements according to who is doing the telling, is all over the squadron. Probably known in every one of our ships in the Caribbean by now, and it will provide wardrooms with gossip for months to come, I am sure." He tossed a crumb of salt pork to Gypsy, who sniffed it and then decided it was edible.

"At any rate, where was I? Oh yes: 'That fine young fellow,' said he—his very words. You are gaining a sweet reputation! Truxtun gave us all up without a word in our favor, it seems, but all's well that ends well, as the Bard says." He ended the flood of words as suddenly as they had begun by shoveling a great forkful of hash into his mouth.

"Yes, sir," I said. I was pleased for him, for I believed he deserved command of the schooner, and that Billy had fallen into a stew of his own making—but I couldn't help feeling that even though Billy was determined to drown himself, I was somehow helping to hold his head under. But before I could say it, or rather decide whether I should worry about it, there was a knock on the hatch, which had been hooked open to allow for some air, and in the low doorway crouched a midshipman who carried himself with a subtle smugness that made me want to spill something on his snowy britches.

"Beg pardon, gentlemen," he said, holding out a note to me. "You are Mr. Graves? I'm here to collect you."

"No, no," cried the coxswain as we approached the *Columbia*, and the officers and sideboys turned away—as they would have anyway, as we were heading around to the larboard side.

"You'll admire," said the smug midshipman, as we rounded the bow, "the Amazon figurehead with her gilded sword and red, white and blue shield." Like her sisters the *United States* and the *Constitution*, the *Columbia* was rated as a forty-four and was considered a frigate, but she was nearly the size of a seventy-four, with spars and scantlings to match. "She's forty-three feet, six inches in the beam," he said, which wasn't much narrower than the *Breeze* was long, "and a hundred and seventy-five feet from stem to stern; and she displaces some fifteen hundred tons. What's *Breeze* displace?"

"About seventy-five tons," I said glumly. Gaswell could just about have had the sloop whipped aboard and stowed on his spar deck, if he'd wanted. Despite her rating, the *Columbia* actually carried thirty 24-pounders and twenty-two 12-pounders, which meant that a single gun from her main battery could throw half again as much metal as our entire broadside, and farther, too. On the other hand, she required more than fourteen feet of water to swim in, while *Breeze* drew less than a fathom. None of which is of any particular moment, except to say that even in my best uniform, and with my journals and certificates under my arm, I felt like a bug as I clambered up her side.

My first impression as I stepped onto her deck was of an almost painful brightness, even in the shade of the canvas awnings. Her decks were sanded to a soft snowiness, of course, and her bulwarks and masts gleamed with fresh white paint, with nary a finger mark or footprint to be seen. Some acknowledgement that she was crewed by human beings could be seen in the pinrails, which were painted a dark yellow—which they'd soon be discolored anyway, what with constant contact with tarred ropes and tar-stained hands. But the enlisted men all wore immaculate slops of white duck, and the officers on the quarterdeck looked like they wouldn't dare to sweat in their white britches and tropical-weight blue wool coats.

I raised my hat to the quarterdeck and to the officer of the deck, an amiable-looking sailing master, who glanced at my letter.

"Carry on, Mr. Bowman," said he to the smug midshipman, handing the letter back and giving me a look that I couldn't decipher.

"This way," said Bowman. He led me down a white-painted corridor, where he knocked on a black jalousie door with an eagle and fifteen stars painted on it. There'd been sixteen states since Tennessee joined the Union in '96, but with Ohio agitating for admission it had become apparent that adding a star and a stripe for each new state would make Old Glory look as tawdry as a whorehouse bedsheet in time. I guess flags with sixteen stars and stripes may have flown over Tennessee, but nowhere else that I ever heard of.

"Come in," said a gruff voice in response to Bowman's knock, but it was only the commodore's clerk in a sort of partition that was bigger than *Rattle-Snake*'s great cabin. "No, sir, he's very busy," he said without looking up. But when I stuck my magic letter under his nose he said, "Oh. Yes. One moment," and stepped through a door behind his desk. After another moment he popped out again, saying, "Come along, come along! Don't keep the commodore waiting," and snapped his fingers to show that I was being contrary and foolish and wicked all at once.

But the commodore weren't behind that door, neither. Instead there was a lieutenant who was even more gorgeous than the officers I'd seen on deck. He twitched my neck-cloth straight, plucked a piece of lint from my shoulder and then pulled my ears, apparently to see if I'd washed behind them.

"Have you all your books and papers, Mr. Graves?" he asked. "Testimonials from previous commanders? Leave them here on this desk." I could have told him that Captain Malloy wasn't likely to give me a kind reference, and that Mr. Trimble wasn't very likely too, neither, not now, but he wasn't listening to me anyway. "Step along," he said, knocking on the door behind his desk. When a roar came in answer, he opened the door, announced me and said, "In-you-go-then-best-of-luck," shoved me through like the lion's breakfast and closed the door behind me.

And here everything changed. Here the pretense fell away, as if I'd been allowed backstage at a play. Cyrus Gaswell was an old warhorse as well as an old sea dog. His sloop during the Revolution had been attached to the Continental Army rather than the Continental Navy, which was the crux of Truxtun's complaints about being placed below him on the captains list, and he'd even fought at Yorktown with my father. And he was nothing like his officers, or rather looked nothing like them. He was barefoot, for one thing, and wearing a well-worn pair of nankeen trousers and an old checked shirt, with the tails comfortably out over his paunch. Silver stubble glinted on his cheeks and chin in the sunlight that came in through the open stern windows, and what hair he had was rumpled. A pair of smudged spectacles gripped the end of his fleshy and pitted nose, and he had a smear of ink on his right temple from the quill behind his ear. He was sitting with his chair tilted back at a desk covered with papers.

"Well, sir! Well, well!" he boomed, all smiles, holding out a massive hand for me to shake. "How'd ye like to be my acting fifth lieutenant? Plenty of lieutenants in a flagship, y'know."

Sudden visions of myself in a lieutenant's uniform played very well across my mind's eye. I wouldn't draw a lieutenant's forty dollars a month, of course, being brevetted rather than promoted, but I would be entitled and required to wear a gold-laced coat with an epaulet and a hanger instead of a plain round jacket and a dirk, which would impress the young ladies of Baltimore-Town no end and Arabella Towson perhaps a little. I imagined her in a gauzy gown, with just a glimpse of *décolletage* as she curtsied. I wondered if her bosoms had ripened yet, which made me think of her redheaded stepmother. *She* certainly had . . . But Gaswell was waiting for my answer, his eyes looking as big and blue as plums in the lenses of his spectacles.

"I . . . I'd like that right well, sir."

"Course ye would," he said, taking a paper from one stack, glancing at it with his head tilted back and his eyebrows raised, and then placing it on another pile. "Listen, I knew your father lo these many years ago when we were both in Congress and when we were in the Continentals before that. Now I've got a chance to repay an old debt and settle a score, all in one swoop."

He looked at another paper while I calculated whether that was good or bad, and then he said, "I'm about to give ye some straight talk, see, and I don't expect it to leave this cabin."

"Aye aye, sir."

"I'm going to give ye a job to do, and three days to do it in. To help ye pull it off, I'll give ye an acting-order as lieutenant. Are ye with me so far?"

"Yes, sir."

"Good. I talked to Trimble and Wickett both, and I'm pretty sure I've got the straight goods on what happened off Guanabo with the picaroons. It's amazing how two independent and of course un-self-interested reports on the same sequence of events can vary so remarkably. Three, when ye throw in that boy's adventure tale concocted by that politico, Mr. Thingumbob. Now, as to why your old man ain't pulling for ye beyond securing a mishipman's warrant for ye ain't no affair of *mine*, but I'm prepared to think well of ye, Mr. Graves. Anyone reading between the lines of Trimble's reports couldn't help but do so, and Wickett's report praises ye very highly indeed. And your handsome conduct with the *Jane* is the talk of the Navy. *Don't hang your head and scuff your feet*—sea officers are always jealous of other men's exploits, and they don't praise 'em unless they God-as-my-witness believe it's true. The papers have heard of it too, and some are even beginning to sniff out the real story. One or two might even print it—or threaten to, anyway, unless they get certain considerations. It's binding the Navy's bowels something fierce."

Before I could think of anything to say to that, he looked at me over his spectacles and said, "Why d'ye think Truxtun gave the *Rattle-Snake* up to me? Answer honest, now."

Orders is orders, and though I was wary at his talk of "straight goods" and "reading between the lines," I was feeling pretty fond of myself. So I piped up: "He wants to get shut of a problem and give one to you, sir, and he sees a chance to do both at once."

"Smart chap!" He beamed at me fondly, which made me nervous. "He thinks I can't get ye without I choke down Trimble as well. But I'm a cunning old fish. I'll take his bait, by gad, but not the hook—no sir. And that's where you come in. You were wondering about that, weren't ye?"

"Yes, sir."

"Course ye were. Now listen." He waggled a finger at me. He was about fifty, and the back of his hand was mottled with liver spots. "You're about to learn a few things about how this game is played.

And I tell ye true, if the game goes bad I won't hesitate to maroon ye. I will set ye adrift on a lee shore with a falling tide, unlessen ye deliver the goods *in*tact, *on* time, and postage paid."

"Aye aye, sir."

"Good boy. Now hark'ee." He took off his specs and smeared them on his shirttail. His eyelids were red and puffy without them. "Your cousin may claim that ye conspired against him. He won't want the whole story to get out, I don't think, but if he decides to, might be he could take ye down with him. Might be he could make a case for mutiny."

"Might be he couldn't, sir."

"No? Why not?"

"Because he refused to fight, sir."

"Refused, or weren't given the chance?"

"He asked us all around had we determined to fight, and we said yes, it was our duty and we were honor-bound." I didn't guess Gaswell wanted to hear about *rights*. "Then he told us to do as we saw fit and went below. Nobody touched him, sir. Nobody forced him to go."

"Captain Trimble claims he was locked in his cabin. Y'know anything about that?"

My heart like to stopped. "Yes sir. I done it."

"Now why in tarnation would ye go and do a fool thing like that?"

"He'd pissed his britches, sir. I wanted to give him time to sober up before anyone found him that way."

Gaswell just about busted his sides not laughing. He choked into his handkerchief awhile till the fit passed him by. Then he folded his hands across his belly and said:

"I guess I might be holding trumps, should he care to play that card. Well sir, let's get down to business. I have a very tough nut to crack, Mr. Graves, and I expect ye to give me the leverage to do it. You're his cousin, after all."

"Yes, sir." My stomach was churning and a band seemed to be tightening around my skull.

"Now, I ain't accusing your cousin of filing a false report. I just about *can't,* because it's wrote nearly entirely in the passive voice: 'the guns were run out,' 'the schooner took up position,' and so on, till ye can't tell who did what, and I don't think he mentions himself at all but once or twice. As far as the bare bones of it goes, it jibes nearly entirely with Mr. Wickett's report, except as to where Trimble was. And with that diplomatic cove, what's his name—"

"Mr. P. Hoyden Blair, sir, assistant U.S. consul to San Domingo."

"Yes, *him.* He's out and out lying about it. He and Trimble held off about six thousand bloody-handed pirates all by themselves, the way he tells it now."

"Him! He was hiding too, sir. He's as much a coward—" I slapped my hand over my mouth. It was a monstrous thing to say about a captain.

"Yes, well, we don't need cowards," said Gaswell, clamping his specs back onto his nose. "What we need is heroes, and you and Wickett are handy." He scribbled a note on a piece of paper and signed it.

"So what d'you want me to do, sir?"

He scattered sand on the wet ink. "What, ain't ye smoked it yet?" He shook out the paper and poked it at me till I took it. "I want ye to make sure your cousin never wears our uniform again. Make dead sure he don't, by gad, ye hear me?"

Billy was drinking coffee in his cabin when I went over to the schooner. He was shaky and pale, but sober although it was nearly noon. His desk was as covered with papers as Gaswell's had been, but in great messy heaps instead of neat piles. He had neither a clerk nor a purser to help him sort things out, and I guessed he had let things go until now. We sat in silence for a while, and then he looked up at the noise the bosun's and carpenter's crews were making on deck and said, "The work would go faster with Mr. Wickett aboard. I've let the schooner fall into sad disrepair."

And it'd go faster with you on deck, too, I thought.

"I'd be glad to help, sir," I said.

"No, no, you ain't dressed for it."

I was still wearing my number-one uniform, with the order as acting-lieutenant that Gaswell had given me crackling in my pocket. I hadn't told Billy about it yet.

"I'm sure I could find some slops, sir," I said. "I don't mind getting my hands dirty."

"No, you never did." He held out his hands, palms up. "Look at mine. Soft as a milkmaid's." He folded them in his lap under the table, out of sight. "You've been to see the commodore."

"Yes, sir. Billy, I'm going to be transferred."

"Are you, Matty?"

"Into the *Columbia,* Billy. The commodore asked for me himself."

"Taken you under his wing, has he? That's good, Matty. I'm glad to hear it, honest I am."

Then, to my horror, he began to cry.

On deck, the crew had knocked off for dinner with the usual stamp and roar and a clatter of tin plates and cups, and the captains of the messes were bringing up wooden buckets of cheese and boiled peas, Monday being a banyan day, a meatless day. Midshipmen dine at noon as well, and my belly was empty despite my second breakfast. I found Dick sitting in his shirtsleeves on the carriage of Number Ten gun, being fed on salmagundi.

"Matty, you old cuss-fire!" said he, grinning. "You've been laying mighty low. Pull up a plate. Jubal, there, fetch him a plate." He eyed my uniform. "I saw you being pulled across from the flag. What news, that the commodore would send a boat to fetch you and send you home again?"

"Can you keep something under your hat for a few days?"

"Sure I can."

"Swear it."

He crossed his heart and spat in his palm and shook my hand. "I swear."

"Gaswell's given me an order for acting-lieutenant."

He was grinning like a possum now, all teeth and no joy, but he eased up on it till he got a normal look back on him, and said, "I'm glad to hear it! Here's my hand again. Now let me see your order." He peered at the scribbled writing and laughed delightedly. "It don't look like much, does it? But I'd do anything to get one." Then he frowned and said, "So what's the big secret?"

I looked at my plate. The chopped fish among the boiled eggs stank in the heat. "The commodore wants me to . . ." I nodded toward the quarterdeck, where Billy was supposed to be. "And if I don't come through he'll take that order back. Or worse. Listen, I ain't supposed to talk about it, but I don't know what to do."

"Well, I know what I would do." He refolded the acting-order and handed it back to me, glancing forward to where the bosun's and carpenter's crews had finished gulping down their dinner.

"And what's that?"

He wrinkled his nose in scorn. "He let us all down, and if he won't quit he needs to be removed. He's a bent nail. Hammer him flat or yank him out, that's what I say." He set his plate on the deck. "Well, I guess I'd better get back to work. The jib boom's sprung and the fore-rigging all needs to be rerove." And with anger and envy mixed in his face, he got up and walked away.

Fifteen

Wickett looked over my acting-order in his cabin. He was in his shirt-sleeves and had one foot up on his desk. I was looking out the scuttle to see what progress Dick and the others were making with the *Rattle-Snake*'s bowsprit.

"He can take this back any time he wants," said Wickett, "even if it is in writing." He tossed the paper onto his desk. "My very best advice to you? Hold out for an actual commission. You ought to consider it your just due for services rendered."

"Right," I said, turning from the scuttle. "Billy gets the black ball and all is forgiven. What am I supposed to tell my family?"

He held up three fingers, one after the other. "One, of course he does; two, that is essentially correct; and three, that is your affair. Oh, and four: call me 'sir.' I'm still your superior officer, even if you are an acting-lieutenant." He waved at the other chair. "Sit down."

"Aye aye, sir." Now that I'd had time to think about it, I could imagine what life as the junior-most lieutenant—*acting*-lieutenant—would be like in a flagship: the constant butt-boy of those officers who held actual commissions signed by the president, forever set to the hardest and dirtiest tasks, kept continually on watch-and-watch, with little sleep, subsisting off the leavings of the wardroom table yet expected to pay a full mess share out of my nineteen dollars a month—eight dollars and fifty-two cents of which was in the form of ship's rations.

"Billy will not be shot, sir?"

"Good God, no." He took his foot off his desk. "Where did you get such a notion?"

"The passages you read in the *Rules and Regulations* make it pretty clear . . ."

He put his foot back up. "Those are ideals, Matty. We—the Navy, the officer corps—we are a society of gentlemen engaged in an honorable profession. We regulate ourselves. There is no need for drastic measures when quiet persuasion will do. So long as your cousin doesn't make this matter public, so long as he can make himself a forgotten man, he is perfectly safe."

He poured me a glass of cider. It was lukewarm and going sour. I said, "Mr. Wickett, there's something I have to do to keep that lieutenancy."

"And I can guess what it is, Mr. Graves. The commodore took you into his confidence?"

"Yes." The hell with "sir," I thought.

"I can guess what he wants you to do," said Wickett. "And between you and me, I have the same job. You are just insurance."

"Can't Gaswell just relieve him of command? Can't he just make him resign?"

"You know how it works."

"No I don't." But I did.

He told me anyway.

"The Navy Board gave him the *Rattle-Snake*. Only they can take her away from him. And Congress gave him his commission; nor can Gaswell take that away. Sure, Gaswell can send him home in disgrace, but then the entire service would be shamed. Not that I say the commodore discussed any of this with me, of course."

"Of course," I said.

"Exactly," said Wickett. He held up his glass. "I merely observe." He drank off his cider and made a face. "But the question is, is this how you want to make lieutenant? Everyone will always remember it, you know. Even if they never say anything."

"I came into this war to make me a name, Mr. Wickett. A good name, which I'll never get by stabbing my cousin in the back. But how can I say no to a commodore?"

"By adding 'thank you' afterwards. The pen and the inkpot stand ready. Write him now while it is clear in your mind."

"How should I begin?"

"*Sir* is the customary salutation."

He helped me write it, did Peter Wickett. "Grateful for the chance to Serve . . . proper place is in the Vanguard against the despis'd Foe . . . profound Regrets that I cannot avail myself of the great Honor and Opportunity," and that sort of rubbish. I never once flat-out said Gaswell could take his bribe and stuff it up his chimney, which is what I should have said if I said it at all, but I intimated it with all the weaseling of a music-hall villain.

After I had written it, Wickett tore it up. "Is it out of your system now?" he asked.

"Yes. But why did you say—"

"I wanted to see what you would do. Once again you have proved your sense of honor and duty to my satisfaction—but in this case I think you are being entirely too honest. Shall I tell you something?"

I eyed him suspiciously. "If you want."

"When I said I had been given the *Rattle-Snake,* I was not completely truthful. I will get her *if I can dislodge your cousin within three days.* And I mean to get her. And if I do, you will have accomplished your object without getting so much as a fingernail dirty. So just let me play the villain in this farce. Once the last act is over and I have been hissed into the wings, you will have your lieutenancy and a clear conscience, and I will have my command and bedamned to my conscience. Is it a deal?"

"Deal." I put out my hand and we shook on it.

"I am glad. I have grown fond of you, which is something I have never had the opportunity of saying to anyone before. Oh, something has occurred to me." He rummaged around in the locker under his bunk and brought out a bundle wrapped in cloth. "There is no point in tempting fate by buying one just yet," he said, handing me the bundle, "but you are out of uniform without it. I will expect it back eventually, but I hope later than three days from now."

I unrolled the bundle and a golden epaulet fell into my hand. It was heavier than it looked.

Wickett lent me a sword and a fore-and-aft hat as well, and in my best white britches and silk stockings I guessed I cut a pretty good figure. I could have a proper lieutenant's coat made when and if the time came. We slipped pistols in our pockets and had ourselves landed at the d'Estaing Reservoir, marking the occasion with a visit to the marble baths in Saint Peter Street. Refreshed by the scrubbings and shall we say other ministrations of the young women employed by Madame le Doux, a Martinican *femme de couleur* of good reputation, we sallied forth to view the city before taking our supper.

Everywhere ranged people of all shades imaginable, from charcoal black to the palest cream, dressed in everything from bright silks to dingy homespun, with yellow and red turbans or shaggy straw hats on their heads, and just about every one of them gnawing sugar cane with great white teeth. The discarded husks and chewed pulp of the cane made a sort of carpet underfoot that infused the air with a sugary perfume.

Many of the French colonial buildings were in ruins. Among the rubble, wooden hovels and grass huts had sprang up, but many of the better-built residences had escaped the torch during the riots and wars that had swept the colony these ten years and more. And the noise was tremendous, with hawkers and shoppers jawing away in musical Creole—which is a dialect of French laced with Spanish, English and various African tongues—and parrots squawking and dogs barking and asses braying, and American and British liberty men jabbering in what they thought was French.

I was laughing at a couple of drunken sailors who had been chasing a pig, and who were now giggling helplessly while an angry black woman beat them with a stick and the pig shrilled indignantly at them from behind the woman's skirts, when a white man plucked at my sleeve. He was bruised and dirty, and he stank.

"Please, monsieur," he said, "I give on' t'ousand dollar to carry me and my family back to France."

I gaped at him, but Wickett stepped between us. "My friend regrets that he cannot help you," he said in French. "But I beg you will accept this small gift as a token of goodwill."

"Fah!" said the man, slapping the silver out of Wickett's hand. "I have money! Did I not just offer you a tremendous sum to take me and my family away to safety?"

"We cannot help you," said Wickett. He took me by the arm and led me away. As soon as we were clear, one of the drunken sailors pounced on the coins and ran with his mate over to a stand selling "monkeys"—coconuts whose milk had been drained out and replaced with rum. The woman and the pig retired in triumph.

In the Jesuits' building with its casement windows, the government clock was keeping time in the garret above the scorched balcony door—it was off only a few minutes from our own timepieces, which we of course reset every day at noon. Along the old promenade near the rebuilt theater a breeze found us, cooling us in our coats, and from its height we had a wonderful view of Cap la Grange nearly forty miles away. As we wandered past the prison in Cat Street I amused Wickett by pointing out that, according to Moreau, the local name for the next street over was the Rue de Pet-au-Diable.

"Street of the Devil's Fart, ha ha!" said Wickett, plucking his handkerchief out of his sleeve. "Does Moreau say how it got its name?"

"No, but—"

"—But I can well imagine how," he said thickly through the handkerchief. The sweet-smelling carpet of cane husks had thinned out as we left the marketplace. Most of Le Cap's pebbled gutters and dirt streets were rimed with decaying excrement, and the alleys were slick with fresh stuff, but the deposits at the base of the jail's walls brought filth to a new and unbearable height. We fled.

At the corner of Cat and Providence streets we came to a fountain. The gang of boys that had taken possession of it insolently ordered us away—as if we'd have risked our health by drinking water when anything else was available—but we kept one hand on our money and the other on our pistols, and no harm came to us.

In a lower street near the Place d'Armes we passed by an apothecary's shop with a curious sign in the window, advertising "certain small contrivances suggested by the stork." These turned out to be sheaths of gut whose use the apothecary demonstrated by stretching one over a pair of up-thrust fingers and waggling his eyebrows. "Proof against pregnancy and the pox," he said. They were reusable, too, with proper care. We each bought one and a velvet bag to keep it in.

"If they perform as promised," said Wickett, "it would be a wise captain who supplied them to his men—assuming he could convince them that the indignity of wearing one during congress is better than having a dose of mercury shot up the urethra a week or two afterwards."

The Place d'Armes, the parade ground, was only four blocks from the waterfront, and we turned our steps in that direction. We could have stopped at any number of tafia shops along the way—tafia being a cheap and vile species of rum—but we continued in search of someplace where we might not be murdered if we got drunk. The small city blocks of Le Cap held only four houses apiece, each of them surrounded by a wall enclosing a courtyard, and many of the houses seemed to contain a tavern or a bawdy establishment or both. Toughs guarded the quieter houses, which we avoided. Quiet houses were respectable houses in Le Cap, and white men didn't visit without they were invited.

As the sun went down, bands of bravos armed with clubs and knives began to appear in the darkening streets, taking small things from passersby and shouting slogans. We had loosened our swords in our scabbards, and were carrying our pistols in our hands where they could serve as a warning, when we happened at last upon the Amiral de Grasse.

The Amiral de Grasse was a well-lighted house in Place Christophe, with black letters swabbed across its whitewashed façade proclaiming more or less in English: "We welcome to our Friend Americane & Britannick."

A happy hum of voices Americane and Britannick spilled through the open doors, and the lamplight in the room sparkled on officers' gold lace. A group of His Majesty's sea lieutenants and redcoated Marine officers were drinking cans of champagne around a table on which they had perched a fat and damp child midshipman, who was squeaking out verses of "To Anacreon in Heav'n" and dodging the coppers the American officers flung at him.

"Stop that goddamn caterwauling," roared one American. "The boy screeches worser'n a buggered pig," said another. "Sweet Christ a'mighty," said the first, "what a miserable tune. Let's have one we can sing," but the British officers just laughed and called for another verse.

Wickett hefted his purse and smiled at me. "I have any number of pesos, pistareens, livres and whatever else passes as legal tender in this island, my friend," he said with mock pomposity. "Our tramping has given me a thirst and a hunger. Shall we enter?"

I pulled off my borrowed hat with an elaborate flourish and made an elegant leg, bowing him through the door. "By all means, dear sir. Pray lead that I might follow."

As a black man in velvet breeches and a boiled shirt ushered us to a table in the back of the room, the American naval officers eyed us with curiosity, with hostility, with amusement and contempt—veiled and subtle, of course, but perfectly evident to me. They didn't know us by sight, most of them, but ours was a small service and it was easy for them to guess who we were. An American lieutenant of Marines, glorious in his red collar and lapels and the gold epaulet on his right shoulder, propped his foot on a chair as I reached for it, and sat staring at me over his wine. Before I could hesitate, Wickett gave him a "By your leave, sir" and pulled the chair out from under his foot.

The Marine shied away from Wickett's look. "Beg pardon, sir," he said, and turned back to his friends.

Wickett waved me into the chair. "Shall we chance the punch, Matthew?"

"If you don't call me Matthew. I'm Matty to my friends."

"Your pardon; I did not realize. Since we *are* friends, I hope, you may call me Peter. Where was I?"

"You were pondering the pros and cons of punch, Pete."

"Oh, yes. The fruit will be sublime, no doubt, but I despise rum even more than I do the name 'Pete.' God damn me," he said, slapping at the mosquitoes that had discovered us. He called for cigars ("That should keep them out of range") and in the end we decided to have the punch anyway, and two plates of whatever the best supper was.

The punch was a pleasant surprise. It had some rum in it, of course, but its main thrust was carried by red wine cut with lemon juice and water, with generous slices of orange, lime, yellow melon, guava and mango, and dosed with sugar, clove and cinnamon. *Sanguinaire,* the fellow in the boiled shirt called it, meaning "bloodthirsty," and it was cold, too.

"Yankees must be shipping ice," said Wickett in wonder before gulping down a can.

The comestible was some kind of pepper pot of stewed goat and cassareep and God knows what else. The hot spices and bitter cassava went well with the cold punch, and the soft-tack was every bit as good as bread could be in a French-speaking country.

A ninnyish twittering caused me to look up. Our brother officers were grinning behind their hands and looking expectantly over at Dick and Billy at the bar. I sat with my spoon halfway to my mouth, wondering what to do, when Dick caught sight of me and waved. I glanced at Wickett. He was preoccupied with his stew.

And here I had a tremendously good idea. Wickett was in rare good humor and had declared himself a friend. There could be no better time to bind new blood with old. He and Billy had settled their differences amicably enough before, when we had captured the *Breeze.* Each could profit so long as he didn't mind that the other did. And if Billy resigned, we all would profit: Wickett would get the *Rattle-Snake,* Billy would have his reputation dusted off and handed back to him, and I would have my promotion. *Et voilà,* thinks I.

I signaled Dick to bring Billy over.

Sixteen

Billy turned from the bar with two glasses in his hand. He followed Dick's glance and flushed as his eyes met mine. He turned away, but when Dick touched his elbow and whispered something to him, he downed both drinks, bought a flat-bottomed bottle and weaved his way through the crowd to our table.

Wickett ignored him, but I was determined to make peace.

"Hello, Cousin Billy!" says I, maybe too chipper. He looked like he'd gotten over his mope. "Will you join us?"

Wickett looked up. "Yes, please do, Mr. Trimble," he said, and called for another pair of chairs.

"Will you drink . . ." Billy paused while his brain reminded his lungs to breathe. "Will you drink with me?" he said, waving his bottle.

"By all means," said Wickett. "We are wetting the swab today, and tradition calls for a great deal of drink." He passed his glance around the room, and our neighbors pretended to mind their own business.

Billy ignored my swab—my epaulet. "I was speaking to my relation, sir," he said to Wickett, falling into his chair when it arrived, and Dick didn't look any too stable himself. Billy poured generously all around and held up his glass, staring at Wickett. "To your continued good fortune, sir. And yours, cousin dear."

We couldn't very well drink his good fortune in return, as he had none.

"To your health, Cousin Billy," I offered, and he drank off another glass.

"The *Breeze* will be bought into the service, I suppose," said he, looking at his former lieutenant. "She will be yours, I take it. An official command for you at last. How jolly."

"Perhaps you have forgot, Mr. Trimble," said Wickett. "I am to have the *Rattle-Snake,* which is of a proper size for an officer of my rank and experience. Do you propose to vacate anytime soon, may I ask?"

"She's a junior officer's command," said Billy into his chins. "Very junior officer, which makes about right."

Wickett gave me a puzzled glance. We both looked at Dick, who shrugged, and then Wickett said, *"Rattle-Snake* a junior officer's command? Our commissions are dated the same day, and yet you commanded her once upon a time. I don't know what you mean by 'junior officer.'"

"No, no, don't distract me," said Billy. "I'm talking about the *Breeze,* damn you! A rum boat. A piker. A cockleshell with popguns."

"No doubt that is how you were able to take her," said Wickett. He looked more amused than angry.

"Gentlemen, please," said I.

"I resent that," said Billy. "Whatever do you mean by it?"

"If you do not know what I mean by it, how can you resent it?" said Wickett. "It is a statement of fact. We were the larger ship and we took her. What else could I mean?"

"Gentlemen—"

"You could mean any number of things," said Billy. "You're pretty damn fond of alternate meanings." He laid his finger alongside his nose. "When I sent you signals, you both thought 'twas pretty amusing, finding all possible interpretations rather than obey the simple intent of the command."

"*Simple intent.* That is accurate."

"You mock me, Mr. Wickett?"

"Oh, no, Mr. Trimble."

"*Captain* Trimble to you, Mr. Wickett."

"I beg pardon: you have a new command?"

"I have not, thanks to you."

"Come to think of it, *you* should address *me* as captain."

"Never!"

"As you wish. Matty, shall we withdraw?"

"The boy is my junior relation, sir," said Billy. "He will sit until I give him leave." He sloshed out more liquor and held up his glass. "To family: our refuge in time of trouble and bosom in time of plenty."

That was a step in the right direction. "Hear, hear," said Dick and I.

Wickett let his glass sit untouched.

Billy peered at him. "You do not drink, sir?"

"I thought it was a family matter."

"There you go again, twistin' things around."

"You see things that are not there, Mr. Trimble. I merely do not wish to intrude."

"Things that are not there," repeated Billy, aping him. "*You,* sir, have a fondness for seeing things that ain't there."

"Such as?"

"Such as—such as vessels that conveniently run 'emselves under, when I have clearly signal' you to rejoin me."

"But you never did, Billy," I said. "It was rainy that day. I couldn't read your flags half the time."

"Aha! So you did see me signaling. An' if you didn't see it, how you know I didn't? Hey?"

"I just told you, Billy . . ." I had to rub my head before I could straighten out his logic. "I saw some bunting as we commenced the chase, but I couldn't read it. We were twelve miles to windward, don't forget, and the flags was blowing near straight away from us. We hoisted *Strange sail in sight* and waited for your reply. A squall hid your next signal, so we stood toward what we thought was the enemy. It was that or let her go."

"But she *wasn't* the enemy, was she. Assuming she even existed." He gave me a triumphant smirk.

That was too much. I stood up.

Wickett raised his hand, and I sat down. "Never mind, Matty. Now listen here, Mr. Trimble, do you suggest that *La Sécurité* was an hallucination? Do not trifle with tragedy, sir. She went down with all souls. If you had troubled yourself to come up to us, you would have seen the bodies of the mothers and babes yourself."

"I don't like your tone, sir."

The port-wine stain grew dark on Wickett's brow. "If you mislike it, sir, there is the door."

"There is the door," Billy repeated in disgust. "I know where the fucking door is. Ain't I off to Philadelphia to be cut up for bait? You are to blame for that, but I welcome the screw—" he belched "—the scrutiny. When I've told my story, sir, you'll wish you'd been pulled apart limb fr'm limb by the picaroons!" He made a tearing motion with his hands. "Limb fr'm limb, ha ha!"

Wickett smiled. Billy's bottle was empty. "A glass with you, Mr. Trimble?" He signaled for the waiter.

"Don't you smirk at me," said Billy, but he shut up when I set my hand on his sleeve.

"Please, cousin dear," I said, "pray mind what you are about." Well, no. I didn't put it quite as genteel as that. What I did was, I grabbed his wrist and hissed, "Shut the hell *up*." And then while he was still goggling at me, I patted the epaulet on my shoulder and said, "Drink me joy of my promotion: Gaswell's making me fifth of the *Columbia*."

Dick did his best to smile, just as if it was news to him, and thumped me on the back so hard that my drink splashed on my nose and chin. He said:

"I noticed your swab right off, Matty. Good on you!"

"Only an acting post, obviously," I said, offhand. "I got half a mind to turn him down."

"Yes," said Billy dryly, reaching for his glass and missing it. "Good on you. 'Tis better to reign in Hell than serve in *Columbia*. Whosoever should wish to be a lieutenant in the most powerful frigate afloat?"

Someone nearby laughed and was shushed.

"I might like to stay in the *Rattle-Snake,* sir," I said.

Billy focused on me as well as he was able, under his weight of alcohol, and said, "Do not do this, Cuz. Oh, no no no. This man is a scoundrel an' a liar. He will drag you down with him. Steer clear of him, if you love me."

Wickett had bitten the end off a fresh cigar. He stopped with a candle halfway to its end, and the men around us were suddenly silent.

"I do beg pardon, Mr. Trimble," he said. "It is noisy in here and perhaps I did not hear you aright. Surely you did not call me a scoundrel and a liar just now."

Billy blinked, his lids puffy over his pop eyes. He seemed surprised by what he had said, once he heard it tossed back at him, but he repeated it. "A scoundrel an' a liar, yes. That's what I called you, sir, and that's what you are! Then an' now, always an' f'ever!"

"He's drunk, Peter," I said. "He don't know what he's saying."

Billy drew himself up and stared at me. "Listen at you, callin' the devil by a Christian name."

"Captain Trimble does not mean it, sir," said Dick. "He's overwrought. The strain of the cruise has taken him aback and spirits have loosened his tongue. His wits have cut and run, but he'll collect 'em again by morning."

But Dick was just a midshipman. His words carried no weight.

"Billy don't mean it, Peter," I said.

Wickett blew smoke, one arm hooked over the back of his chair. He said, "Pray enlighten me, Mr. Trimble: If you do not mean a thing, why would you say it?"

"Said it 'cause it's true." Billy's lip trembled. "You mutinied, sir. Refused my orders and locked me in my cabin."

"I refused to ignore my duty, yes. So did every man and officer, from the sailing master right on down to the smallest ship's boy. With the obvious exceptions of you and Mr. Blair, of course."

"You admit you refuse' a direct order?"

"Do you admit you ordered us to surrender without firing a shot?"

"You admit you locked me inna cabin so I couldn't take the deck?"

"No, Billy, no!" I said. "*I* had your key. *I* locked you in."

"Oh!" He turned to me. "So, was you, hey? Pirates attacking my convoy, and my own cousin, a wet-nosed, snot-faced, mewling—not even officer but a, a—" He paused to catch his bearings. "A mewling, flux-bottom, snot-face *reefer*, who bangs me onna head, throws me inna cabin and locks me in."

"No one banged you on the head, Mr. Trimble," said Wickett. "You tried to turn the ship over to murderers and we prevented it. The men insisted on defending themselves, as well they should, and as I had insisted they ought from the outset. You chose to go below, saying, 'I leave the fighting of the ship to you, Mr. Wickett,' and that is just what I did. And while we were fighting, you and Mr. P. Hoyden Blair were hiding in your cabin with your lips wrapped around a bottle."

"Gah!" Billy banged on the table till the glasses spilled and the child midshipman trailed off just before the sons of Anacreon had agreed to entwine the myrtle of Venus with Bacchus's vine. "You're a goddamn liar!" roared Billy. "Your impertinence is beyond bearing. You been against me from the moment we sailed, God *damn* you. You have repeatedly countermanded my orders, plotted behind my back and laugh' in my face. I say again, sir, you are a liar an' scoundrel, a *dog!* And the sooner a dog is shot, the better for his betters. Stick *that* in your pipe, sir!" He lifted his glass, saw it was empty, and looked around for the barman.

Around us, British and American officers alike sat aghast. I touched Billy's sleeve again, but he pulled his arm away. I tried one more time, but I knew it was useless.

"Please, Cuz," I said. "You're tired and distressed. Please tell him you don't mean it."

"Yes, well," murmured Dick. "Perhaps Mr. Wickett will accept an apology."

Wickett tapped a coil of ash off the end of his cigar. He drew on it and blew a cloud of smoke, and the smoke billowed around Billy's face.

"*God* damn it," cried Billy. "I'll rot in hell before I apologize to this, this upstart! I am your superior, sir, and I demand that you tell these gentlemen the truth, or so help me God I'll shoot you down where you stand!" He patted his pockets. "Somebody gimme a pistol!"

Wickett fished his pistol out of his pocket and set it on the table with the butt toward Billy. "I'm sitting, actually," he said. "However, there is a pistol, and I *shall* tell you the truth. The truth is that you are an infamous coward, a liar and a tosspot. But there is no sense in—"

"The man has drawn on me! A pistol, I say!"

"But there is no sense in calling names. A pistol lies before you, sir—"

"Damme, a pistol!"

Wickett put the pistol back in his pocket. "No one else will lend you a pistol here. But if you have a friend, or can borrow one, I should be glad to meet you at a time and place of your choosing to resolve this matter."

"I do have a friend," said Billy. I turned to him, reluctant but knowing my duty, but he looked at Dick instead. "Mr. Towson," he said, "would you do me the honor of calling on this gennelman's friend, if he can find one lying about that no one wants?"

Dick at last had his chance to participate in a duel, but he didn't look like he cared for it right then. "Of course, sir. Mr. Wickett, do you—"

"You are familiar with the Code Duello, I believe you said once upon a time, Mr. Towson. I myself know little about it, but I do know you must speak my second, not to me."

"That's right, sir," said Dick. "Who—"

"I refer all matters to a steady chap of my acquaintance, if he will. Mr. Graves?"

My chair clattered against the table behind me as I jumped up. "The hell you say! He's my cousin, for chrissake!"

Billy grabbed my shoulder and shook me till the epaulet tore off in his hand. "Go on, accept, you treacherous pipsqueak!" He threw the epaulet in my face. "Go on! Accept! The Code Duello says you must!"

So I did. I picked up the epaulet and told Dick he'd better get Billy out of there. "We'll talk in the morning," I said. "I guess he'll want to explain himself."

Seventeen

"What do you mean he won't fight?" I was sitting in a hired boat in the middle of the harbor at Le Cap, looking up at Dick leaning over the *Rattle-Snake*'s rail. The sun bore down on our heads and glittered off the wavelets. I could feel the beginnings of a headache behind my eyes. "Has he lost his nerve?"

"Lost his wits, more like," said Dick. "Listen!"

"Singing chip chow, cherry chow, fol-de-riddle-de-ido!" sang Billy in his cabin.

"It's been that or 'A-cruising we will go, oho oho oho' for this hour and more," said Dick. "That cat of his turned up all skin and bones at last. The watch below caught a mess of flying fish this morning. I guess it was the noise of 'em flapping around on deck that brought him out of hiding, and Billy had a bunch of 'em minced up and has been stuffing Greybar silly ever since. Between bottles, anyway."

"Well listen, let me come up out of the sun and maybe I can talk some sense into him while he's in a good mood."

"No sir, stay where you are," said Dick. "You can't talk to him till after the duel, y'know. Besides, he says you're not to come on board, nor anyone else, neither. He's even got the Marines out again." He looked embarrassed. "He says only gentlemen can fight duels, and since Mr. Wickett has behaved dishonorably, he's no gentleman. Ipso facto, there'll be no duel."

"We'll wait till he's sober, then."

"It'll be a long wait."

"Well, we've got to have some sort of answer, Dick. The commodore's sent the *Breeze* to Charleston to be condemned, so we're at the Amiral de Grasse in the meantime. I'll have to post him if he won't come."

"Ben Backstay was our bosun, and a very merry wreck," sang Billy.

"I know," said Dick. "I'm going to talk with him, ain't I?"

"For no one half so merrily could blow 'All hands on deck'!"

The hands on deck busted out laughing and laughed even harder when Dick told them to shut up.

Billy sent Dick to the Amiral de Grasse with a refusal to apologize or to meet us. His actions spoke for themselves, he said, which was true enough. So I was obliged to "post" him, tacking up a notice on the barroom wall:

> Le Cap, Tuesday
>
> Duty & Honor compel me to discover the following
>
> *NOTICE*
>
> Mr. William Trimble, lieutenant, late commander of the U. States schooner *Rattle-Snake*, having publickly charged me as a Liar, Scoundrel, and other Charges too infamous to list, including Mutiny, none of which he has ability to Prove, & having refus'd to render me the Satisfaction demanded and expected; I have no Alternative than to publish him to the world as a *Liar & Coward.*
>
> *P: Wickett, lieut., U. States navy*

Dick replaced the notice that evening with a reply:

> Peter Wickett having ungenerously held me up to public view without Advertising his intention shews a heart devoid of Honour.
>
> *Lt. Wm. Trimble*

"How he lies," said Wickett, staring at it with his hands clasped behind his back, as the man in the boiled shirt went around lighting the lamps. "You told him you would post him?"

"I did."

"You will notice he does not deny the charges, anyway. Just resents my mentioning them."

I started to take Dick's notice down, and then decided to leave it. I wasn't sure what to do.

"There's so many rules that somebody ought to write a book," I said. "Take the choice of weapons, for instance. Since you challenged him, he gets to choose. I think."

"What stuff. It is whatever you and Towson agree on, I know that much. I shall use sword or pistol or tomahawk—I care not. I will even stand in a hole and throw cow patties at his head if he wants. Lord, this is entirely stupid. Look here."

He took a letter from his pocket and waved it at me, and then as if suddenly remembering that we were standing in a public room where anyone might hear him, and probably would try to, he handed me the letter and lowered his voice.

"New orders from the commodore," he said. "Came this morning. I'm requested and required to go aboard of the armed schooner *Rattle-Snake* immediately, there to take charge and command of her, whereof I nor any of us may fail at our peril, et cetera, et cetera and so on." I'd have given my right arm to hear those words coming out of my mouth, but Wickett said them as if they sickened him. "On my honor, Matty, I never thought it would come to this. And now I cannot set foot in her because of this impending duel. Presumably Trimble has gotten more explicit orders, as well. And yet he remains aboard, the ass."

"I thought it was what you wanted."

"And so I did. So I did, and yet it turns to ash in my mouth."

I handed the letter back. "Gaswell don't give a hang what you think of it or how you do it. Go read yourself in and then heave Billy over the side. I'll help if you like. I'm tired of him."

"Nonsense. How would that look?" Suddenly he grinned. "Pretty damn funny, really. I know I would laugh were it not me. Well, how about you? Any further orders?"

I showed him Gaswell's most recent note. "I report aboard the *Columbia* as soon as—as soon as a certain obstacle has been removed. In the meantime I'm to help you in whatever capacity you see fit. I bet Gaswell knows something's up."

"Oh, to a certainty he does. Toadies and spies abound, you know. I should keep that letter, was I you."

I let that lie for the moment, following my own thoughts. Gaswell would not, could not, intervene in an affair of honor, but if Wickett killed Billy his problem was solved. And if it went the other way around, Billy could be had for manslaughter—a conviction wasn't very likely, but Gaswell would be within his rights to arrest him.

"Seems to me, this duel suits Gaswell's purpose pretty well," I said.

"And ours. Yet one hates to be a tool in another man's hands, even when it brings about the heart's desire," said Wickett. He smiled sadly. "No doubt he has heard those lies about my having killed the *Rattle-Snake*'s previous captain."

"About your duel? They're not true then?"

"No. Captain Tyrone shot himself."

I couldn't tell if he was lying. "Why'd he do that?"

"You would have to ask him," said Wickett, "for I swore to him I would not tell. Come, let us sit."

"You have to tell me *something*," I said, following him to a table. "I don't know anything about duels."

"What's there to know? You sneak out to a dark and lonely place—"

"Yes, and one of you has breakfast after. You said that once already."

"Then obviously it is all I have to offer on the subject. You know, I think I want some beer. Should you like some beer?"

"But what about the rules? You're bound to try to kill each other, and I don't know how to stop it!"

"Why should you want to stop it?"

"Because that's what seconds are supposed to do. 'Seconds are bound to attempt a reconciliation'—that's in the code. Dick says so. Only I don't think he's trying very hard at it. He wants to see a fight. He don't like Billy any more'n you do. And he ain't too fond of you, neither, come to that."

"I am not surprised—I rode him hard. But if Towson knows the code, where are you perplexed?"

"He don't know all of it, you see. He's full of 'the first offense requires the first apology,' and 'the lie direct,' and 'disarms' and 'disables,' and he's pretty sure there's rules about how many shots you've got to take—*shall* take, not *may* take—but he don't remember how many or under what circumstances. He's so taken with the— the elegance of the trappings that he don't see the nastiness they cover up."

Wickett had ordered a bottle of wine instead of beer, and he stopped with his glass halfway to his lips.

"Nastiness? That is coming it a bit high. It is my honor at stake, you know."

"No, Peter, it's your life!"

He made a dismissive gesture.

"Or Billy's!"

"Oh, fie. I shall shoot wide."

"But you can't! If you do, I'm supposed to shoot *you*. Jesus, Peter, if you weren't offended you shouldn't have called him out. And now one of you is going to die. Billy's an excellent shot. Don't you know anything?"

"I know my *memento mori*," he said. He fixed me with a look, and he was the old Peter Wickett again, bleak and forbidding. "I know that we all die sooner or later, and that we must make the best of it while we are here. I also know that you are just like me: we risk our lives so we can kill. You enjoy a good fight—I saw your face when you discharged your murdering pieces into the picaroon longboats."

"How did I look, then?"

"Like a man in the throes of coitus."

"Now that's an odd notion," I said, and we both laughed so hard that the man in the boiled shirt joined in from across the room.

After he wiped his eyes, Wickett said, "And I want honor the same as you do, the same as any sea officer does. And glory too I suppose, though the glory of the world is fleeting, let us not forget. Regardless, without a good name these things are unobtainable."

"Oh, speaking of good names, Greybar's come back."

"Who?"

"Billy's cat."

"I am gratified to hear it. I did not dislike the beast. But what has this to do with good names?"

"Well, now Billy can't roar around saying you scruffed his cat."

"Ah." He looked up toward the ceiling and said, "Gypsy will be glad to be aboard of the *Rattle-Snake* again. She dislikes being cooped up indoors."

Yes, and she showed it by thundering around our little room all night like a lunatic. I'd be glad to get her back aboard, too.

"You'd think she'd be used to confined spaces, having spent all her life at sea," I said.

"Cats pine for company, though they rarely show it. I am not her only pet, you know."

"She's never shown any particular fondness for me."

He finished his glass and pushed the bottle away. "Perhaps you have never shown any fondness for her."

"I'll go see Dick again," I said. "He's waiting down at the quay."

"He says pistols," I said when I came back. "I told him we're agreeable. You sure you don't want swords?"

"I am a better swordsman than he," said Wickett. "And my reach gives me a decided advantage. I will not have it said that I prevailed upon a man unfairly. But, listen, it has just occurred to me: ought we to shoot until someone is dead, until someone is wounded, or just one shot apiece?"

I had to go out to the *Rattle-Snake* to ask.

"Oh, I don't guess he'd be satisfied with just the one shot," said Dick. "I mean, really."

"But what about 'first blood satisfies honor'? I'm sure I heard that somewhere."

"Let me just duck below stairs." He came back looking prim. "He says Mr. Wickett is free to stop firing anytime he wants, or not fire at all if he wishes. He says for his part he intends to see the business through."

"Idiot!" said Wickett when I got back. "All he has to do is say he was drunk and did not mean it. I should be satisfied with that, as long as he said it in public. Go back and say first blood only. I do not intend to kill him, dammit."

It was pro forma, of course, and Dick shook his head when I put it to him. He went below to ask anyway. He came back and said, "There'll be blood for breakfast. That's his very words, Matty: blood for breakfast."

"Ask him again, man. Tell him I said please, for the family's sake. Tell him I couldn't go home again, was he to get killed."

"Half a minute."

Dick's half a minute stretched into half an hour, and while I waited a boat came from the *Columbia*. Mr. Bowman, the same smug midshipman as had fetched me aboard the flagship, climbed over *Rattle-Snake*'s rail, carrying a dispatch bag over his shoulder. He came back again a few moments later, gave me a wink and a wave, and shoved off.

When Dick returned, he had a thoughtful look on his face and a letter in his hand.

"Dick," I said, "something occurred to me while I been sitting here." I laughed. "I can't believe I forgot. All participants in a duel must be of equal rank. I know it for a fact. It's why I couldn't call out Malloy! You can't be Billy's second. Hey presto, no duel."

He shook his head, holding up the letter. "Gaswell's beat you to the punch, brother. This here's my order as acting-lieutenant in the

Croatoan. Captain Block says his third lieutenant dropped a twelve-pound ball on his toes last week and died while the surgeon was taking his foot off. Block swears his son Oliver is his only mid worth promoting, but he's only fourteen and Gaswell won't allow it."

A bleak fury rose in me. "Well I'm sure I wish you joy of your promotion, Dick. We'll wet your swab in blood."

He leaned on the rail with his chin in his hand. "I could take that unkindly, but I won't. Anyway, Billy still says no to first blood."

"Well, shit and perdition! Tell him go fuck himself." I rubbed my temples. "No. No, wait." I snapped my fingers. "By Jupiter, I have it! Tell him he's a better shot than Wickett. Tell him his first shot'll probably kill him anyway."

So he left and came back again. "First blood it is," he said, and we shook on it.

Billy looked drawn and gray in the golden morning light. He and Dick stood together at one end of a little clearing in the woods near the shore, Peter and I stood at the other end, and Quilty, the surgeon, stood off to the side.

Billy wasn't bothering to slap at the mosquitoes. He was as pale as a pudding, but I could swear he was sober.

Following the formula, I asked Dick if his friend had anything to say.

"My friend wishes the incident had not occurred."

"As does mine. Will your friend deliver a retraction in front of the gentlemen who were present when the affront was delivered?"

Billy's lips quivered. "There never was an affront! How can a man be offended by the truth?" Little drops of blood stood out on his cheeks and hands where the mosquitoes had bitten him.

"My friend says no," said Dick.

"The gentlemen are determined, then?" said Quilty. He swatted himself in the face. "Damnable pests. Very well. Let the foolishness proceed. I have here the weapons the gentlemen have agreed upon, and I might say I find this business repugnant."

"If you find it repugnant, Mr. Quilty," said Dick, "you should withdraw."

"I find it fascinating as well as repugnant. I wouldn't miss it for worlds."

He held out the case containing my set of dueling pistols. Dick had insisted on them as the only proper tools for the job, and when he and I had loaded them and checked the flints, Quilty took the pistols from us and switched them several times behind his back before returning them. We primed them and put them on half cock. I took one to Wickett while Dick took the other to Billy.

"Take your places, gentlemen," said Quilty.

In their shirtsleeves, the gentlemen advanced to the markers that Dick and I had laid out a dozen paces apart in the little clearing. There was a chance, a small chance, that they'd both miss at that distance, but I wished I could have gotten Dick to agree to twenty paces. Or fifty.

"I shall count three," said Quilty, "after which the gentlemen will have a further count of three to fire. The seconds shall shoot their man down should he try to fire except during the allotted time. A misfire counts as a shot. An accidental discharge counts as a shot. First blood satisfies honor. These are the rules of the Code Duello as the gentlemen understand them?"

"Yes." I got out my pocket pistol and cocked it. I imagined the blotch on Wickett's forehead was a bullet hole.

Dick cocked his own pistol and nodded, breathing through his teeth.

The surf hissed and puffed beyond the mangroves. A flight of sea ducks powered their way across the bright sky. Wickett followed them with his glance, his pupils as tiny as pinpricks.

There was a lull in the sound of the sea. Billy full-cocked his pistol, and the metallic *click* seemed to echo against the trees.

"I have you at last, Mr. Wickett," said he.

Wickett thumbed his lock the rest of the way back and smiled at me. It was like being smiled at by a corpse.

"Ready?" said Quilty, and Wickett and Billy raised their pistols. "One . . . two . . . three. One—"

Wickett jerked as a mosquito flew into his eye, and his pistol went off with a flash and a bang. He let it dangle in his lowered hand and stood still, trying to blink the speck out of his eye as he waited for Billy to shoot.

"Two—"

Billy kept his stance for a moment, one hand on his hip and the other outstretched, his pistol steady, and then he too lowered his weapon. A red flower was blossoming on his breast.

"Three," said Quilty.

Eighteen

As I packed Billy into his last barrel of Monongahela rye, I thought of the many ways I could have stopped his death. Billy had steered his own course, but by God I wished he hadn't enlisted me for his crew. I looked down at him in anger, his thin legs bent double against his paunch, his kindly protuberant eyes half-closed beneath long pale lashes, his lank hair wisping to the surface of the spirits as I set the lid in place and the cooper nailed it down. Billy crouched in his whiskey in death as he had lurked in it in life: insulated by it, preserved by it, drowned by it. "And now it's your preservation at last," I thought. He'd be well pickled by the time he got home, so I guessed he was content.

Greybar hopped up on top of the barrel and rubbed his cheek against my hand. I felt his teeth on my skin, and I snatched my hand away. He made a chirping noise, like a question, and blinked at me. Never having petted a cat before, I touched him between the shoulder blades by way of experiment. He thrashed his tail, surely a dangerous sign, but when I did nothing further he paced around the perimeter of the barrel top and then bumped his head against my hand again. He was purring. I tried scritching him behind the ears. He purred louder. Then, satisfied or bored, he jumped down and trotted off toward the after hatch and went below.

I chalked the destination on the side of the barrel and stood back.

"Hoist away, handsomely," said Horne. Billy rose aloft and then settled with a gentle bump on the deck of the *Harold* standing alongside.

"Don't you worry none," her captain called up to me as the Harolds trundled the barrel away. "My boys won't drink him dry, upon my honor."

"Thank you for your kindness, sir."

He gave me a casual wave instead of a salute and bawled, "Let's get some cloth on her, boys! Course nor'-nor'east or as close as she'll lie."

"Well, that's my ride," said Dick. Jubal was already in the *Harold*, stepping lively between the rushing men with a sea chest under each arm. The *Harold* was bound for the Mona Passage, where the *Croatoan* was said to be cruising between Hispaniola and Porto Rico, and then off to fetch the squadron's paychest from Gaswell's agent in Baltimore. "Are you sure you ain't going home, Matty?"

"No, I don't think I will. I ain't ready yet."

"But what'll Phillip say? What'll your father say?"

"I expect they'll be happiest not to see me."

"But you'll have to face 'em eventually."

"Eventually, Dick. Let it lie."

He held out his hand. "It was an affair of honor between gentlemen, Matty. No hard feelings, I hope."

"I reckon not." I shook his hand. "Well, good-bye, Dick."

"Brothers don't say good-bye." He grabbed me in a hug while I hung onto my hat, and then he leaped across the widening gap into the *Harold*'s shrouds.

The cutter fell away, gathering speed, and I watched Dick fading away into the distance and waving his hat in farewell. My brother Geordie had waved his hat just like that, as he marched backward up the lane on his way to take a stand with the Whiskey Boys.

"You got a man's work to do now," my father had said. "If you're up to it." At the time I'd thought he was taunting me, but now I wondered.

"Woolgathering, Mr. Graves?" Wickett stood beside me, gazing down at me as if from very far away.

I scrubbed my handkerchief across my face.

"I calculate I was, sir. I was just thinking."

"About what, if I may be so bold?"

"It was an accident."

"Well, yes." He was standing unnaturally straight, as if was he to bend just a little the whole world would come crashing down. "A mosquito flew into my eye. But I thank you for saying it."

"Oh. No, sir, I meant about my brother Geordie."

"Ah." He gave me the old empty look. "So his death was an accident. Does it change anything? Is he not still dead?"

He put his hands on the rail and stared at them. I raised my hand to touch his shoulder, but then I put it down again.

"I'd taken the wagon and gone to fetch him home," I said. "The Virginia militia was raiding the village when I got there. He was in a little house. I remember it had a white fence." Hatred had kept the incident burning bright in my mind for years, but now I found I had to struggle to blow life back into the truth of it. "The dragoons dragged everyone out of the house and lined us all up in the yard. But Geordie was so sick. He couldn't stand up. He kept falling and I couldn't hold him up. I tried to help him back into the house, but a trooper cocks his pistol and says, 'Stand fast. Stand fast or I'll shoot,' he says. And I said, 'Can't you see he's sick?' Then an officer comes up and says, 'If he is sick, let him lie in the dirt.' So Geordie lay down in the dirt. And then the trooper's pistol fired."

"You mean he shot him while he lay on the ground?"

"I mean his pistol fired. He jumped off his horse, swearing he never meant to shoot."

"Comes from putting weapons in the hands of untrained militia, the dogs."

Peter was missing my point entire—was listening with only half an ear, even. He had his troubles, and I had mine.

The officer had sent for a surgeon, but there was nothing he could do. The ball had pierced the artery in the thigh.

"Geordie never said a word. Not at first. Just stared at me . . ."

Wickett was watching a cutter running down toward the *Columbia*.

Faintly from across the water came the sound of her crew, hollering and carrying on. Men were lining her sides and waving from her rigging.

"Never said a word, just stared at you, yes," said Wickett. "I realize this is an inopportune time, Matty, but I must fetch a glass."

I followed him up to the quarterdeck.

"He was scared, Peter. He was *scared.*"

He trained his glass on the cutter. "It is a difficult thing, to see fear in the face of a man one admires. No doubt he knew he was dying."

"I told him there was nothing to worry about. He would be fine."

"And what did he say to that?"

"He said, 'Of all people, I never thought I'd hear that from you.' Then he turned his face away and wouldn't talk no more. And then he was dead."

Peter lowered his glass. "A hard lesson for the learning," he said. "For you and the trooper both. But you were a child of twelve, if my mathematics have not failed me, and surely you can be forgiven."

"Me? Forgiven? For what?"

"For lying to your brother when he needed you to help him face the truth." He swept his glass across the squadron, hove-to on the starboard tack with the mountains above Le Cap François peeping over the horizon astern. "The *Congress* is getting out a boat. Mr. Klemso! Mr. Klemso there, hoist out the gig."

The cutter came up into the wind alongside the flagship. A moment later the Columbias joined in the general hallooing.

"I wonder if the war is over," said Peter. "Look there— *Columbia* signals."

I picked up a glass. "*All captains,* it says, *send boat.*"

"Ah," said Peter, setting his glass back in the beckets. "It would be *All captains repair aboard flag,* was the war over. Mr. Graves, light along to the *Columbia,* if you please, and find out what is what."

The trooper who'd shot Geordie drove us home. I expected my father to horsewhip him at least. But he'd gathered Geordie into his arms and carried him into the house without a word. I told the trooper,

"Why don't you go home? What're you doing here, anyway?" He looked at me like the thought had never occurred to him. "Because the president asked us to. He's *General Washington*," he said, and I said, "Fuck General Washington."

I was giving him as good as I got till my father dragged me off.

And although my father had already paid his tax, the dragoons came by that night and burned our barn.

"What news?" I called as we approached the *Columbia*. Boats from all around the squadron had converged on the flagship. The men were huzzaying, and some intemperate souls were throwing their hats in the air. A growing squadron of hats plied the waves to leeward.

"The *Constellation*'s fought a great battle off Guadeloupe," said a grinning lieutenant. "The *La Vengeance* of fifty-four guns or more, and heavier ones than *Constellation*'s at that. Truxtun lost his main-mast and the Frenchy escaped in the dark, but he mauled him, sir! *Mauled* him!"

"Make way there," I roared. "I belong to this ship. You sir, back water! Make way!"

A sweet-smelling lieutenant met me at the entry port. He settled his hat back onto his carefully brushed blond curls and said, "The commodore has been expecting you all morning, sir. What d'ye mean by making him wait?"

"Sorry, sir. I was seeing off my cousin."

"Oh. Yas," he drawled. "My condolences, I'm sure. Well, shake a leg, sir, shake a leg."

"Just between you and me," said Gaswell in his cabin, and there was something rehearsed about the way he said it, "the Secretary will probably be more interested in what happened in the bight with them picaroons than in any duel, if he thinks about it a-tall. He's got a lot more on his mind than a spat between gents."

"I'm glad to hear it, sir. But what's this about the *Constellation*?"

"Oh, *that*. The Congress will vote Truxtun a medal, I expect, and he'll never let me hear the end of it."

"But what was the butcher's bill, sir? I have a friend aboard."

"Pretty light, considering," he said, extracting a paper from one of the piles on his desk. He settled his specs on his nose and tilted his head back. "Chased 'em for twelve hours, and fought for five hours once he'd hauled alongside. I have no love for Tom Truxtun, but I guess he can dish it out and take it too, the old cuss. Let's see now. Eleven seamen killed outright and thirteen wounded, one of which has since died—arm shot away. One Marine killed and three wounded. One boy killed and two wounded. One of 'em got his leg shot off, poor kid. But your friend is one of the officers, I expect." He ran a blunt finger along the lines of script. "None of 'em killed, says here, but let's see now. Mr. Shirley, the second lieutenant, received a slight wound to the leg." He glanced at me over his specs. "But I expect you're more concerned with the mids and master's mates. Hmm. Wederstrand, Warren and Comerford, all got knocked on the head but not seriously. No worries there, eh?"

"My friend's name is Jarvis, sir."

"Jarvis, Jarvis. I know him—cheerful young fellow. No, he ain't among the wounded." But before I could relax he said, "Here he is— missing, along with several seamen. That rings a bell."

He pulled out a packet of papers, three closely written pages. "This here's a copy of Truxtun's journal from February second. I allow I only glanced through it before to get the particulars of the action itself, y'understand, as the boys was all with child to hear the news."

He scratched his nose, skimming through the lines. "He'd silenced the *La Vengeance*'s guns and was about to receive her surrender, it says here, when he discovered that his mainmast was 'totally unsupported by rigging, every shroud being shot away.' Sent the men aloft to save it if they could . . . 'every effort was in vain.' Ah, here 'tis: 'The mainmast went over the side in a few minutes after, and carried with it the topmen, among whom was an amiable young gentleman who commanded the maintop—Mr. James Jarvis. This young gentleman it seems was apprised of the mast going in a few minutes by an old seaman, but he had already so much of the principle of an officer engrafted on his mind, not to leave his quarters on any account, that he told the men if the mast went, they must go with it. I regret much his loss as a promising young officer and amiable young man.' Well, now," he said, pretending like something had got in his eye, "I don't suppose I need to go on."

Through the great stern windows I could see the *Rattle-Snake* rising and falling on the swell. Peter had dropped down to leeward, as if he was waiting to pick me up again.

Gaswell followed my look. "Well sir," he said, "it's come to my attention that I can scrape along just fine with only three working lieutenants and a flag lieutenant. So I'm going to keep you in the *Rattle-Snake* awhile. Wickett needs a lieutenant, and you two get along well." He looked at me over his specs. "Or do I miss my mark?"

"No sir, we get along well."

"No lingering resentments about your cousin?"

"No sir. It was an accident."

"An accident? Playing about with pistols in the first light of dawn, an accident?" He shook his head, no doubt wondering about the intelligence of the officers who worked for him. "Any rate, though you'll be listed in the *Rattle-Snake*'s books as her first lieutenant, I have a job for you. It'll take you into the interior for a time. Dangerous work and little glory in it, but a very important job."

"I'll take it, sir."

"Don't ye want to hear the particulars?"

I didn't because I didn't care, though it would never do to say so. I just wanted to go away awhile, and the interior of San Domingo with its black maroons—runaway slaves who killed strangers on sight—seemed an appropriate place to find the mayhem I needed to cleanse myself. But it wouldn't do to say that either.

"If you please, sir."

His little job took me to Jacmel, as it turned out, down on the south coast of San Domingo, where General Dessalines had trapped a mulatto army in a bloody siege. I was held prisoner a while and near-about killed by a secret society of assassins—François Villon Deloges's letter having provided all the mayhem I could have wish for—but that, as they say, is another story.